The Great North Road

Annabel Doré crossed the Great North Road daily to get to school. She now lives on the North Yorkshire coast. Her career as a vocalist spanned twenty-seven years. She has studied art and design and has a degree in contemporary theatre.

ANNABEL DORÉ

The Great North Road

PICADOR

First published 2007 by Macmillan New Writing

First published in paperback 2008 by Picador
an imprint of Pan Macmillan Ltd
Pan Macmillan, 20 New Wharf Road, London N1 9RR
Basingstoke and Oxford
Associated companies throughout the world
www.panmacmillan.com

ISBN 978-0-230-53127-7

A CIP catalogue record for this book is available
from the British Library.

Typeset by SetSystems Ltd, Saffron Walden, Essex
Printed and bound in the UK by
CPI Mackays, Chatham ME5 8TD

Visit **www.picador.com** to read more about all our books
and to buy them. You will also find features, author interviews and
news of any author events, and you can sign up for e-newsletters
so that you're always first to hear about our new releases.

For Eden

Acknowledgments

For help along the Road, I thank:

Will Atkins, for the pantographic hook-up, which powered, inspired and generally kept my trolley on course,

Mike, my husband, ever supportive, patient as Tempus, for a research detour to Scarborough during which we bought Italian ice-cream and a new home,

Tamsin and Kathryn, daughter and god-daughter, for enthusing over early drafts and debating the characters so vigorously that they sprang out of the pages and sat looking at us,

Ann Cochrane, for shared childhood memories giggling secretly between the lines,

Bob Merrilees, for characterful reflections glinting like sixpences in the Geordie lads' pockets; also for a timely bob's-worth of motivation;

most importantly –

Jamie, Amy, Lauren and Lydia, for reminding me how eagerly children love.

❖

Two brave women talked to me about the reality of caring for a loved one suffering from the condition known as 'schizophrenia'. *The Great North Road* is a story conjured in the mind of a reasonably sane, if rather theatrical, author; it doesn't even begin to describe the real distress which the illness can cause to sufferers and their families. It is with humility, therefore, that I thank these ladies.

I am also extremely grateful to Dr Janice Sinson, Research Psychologist, for her professional insight into the emergence, symptoms and treatment of schizophrenia.

Come

with me. Slip between the oak doors and tiptoe down the left aisle. Slide into the front pew, next to the girl, Alexandra. Don't worry, she can't see us.

I wish we could warm her up. There's not much flesh on her twelve-year-old bones, and it's chilly in here. I wish we could each take a hand and rub it warm, but we can't. Nor can her poor mother, Sophia, who is lying on ice-blue satin with her arms folded over her chest, colder than any of us.

Or is Sophia sitting quietly, invisibly, next to you?

Look how tight and white the child's lips are, and how she hunches her shoulders protectively around her narrow chest. Watch her red-rimmed eyes as they wander upwards, over ruby and royal stained glass, the golden nails in His feet and thorns around His head.

Mighty organ pipes thunder. That organist must have eaten a hearty breakfast! Come on, shuffle to your feet. Pick up a service sheet. Notice the date on the front – 15 May 1937. Cough and clear the cobwebby larynx. Sing up! The vicar thinks he is a tenor, but he certainly isn't, and the choir trebles need all the help they can get to drown out the vain wretch.

'Yea, though I walk through death's dark vale.' Lord, how hard it is to sing that hymn when one's throat is aching.

While we are on our feet, just glance along at Alexandra's father, Douglas Hythe. He is standing slightly away from her, not touching, his handsome face a complicated manuscript. We can't quite measure his grief. He isn't singing, but his restless, strumming fingers betray a love greater than anything he has ever felt for a woman. Hythe is a concert pianist, a composer. Perhaps it is the eternal clamour inside his head which deafens him. Perhaps music transports him to a private place of thunder and discord, where passions collide, where enemies and lovers entwine, where furies, frustrations, adoration, violence and sex all transcend into an elevated emotion so wondrous that actual human experience is rendered dull.

Or perhaps not. You see, his proud, silver-blond head is tipped at a suspiciously dramatic grieving angle, and I suspect Hythe is as good an actor as ever his wife was.

Goodness, I sound cynical. No. Let's not judge him. He must survive in an era of intolerance, when society crushes people who are simply 'other'.

Now, look over your shoulder, past the pew of snivelling household staff, right to the back of the church, where the 'uninvited' mumble into hymnbooks. On the end of one row is an olive-skinned man wiping his nose on a grubby red handkerchief. Antonio Torricelli. There are no heroes in this story, only people with heroic hearts, and this Italian ice cream-maker is one of them. I'll introduce you properly, later.

It's no good looking for the butler (there's always a butler). Martin is polishing teacups back at Halstone House. And by the way, he didn't kill Sophia. She died of cancer.

The vicar mounts the pulpit, spreading his arms like a red-nosed angel. Heaven help us all! Flushed with sanguine sincerity, he begins on a bellow.

'SOPHIA!' he cries. 'A special soul. A fine and beautiful actress. Yet also . . .' (Don't you just loathe the way his fluted voice plummets dramatically to bass? So contrived!) '. . . beautiful in here.' With Shakespearean declamity he is banging his fist against his ribs – bomp, bomp, bomp. Send him to Hell, I'm sick of him.

Alexandra is sucking her cheeks. Trying not to cry? Or is she fighting down that awful giggle which bubbles up when one's emotions are utterly confounded?

What about that poor old man behind us? His tortured sobs send shudders down my spine. That's Alexandra's Italian grandfather – her nonno. Visibly trembling, his arthritic, Catholic toes are curling with revulsion in this Episcopalian church, yet this is the moment when he can no longer deny the unthinkable. He has lost his daughter, his princess.

I do feel sorry for him. I do. But I also know rather too much about him. His gasps, however despairing, are also feverish with fury. Believe me, the eldest living Marletti, isolated from the other mourners by language, culture and politics, is not rendered helpless by his dreadful grief.

The bearers have lifted the coffin. Shall we walk next to Alexandra? No one else takes her arm. Her chin is well down now, as if she daren't look down the aisle and out into tomorrow.

Oh, God! Where did all those photographers come from?

Douglas is squaring his shoulders. 'CELEBRATED PIANIST', the papers will read, 'GRIEVES IN DIGNIFIED SILENCE.' I reckon his grief is somewhat tarnished with anxiety. In the churchyard, as he looks down into the grave, he must surely be pondering the Inferno.

There is a chill draught around my legs. Can you feel it, whipping between the gravestones? Could it be Sophia's final whisper of dismay as her husband's arm stretches gracefully around Alexandra's bent shoulders?

Or is it just a sprinkle of authorial glitter in the eternal breeze?

❖

Welcome to the party. Have a sherry. Have a sandwich. Let's join the pecking vultures in Halstone House. Plates and glasses are clinking. Alexandra is staring at crumbs on the carpet, while her father approaches the piano. Elegantly he seats himself and pauses with his fingers over the keys. Ah. Soft smiles are settling across his audience. Notes of exquisite melancholy trickle into the room.

But look at Alexandra – her teeth are so tightly clenched that her neck must be aching.

I want to cry. The music seems to drag something out of me, something which has more to do with the future than the past.

At last the chords are doing a final stomp, stomp.

Don't you dare applaud!

The mourners have snivelled through their cabaret, they have munched and supped and are now indulging in a fanfare of back-slapping. Wait with me, behind the door, until they have gone. Shh! Let's just ease towards the fireplace and sit beside Alexandra for a moment. She is crouching on a footstool, her forehead heavy on her forearms.

Quiet, isn't it?

Tick, tick.

Why doesn't Douglas say something loving, something kind?

No. He is indulging his own gloom.

The corny old clock dongs seven.

'Why?' Alexandra is speaking suddenly, her voice more adult than her body. 'Why did you send Nonno away?'

'I've explained. There's trouble between your grandfather's country and ours. Best he gets home quickly. Anyway, Halstone House has never held any attraction for Mamma's family. Not quite a Venetian palace.'

Now –

enter that butler. Into the drawing room sidles a young man with an oil-slicked head and shiny tray. He bows, proffering Douglas a balloon of brandy.

Can you shield Alexandra, turn her flushed face towards the fire?

'Martin.' Douglas sounds abrupt.

'Saddest of days, sir.' Starched cuff to glistening eye. 'Truly unbearable.'

Oh, I know Martin. Let's just say that for him servility is delicious.

'Organization impeccable,' Douglas mutters. 'I'll thank the staff tomorrow. I'm exhausted.' He downs the brandy in one. 'Put that bottle in my room.'

Her toes are too icy for sleep. We are no use. Ghosts of tomorrow, we can give no warmth to the past tense. Alexandra is awake in her vast bed, the feathered mattress enfolding her. She crosses her arms over her chest and tries to stop breathing.

With a gasp, she suddenly flings away the covers and crawls towards the embers in the hearth.

Get back into bed, girl. Sleep! But no, she is hollow with grief and loneliness. Restless, she leaves her room. We know, don't we, as we follow her along the dark corridor, that something bad is going to happen.

She presses her face against her mother's bedroom door. Oh, why didn't someone lock it? At the dressing table, she picks up Sophia's hairbrush and tugs at the black threads. Dead hair from a dead head, brittle between her fingers.

A soft wedge of light is glowing beneath the interconnecting door to her father's room. For goodness' sake, why can't he be quiet? You and I recognize the muffled, guttural whine, but Alexandra mistakes it for a sob.

Nervously, she pushes the door and peers into his private domain. An oil lamp flickers over an empty bed. Douglas is standing in the centre of the room, tall and strong with his back arched and his face turned to the ceiling. He is completely naked. A golden rose with a single thorn.

Behind Alexandra's camera eyes, an internal shutter clicks. Picture taken, film exposed. She steps back. Back again.

As she stumbles blindly down empty corridors, the photograph develops. Most of the room darkens away into sepia shadows, but Hythe's ivory skin glows brighter and brighter. At the precise centre of the tableau, framed in mysterious triangles, an intumescent image that will permanently etch obscenity over this child's perception of male.

At the bottom of the snapshot, another man's flesh curves over folded thighs, knees and knuckles. Wetted by candlelight, a servile mouth opens wide, wider still.

❖

It is a relief to float now. Under the stars, we hover above the poplar trees which line the driveway. See there? A shadow is slipping between them. Young Alexandra is running, feet skimming the ground as if flight is real flight. Skinny shoulders forward, pelting through blind night, she pants on, wrenching herself away from the nightmare which bites at her heels.

With stolen money from her father's desk she is clinging to one last sanity – Nonno. Dear Nonno, on his way to Dover. If only she can catch him! Run. Run. To Italy. To Venice . . .

❖

Enough! Bring down the curtain! That's it. All over.

We must dash too. Escape the damned gloom.

Come on . . . run . . . RUN . . . are you keeping up? Flee across the Wiltshire Downs on the wondrous wings of typesetters' words. Dawns and days hurtle past. History blurs.

Bombs rain down as we vault over the appalling thunder of the Second World War. Years are puddles beneath our flying feet.

Now, breathless, we're sprinting up the Great North Road, across the shoulder of England, in relentless pursuit of higher skies.

Culture somersaults. Hang on to your ears, folks – our language has turned inside out.

We've leapt over time, almost fourteen years,
and over the distinctive girders of the Tyne Bridge,
to land in . . .

Part One

. . . Newcastle,

December 1951, on a freezing night, when black clouds came creeping in from the North Sea to deposit a blanket of snow over the sooty city. Under orange sodium lights, flakes fell like showers of gold dust, settling soft and clean on inky pavements. High above Haymarket, perched on her obelisk, the winged Goddess of Victory was feathered and draped in heavenly white, her frosted sword at rest. For a few quiet hours the land of the Geordies lay as serene as a silent night in Bethlehem.

A brittle illusion.

Granite-grim, the city woke to revving cars and lorries trundling up the Great North Road as it passed right through the city centre, calling itself Northumberland Street. By the time the Goldsmiths' Clock said nine-thirty, the gutters were heaped with mucky slush and an icy north wind was cutting through the streets, chilling the bones of shoppers 'doon toon' for their Christmas bits. Outside Fenwick's, runny-nosed infants had gathered to gaze at the great glass windows, where teddies and dollies had magically come alive in Santa's grotto. And there, among the enchanted, shivering crowd, stood a tall girl in a royal blue pompom hat.

Sylvia Sharp pulled a matching scarf around her ears and tucked her long streamers of springy red hair into her collar. Unusually tall for her age, the teenager stood giant among the toddlers, yet equally mesmerized by the fantasy, her eyes dreamy with Christmassy spirit, until . . .

Was that?

Her focus sharpened, and for an instant she was shrinking back into infancy, back into a time where imagination permitted other realities, other worlds, other magical possibilities.

Was it . . . ? Was that Dothy? Had she just glimpsed her long-lost childhood friend tiptoeing among the plastic fairies in the window, wearing her lavender ballet dress, with a tinsel tiara in her hair? Dothy, her faithful, dimple-cheeked companion, apparently still invisible to the whole world, apart from Sylvia herself?

No. She blinked, and the child slipped away, as invisible friends must, on quicksilver dance shoes. Dothy could never grow up – but Sylvia had.

At thirteen and a half, she had finally been allowed to come into the city, all by herself! In years to come, Sylvia Sharp would remember this day as the last time when being alone was not pierced with the icicle of loneliness.

She did her Christmas shopping in Farnons: talc for her mam – violet, because she was called Violet – a diary for Dad and, for her younger sister, Katherine, bath cubes which turned the water blue.

Nose tucked into scarf, she waited at the trolley stop,

stamping from one achingly cold wellington to another, wishing she still wore a liberty bodice. Better still, she wished she had worn the new size 34A bra which was waiting in her top drawer, ready for its debut at the Youth Club Christmas party.

A yellow, flat-faced trolleybus, with its long antennae grasping at twin overhead cables, came gliding through the slush. Sylvia clomped up the stairs, rushing for a front seat. At Haymarket the conductor leapt down from his platform and, poking and prodding with his long pole, hooked the pantographs over the points. He rang the bell; the number 31 slid up, out of the city and into a broad, tree-lined avenue, where black branches clipped against the trolley's upstairs windows. Sylvia did not glance east towards the Victorian elegance of Jesmond, nor west, where the delicately wrought bandstand in Exhibition Park glistened like spun glass. The Town Moor rolled whitely, innocently by. She had no premonition. Yet here, on either side of the Great North Road, her own story would be rooted, a drama in which Katherine would also be wretchedly drawn.

Happy Christmas.

Happy, naive, childish, fairytale, romantic Christmas.

Thirteen. A year of firsts. First kiss. First suspender belt. First pair of stockings. A burning taste of sherry. A drag of a fag. First period.

First bra. The same 34A which her younger sister was, at that very moment, trying for size. Sylvia would have been doubly horrified to know that Katherine, puffy with puppy fat, filled the cups quite well.

Blissfully unaware, both.

As Sylvia sat daydreaming about a boy called David

Linden, it never occurred to her to distrust her sister. Nor to distrust her own body, which harboured a threat more devastating than any passion. Small signs of it had slipped through her childhood, unrecognized, unlabelled and menacingly potent.

Almost home. Past Tittybottle Corner, the Great North Road narrowed into a suburban High Street. GOSFORTH. 'The Village' they called it then. Toytown. Fire Station, Police Station, Church, Chapel, School, Clinic, Library, Cinema, each building a gem, everything in its place and as it should be.

❖

The church hall was decked with its requisite boughs of holly and a hundred colourful paper chains. David Linden helped his two friends, cheeky little Alan Watson and huge, hirsute Terrence (Hendo) Henderson, to hang mistletoe over the door. Trap set, the three lads stood beside a trestle table laden with paste sandwiches and coconut mountains, surreptitiously eyeing the giggling girls on the other side of the hall. David rocked casually on the sides of his feet while Alan combed his blond hair and Hendo flapped his sports jacket.

'Me armpits stink. A'm sweat'n like a pig.' Hendo's hairy, bull-necked frame was hot with anticipation.

A black forelock fell over David's nose. He flicked it away from his brow, but it fell straight back down, so that one amber eye glinted through lank strands. Oh yes, even at fourteen David Linden knew he was handsome.

Alan, who only knew he was shorter than most of the girls, picked up a pickled onion, then, remembering the mistletoe, put it down again. 'Hey, look at Sylvia! She's got her hair up.'

David spotted the emerald dress. His heart thumped jaggedly, undecided whether to pump blood to his head or his loins.

'Bloody hell,' said Alan. 'She looks about twenty.'

'MINE!' declared Hendo. 'Howay, lads. A'm a big lad what needs a big lass.'

David looked sideways at his tall mate's heavy chin and the wisps of chest hair straying though his shirt buttons. Surely Sylvia wouldn't prefer Hendo's cheese breath to his own darkly romantic stares? Tonight was supposed to be the moment when all his cool glances, shy smiles and zesty moments of feigned indifference would culminate in a kiss – at least. The thought of Hendo's big hands touching the glorious redhead filled David with Byronic jealousy. He wanted to punch something. Hendo.

His jealousy was not unfounded. Sylvia and Hendo were comfortable friends, having grown up as next-door neighbours, sharing roller skates, mischief, bogies and blame. These days David found any excuse to call for Hendo, just so that he could covertly gaze up at Sylvia's window, lusting for knowledge of her secret world, a heaven of brassieres, pants, female smells and talcum powder.

Alan, craftily watchful and disarmingly outspoken, sniggered, 'You fancy Sylvia yourself, divent you, Davy lad? Aye, I confess – me anall. Dibs on who takes her home? Half a crown?'

David flicked his fringe.

And Hendo smiled. The big lad held an ace in each of his

shoes. He could dance. Secretly, Twinkle-toes had spent several evenings with his left hand in his father's right, learning the pretty art of knee-bending, hip-twisting, and taking one permitted step backwards for a reverse turn. Father and son had stumbled and laughed, shoved and shoved back, until Hendo could waltz, foxtrot and canter a long-legged quickstep.

Generously, Hendo had even taught Alan a couple of bits of crafty footwork, on the grounds that Alan didn't have a father of his own. Alan didn't have much at all really, except a vicious tongue and too many opinions. David, on the other hand, seemed to have everything: big house, big brain, two parents, a rich grandmother, a dog.

There were, however, private facets of David's life which his mates never imagined: the sharp pangs every time he walked through his front door, the twisting frustration of trying to concentrate on homework while his parents spat and bellowed, the enigmatic poetry he wrote and hid on the top of the wardrobe, and the weekends spent locked in his room, spilling his artistic soul through the bell of a saxophone. No one at school or at the Youth Club knew he could play; his only audience was his family. David's fingers, when spread down the brass keys, had a dexterity and sensitivity which could send his grandmother into girlish dreamland, send his father into a passion of regret – and send his irritable mother out shopping.

Hendo was still flapping his armpits. Alan, blessed with more gob than stature, scratched his floppy blond hair, while David leaned against the wall with an air of superior melancholy. A spindly Christmas tree twinkled over the party. Someone changed the record and the boys surveyed the girls who were lined up like fillies at Gosforth Park Race Course.

'Gan on, Hendo,' urged Alan, 'ask Moira.'

'Wharaboot, Denise?' Hendo's accent was stodgy as his mam's dumplings. 'Mind . . . you'd need scaffold'n to get around that frock. What's she got underneath, to make it stick oot like that?'

'A bloke could get lost in them petticoats. Netted like a haddock.'

'Have you seen the titties on Jean? Christmas bloody pudd'ns.'

'Another Christmas miracle,' Alan giggled. 'She was flat as a cowpat yesterday. Hockey socks, my guess.'

The banter went on, until couples began to pair up and step awkwardly around the hall. Alan trotted around with his nose between Jean's sock-stuffed puddings and Hendo went straight for Sylvia.

Astonished to witness them gliding around the floor with unexpected grace, David retreated moodily into the shadows. He closed his eyes and let the music flow through him. Wilful muscles in his arms and legs tugged gently, responding to the rhythm, and for a second he felt the strangest urge to leap, like a ballerina, into the fray. Grunting at his own madness, he schooled himself to wait. Sylvia would be his girlfriend by the end of the night. And somehow, in the future, David promised himself, he would learn to dance better than Hendo. Actually, he would.

❖

Sylvia matched Hendo's long stride, knowing that boys were watching her stocking seams. Her instinct for seduction, still pubescent, felt the novel sensation of nylons shifting behind

17

her knees and up her thighs. Red hair twisted on top of her head, she arched her slim neck and gazed around Hendo's arm, to turn pale, aqua eyes on David Linden. When he stared back, she licked her smooth lips, tasting her mam's peach lipstick.

The music paused, the lights went out, and someone announced, 'The Bradford Barn Dance!'

Two in, two out, turn around.

Two in, two out, change partners.

Everyone could do it. Everyone wanted to. Those simple steps were an excuse to rest brow against chin, breast against chest, sometimes even lips against lips, as partners shuffled and swapped in the darkness.

Sylvia entered the circle with Alan, who, being several inches shorter, tucked his clean blond head neatly into her shoulder. On the other side of the hall, David pulled Denise towards his tall frame.

Teenage hormones raced, as dancers savoured a procession of differing bodies, squeezing fingers, sniffing necks, comparing intimate smells of sweat, talcum powder, Soir de Paris and mothballs. In a gentle wheel of flirting, laughter and swift kisses, turn by turn, step by step, Sylvia and David approached the moment when they would finally touch.

The fairy on the Christmas tree twitched her wand.

A handsome lad and a girl in an emerald-green dress stepped towards each other, lifted their arms and drew together. He was trembling. She felt the message in his quivering muscles, and pulled back to stare at the dark smudge on his upper lip. As she squeezed his hand, and he pulled her so close that he could smell her shampooed hair, a dance of dangerous emotions was just beginning. Mistletoe and Mother Nature were potent, yet, in their carved future, this pair of beautiful teenagers were not destined to be entwined like ivy on ash, because the ivy would be deemed destructive and hacked away.

❖

This would be remembered as the night of the Great Christmas Battle. Around ten o'clock, right outside the church doors, a jeering crowd gathered around Alan and another spotty youth, who were rolling about on the cold stone slabs, kicking and punching with vicious abandon, struggling from one wrestling hold to another.

'Why does he do this?' yelled David, as he and Hendo elbowed through the rabble.

'Bad-tempered little bastard. He can vex a feather.'

'Grab him!'

'It's his gob. His bloody gob.'

'Tynemouth.'

'And just as full of shite.'

David pushed between the two assailants, but found his own temper rising as he was pummelled. Hendo grasped the back of Alan's shirt – which ripped. The original opponent then began jumping and jerking around, trying to head-butt everyone. Alan swore and thumped furiously at Hendo, who was trying to wrap him in a bear hug. Curses rent the air. Someone tripped Hendo. The head-butter cracked another boy's chin. And so the fight doubled and trebled until several boys were laying into one another, knuckles crunching in cowboy savagery.

Eventually it all began to hurt too much. Tempers melted in pain.

Alan sustained more than the injuries to his elbows and knees – he also took a verbal battering from Hendo, as the bigger lad carried him along the High Street.

David bled profusely from a split on his head, which gave Sylvia an excuse to fuss with her handkerchief. When the bleeding stopped he took her hand. The half crown would be his.

In Woolworth's doorway they shared their first exquisite tingle of mutual arousal.

'I'm freezing.' Shivering, Sylvia slid her hands beneath his jacket, and lifted her face.

There were dark hooks in those kisses.

❖

Spiced by secrecy, hidden from two sets of very strict parents, this raw romance, fresh and frank with holy naivety, itched with eroticism. As the clandestine months slipped by, young passion took its inevitable course.

One brilliant summer day, just after Sylvia's fourteenth birthday, the young lovers lay at the edge of the golf course. At their feet a stream slid sensually by, a thousand tiny suns glittering in its glassy, ochre flow. Sylvia's russet hair hung around their faces, hiding slow, earnest kisses. Her school blouse was unbuttoned and David was lifting the hem of her skirt.

The gypsy

gripped her hard, distended belly with dirty fingernails, closing her eyes and wincing, as the first contraction tightened.

'Perfect timing, little bastard.'

She was sweating. A massive, low-slung pregnancy distorted the contours of her splendid body but, beneath layers of slovenly neglect, lingered tracings of a younger beauty – a strong jawline, mobile mouth and straight neck.

Long grass dragged at Greta's old shoes as she lumbered across Newcastle Town Moor. Head down, back arched and hands protectively supporting her huge abdomen, she trod carefully to avoid cowpats in the rutted ground.

A pair of youths almost collided with her. They apologized, then sniggered. The gypsy lifted tangled black locks from her brow and stared at Alan and Hendo, her gaze as unreadable as a glass ball.

No mystical communication passed. No inkling vibrated though the thick, hot June air. Perhaps the dusk was already too turbulent with fairground screams; or perhaps, like Greta's baby, the story was not yet breathing.

Alan and Hendo, now fifteen, strode happily towards a moving canvas of whirling rides, stripped tents and throbbing traction engines.

Behind them, the pregnant gypsy called Greta was planning to escape it.

❖

Newcastle was hot – for Newcastle. This was Race Week, June 1953. As always, it was celebrated on the Town Moor by the arrival of a fair to surpass all others – the HOPPINGS.

Chugging up the Great North Road they had come, a colourful armada of lorries, caravans and traction engines pulling huge, fabulously painted loads, as showmen and gypsies from all over Europe gathered for their own annual summer party. After a professional frenzy of lifting and hammering, almost a mile of the moor was now ablaze with a fearful feast of whirling rides, gruesome exhibits and gaudy sideshows. Three Big Wheels! Three helter-skelters! Parents had saved for weeks. If the nippers didn't have a few sixpences to take 'owa the moowa', it was a 'poowa lookout'.

'Let's see that woman with two heeds,' urged Alan.

'She's not really got two heeds. She's two women stuck together. Siamese.'

'Howay, man! On the skyrockets! Ah, yer a sissy!'

'A'm not!' Hendo lied. 'A'm just lett'n me tea go down.'

'Look, there's them posh lasses from the Convent. Let's get them on the dodgems.'

The girls were only too willing to be swung and bashed on dizzying rides, especially the Caterpillar. On a torn leather seat Alan cuddled up to girl in a silly, frilly dress. In the carriage behind, Hendo slid his hairy arm around a narrow waist. As the ride began to undulate around the track, rattling, picking up speed, a siren blew and the caterpillar skin, a continuous umbrella of green tarpaulin, lifted over the carriages. In the darkness, both lads kissed their enchrysallized butterflies, waiting for the fan in the thundering machinery below to gust through open grilles, blowing the girls' skirts up.

Queues for the Caterpillar were always long.

At the Wall of Death, Alan gripped the viewing rail and looked down the vertical track, willing the flash riders to fall off. One of the girls was standing between him and Hendo. 'Last year a bloke got his leg chopped off,' she said, chomping on a toffee apple.

Hendo raised an eyebrow. Lies and exaggeration were all part of the Hoppings frisson, in an atmosphere where dirt was deliciously touchable.

Another girl, curling her pink tongue around pinker candyfloss, suddenly screeched, 'Ouch! That bloke just twitched my bum.'

'Dirty gypo!' yelled Alan.

'Wishful thinking,' murmured Hendo. He suddenly felt reflective. He had moments like this now, when he could remove himself, stand back and look. The girls were drifting off, and he was glad. He didn't understand why the sensual earthiness which tickled the evening also shamed him. Was it the rides which made him feel a bit sick, or the lust of excess?

Or was it just lust?

Women seemed dangerously stirred by the raw tension around them. He watched one young mother meeting the gaze of a dark-skinned man who was leaning against a booth, and he wondered if she was fantasizing about forbidden sex in a dark caravan. As Alan hauled him towards the (secretly dreaded) Big Wheel, Hendo looked behind the garish facades, sensing superstition and desperation lurking in the shadows. Did pickpockets actually enjoy their work? Did gypsies really lure away helpless virgins, or did they go willingly? Could Romany women in tasselled shawls honestly see the future?

Twilight was falling, blurred by thousands of spinning lights. Hendo heard the screams of the women on the rides, and suddenly felt that everything was wrong, distorted.

'I miss David,' he said.

Alan stopped for a moment, shook his head, and looked at his friend with a terrible mix of anger and sadness.

❖

Greta knew that same terrible mix. Breathless, she paused at a circular stall where an old woman was handing out six marbles for sixpence. Twenty to score, prizes galore!

'Time, Binnie.'

'Go. Hurry. I know what to do.' The old woman stared into Greta's face.

'What do you see, Binnie?'

But the old Romany woman would not be drawn. 'Be sure, Greta. Very sure.'

'I am.'

'Quickly now.'

Back aching, Greta staggered to her caravan. At the steps another contraction clutched her whole body. After a few seconds it subsided, leaving her surprised and fearful.

It was time to cross the Great North Road to Princess Mary's Maternity Hospital which stood, in awesome Victorian pomp, so conveniently near the Town Moor that Geordies believed gypsies deliberately contrived their pregnancies for delivery to coincide with Race Week. Not Greta. Her child was not planned. The twenty-seven-year-old had enjoyed her fabulous body too much to want it impregnated. Unfortunately HE had enjoyed her body too. At this precise moment her hands were shaking with fear, not just of the delivery, but also of the man who raped her daily, her husband, Dick Korda.

So little time left. The child was impatient, yet even now Greta muttered bitterly, 'How did I let this happen? How have I allowed the bugger to crush me, to bloat me with his filthy child?'

Three dirt-grubbing years. Yet, before that, she had been a daring, defiant trapeze artist, her hard, muscular body sparkling with sequins, a feathered headdress floating behind her as she flew over the heads of entranced audiences. In the air she was supple and strong, sure-handed, perfectly timed. Gutsy Greta never missed a catch because mistakes were unthinkable. Until Dick. Now Greta was tethered to the mud by the deceit of her own body. Pregnancy had suffocated that fierce spirit under a weight of lethargy and self-loathing.

The shell of the caravan was dirty, paint cracked and peeling. Inside, the rancid smell of Dick's unwashed body clung to faded crimson fabrics.

Greta carefully eased herself into a sitting position on the unmade bed, legs apart, belly between her knees. A lumpy foot shifted under her skin as the baby moved, restless to be born. Looking around in despair, she thought about the small unwanted life, warm and protected in her womb, and vowed that this caravan would never be its home.

Hurry. Hurry.

Greta pushed herself into a kneeling position on the bed. She stretched up towards a cupboard over her head, fingernails just touching, but another contraction drew her hands into claws and she curled into a ball. Puffing, she waited until peace returned, then tried again. There was something she had to get. Then she would hobble over to the Maternity Hospital just late enough so that they couldn't turn her away.

The next contraction bit down. She arched her back, trying to escape it. Dick's child. Undoubtedly a boy, with his father's sadistic leer and terrifying temper.

Dick should be busy working his ride, the Zipper, for the next few hours. She raised her head to look out of the little windows. No sign of the soiled checked shirt, the broad shoulders, the oily curls or the sensual swagger. It was a busy evening, so the Zipper would be running full every two minutes. She should be safe for a while.

Again she tried to reach up to the secret place where Dick kept the money. Standing on the bed had been easy until about the sixth month. Now she rolled herself forward and lifted a knee, but her muscles would not respond properly. Breathless, she fell against the window and pressed her brow hard on its cold surface.

❖

Dick saw her face braced against the glass. He stopped and watched her, hating the spirited beauty he had married for becoming an old frump.

26

But, Greta as he had first known her! A beauty with icy, slanted eyes and deep ruby lips, smooth, tanned skin covering curves ripe with the promise of passion, every muscle, every nerve finely tuned, as she stretched and contorted on the dangerous high swing.

Now, with this obscene growth in her belly – Christ, she was repulsive! The crafty bitch had tricked him into fatherhood. He wanted no baby. But nothing had shifted the little bastard, however hard he had tried to bash it out of her.

Was it even his? How many times had she rejected him? Enough to make a bloke wonder. Had she been doing some other bugger? Is that why he had to force her these days?

Irrational suspicion chewed at his drunken brain cells.

Dick Korda was only once removed from reptile. Others had seen it when Greta had been blind to everything but sex. 'Possessed of a thousand devils' (as Binnie described him), the madness was growing, fuelled by greed, power and whisky.

Dick leaned against a lorry and dragged on his cigarette.

❖

As her belly squeezed, so did Greta's resolve tighten. Why, oh why had she married him? The itinerant nature of their existence hardly demanded legal niceties, and although real gypsies were proud of their Romany heritage, the hundreds of caravans assembled on Newcastle Town Moor housed many a fugitive from the real world. Dick Korda was no Romany. His background was as dark as his scowl. Yet there she had stood, drunkenly swaying beside this vulgar, aggressive man, before a registrar in Bath. Now the law gave the bastard rights over her child – and she couldn't bear it.

Her own fault. Her own bittersweet sin, which strapped her to him.

At first she had liked it. An athletic young woman, her wildness craved and courted sexual ferocity. But gradually Dick's taste for dominance had tipped over the edge, changing from titillation to gross humiliation. If anything, the pregnancy had increased his lust. It was a miracle that the baby had clung to her insides to full term.

She knew the exact moment of conception. An afternoon of shifting gears and sexual acceleration. It had been cold, she remembered, and wet. The floor of the caravan was perpetually slippery with muddy footmarks . . .

❖

If only she hadn't slipped. If her ankle hadn't turned. If her skirt hadn't tangled on the drawer handle. But the devil had tempted the moment. Dick towered over her, laughing. A kick. A push. Frenzied slapping and shoving on both sides.

She remembered him pinning her to the ground, his weight crushing. As always, she fought – that was the game. Her master punished her by binding her hands with his belt and hooking the buckle on a clothes peg above the bed. Then began the taunting, the sweet, shameful torture. His dirty hands poked and pinched while she twisted and turned her torso, hurling abuse at him. She spat in his face. Greta hated it . . . and yet . . .

His lips were slack with lust as he knelt on the bed and thrust his filthy fingers into her mouth. She tried to avert her head. He smacked her across the jaw, then grasped her scalp. This was new. Greta recoiled. She didn't want the foul-smelling pubic hair thrusting into her face. She gagged. The temptation to bite was insistent, but she dreaded the consequences.

Afterwards she had been left to weep and dangle. Dick, however, was gluttonous. Greta remembered the endless afternoon of rape which followed. She also remembered her own guilty, sucking orgasm. From that day on, Dick's appetite for abuse became insatiable. Greta endured it, bruised physically and mentally, never healing enough to find the strength to walk away.

Once she missed a period it was too late. She had no home, no money, no one to turn to.

❖

Shamed tears slid beneath her lashes. Hold on to the happier times, she told herself, keep the memories safe and pure. Remember, remember . . . body stretched in a graceful crescent – hanging somewhere between heaven and hell. Swinging from one side of the big top to the other. Letting go. Flying . . .

Memories faded as her bulbous body began squeezing once more.

The pains were too close. It was happening too quickly. The money would have to wait. Thank God she'd left her case with Binnie. Hidden under her friend's divan was a battered brown leather suitcase containing a few baby clothes, some of her own tatty garments and a tiny, multicoloured teddy bear with black glass eyes, which she had knitted herself, as a child. The suitcase could not have stayed in Dick's caravan. He destroyed anything she cherished. If he found out about the ten bob notes sewn into the lining he would destroy her.

A hard slap on the window vibrated through Greta's skull. Her eyes, dilated and unfocused, flew open to meet Dick's scowl on the other side of the glass. Stomach churning, she cursed herself for lingering. In a flash he was at the door.

'Not got rid of that ugly lump yet?' His eyes glittered craftily under hooded lids.

'Tea?' Greta tried to sound normal. 'Busy night to be leaving the ride.' Another spasm was building and she turned to the stove to hide it. 'I've run out of matches.' She could barely get the words out as she clawed for the kettle.

He reached over and threaded his fingers through her jet-black hair, then grabbed and tugged.

'What's to be done then?' Stale breath hissed against her ear. 'To get this lump out of the way?' There was a quiet, petulant rage under his voice. 'How can we wake the bleeding brat up?'

'Jesus, Dick, not that. For Christ's sake, I'm past my time.'

The contraction melted away, but every other muscle tensed.

Dick sneered. 'Scared, Greta? In case I want to play with your great ugly body? I'm not drunk enough.' Vice-like fingers bruising her arm, he dragged her towards the door and pushed her down the steps.

Greta fought him clumsily, her arms as muscular as his, but she couldn't kick because a baby was pressing on her pelvis, and the exhaustion of late pregnancy had sapped her strength.

Folk were used to strange things happening at the fair. Heads turned as a strapping bloke dragged a hugely pregnant woman behind him, but – well, 'gypos' did things like that.

Dick's face glowed with mischief, his gold tooth glinting. He pushed her to the front of the Zipper queue, hauled her into a carriage, and bashed the metal bar down on her belly.

'Give us a good shove,' he shouted, 'Greta wants to get going.'

A laughing urchin stationed himself behind the car, swinging it round as it began heaving up and down the undulating circuit.

The ride picked up speed, and the next excruciating contraction hit. Dizziness brought bile into Greta's throat. She longed to pass out, for her mind to escape, even if her body couldn't. Round and round she was hurled, first one way, then the other. Pain and panic began to push her back inside of herself, into a dark place where all she could think was, 'Survive. I must survive.'

Tortured minutes passed and finally the ride slowed. The pain was easing but her mind was trapped in the dark. She was only vaguely aware of being pummelled and pushed out of the car. Her legs gave way. Dick propped her up from behind, hands roughly clenched under her swollen breasts. The world was still spinning. She felt sick. From far away she heard his voice, 'Big Wheel.' Disoriented, she staggered along, and after being pushed into a carriage, she was trapped once more behind a weighty steel bar. Again, the pressure triggered another agonizing cramp, as the great Wheel lifted her backwards and up.

Flying! She was flying again. But now she was terrified and she didn't want to fly ever again. Over the top, the sickly lunge downwards. Down. Back. Up and . . . over again.

Vomit fell into the air, splattering the riders beneath.

Drops fell on Alan and Hendo, who recoiled in disgust. Fascinated, they retreated with other spectators to stand at a safe distance and watch the pregnant woman spray crescent streams into the sky.

The operators brought the ride to a halt, with Greta's chair at the bottom. When they lifted the bar she slumped out. Groups of people gawked as the huge, filthy woman was shunted over the red platform. There was a general snigger as Dick furiously stripped off his evil-smelling shirt.

Oblivious, Greta fell to her knees, clutching her belly. A grinding pressure was building near the base of her spine, enveloping her whole body in a tension which felt beyond endurance. Suddenly her feet were drenched. The whole world and his brother witnessed the breaking of Greta's waters.

❖

'Some show, that.'

'Pissing herself!'

'Alan, you silly bugger, that wasn't piss, that was amniotic fluid.'

'Just cos you've done biology!'

'Be thankful, lad, that you're a stigma, not a stamen.'

'I am. Poor lass.'

'Aye, poor lass.'

Neither of them was really thinking about the gypsy woman.

❖

Greta lay in the mud, gulping for air. They had managed to

get her behind a caravan, but it was happening too quickly. The rolling, clamouring urge between her splayed thighs meant that time had run out.

Watchers were circling, grandfathers in blazers and mothers in sandals, standing on tiptoe, men looking sideways, teenagers ogling, while children clutching toffee apples wriggled between legs for a better view. If Alan and Hendo had waited a little longer they would have seen old Binnie lift Greta's skirt and place a shawl beneath her open legs. And if they had stayed in the front row, they might have glimpsed the gypsy's pubis stretched and swollen.

The gypsy covered her face with her hands. She writhed and screamed as the basest of animal instincts made her contract every muscle in her body. The voyeurs' curiosity was sated. A black head crowned between Greta's shuddering thighs. Seconds later a purple mass slid on to the bloodsoaked shawl. The baby was as floppy as a rag doll, and silent.

Desperately trying to cover herself Greta let out a gurgling howl. 'Was that worth sixpence, you bastards?' she yelled, 'A dead baby?'

Binnie gathered Greta's inert baby into the dirty shawl. Across the old woman's soiled palm lay the umbilical cord. She curled her fingers around it. Closing her eyes, she began muttering softly. The audience watched, fascinated, as some private horror shuddered visibly across the fortune-teller's bent shoulders.

had a gentler premonition – no more than a stomach flutter, a sense of pathways shifting beneath her feet.

She entered the ward cheerfully, only to be met by the wrath of Midwife Ada Parks.

'Gypo in. Hacky! Foul-mouthed. Violent. Clouted me! Kept screaming that the Devil had killed her kid. We've scalded and scrubbed her and put her in the side ward.'

'The baby?'

'Fine, considering what she arrived in. The gypo won't feed. Won't even pick the bairn up. Seemed happier when she thought it was dead. Ranting about curses. Crackers!'

'Poor woman.'

'I hope her bust bursts.'

'Not on my duty, please.'

'They're bringing down one of the "naughty girls". Midwife at St Hilda's can't cope tonight. Breech. Sister says to put her in with the gypo. Two mucky bitches together.'

Janice felt the flutter again. 'There but for the grace . . .' she snapped.

34

'Pardon?'

'Children only get pregnant because they don't understand what they're doing.'

'Aye. But they enjoy doing it.' Ada picked up her bag. 'Into the breech for you tonight, petal. Tarrah.'

Janice went straight to the nursery. Her secret relish for this part of her job bordered dangerously on fetish. Cradling the babies, she temporarily possessed every child. Each week she had a favourite – a boy with huge eyes, a girl with a strawberry birthmark, a lamb with a twisted foot. Sometimes, when no one was looking, Janice would pick them up and covertly kiss their foreheads, then hold the bottle close to her own nipple.

Janice's own breasts would never flow. God's law of random selection was cruel. She had menopaused prematurely, at twenty. A devout Christian, she labelled herself 'biblically barren' and indulged the minor sin of envy. Although she knew the theory of postnatal depression, a mother's rejection of a baby was utterly beyond her comprehension. It was evil.

So, as she changed and fed the gypsy's baby, Janice had little compassion for the dark-skinned woman who lay unusually still, her closed face deathly and forbidding. With the warm bundle in her left arm, the nurse laid her right hand on the gypsy's shoulder.

'Mrs . . .? We need your name, pet, for records. And one for the baby.'

A long brown arm lifted from the bed and flipped Janice's gentle hand away.

❖

Just before midnight, the under-age pregnancy was trundled into the side ward with the gypsy. Janice pulled gingham screens around, in a farcical attempt to give the child some privacy.

'Am I going to die?' Sylvia Sharp's russet hair stuck to her head and a waxen glaze sweated across her pale skin. She was clutching her vagina, like a toddler who wants to wee. 'Get it out! Please. Help me get it out.'

'That's your job. And it's hard work. That's why it's called labour.'

Sylvia was pounding her fists on the bed and arching her back.

Janice tried to calm her. 'Try to relax between the pains, pet. You're in hospital now. We'll look after you.'

'I'm supposed to have it in the Home.'

'Baby wants to come feet first. You might need extra help.'

'It hurts! Where's me mam? Ow!'

❖

God hates me, thought Sylvia, in a brief moment of respite while her body paused between contractions. He's broken my heart, and now He's breaking my body.

Oh! Oh, no . . . It's coming again . . .

'Mam!'

But her mam wasn't there, and neither was God. She was alone, behind a gingham screen, terrified because she knew that, bad as the pain was, it could still get worse before she died. This time she yelled from the bottom of her soul. The yelling gathered momentum, taking over her body, her lungs involuntarily drawing and expelling gusty yowls.

The screen was suddenly yanked back. Framed in the artificial light was a wild-looking, black-haired woman in a hospital nightie. The woman came forward and stared down at Sylvia with eyes like frozen sky.

'Here. Hold my hand.'

❖

When Janice glimpsed, through the screens, the gypsy woman wiping a flannel over the girl's brow, her first reaction was revulsion, as if she was witnessing some foul corruption – evil anointing an innocent. Again, the ground seemed to shift. Uneasy, Janice stood quietly for a moment and listened, but in the gypsy's murmurs she only heard kindness, and Sylvia Sharp was coping more calmly, her knees up, bent, ready.

An hour later Sylvia's baby daughter was born – head first. Despite her tender years, tender flesh and demented screaming, she had delivered relatively easily, requring no stitches and being left with an instantaneously deflated belly. The child weighed six pounds six ounces, heavier than Greta's by half an ounce and younger by just one day.

With her red tresses spilling over the pillow, the teenager looked like an exhausted movie star. Janice slipped a tiny nightie over the baby's head, wrapped her in a sheet and placed her in Sylvia's shaking arms.

'What will you call her?'

The bundle wriggled. Sylvia kissed her daughter's little round head, which was dusted with hair as coaly-black as David's.

'Alice. Yes, Alice.'

'Little sweetheart. Tomorrow they'll show you how to feed and change her.'

But Sylvia was crying. Huge tears were welling and spilling on the baby's face. Janice took some cotton wool and wiped both children's eyes.

'Are they making you give her up?'

Sylvia nodded, hupping and gulping. 'But not properly, through the Home. I think my dad's sold my baby. To a baker's wife.'

Janice felt a breath on the back of her neck, and sensed the gypsy standing behind her.

'Oh, pet,' said Janice, biblically barren, 'hard though it is, you'll be giving a sad lady the most wonderful gift.'

'A gift she can never ever have back,' snapped the gypsy.

After her shift, Janice went home to sleep. Even with the sun streaming through the gap in her curtains, she had a series of nightmares.

Katherine

dawdled home, grumbling about this afternoon's horrible Maths test. 'What use is trigo-sodd'n-nometry anyway? Sin should be a damn sight more interest'n and the only tan I want is on me legs. God, I'm starv'n.'

The back door was locked. She found the key in the shed and let herself in. On the kitchen table was an artfully penned note.

Dear Kath,
You know WHAT has happened. Have gone
to visit.
Peel some spuds for tea. Ta.
Mam.

'Small mercies,' Katherine said, licking jam off a spoon. Was it a boy or a girl? Why did no one tell her anything?

She didn't feel sorry for her sister, in fact she was glad Sylvia was going away to Lincoln, but it seemed odd, just handing a baby, like a cup of sugar, over the back fence.

Head averted, Greta tried to doze, willing her breasts to shrink and her vagina to stop bleeding. Her heart, she knew, would never stop aching. But maternal love was simply too powerful and too dangerous to be indulged.

❖

Sylvia clutched Alice to her chest. Her mam sat staring at the floor, and her dad, Cuthbert Sharp, went to look out of the window. He had called her 'dirty' so many times that Sylvia had started to believe that there was something bad inside her, giving her rude urges, something dirty passed to this little baby who he had called a bastard.

'I've called her Alice, Mam.'

'Oh, love. You can't call her anything,' Violet Sharp hissed through taut lips, like a bad ventriloquist. 'The other folks have made a nursery and bought her clothes and everything. They'll pick baby's name.'

Across the ward, the gypsy caught Sylvia's eye, and put her finger to her lip.

Yes, thought the teenager, words sounding unusually loud inside her mind. Silence is power. Silence is the last thing they'll expect.

It was surprisingly easy, saying nothing. It distanced her and punished them. What no one could have imagined, however, not Greta, nor Violet, nor Sylvia herself, was that clicking in that silence, a trigger, balanced delicately in the girl's head, was already cocked, ready to fire.

❖

Violet always felt her emotion in her bowels. They rumbled loudly as she whispered, 'They're good folks. Desperate for a bairn. Lovely little house behind the bakers' shop. She'll never be hungry.'

Crumpets and teacakes and strawberry tarts. Violet felt sick, but she carried on, 'It's time to sign the paper, love. Then it'll be all sorted. Just let them . . .' she nodded towards the door, 'think you're keeping it. You'll be out in a week, and straight off to your auntie's in Lincoln. Fresh start for you, love, and nobody none the wiser.'

None the wiser? Violet thought she was being wise; setting her daughter back on a right path. But in the bitter silence, while the girl's eyes pleaded, and the baby who must not be called Alice waved a small, pale, helpless arm, Violet was thinking that it was Sylvia she badly wanted to hold. Her own little lass, too padded and swollen with womanhood for an innocent cuddle.

'Oh, pet. It's for your own good. And the bairn's. Clean, quick break.'

Still Sylvia would not speak.

'When the right time comes, in a few years, I'll be the best grandma ever. But not now. Not like this. When the baby's father is fifteen and his family has called you such awful names.'

Violet's bowels churned again. She met her husband's glare, noticing the oiliness of his red hair, the dandruff on his jacket collar. Face set hard, Cuthbert pulled the buff envelope out of his pocket.

'You'll sign this for the solicitor.'

There was no cussing, no shouting from the teenager. Nothing at all.

A fresh gush of pitying love flooded over Violet – yet still she could not touch her daughter. These days she hardly dared touch anyone. Only by keeping her body tight as swaddling could she cope.

None the wiser. The baker, his jolly wife and all their blessed buns were waiting. The form must be signed.

'You're such a clever lass,' she heard herself saying. 'Your auntie's bought you a smart new school uniform. And one day, when you're a bit more grown up, and a nice young man takes you out dancing, you'll understand . . .'

But Sylvia had pushed herself out of bed, heedless of the blood running in trails down the inside of her thighs and into her slippers. She stood directly in front of her mother, with her baby in her arms.

'Come on, lass, you should be in bed.' Unable to resist any longer, Violet looked down at her cherubic granddaughter. 'I'm so sorry, pet, that it has to be like this.' Tenderly she took the baby, in her bundle of blankets, kissed her tiny, innocent forehead and placed her in the crib. Then Violet pulled her silent daughter towards her and, for the last time ever, the girl came willingly into her arms.

But Cuthbert placed a stern hand on her shoulder, and Violet stepped back to let him have his say. His frustrated vocabulary made her shiver with shame, even if his only audience was a dirty gypsy. 'Whore.' The unforgivable word ricocheted off bare walls, polished floor and sterile sink.

. . . hate it here! Snobs, bullies . . . headaches . . . Matron's a cow. Headmaster abhors me.

David's father, Arthur Linden, smoothed the crumpled letter.

'What have we done, Mary?' he asked his wife.

'They'll make a man of him.'

'What sort of man? This is the first letter he's written to us, after all these months, and it's full of begging. I'm appalled.'

'He's soft. Cowardice, it seems, runs in your family.'

'Never miss a chance, do you? I don't think David's a coward. But maybe I am. Only crippling weakness could have made me marry the snottiest, most selfish woman in the whole of Tyneside!'

'I BEG YOUR PARDON?' But Arthur had walked out of the room. Mary Linden listened to the telephone click and muttered under her breath: 'Ringing his flaming mother again!'

❖

'What a bloody afternoon!' moaned Ada, as Janice came back on duty. 'The gypo still won't look after her kid. Some filthy old biddy from the Hoppings came in. I had to wrestle the bairn out of her hacky mits! The colour of her fingernails! Then Sister and me chucked Sylvia Sharp's dad out. I quite enjoyed that. What a racket he made! Bad-tempered, foul-mouthed git. I actually feel sorry for that lass, now.'

❖

Violet sat grimly darning a sock over a wooden mushroom.

'Turn that flam'n radio off, Kath. Get on with your homework.'

'Mam?'

'What?'

'Is owa Sylvia definitely going to Auntie's?'

'Aye.'

'Can I have her bedroom?'

'You can't.' Violet threw down her work and crashed out into the kitchen. Opening the back door, she slumped down on the step.

'It's a wicked thing – love,' she murmured to herself. 'A wicked bloody thing.'

❖

Janice Kirkstone looked up. On her lap was a dark-haired baby.

'Is that mine?' The gypsy stood swaying at the nursery door.

'No. This is Alice. Your baby is over there.'

The strange woman looked into the cot where her own baby lay sleeping.

'Is she like me?'

Janice shrugged. 'What are you like?'

Greta left the nursery with a stiff back and a wide gait.

❖

The Zipper ran fast and furious as Dick hopped from car to car, flirting with screaming girls and pocketing their money. One particular lass with ample breasts must have spent nearly ten bob, coming back time after time to roll around in the undulating car like a cuddly puppy. When the Zipper stopped he helped her out and she fell against him, feigning dizziness. She didn't seem to mind when the back of his hand brushed against her blouse.

❖

At two in the morning, while Janice sat beside Greta Korda, feeding the unnamed gypsy baby, she found herself disturbingly fascinated by the sight of the teenager, Sylvia Sharp, trying to offer her nipple into her tiny daughter's mouth. A glow of intimacy between the young mother and child reminded her of Mary and Jesus. Blasphemy! the nurse chided herself. But a surge of guilty superstition kept her eyes locked on the pale, freckled breast. This moment was, for some reason, either holy, or abominably unholy.

Why am I thinking like this?

Beside her, the gypsy mother was lying on her stomach, apparently sleeping. Looking down at the unloved babe in her arms, the kind nurse felt overwhelmed by something far beyond pity. This was not emotion of the heart, it was of the soul. God, she was sure, wanted something from her. So she tucked one contented baby into her cot, and went to rescue the second.

'You shouldn't be nursing, Sylvia. Your breasts will become very painful when you don't have baby any longer. Let me give her a bottle, pet.'

With gentle compassion, she took the baby out of Sylvia's exhausted arms.

Alice. So sweet. So alert. Janice sat with the bottle tilted and her head bowed, so that she didn't have to witness the young mother's pain.

When tiny Alice was settled, this God-fearing nurse brought crêpe bandages and bound them tightly around Sylvia's chest. The girl seemed acquiescent enough as she lay down to sleep. Janice checked both babies, turned out the light and closed the door.

❖

Sylvia dreamed words. They echoed from somewhere behind her head: 'I am the bread of life. He that cometh to me shall never hunger. Four and twenty blackbirds baked in a pie.'

Out of the voice came a picture. An oven, and a tray of baking tins, some lined with pastry, some bulging with white dough. In one of the loaf tins lay Alice.

'Pat-a-cake, pat-a-cake!'

High above, a giant bird was beating the air. It swooped down and rested its ticklish head on Sylvia's shoulder. As she cringed, a pair of black wings, as huge as an angel's, all feather and spindly bone, swept around her body, enfolding her, pinning her arms to her sides.

Heat blasted out of the oven door. Frantically, she tried to kick herself free, but she was being squeezed by the wings, tighter and tighter. The oven door was closing. Sylvia's body slackened in despair, and she was in a hospital bed, gripping a twisted sheet, staring at a cot, where her newborn baby lay quite safe, wide awake, strangely alert.

As the innocent child stared back at her, the shock of grief hit Sylvia so hard that a pain in her core, worse than any physical contraction, drew her knees up to her chest, and she began to whine.

'Sylvia?'

The gypsy limped across the cold floor, her own stitches biting. 'I know, lass. I know.'

❖

At six a.m., Janice Kirkstone reopened the door of the side ward, and stopped. Every instinct, every twinge of doubt and premonition, gushed into the silent room. Both of the mothers' beds were empty. Worse, their babies, so alike in colouring, were lying top-to-toe in the same cot, all identifying tags removed. The babies' charts had also vanished. In their place, a note:

> This baby is called Alice Sharp. I forbid anyone to adopt her! I have run away so that my father can't make me sign the papers, but I will come back for her as soon as I can. Please look after her kindly.

> Yours faithfully, Sylvia Sharp

Janice touched each child, lifting blankets, stroking, saying soundless sorrys for things which were not her fault. Then she ran out into the corridor, shouting.

One baby slept on. The other stared at an empty bed, disturbed by gypsy hands which had cheated her from cot to cot, when the younger mother was already half-way down the corridor.

Two daughters abandoned. One would never forgive, and one would never have the chance to.

Unable to run,

two weary, childless mothers sat on a park bench, staring across the Great North Road, where a low June sun burnished the colours of the sleeping fairground rides.

'Sorry. Jelly legs.' Sylvia had barely walked any distance before needing to sit down. 'Can you get me a job at the Hoppings, Greta?'

'I could send you to friends, but I'll never go back. It's taking me all my courage to walk away from my baby so she won't be raised in the muck by a father who'd beat her.'

'Why does a man do that?'

'Because he enjoys it. Come on, girl; keep walking. That life's not for you, either.'

They made an incongruous pair, limping towards Newcastle, with their pelvises still stretched and their empty maternity dresses flapping; Greta carrying a battered suitcase, Sylvia her mother's vanity box.

'It's miles to Central Station,' the young girl moaned. 'We'll have to catch the train, won't we? Get away quick.'

'Can't leave Newcastle. Not yet.'

'But shouldn't we go to London or somewhere?'

'Never do what people expect, Sylvia. First lesson of survival. Anyway, you're dead on your feet. We need to hide and rest.'

'Where?'

'Keep walking while I think. It's you they'll be worried about. Gypsies hardly exist.'

'That's awful.'

'Useful.'

Sylvia sagged against a tree. 'Go on without me, Greta. I can't leave Alice.'

'They're taking her away from you, anyway.'

For a moment Greta kept walking. Then she stopped and turned. 'Come on, girl. Put one foot in front of the other.'

Sylvia began tottering as quickly as her jittery legs would allow. 'Will the police stop Dad doing this secret adoption?'

'Don't know.'

'Will the hospital look after the babies?'

'Yes.'

'Just for a fortnight or so,' Sylvia promised herself. 'Until we've got jobs, and somewhere to live.'

The two mothers trudged on, Sylvia sniffling with terrified sorrow; Greta sucking private tears behind her nose, into her throat. Each in their own way was ripped apart emotionally, too raw to measure their actions. They thought what they were doing made sense.

'The hospital will call the police,' Greta reasoned. 'They'll put a watch on Central Station. We need a car. Tomorrow's problem. Today we go shopping.'

'Shopping?'

'We're a bit shabby, girl.'

Greta smiled. A shocking smile. White, wide and surprisingly clean. Something lifted under Sylvia's breastbone. A judder of hope, or an oblique dawning.

They rested briefly beneath the outstretched wings of the verdigris goddess in Haymarket, before dragging their bones down the deserted parade of department stores. Sylvia's stomach was cramping. In an underground public toilet, seeing how much blood was draining out of her, she wailed, 'Bloody hell, bloody hell.'

Greta shouted through the cubicle wall, 'Normal. For a week or so. Let's clean up and find a cuppa.'

'What if I bump into someone I know?'

'Look, if you want to, catch a bus and get clear of Newcastle. But I can't leave the city yet. I must work something out.' She was smoothing down her voluminous dress, as if trying to find the figure beneath it. 'Have you got somewhere you could stay?'

'No one. Nowhere.' Sylvia's confidence was ebbing away with her blood. 'Where will you go?'

'To a friend. I trust him.'

'A man? Would he help me too?'

'Maybe. He lives in Yorkshire. But tonight we need somewhere very clean and very private.' Hesitating for a moment, Greta said, 'They'll blame me, you know. Say you were lured away by a wicked gypsy. That I cast a spell over you.'

'Have you?'

'I'm not really a gypsy and I can't cast spells.' She looked right into Sylvia's eyes. Again, the young girl felt a stir. There was something unexpected, something hidden behind tangled hair and tatty clothes. Was it, perhaps – beauty? Uncomfortable, the teenager looked down at her own huge brown smock and horrible flat, schoolgirl sandals.

Greta touched her arm. 'I've got a little money. Would you like a new dress?'

Oddly, Sylvia felt choked up again, as if kindness was unbearable.

'What do you think will be happening at home?'

❖

The door knocker reverberated around the house.

'Mam!' Katherine was simultaneously stuffing toast into her mouth and schoolbooks into her satchel. Before Violet could answer the door, the hammering started again.

'Mrs Sharp?'

With a deep flush rising in her chest she ushered the blue uniform in, then popped her head back out to scan the street for nosy neighbours.

'About your daughter,' the officer began.

Violet's mouth was open but she couldn't speak.

'Sylvia Sharp?'

She nodded rapidly.

'She's left hospital. Run off. Fourteen, isn't she? Has she come home?'

Home? Guilt hit Violet like a hammer.

'No . . .' Then, in a rushing, frantic gabble of shocked grief, 'Where's she gone?' Thoughts and words tumbled together. 'She's only a bit lass. Just had a bairn. I haven't done right. Haven't done right at all. Oh, God, what about the baby? Did she take the bairn with her?' The officer was shaking his head. 'Or . . . the baby died?' She clapped a hand over her mouth. 'Did the baby die? Oh, me lass.' The policeman tried to penetrate her gibberish but Violet was lost to panic. 'It's me man's fault. Not mine. Not mine.'

She already had one arm in her grey coat and was grabbing purse and shopping bag.

The policeman blocked the door.

'Your man at home?'

'No. He's on nights. The pit.'

'I'll walk you to the station.'

Half an hour later Violet formally reported her daughter, Sylvia Sharp, as missing.

'Red hair. Tall. I don't know how tall. Yes. Got in trouble with a lad. But a good girl . . .'

❖

The good girl was sitting in Fenwick's' Powder Room, where mirrored walls reflected her drawn face. She had removed the painful binding and stuffed the bandages in her box, but rhythmic belly cramps kept bending her double. Struggling to focus, she thought, I look awful, yellowish. My bosoms are enormous. My hair! I look as wild as her. A gypsy, I've run away with a bloody gypsy!

Behind her, the shabby gypsy was slouched, trance-like, on a velveteen seat. In these plush surroundings, her long, matted black locks and dark complexion were out of place.

Further along, a middle-aged woman was fluffing her perm. The hairstyle was almost identical to her mother's. Sylvia rummaged in her mam's vanity box for a hairbrush.

❖

Greta watched Sylvia tugging lethargically at red curls, folding strands around fingers. Such beautiful hair! Moving to the mirror, the gypsy scowled at herself. A wart on her chin and she'd look like a witch!

'Can I borrow your brush?'

Sylvia pulled out a handful of red threads and passed it over. They both knew she was wondering if it would come back crawling with nits. Greta stroked the brush through her heavy black swathe. Suddenly she brought her dark face close to Sylvia's pale cheek and whispered, 'They'll be hunting for a young girl with a gypsy woman. Look.' Their eyes met in the reflection. 'That's exactly what we are. But with high heels and makeup – you'll look three years older. For me,' she murmured, twisting the black mass of hair into an untidy knot, 'a hat, a suit . . . a little class.'

'I'm too tired,' Sylvia groaned.

Greta returned the brush thoughtfully. Mischief tilted the corners of her eyes. 'Tonight – the last place they'll look – the flashiest hotel in the city.'

They waddled up to the fashion department where Greta selected a powder-blue linen suit and matching pillbox hat. Navy netting fell across a down-turned brim, veiling her wide forehead. Dramatic black locks were twisted into a chignon. She straightened her back, lifted her chin. Forgotten grace and beauty emerged from the ashes of her shame, to glow in her tanned face.

'Where shall we go tomorrow, girl? York, or New York?'

'Across the Atlantic on the *Queen Elizabeth*.'

A bubble of laughter hesitated behind Sylvia's smile. Standing even taller in white court shoes, she was wearing a full-skirted cotton dress splashed with overblown apricot roses. Gloves, a wide-brimmed hat which flowed in a luxurious wave across one side of her face, swollen breasts pushed into a low neckline – she looked even older than the assistant who was picking their tatty maternity garb off the floor.

The transformed women paused their affected, wobbly saunter to buy powder compacts, lipsticks, pants, stockings, and two brown paper bags of STs. But 'Sophisticated Sylvia', who had given birth less than twenty-four hours ago, began to sway.

'My niece is unwell. Fetch a chair!' Greta commanded, sounding as posh as the Queen.

A woman bustled from behind the counter, flustered at the prospect of clearing up vomit.

'Ee, pet. Will I call a doctor?'

'No, no! A taxi!'

With an absurd lack of decorum, Greta pushed Sylvia's head between her knees: then she opened a shiny new compact and powdered her haughty nose.

❖

Student Midwife Kirkstone rocked both the babies together, one on each arm. In her pocket was a clumsily knitted teddy bear.

Matron had been livid when Janice said she wasn't sure which baby was which.

Vanished

POLICE FEAR FOR TEENAGER'S SAFETY

In the offices of the *Evening Chronicle* they were shuffling photographs of Sylvia. She was a minor, and they were required to protect the identity of the babies, so they decided to divide the facts between two stories. The second headline would read:

TWO BABIES ABANDONED BY GYPSIES

❖

Hendo had a soft but brave heart. He feared nothing – except weeping women. Standing with one leg hooked over his crossbar, he looked down dubiously at Sylvia's sister Katherine who was sitting on her garden wall.

'Think she's gone to find Davy?'

Katherine sniffed. 'Mebees. Where is this posh school, anyhow?'

'Me and Alan'll find out.'

'Mam's mental with worry.' She raised her tragic eyes. 'What if she's dead? Murdered by gypsies?'

'Your Sylvia's not daft enough to bugger off with gypos.'

'It's me dad's fault. Bloody bastard!'

Hendo winced. Boys swore, girls shouldn't. It was a pity, because he was attracted to this cheeky, pubescent lass with springy brown curls and freckle-dusted nose. But Sylvia's sister was only thirteen. If he asked her out the lads would think he'd gone off his rocker.

Katherine sighed. 'She's a right cow, owa Sylvia. But she is me sister.'

Hendo watched puddles form beneath dark lashes and decided to clear off before anything embarrassing happened. Leaving Katherine fiddling with a hanky, he scooted off on his bike.

In Gosforth High Street he paused to scan the posters outside the Royalty Cinema. Which girl should he ask out this Saturday, to share one of the double seats in the back row? His eyes wandered upwards to admire the stained-glass dome which gave exotic mystique to the deco whitewashed building.

Hendo had a secret, so private that it hurt. He was blessed with an abiding appreciation of buildings. This one puzzled and fascinated him. Who had designed it? Why? All around him Hendo noticed things – the intricacy of fascia carving, the distortion on an old cottage window frame, the spindles on a staircase, the turn of one roof against another. His happy soul could sprout wings as his gaze ascended a church spire.

A cheerful, optimistic lad, he couldn't bear witnessing the unhappiness of the Sharp family next door. So, turning into a tree-lined avenue, he pedalled towards the ponderous Victorian terraces where Alan lived. He found his mate, as usual, doing homework.

'Yu'll never guess what!'

Alan reacted to Sylvia's story as Hendo expected, furiously. Resolve pushing at young legs, they raced together up elegant avenues to the part of town where large houses hid behind old trees and high stone walls.

Each of the three friends was acutely aware of the social differences between them, with David at one end of the spectrum and Hendo at the other. Unspoken envy wriggled eternally around the trio. Alan coveted David's new bike. He also envied Hendo his dad, who laughed a lot and boozed down the Club. David, on the other hand, would have cheerfully swapped his bike for some of the peace which both the other boys took for granted.

Hendo would have been amazed to know this. With private, jealous longing, he daydreamed about David's HOUSE. Regularly he spent those last few moments before sleep imagining seducing the busty Sabrina in a bedroom with a cantilevered bay window overlooking a huge back garden.

Now, beneath the Lindens' neo-Gothic porch, the two friends stood sweating. Things had changed since Davy went away. They knew that Cuthbert Sharp had returned from his one brief visit to this big house with his ruddy cheeks burning and his eyes like cinders.

A minuscule elderly lady answered the door, accompanied by an equally aged spaniel. David's grandmother looked up at them through small round spectacles.

'Now then, Hendo, what's a big lad like you doing, hiding behind Alan?'

Born charming, born dignified, born into money, Ethel despised affected airs and graces. On this June afternoon, there was little warmth in her pale eyes.

Hendo mumbled, 'Is David in?'

'No. As well you know.'

'We want his address,' Alan, ever confrontational, demanded.

'Wanting doesn't get. Come in. You look thirsty.'

The boys hesitated. Hendo stroked the spaniel and stared at the black and white tiled floor.

'It's all right. David's parents are in Cornwall,' the old woman reassured them.

The kitchen was cool, the dandelion and burdock fizzy. David's gran took them out into the garden and eased herself into a wicker chair.

'You want to write him? What about?'

'Oh, just . . .'

'Has that lass had the baby?'

Two heads studied clipped grass. All this baby stuff was bloody embarrassing. Alan mumbled that yes, she'd had a little girl. They watched with fascination as Ethel slumped in her seat and closed her wrinkly eyes.

❖

A GIRL! The breath at the top of Ethel's chest felt hot, as if she had drunk gin. 'Is she all right?'

'Sylvia's run off. Done a bunk with some gypo woman . . . left the baby behind.'

Ethel felt the lads' anxious faces studying her reactions. A GIRL! At last! But what bitter injustice! She, the great-grand-mother, would never even have the chance to hold the child. Very slowly the boys' words began to sink in. The hussy had abandoned David's baby! Ethel's own great-granddaughter! The first Linden female for three generations. Poor innocent little thing. Oh, the absurd irony.

A lifetime ago Ethel's own daughter had died in her womb, just hours before she was born. The baby, Matilda, had been perfect, but Ethel's womb had not. Matilda and womb were disposed of and Ethel went home to her callous husband and her sad little son, Arthur. Battling privately with her terrible loss and yearning, depression set in. During the day she overwhelmed Arthur with adoration, but late at night the memory of the dead child's face haunted her. Wakeful, resentful of something impossible to repair, she would look down at her sleeping husband and, although none of it was his fault, she fantasized about killing him.

Little Arthur was a good boy who grew into a pleasant young man. Finally, with Ethel's middle age, her son began bringing home young ladies for inspection and she became hopeful that soon she would have grandchildren.

Sadly, on the day Arthur walked down the aisle with Mary, Ethel knew that her daughter-in-law was no blessing. She could only count months, waiting now for a grand-daughter, a doll creature – who was alive, not dead. A child she could dress in pink frills and burp on her shoulder. But there was only to be one grandchild, David, a boisterous tod-dler utterly suppressed by a mother who was constantly slapping him for climbing furniture.

Dear David! Ethel prayed that he would develop more character than his father. Under Mary's domination, Arthur had become as spineless as his own father, who had survived Ethel's murderous urges more by luck than wisdom.

In widowhood, Ethel was now reasonably content, living alone in Corbridge, where the river danced past her home, Twin Elms. She only visited Gosforth occasionally and when she did she generally managed to stir up much (very satisfactory) ill feeling.

With uncharacteristic pity Ethel wondered how Sylvia's mother was coping. The elderly understand humiliation, the powerlessness of diminishing choices. Shame, shame, she thought, it's all about shame.

Hendo broke the silence.

'Me mam says she'll bust herself and bleed to death.'

Alan became insolent then, his faulty posh accent punctuated with finger-pointing. 'David has a right to know! It's his kid!'

'What business is it of yours?' It took more than a cheeky teenager to intimidate Ethel. 'Is that the doorbell? Go get it, Hendo. Thank you.'

The big lad loped obediently across the lawn. He returned to the garden followed by two men.

'It's the police, Mrs Linden.'

The man with the air of a colonel introduced himself: 'Detective Inspector Howard. I need to speak to your grandson, urgently.'

Ethel's frail heart fluttered. 'Ah. The Sharp girl? I've just heard. Do come indoors.'

The second, tubby policeman scanned the faces of the two lads, before following his boss.

When DI Howard and DC Butterwell left, Ethel rushed into the garden, where Hendo and Alan were patiently waiting for information.

'Did Sylvia have intercourse with other boys?' she demanded.

Simultaneously they shook their heads, in quick denial for themselves.

'This baby is definitely David's?'

Nods.

'Then I'm going to write to Sylvia's parents. Will you deliver it, sharpish?'

After they had gone Ethel wrote four more letters: David, Arthur, Hospital, Solicitor.

Exhausted, she fell asleep in her chair.

❖

Violet was knocking desperately on the toilet door. The shock of Sylvia's photograph on the front of the *Chronicle* had set her bowels on fire, but Cuthbert had got in first. He was sitting with his trousers around his ankles, looking at Ethel's note, thinking he might wipe his backside with it.

But, on the other hand, what if David Linden knew where Sylvia was? What if the old biddy had information? He flushed the chain and scrubbed his black fingernails with coaltar soap. A man had his pride.

Marching across Gosforth in his Sunday suit, the miner prepared himself for confrontation with the Linden family. How could he forget the mortification of his last visit? His perfectly reasonable demands (he was conveniently forgetting his threats to throttle young David) had been met by arctic snobbery and foul counter-accusations which had left him feeling as dirty as his pregnant daughter. Bastards!

At the door, the bespectacled old Linden woman had the nerve to smile!

'Thank you for coming. Don't worry; Arthur and Mary are on holiday.' She led him into the formal sitting room, saying, 'I'm minding old Lucy here.'

The spaniel on the moquette sofa opened one eye. Cuthbert returned Lucy's suspicious stare, while Ethel Linden dropped into an armchair and sat twitching at the arm covers. On the small table between them lay the *Chronicle*. Sylvia's face, a child in pigtails, grinned innocently from the front cover.

'She's gone then.'

'Aye.'

'With some gypsy woman?'

'Seems like. Was your David in on this?'

'I don't know. His letters are full of his own misery. He never mentions Sylvia, even to me.'

'Then you've wasted me bloody time.'

'Where've you looked?'

Cuthbert's worry spilled. 'Been all over the Hopp'ns. Ne hide nor hind of owa Sylvia. Looked through caravan windows, under wagons. Walked me feet raw, check'n every face. Twice I rushed after a young lass – what wasn't her. Made a right charlie of meself.' He coughed to cover a choke. 'Aye, she's away. And of her own choice, missus, not abducted like what it says.'

'And the baby?'

'Owa business.'

'The child is David's daughter.'

'DAVID'S DAUGHTER!' Rage purpled his face. 'The same lad what zipped himself back up a bit quick and called owa Sylvia the Gosforth BIKE?'

'David did not spread that rumour. We both know that.'

'Where was the precious boy when owa Sylvia got put inside?'

'He was locked in his room for days. They told him she'd been sent away, that he could never find her. He was only fifteen, Mr Sharp. His parents took over. But he went off to that school bitter as a lemon. What will happen to the child now?'

'None of your sodd'n business.'

Cuthbert made to leave, but when the old biddy shouted for him to stop, he paused with his back to her.

'Mr Sharp, I think we can salvage something from this tragedy.' She measured her words like ladling treacle. 'Let me take care of Sylvia's baby. Just for now. Till everything is sorted.'

'Over my dead body.'

'Why?'

Cuthbert Sharp struggled to find a good reason. Something was nagging at him, something emotional and passionately wordless. He was all off balance.

'Be reassured, I would never let my daughter-in-law touch this precious baby. The wretched woman is utterly egocentric.'

'A cow.'

64

'The child would be looked after at my home in Corbridge. To be truthful, all through Sylvia's pregnancy, I've wondered about asking, but I schooled myself that the baby should be adopted into a normal home with a younger family. Now, with all this publicity, I'm guessing that adoption may have to be postponed. Rather than have my great-granddaughter put in some institution, why not let her come to me, in Twin Elms? A woman from the village, Daphne, comes and does for me. I could even hire a nanny. No one could have more time or more love to give a child. Our little girl will have everything.'

Our little girl? Cuthbert stared at the old lady, who was smoothing her smart skirt with bony old fingers. A newly forming ulcer cramped under his ribs.

'Got a few bob, have you? Posh house along the valley?'

'If it helps, I'm sure we could discuss some – remunerative arrangement.'

Remunerative arrangement? Seconds ticked by as his thoughts hovered between essential practicality and outrage.

Ethel Linden lifted her sagging chin, making her look younger. 'The authorities will surely sympathize with my wish to care for David's baby. Unless you think Sylvia will come back?'

And suddenly Cuthbert knew what had been troubling him. Bowing his head, he closed his eyes and saw her. Saw Sylvia walking up the garden path, opening the kitchen door, and shouting, 'Dad!' Sylvia sitting at the kitchen table doing her homework. Warming her toes on the mat in front of the fire, playing with the cat. If she came home, if she ever walked up the garden path again – what would he say to her?

Leaning against the doorjamb, he crumpled as if he had been kicked in the gut.

Clutching at the arms of the chair, Ethel rocked until she pushed herself upright. 'If we must barter, let's be dignified about it.'

Cuthbert ran his hand through his red hair. Why could he take money from a baker, and not from a Linden? What had happened to him? How was he here, in this house, selling a baby?

He pointed a finger in her face. 'I wouldn't take a bloody farth'n out of your wrinkled awld mit!'

Ethel's voice wavered. 'I've no wish to insult you, Mr Sharp. I simply thought it might make things . . . easier. Oh dear! This has all gone wrong!' Her face looked old again. 'You see, it's really a question of . . . love. I want to love the child, to look after her. Poor mite, she's my own flesh and blood. I couldn't bear for her to grow up thinking no one wanted her.'

The old lady looked too near tears for comfort. Cuthbert shook his obstinate head, sniffed long and loud, then sighed, 'Divent get yourself in a fettle, woman.'

'Don't give that little girl away to strangers. Please.'

❖

'Will I get a reward?' The teenage shop assistant fluttered her eyelashes at a young constable as she described the clothes which the two shabby women had bought.

'That's definitely her. The lass in the *Chronicle*. And the older woman was trying to talk posh, but I wasn't taken in.'

Olive-green curtains were closed against too cheerful sunlight. Violet listened to her husband's blasphemies as he paced the floor, every stomp echoing through her bones as he stamped on Ethel's proposition.

Sylvia's mother was beating herself with a prickly guilt stick. Mistakes must be corrected. Punishments meted. And her husband's conscience needed stripping down and laying bare.

'Mebees it would be an answer. For now,' she ventured.

Cuthbert's face was redder than his hair. 'Mrs Moneybaggage can gan jump off the bloody Bridge. I'll not give the Lindens me bloody spit.'

'Give? What's yours to give? It's a baby you're talking about. The one you want nowt to do with.'

'Aye, but it's owa responsibility. And if we don't watch out, it'll be landed on us. But I'll never let that grasp'n auld cow lay hands on it.'

'It? Your granddaughter?' Violet shouted. 'Doesn't it occur to your ignorant, bigoted brain that Ethel Linden just wants to do the right thing by the bairn? YOU don't want her. I'll say it again – You Don't Want HER.'

'Well, neither do you. Your decision as much as mine.'

'So why not let Ethel take her?'

'What's happened to your own morals, Violet? We picked them people to adopt the kid because they was good. Call uz ignorant, but it would be a darn sight worse to let the Lindens have it, when we can't even be certain it's Davy boy's. We'll never be sure . . .'

'What?'

'. . . how many lads owa Sylvia did it with.' He pointed his finger in her face, as if it were Violet's fault. 'Face it, woman, she's went bad.'

Furiously, she slapped his finger away. 'No!'

'It's the truth, Violet! Your daughter's gone mucky bad.'

'Mine? Not yours?' She narrowed her eyes and dug into the murkiness of Cuthbert's own sexual guilt. 'There's summut wrong with a man who prefers dirty lies to the truth. Mebees it's a sign of how dirty you are yourself. Inside.'

'Bollocks!'

'You've got none,' she shouted. 'You've disgusted me and you've disgusted yourself, gett'n Sylvia's problem all mixed up between yer own mucky urges.'

Cuthbert's glower was becoming dangerous, but Violet wasn't finished.

'You treated owa Sylvia like shite.'

'She turned whore.' His voice was rising on a crescendo.

'She's owa little girl.'

'Sex-crazed!'

'In love.'

'Call that love? Kick'n her knickers off in some alley?'

'Lost your memory, Cuthbert? We did it all ourselves.'

'Aye, I remember. You chas'n uz like a bitch in heat with your brassiere round your waist. YOU she gets it from. YOU!'

Violet lashed. Washday-red hand slapped hard against his jaw. Not hard enough. The look of innocent outrage on her husband's face was maddening. She balled her fist and caught the other side of his face with a second blow. Her hands seemed to have a will of their own, fingers curling into claws as she grabbed at his shirt and ripped at the fabric. Cuthbert had to use coal-hauling strength to free himself. Pushing and shoving, they struggled in a ridiculous, violent dance, lurching around the room, hurting each other, letting the agony out.

A scream stopped them both in their tracks. Katherine was standing at the door, knuckles pressed into her mouth.

Violet felt as if she was sinking into the earth. Her knees buckled and she crumpled to the floor, hands holding her own head, fingers pressed into her scalp, tugging her hair. She was going mad. The world was going mad. Her baby had run away. Enveloped by a wave of wracking wails, she curled up into a foetal position on the carpet. Father and daughter watched impotently, until finally her shoulders stopped heaving.

A stillness fell upon the three. Katherine made a move towards her mam, but Cuthbert gestured her to wait. He edged slowly towards his wife and put his hand on her rounded back.

The fugitive mothers

floated on soft hotel beds, while the sun burned its way through the first hot afternoon. On they slumbered through a short midsummer night, until dawn rubbed at Newcastle's sooty buildings.

They would wake to a day when each must begin to circle around the seductive well of postnatal depression, the athletic gypsy dodging and leaping, the naive teenager walking blindly, unaware that her demons' cages were already weakening.

Somewhere around six o'clock Sylvia dashed for the bathroom, waking Greta, who lay staring at the moulded ceiling, trying to conquer the fearful rawness of her emotions. The harder she tried to remember her daughter's face, the more she saw Dick's depraved smile.

She stroked the bruises on her belly. Sensual to the point of eroticism, she was acutely aware of the tingles across her skin, the powerful pull in her thigh muscles. Now, as she flexed tendons and ligaments, familiar sensations of athletic grace flooded back. Yesterday's exhaustion lifted and although her abdomen kept cramping, the pain felt like stiffness after healthy exercise.

She went to the dressing table, picked up a pencil and a piece of hotel stationery, then began to write.

Sylvia emerged from the bathroom, her red locks falling in wet ringlets.

'My bosoms feel as if they are about to burst. And I'm starving! I can't even remember getting into bed. You were hilarious, acting all hoity-toity with that man on the door. What did you write in the register? Madam Muck and maid?'

They laughed then, as strangers do, too hard.

The teenager's eyes were round with sincerity. 'If they think you somehow kidnapped me, you could go to prison.'

'We won't get caught.'

'I'll never be able to pay you back.'

'Don't worry about the money.'

'But you haven't got enough for two. Not for long.'

'Then we'll steal some more.'

Sylvia brought her fingers to her lips, as if the act of theft would burn them.

'Listen – if you want to be moralistic, go back to Gosforth and fight for your baby. But ask yourself, who taught you that working-class morality? And do they live by it themselves? Look at yourself,' Greta urged. 'You're stunning. Not a child any longer. Go forwards. Backwards will only bring blame, guilt and embarrassment.'

She drew them both towards the mirror, so they were framed as a contrasting pair. 'Look at me. A traveller. Scum. I'll tell you how it feels, to lose your pride. Imagine – folk spitting on your feet. Children jeering and pointing, as if you're

71

a freak. "Respectable" women backing off when you try to make conversation. Men slapping your backside, as if you're a dirty joke. Imagine living with a man who stinks, who abuses you until you hate yourself even more than he does. The day you start devaluing yourself, Sylvia, the rest of the world will wade in and trample you down.'

'I'll never devalue myself.'

'Haven't you already? If you go back to Gosforth you'll spend the rest of your life apologizing for one mistake. You might get a job, but you'll be praying your boss won't find out you've had an illegitimate baby. In the end you'll marry the first lad who asks, just for the sake of some self-respect.' She curled her fists around Sylvia's shoulders. 'Hang on to your pride, girl. It's what keeps a woman beautiful.'

Sylvia rubbed the crease between her eyes. 'Come on, Greta, let's get out of this bloody city.' She began throwing her things into her vanity box, stimulated by a reckless surge of tricky optimism. 'When we get to Yorkshire I'm going to change my name to Evette or Nicola.'

'And maybe one day I'll get to New York . . . Shh! Shh!'

Someone was hammering on the door. Adrenaline took a reverse circuit round Sylvia's nervous system.

With amazing calmness, sounding sleepy and bored, Greta answered, 'Yes?'

'Madam? Some gentlemen downstairs are asking to speak to you.'

The haughty gypsy, slightly irritated, demanded, 'Who on earth is it? Ridiculous hour to call. Tell them to wait.'

'Madam, they appear to be policemen.'

❖

The hotel's assistant manager trotted downstairs, congratulating himself on his powers of observation. Excellent way to start the day. His manager would be livid!

After seven minutes, when neither woman made an appearance, he raced back upstairs even faster, behind two leaping policemen.

The room, of course, was empty; the bill would never be paid.

❖

A sleek black Lagonda slid across the Tyne Bridge, through Gateshead, and continued southwards on the Great North Road. Greta, who had been driving trucks for years, handled the car easily, but Sylvia's sweating hands gripped the leather seat. She hadn't been in motor cars much, and the gypsy woman was driving so fast! Nearly sixty miles an hour. A mile a minute! Corners rushed towards them and Greta kept taking her eyes off the road to look in the mirror, to check if they were being followed.

Birtley, Chester-le-Street, Pity-Me. Just before Durham, Greta pulled the handsome vehicle off the main road and down a lane. Suddenly, she spun the wheel, ploughing into a field of ripening barley. The car bounced, tearing at the feathery cereal, gathering a bumperful of the stuff.

Stalling the engine, Greta climbed out and stretched her long brown arms as if she had driven to the Mediterranean and felt like sunbathing.

At last Sylvia breathed. Disoriented by a clash of

exhilarations, she stumbled out into the pleasant morning sunshine. A light breeze rippled softly across the barley, wafting a countryside bouquet over her troubled nerves. The shiny bonnet of the Lagonda was warmly comforting as she leaned against it.

'Sheer luck,' Greta trilled. 'This marvellous beast, just standing there waiting to rescue us.'

'We stole it.'

'Borrowed!'

'That poor chauffeur will get the sack. There's even luggage in the back.'

'Welcome to my world.'

Greta lifted the boot. There were two matching tan leather suitcases, a hatbox, a shooting stick, also a small trunk containing all the paraphernalia of a gentleman's toilet – clothes brush, hairbrushes, brilliantine. Plus a hip flask. She tugged the stopper and put it to her lips.

'Want some?'

Sylvia sipped. The whisky rolled across her tongue, warming throat, chest and belly. Suddenly Greta was laughing aloud, a great bubble of joy for the sparkling day.

'Life will be good again.' She threw her arms in the air, dancing around like a giant fairy.

For a second it seemed Sylvia was the elder, regarding a mischievous child with dismay. Unperturbed, Greta was dragging out a suitcase, flipping the catches and examining the contents.

'Yes!' she cried. 'Will they fit?' She pulled out a blouse of soft white linen and held it against Sylvia, who flinched as her milk-tender breasts were brushed. Out too flew a sunshine-yellow skirt, thrown into Sylvia's arms.

'I can't wear someone else's clothes . . .'

'Well, I can.'

Sylvia turned away as the excited gypsy thief stripped off. There was a swish of taffeta and Greta was twirling in a concoction of shimmering grey which flowed through the air like an errant rain cloud on a sunny afternoon.

She had good taste, that poor lady in the Turk's Head.

'Never look a gift horse in the mouth,' chanted Greta as she shared the woman's clothing between two quality leather suitcases. Sylvia, however, hung on to her mam's vanity box. Greta slammed down the boot and took one more deep breath of fresh air.

'We'll drive into Durham and catch a train.'

She backed the vehicle out of the field.

'This man friend, in Scarborough . . . ?' asked Sylvia.

'Twice my age and three times yours.'

'Oh.'

In Durham they left the Lagonda shining conspicuously beneath the railway viaduct. Several little boys viewed the car with awe, whispering that one of the two women MUST be the new Queen Elizabeth.

After a wretchedly long climb to the station, hauling stolen suitcases, Greta purchased tickets, while Sylvia rested her shaking legs on a bench. Thirsty, she sipped at the whisky and, through sleepy eyes, gazed across the river's gorge to where Durham Cathedral squared its majestic towers heavenward. God, she decided, liked very big houses . . .

'Wakey wakey.' Greta's voice woke Sylvia from her sun doze. 'Train to York in half an hour. Scarborough by teatime.'

'I'm so thirsty.'

In the buffet Sylvia drained a teapot and gobbled two scones before the great steam engine coughed into Durham Station. Doors clattered open. Passengers from Edinburgh alighted with much case-thumping. Sylvia stepped into the smoky interior and turned to take Greta's case.

'No, I can manage. Find some seats. Hold this, will you?'

Sylvia took the proffered envelope between her teeth. She hauled her suitcase and vanity box along the cramped corridor until she found an empty compartment. Manhandling her luggage, she turned back to beckon Greta.

But the gypsy had vanished. The whistle blew and Sylvia desperately clutched up her cases. Doors slammed. A large woman was blocking the corridor.

As the train pulled out of Durham station Sylvia was shouting helplessly for it to stop.

Bitch! Sylvia cursed in her head, as she huddled, almost naked, on the lavatory seat, rocking with the motion of the train. The stolen suitcase was propped between her knees; the vanity case in the sink. Terrified, she clutched a towel against her chest, feeling fluid run uncontrollably out of her nipples.

I'll pull the communication cord! NO! Calm down. Calm down.

The envelope lay ripped open on the floor. It contained her ticket to Scarborough, four ten-bob notes and two letters, each written on Turk's Head stationery, one addressed to a bloke called Tony Torricelli, the other to herself. Greta had planned on abandoning her all along! Gypsy bitch!

Another irate knock on the toilet door. Bugger off!

Tucking hankies into her bra, she picked up the letters.

Dear Tony,
Sylvia, who carries this letter, is in trouble. I am too.
Could you please look after this young friend until I get
to you? I hesitate to ask as I have never been able to
repay you for helping me when I was a child, and I
know my leaving must have hurt you. Please forgive
me. My life has not worked out well and there is no
one else I trust. I'll come as soon as I can and will
explain all. I hope to God that this finds you at the
same location and that you and Liz are keeping well.
  With love and great humility,
  Greta

The second letter had obviously been scribbled in haste.

Dear Sylvia,
Sorry! Something I must do. To help us both. I don't
want you involved, so I'm sending you to Tony. Wait
for me there. I'll join you as soon as I can.
  Greta

But Sylvia was too intelligent to be convinced by penned platitudes. Greta had abandoned her, just like everyone else.

Why, how, had she been persuaded to leave Alice? The breathy locomotive was hauling her further and further away! Next stop, Sylvia decided, she would get off and go back to

77

Newcastle. She would take the baby charts and labels to a solicitor . . .

They were in Greta's case! The cheating bitch had stolen Alice's charts!

Sweat dribbled from her underarms and fear pushed up under her ribs. It was stifling hot, and the blouse was tight across her leaking breasts.

Think straight!

Sylvia turned Greta's letter over in her hand. On the back were directions to an ice-cream stand in South Bay, Scarborough.

I'm nearly fifteen, she thought. I can find this Tony. Greta said she would come. I'll wait, get the charts, then go straight back for Alice.

❖

Head high, Greta walked through the portico of Newcastle Central Station as if she owned the city. A photograph of Sylvia grinned childishly from the newspaper which was tucked under her arm. It would be totally inappropriate for such an obviously wealthy woman to stand at a bus stop, so she hailed a taxi.

❖

Scarborough, the seaside town built on dinosaur bones, settled by Vikings and much celebrated by Victorian spa bathers, was thronged today with jolly holidaymakers, all enjoying the rare, sunny weekend.

A row of shops went down, down, towards the sea. Sylvia pushed through the crowds, with her mam's vanity box in front of her and the stolen suitcase dragging on the ground. She felt muddled, detached, distracted by anxiety and bone weariness. Pushing her aching feet down the endless street, she kept glimpsing the sea over roofs and between buildings.

Eventually, she stumbled around a corner and found herself against a railing, still high above the bay, beside the largest, most imposing hotel she had ever seen. The Grand.

High up on her left stood a ruined castle. Below her was a wide beach, packed with half-naked people, some hesitating on the frilled edge of the huge navy-blue sea.

To her left, two piers, like crabs' claws, formed a harbour which sheltered colourful fishing boats. Children queued at small white kiosks along the pavement.

Was one of them Tony's?

She leaned against the metal balustrade, drawing in the mysteriously pungent sea air. Suddenly, with a rush of childish excitement, came a greedy urge to feel the sand between her toes and clear water tingling across her skin.

On her right was a pretty, wrought-iron entrance to a funicular lift, but the fare was just a penny, and she only had Greta's stolen ten-bob notes, which she didn't dare flourish. Swollen ankles burning, she zigzagged down a cliff walk, staggered the last steps across the road, and dropped her luggage down on the sand.

Wet children padded past her, dripping icy seawater. Men with rolled-up trouser legs plodged in the waves. Old ladies sprawled, legs splayed, in striped deckchairs. And the giant North Sea crashed triumphantly above it all.

Soft, warm, golden grains ran between her fingers. Sandals thrown off, she stretched her aching toes. Pushing the cardigan under her head, she eased on to her back, and lifted her skirt to bare her knees. Tension ebbed away with the sun's caress. The anxious gabble in her head quietened, as silken sand moulded to her weary muscles. Sunlight played on eyelids heavy with weeping, and, for a few blissful minutes, fear, guilt, anger, all dissolved.

❖

A cloud flew across the sun. Sylvia woke with a start, disoriented, chilled by a sunburn shiver which fluttered across her skin. Anxious and thirsty, she fastened her sandals around swollen feet, and stood looking at the promenade. Where was this ice-cream stand, belonging to the bloke, Tony?

The architectural hotchpotch flashed with neon: chips, ships, shells, bells. Gathering up her cases, Sylvia stumbled over the sand and hurried past arcades and cafes. There were three ice-cream parlours – Jaconelli's, Pacitto's and Alonzi's Harbour Bar – but no stand saying 'Tony'.

What if I can't find him, she worried. She looked up at the towering Grand Hotel. Do I look old enough to stay in a hotel, by myself?

Now the road was curving inland, under a bridge. Holiday dazzle had petered out. Tony's Ice-cream Stand was not there! Had she missed it? Had Greta tricked her AGAIN? She turned twice on herself, then padded back along the front.

A severe cramp clawed at her stomach and a heavy feeling settled between her legs. Desperate with thirst, she entered a small café called 'T's Teas'.

'Excuse me,' Sylvia asked a stout woman with a teapot, 'I'm looking for "Tony's Ice-cream Stand".'

'Don't do cornets, love. Toasted teacake?'

'I must find someone called Tony Torricelli – urgently. I've got a letter for him. Do you know where his stand is?

'Got t'letter for him, did you say?'

'Do you have his address?'

The broad-beamed Yorkshire woman walked to the bottom of the stairs and bellowed, 'Tony . . . you up there? A bonny lass 'ere's got t'letter for you.'

Cash

was flying from sticky fingers to filthy palm. It was Saturday evening, the last night of the Hoppings – a chaos of speed, exhilaration and noise. Diseased goldfish were crushed on rides which spun faster than ever. The showmen were milking as much money as possible from the Geordies, for this was their best earning night of the year. In the early hours of the morning the rides would be packed away and, by dawn, the moor would be left desolate and dirty for the council dustbin men to clear.

Greta watched a young pickpocket lift a woman's purse – and she smiled. These children had nothing. Unwelcome at local schools, they spent their days playing in mud with junk. Theft was both entertainment and survival.

From the protection of a tented sideshow, her slanted eyes narrowed as she watched Dick's muscular frame balancing on the perilous, swirling Zipper. Oh, how he loved to be King of his beast machine!

The dark exhilaration of the night touched that twisted chord of sexual insanity which knotted Greta to her swarthy gypsy husband. Lingering in the shadows, she perversely tempted his eyes to meet her own. But the ride was running at full pelt and Dick was spinning in his own powerful world.

So she moved away. Sneaking past throbbing motors, she edged towards the caravan. Her key turned. A smell of something foul and sexual hung in the fabrics; memories clinging, stinking rotten. The tilley lamp was within reach but she didn't light it.

She knew what she wanted – the small fortune which the Zipper had earned him – and she knew where to find it.

At the far end of the caravan, where the roof turned down to meet the window, was an overhead band of walnut panelling, housing two shallow cupboards where Dick kept his personal belongings. Working quickly, she grasped the base of the suspended structure and pulled down hard. A click – and the whole contraption dropped away from the roof. Reaching far back behind it she touched the cold, squared corners of a metal cash box. Yes!

Only recently had Greta found the hiding place. During her lonely pregnancy she had searched, muscles sore with hauling linoleum, shifting the cooker, unscrewing wall panels. Always she had come back to these two forbidden cupboards. One day, while she rummaged, the chair had toppled and, as she clung on to the cupboard base for balance, her weight had released the catch.

The bastard owed her. She held the box by its handle, savouring its coin-rumbling weight. How much? No key! Worry about that later!

Hastily she pushed the shelving back, then began to

rearrange the clothing in her suitcase to accommodate the bulky box.

'Unpacking your nightie, Greta?'

Fear streaked through her veins. Damn! How long had he been watching?

'Is that an invitation, Dick?'

'Depends. Did they sew you up nice and tight?' His silhouette was framed in the door. Flashing lights from one of the rides threw alternating slivers of red and gold across his eyes. In the seconds while he adjusted to the darkness, Greta flung herself on to the bed, sitting awkwardly on the box.

'You've remembered I had a baby then.'

'Dead, isn't it?'

'Yes. You killed your own daughter. But you didn't kill me.'

The crack across her jaw was no surprise. Her head reeled and blood spurted against her teeth.

'Liar bitch. I read the paper. You left it in the hospital.'

'Why should you worry, Dick? She wasn't even yours.'

Then he smacked her again and again, right cheek, left cheek. Her vision blurred.

'Who? What bastard poked my wife?'

'You'll never know.'

'Who, Greta?' There was venom on his breath.

She began to feel too vulnerable. Instinctively, she crossed her legs. As his shadowy form bore down on her, she punched both fists into his belly.

Dick doubled and cursed.

The final spiral of violence had begun.

Swiftly Greta twisted her body, pulling a blanket over the

cash box, covering the move by grabbing the handle of the suitcase. It was still open and it fell, littering the floor with clothes. Dick lunged at her from behind. Her arms flailed uselessly as he hurled her against the thin caravan wall.

The stench of unwashed flesh and acid breath was suffocating. His teeth were over her neck, biting like an animal's, soiled hands clawing at her blouse. He used his knee to prise her thighs apart and she could feel his engorged penis pushing at her. Her body sagged. Compliance became automatic. Pain was nothing, a transitory thing. Fighting would only heighten his pleasure. But Christ! She'd just given birth; stitches in the delicate skin would be ripped apart.

He laid one arm painfully across her throat while he lifted her expensive skirt. As Greta's husband tore away the bloody postnatal mess in her knickers, instinct pinched her thighs together. He pressed. She forced herself to open. This was her penance. This was her debt to her child, that innocent, lonely baby, conceived in another hideous, repulsive sexual act, who must, in this last night of torment, be saved from both her mother and her father.

Dick took his conjugal right. A burning, searing pain shot through Greta's core. She stood with her weight against the wall, knees bent, ungainly, inert. As he thrust, she felt his teeth dig deep into her collarbone, but although her body was a mass of agonized tension, she remained dead meat in his hands.

There came a point when endurance was impossible. Her breasts were hard and painful with unspilled milk. As he bit into a nipple and arched his back to press deeper, a wave of agony rolled through her entire body and she screamed. Dick groaned in crude, perverse satisfaction and pummelled on until his final knifing thrust.

The offending flesh withered. Blood and semen seeped between her thighs.

Lights from the rides danced across the caravan ceiling. Dick's body slumped against hers, his foul breath panting against her neck. To her disgust she felt her vagina contract in a spasm of illogical, sexual arousal. She shuddered with self-loathing. Rape should leave the victim cold. As her delicate muscles pulled, Dick sniggered. He dug his fingernails into her backside, but Greta's heart flared with courage and she shoved. Hard.

The rapist gripped her shoulders in his struggle to balance, but behind his feet, the suitcase lay open. One step backwards and he tripped awkwardly. Locked together, husband and wife fell towards the floor. Greta's full weight was on top of Dick as his head caught the corner of the table. His eyes flew open and closed again instantaneously.

She lay there on top of him, trembling, sickened with a hatred that neared insanity, fingernails clawing the hairy flesh beneath his shirt.

Finally, as her pulse slowed and gasps stopped ringing in her head, she listened. He was so still. Breathing? Yes. No. Wild music and screams from the rides echoed in the night and she couldn't hear well enough to be sure. She got up clumsily, untangling herself from his splayed legs. Gingerly she drew her clothes back together. His head seemed to lie at a strange angle. He didn't move. She almost wished he would get up and curse. The warm night chilled.

Dead? Had she killed the bastard?

Horrified, terrified, keeping her eyes locked on his lifeless form, Greta felt for an old jacket in the cupboard and pulled it over her tattered clothes. Holding her breath, she hauled the case from under his legs.

Dick's hands suddenly flew out in the darkness and closed around her throat, choking the life out of her, pulling her down to her knees. A new torment. Heart surging. Wild desperation, the need for oxygen worse than any physical pain. Wriggling, struggling, fingers clawing at the air. The back of her left hand slammed hard against the table. She barely felt the pain. Her right hand curled around the blankets on the bed. Something hard and cold slid towards her. The cash box! Her thumb touched the handle and she grabbed. With all her strength, she heaved the heavy metal box across his shoulders. He yelled, as a corner cut into his shoulder blade, his vice-like fingers suddenly losing their grip. Greta, once a strapping young trapeze artist, felt power returning to her muscular arms and she pulled herself free. She found her balance and wielded the box again. The metal crunched up between his legs, crushing his testicles back into his pelvis. Dick screamed. Gasping for air, Greta heaved the thing at him once more, injuring the hands which were clutched to his groin.

From fear and anger rose the instinct. She bore down on him. As the box swung upwards for a fourth time it whacked his chin. There was an ugly cracking sound as his jaw dislocated. Dick fell to the floor. The next time she wielded her bulky weapon it smashed into his face, bursting his eyeball. The last time it cracked his skull.

Greta found herself on all fours. She shook her head like a twitching dog, trying to clear her brain. Then she felt pain.

Every part of her hurt, inside and out. She curled up against the cupboard and peered into the crumpled shadows.

'Be dead, you bastard,' she whispered, then, 'God forgive me.'

After a while she tried to move one part of her body at a time. She straightened her legs and stretched her arms. Searing agony accompanied every tiny movement of her left hand. Later she would discover that three small bones were broken. The ache deep in her belly was indescribable.

Outside, staggering, she slipped between the caravans towards the avenue of trees which marked the Great North Road.

Her arm muscles were leaden with the effort of hauling the heavy case. In it, of course, was the cash box. Already she had forgotten wiping the metal clean with her good hand, forgotten retrieving the key from Dick's trouser pocket. Mindlessly spurred by dogged, confused determination, she had taken what she came for.

Greta waited, shivering, at the bus stop, surrounded by a floss of shrill young women. As the trolleybus approached she turned slowly and looked back over her shoulder at the Maternity Hospital. The implication of her crime hit her like a blast from Hell. 'Jesus.' she swore silently, 'I've killed my daughter's father.'

❖

Sunday afternoon. The moor was empty, except for filth.

The unforgiving

berth shuddered and creaked, as the night train hurtled south towards London. Greta tossed and twitched, desperate to sleep, but every time she neared the bliss of oblivion, her survival instincts jarred her back into brutal consciousness. Her head rolled with the motion of the rattling carriage, as she tried to forget the slick of Dick's saliva on her skin, his lips wet on her eyelids. She could see his gold tooth glinting as his ghost cursed her: murderess! Terror shuddered through her. Terror, not of being caught, but of being haunted. Dick's grotesque spirit would surely torment her to damnation; his broken, bloody scowl would chase her to Hell.

Her swollen hand throbbed. As she gazed at the fleeing blackness beyond the window, she imagined the police questioning the hospital staff, the showmen and gypsies at the Hoppings, poor Binnie. Dick's vile mouth had earned him plenty of enemies but Greta would surely be chief suspect. A net would be spread across the country in the search for a low-time gypsy named Greta Korda.

Over and over her tired brain replayed those hideous

moments, confusing the events more each time until she couldn't differentiate between what she wished she had done and what had actually occurred. A few angry moments in a lifetime. Shouldn't it take longer to force the life out of a great brute like Dick? Not just a few bashes with a box, then whoops-a-daisy, gone.

Gypsy blood. Dick's blood.

There was more blood – her own. Her whole pelvic area ached with abuse and her belly cramped in great heaving spasms. Limp as a rag, her mind would not rest. In the rushing dawn she imagined prison for one last time. Captivity seemed like a madness. Unthinkable. She had already decided what to do.

The train pulled into Kings Cross. Slowly, with one hand, she gathered her things, the weighty suitcase jarring her shoulder. She thought briefly about Sylvia, but dismissed her, thinking, why drag an innocent girl into her crime? Sylvia would cope. Tony would look after her.

Her knees were trembling as she struggled to lift her case down from the train, one painful, bulbous hand tucked protectively around her waist. Her legs seemed to drag stupidly. The station began to spin.

'Hey! Careful now. You all right?' A firm hand steadied her elbow.

'Thank you.'

'You look a bit pale.'

Actually Greta had two black eyes. She leaned on the kind man's arm, vaguely aware of the prickle of his rough wool jacket as her cheek brushed against it.

'Perhaps if I sit down for a moment. I need to deposit my case in Left Luggage.'

Why was there no strength in her limbs? The young man was searching her face.

'Right!' He took charge. Tipping a porter, he instructed him to deposit the case and bring the receipt docket to the station café. Then he propelled Greta gently along the platform and bought her a cup of stewed tea.

'Samuel Phillips.' He extended his hand. She hid her swollen fingers beneath the table.

'You're very kind.'

Go away, Greta was thinking. Just go away. I don't need your frank gaze, your questions or your charm.

But this Mr Phillips was talkative.

'You look like you've been in the wars. I'm a vet. Damn. Sorry. That sounded dreadful. As if . . .'

'I'm a sick dog and you can mend me?' Greta's eyelids drooped. 'Aspirin would do. Touch of flu, that's all.'

They both knew she was lying. Greta stared at the stained table. Then suddenly she realized. Here was her first opportunity to bury Greta.

'My name is Alexandra Hythe.' The name tasted sour on her tongue, like a forkful of something unpleasant at a formal party.

'Live in London, Alexandra? Or just visiting?'

'Visiting my father.' She licked dried blood from the corner of her mouth.

Samuel Phillips was looking at the livid bruise on the tender flesh beneath the collar of her coat. 'Not here to meet you then? Your father.'

'No. It's a surprise.' And oh what a surprise, she thought. 'He's a concert pianist. Tours a great deal.'

'Fascinating,' said Samuel without much conviction. He had no ear for music at all, but out of politeness asked, 'Famous?'

Her father's name sickened her. 'Douglas Hythe.' She looked down, hating to see even the slightest flicker of awe in the man's face. As it happened, there was none. Chords to Sam were cords umbilical, music, the contented purr of a geriatric cat.

The clouds in Greta's head thickened, like a gathering, oppressive storm. Samuel was looking at his watch, rubbing the scar on his chin. 'I'm down from Northumberland for a conference. Starts at ten.'

His words were echoing. She could feel blood soaking between her legs. Her broken hand, hidden beneath the table, throbbed nauseatingly and the fingers which held the teacup shook, but she tried to make politely banal conversation. 'Have you always lived in Northumberland, Mr Phillips?'

'Sam. Yes. Love it, actually. Hate all this.' He waved vaguely at the city. 'You're not well. Shall I call a taxi?' She nodded slowly, seeing the rough texture of his skin through a shimmering haze.

'Thank you.' She stood up to leave, but the room began heaving again. Beneath her fingers the table swayed like a listing ship and suddenly the floor came up to meet her.

❖

Across Scarborough's wide, blue horizon, the sun rose under threaded clouds, glowing golden on Sylvia's wet shins. She was paddling, her ankles numb in the cold water. As small waves tugged in and out, she felt dizzy, yet amazingly calm. Freedom felt good, the future only a grab away, a new life, one she could share with Alice.

Yet, unconsciously, her hands remained clenched, thumbs curled tightly beneath her fingers, a sign that anxiety and grief were sinking backwards into the waiting recesses of her mind.

The Italian rolled up his trousers and joined her. They made strange companions, alone at the water's edge: a beautiful young girl with a glorious russet mane, and a plump, middle-aged man whose large olive features were split by a huge, shiny black moustache.

Tony (Antonio) Torricelli had heard two sad tales, and he did not like either. Greta's letter was tucked into his shirt pocket, the feel of her words, her handwriting, bittersweetly close to his skin. He didn't want to be involved with this daft young girl, or her dirty laundry. But Greta, the girl he had mourned for over a decade, had sent her message, and he would do what he must – in his own way.

'I cannot believe this dreadful thing. She is married to a monster gypsy who beat her? And a baby. A lost baby.' These revelations about her adult life were deeply disturbing.

And what should he do with this young girl from Newcastle?

'Problem. Story is in paper and every place we see your picture. Who knows you come here?' He was puffing with the effort of walking through the sand and he kept looking over his shoulder.

'No one.'

'Who see'd you yesterday?'

'Most of the journey I hid in the toilet. Nobody gave me a second look.'

Tony frowned dubiously at her ruddy hair, glossed by the sun.

'The only person I spoke to was that lady in the café, Liz. Would she report me?'

'Never.' He shook his head vigourously. 'Lizabet will respect Greta's wish.'

Liz had adored the child who once came to them as Alexandra. In fact, it was Liz who renamed her Greta, after Garbo, and Liz who had mothered the grieving child for two years.

Tony lowered his black bushy eyebrows over his own ruffled memories.

Did all relationships need a name? Some title to permit emotion? That lanky, dark-haired teenager, with secrets in her eyes and a precious smile, had temporarily filled all the mysteriously painful spaces in his heart. With young Greta he could speak his native Italian, tease without offence, share thick coffee, vent his swift, but instantly forgiving Latin temper – and love without the complication of touching, because touching was simply unthinkable.

He remembered returning from Sophia's funeral. Ironically Tony had been on the verge of returning home to Italy. With turmoil building in Europe, English people were becoming very suspicious of handsome Italians, and his small business was not doing well.

But then came that first telephone call from Sophia's brother, Mario Marletti. Alexandra had been picked up at Dover, with no passport and no ticket. Frantic, yet astonishingly crafty, she had deliberately spoken only Italian. Officials, assuming she had been separated from her family, allowed her to telephone Venice. She passed the handset to an officer and Mario's broken English accent had given them Tony's address. A woman PC then escorted Alexandra to Scarborough. Adequately reassured by the warmth and familiarity of Tony's welcome and the presence of the very capable Liz, the PC had left the teenager in their care.

Of course Tony received Sophia's daughter without blinking. Alexandra, however, would not be drawn as to why she had fled her pampered life at Halstone House.

A telegram arrived the next day, from the Marlettis, with instructions for Alexandra to remain in England with Tony, until Mario arrived.

Why should Tony mind? Her sparkle brightened his jaded heart.

Never destined for marriage, or parenthood, Antonio Torricelli had walked crab-like through his own rocky adolescence, never daring to confront a mate, always scuttling away from passion. Adulthood found him under a stone, alone, lacking in confidence with women and sometimes, terrifyingly, attracted to older men. His sexual ambivalence horrified him.

To escape himself, Tony had fled to England, where Yorkshire folk conveniently associated his lack of family with his 'foreignness'. In Scarborough he grew his great moustache, playing his flamboyant Latin role to the full. A big personality hid profound self-doubt.

Mario never came. He wrote that the family was in

political difficulties and it would be best if the girl remained obscure for a few months. Europe was boiling.

It was also clear that Greta's father had never reported his daughter as missing. In the midst of the sensational news of the Duke of Windsor's marriage to Wallis, there were no headlines about the Hythe family. Nor had any policeman knocked on Tony's door.

Two happy years they spent together, Tony, Liz and Greta. Two ice-cream summers and two lazy, cosy winters. Mario's support afforded them luxuries: shows at the Spa Theatre, rides on North Bay's miniature train, concerts in Peasholm Park.

Then, on a sultry afternoon, in July 1939, as Britain stood on the brink of war and Greta was just budding into womanhood, Tony found himself face to face with Douglas Hythe.

Greta was out pushing the ice-cream cart. Perhaps she saw them talking. Perhaps, from some yards away, she recognized her father's back. She must have seen something. While Tony was vehemently denying all knowledge of her whereabouts, she vanished, leaving the cart in the back alley.

Utterly bereft, Tony and Liz waited for her to come home. Day after stricken day.

Mario could do nothing, because suddenly the world was at war. Along with several hundred other innocents, Tony suffered the frustration and indignity of an internment camp in Scotland, where racism tempered his cracked shell. When his precious liberty was finally granted, he chose to return to Scarborough, to wander the damp moors and stormy beaches, nursing a heart grown too cold for the passionate Mediterranean.

Liz, he discovered, had lost both sons in the Normandy Landings. Her husband, in depressive grief, had jumped to his death from Cornelian Cliff. One of her three daughters was widowed; the other two were caring for disabled husbands. The three sisters had decided to live together in York, so Liz, emotionally and financially impoverished, had been forced to sell her home and move into a loft room. With her newly silvered hair plaited around her head like a halo, Liz survived by warming other sad hearts with her mischievous jokes and singing. Her vibrato was now revered and feared all over Scarborough, as was her bacon rolly-polly.

❖

Half a generation later, another girl was now looking pleadingly at Tony, through ginger lashes, with eyes the same colour as the sea.

❖

Sylvia felt uncomfortable, talking about private things to a man she didn't know. His Italian intonation, laced with Yorkshire dialect, demanded so much concentration that it was difficult to avoid his questions.

'You trouble,' he said.

'Sorry.' His pouting moustache made her feel guilty.

Tony sighed heavily. 'You stay with me. Until Greta comes. But if you seen, if police find you here, Tony in shit. They think . . . God knows what they think.'

'I'll tell them the truth.'

'Perhaps. For now, you hide. I have a place. But for how long, Sylvie?' His big brown eyes challenged hers.

'Not long. Greta will come, won't she?'

'I hope.'

'I can't understand why she left me. I know she's your friend, but was I wrong to trust her?'

Tony stopped and looked out across the becalmed sea. 'I only know her as a child. The woman, she will be a different person.'

Wavelets lapped around their feet. Shyly Sylvia touched his arm – and then wondered why she had done it. But the action seemed to awaken something in Tony and he turned sharply, taking hold of her shoulders.

'Go home, Sylvie. Back to your Mamma and Papa. Or maybe you spend the rest of your life like Greta, always running.'

Tears sprang into her eyes. 'I will go back. When I've found a way to look after my baby myself.'

'*La bambina*? She will be crying for her mamma.'

Sylvia clenched her fists even tighter and kicked the eternally slapping waves. 'Stop it! I can't bear to think about her crying. It's for her sake. If I don't sign the papers they can't have her adopted.'

'You sure? You a minor.'

Sylvia frowned, puzzled, thinking he had said 'miner'.

'My guess – it is already out of your hands,' sighed Tony; but he persisted, 'When you go back?'

'As soon as I've found a job and a place to live. I'm nearly fifteen. I just need a little time.'

Time, like a bomb, began ticking.

Tony moved up the beach and plonked down on the sand

with a dull thud. Sylvia could feel him watching her knees, as the sea tipped over them.

After a while she set her mouth, and came to him.

'Please can I wait here for Greta?'

He looked at the horizon. 'You stay hidden. Comprehend?'

She nodded.

The sun warmed their backs as they crossed the road. Tony ushered Sylvia hastily through the café doors and back up to the sanctuary of his flat. A little later he puffed up carrying several Sunday papers which he handed her with a brow-sag, before stomping back down to start frying breakfasts.

By the time he came back up, Sylvia was huddled in a corner of his sofa, her face glistening with tear trails.

'I don't believe it.' She slammed down the paper and hugged her knees. 'My parents are supposed to be heartbroken! Liars! They were sending me away!' She lifted a crumpled page from the floor and slapped it furiously. 'They've given Alice to the Lindens! Listen . . . "Mrs Linden Senior, a woman in her sixties, has advised us today that she will be caring for the child. The abandoned baby girl will be brought up by the prosperous Linden family." BASTARDS! How could my bloody parents have given my baby to them SNOBS?'

'Give me here.' Tony carried on reading, '". . . second baby, left behind on the same night by a gypsy, will be placed in an orphanage." No! Ah! Mario Marletti will be much angered!'

'Who?'

'The uncle of Greta. These mistakes cause problems for generations. You must go back. Now.'

'No!' Sharpy obstinacy pinched her mouth. 'Legally, I'm just a child. The Lindens have my baby, and they're rich. I don't know how to fight them. And Greta has my baby's charts. I'll have to wait for her.'

'Perhaps it is not so bad,' Tony suggested, 'if baby with Papa's family. Perhaps someday you and he, this David, marry?'

Hope flushed Sylvia's face. 'Perhaps . . .'

''Tis better than the baker. Now, you write your mother that you are safe.'

'No!'

'Yes. I send it to friend in Glasgow, who will post on. They not find out you here.'

❖

David slammed his fist into his pillow. He hated this mausoleum, this prison. The discipline was welcome, but he was lonely, traumatized by the rejection of his parents and the loss of his friends. The work he could manage well enough but his slight Geordie accent made him the object of ridicule and he was regularly singled out for typical boarding-school pranks. He yearned for his real mates, his own bed, for Gosforth; but his two greatest losses were his saxophone and Sylvia. He loved both, and could have neither. When David had wailed his terror over Sylvia's pregnancy into his sax, his mother, detecting a musical moan of accusation in his sobs, had confiscated it.

In his hammock-like bunk he longed for the feel of the reed on his tongue and Sylvia's nipples between his lips. Her pretty face eluded him, and yet he could picture every inch of her body. On the other hand, she would be fat by now. 'With child.'

Was it his fault? Shouldn't she have stopped him from going too far? A girl should. Sylvia hadn't. Once they had done 'it', she couldn't seem to stop.

Where was she now? Sent to 'the country'. What country, what county, where? He had no way of contacting her, but he had been counting weeks. It was due this month.

He cursed himself for losing touch with Hendo and Alan. Initially it had been embarrassment, fear of taunts about rubbers on the end of pencils. There was a worse shame. Guilt – for having parents who could buy him out of trouble. Guilt – for betraying Sylvia.

He was getting headaches. At least once a week he was confined to his bed, suffering agonizing cramps across his skull and bouts of debilitating nausea. Matron said it was 'his age' and gave him the odd aspirin, which he immediately threw up. A cloud of self-pity shrouded David, leaving him unpopular and isolated, writing scraps of pathetic poetry in the back of his jotter.

'Linden!' a prefect shouted into the dormitory. 'Head's study. Now! Shift arse.'

Outside the headmaster's study David lifted his fist to knock. He hesitated. He had no intention of coming back here next term. If his parents insisted, then he would do something terrible. Mustering his determination to escape imprisonment, he hit the door too hard.

'For God's sake, don't break the door down.' The Head sounded irritable. He sat behind a large oak desk. A single ray of sunshine, dancing with motes, fell on a newspaper.

David kept his arched nose in the air. He scanned the last few days. Prep handed in. Decent marks in the Science test. A spot of bother with one of the other boys in the lavatories, but he didn't think the tutors knew about it.

The newspaper was being wafted through the air.

'Trouble, Linden.'

'Sir?'

The headmaster sat back in his leather chair and narrowed his eyes. 'Human reproductive system. VERY practical Biology. Sexual intercourse. ILLEGAL. Congratulations, Linden, you've become a FATHER.'

His voice rose and fell as if he were reading Shakespeare.

'Your parents somehow FAILED to tell me that you'd got a fourteen-year-old girl PREGNANT. I was given some COCK-and-bull story about you needing better TUITION. Load of TRRRIPE, wasn't it? Had to get away from the DISGRACE. Leave the girl, as it were, holding the BABY. I despise cowardice, Linden, even more than oversexed boys.'

He stood up and circled the quaking teenager.

David stared at the carpet. 'Sir. I presumed my parents had spoken to you – confidentially.'

Mr Wigson's face was so close that David could smell tobacco.

'Aren't you going to ask me how I know?'

'Sir.'

'Read this.' He pulled the national rag across the desk.

TWO BABIES ABANDONED

TEENAGE GIRL RUNS AWAY WITH GYPSY

David couldn't focus on the small print. He was seeing Sylvia's face, her freckles, her lips. A dagger was gouging behind his eyes and he felt sick again.

'Linden!' David jumped. 'Has this hussy contacted you here? If I find her cowering in some corner of my school, I'll whip you, d'you hear? What do you know about this?'

'Nothing, sir. Honestly, sir.' SYLVIA RUN AWAY? WITH A GYPSY!

Wigson became businesslike. 'I've just received a telephone call from a police inspector, in Newcastle. In case you didn't know, sexual intercourse with a fourteen-year-old is a CRIME! How come you weren't prosecuted?' The man's eyes were bulging with wrath. 'DI Howard was intending to travel down to see you, but I said I'll save him the bother.' He returned to the back of his desk. 'Your grandmother has telegraphed your father in Cornwall. He will collect you this afternoon and take you straight back to Newcastle. Go now and pack. Clear your lockers completely – you won't be coming back.'

The Lindens had been driving all day. David was waiting forlornly under the school portico. He crawled into the back seat, where his mother greeted him with a back-bending glare.

For a full hour Mary berated her son, but when the car slewed across the road after nearly hitting a lorry, Arthur, in a rare show of strength, shouted, 'Belt up, woman!'

Mary's venom only increased by decibels. Mile after mile she ranted, while they trudged up the country until at last they crossed the Tyne Bridge. Passing the Maternity Hospital,

Mary started again, this time berating Ethel for her 'incomprehensible interference'.

❖

Home. Cold comfort, thought poor Arthur Linden. He sent David to bed and tried to stand between his wife and his mother who were rowing with awesome passion.

'How dare you suggest bringing a bastard child into my family?' Mary Linden's fury trembled around her powdered face and stank on her breath, while Ethel's obstinacy was almost sugary.

Eventually Mary flung herself upstairs. Arthur Linden, exhausted, poured himself a whisky and sat in his favourite armchair. His mother faced him.

'She's a bully.'

'Leave it, Ma.'

'She fusses about your "standing in the community". Well, the community will take a dim view of this melodrama. If you had done the right thing in the first place . . .'

'What was the right thing, Ma?'

She sighed. 'If I start telling you what to do, I'm no better than she is.'

Arthur had no desire to share his wife's bed. He rested his balding head on the wing of his armchair and wished he could go to work tomorrow, to hide behind his desk where everything was ordered and where he was allowed to think clearly. He was respected in the office, even liked, especially by his secretary. As he dozed, he drifted towards a fantastical, idyllic life, where women were kind and responsibilities were tidy . . .

David woke him.

'Dad.'

Arthur rubbed gritty eyes until they were raw.

'I'm sorry, Dad.'

Arthur looked up at his six-foot son, a giant child, lost, unhappy, afraid. Impulsively he extended his hand. David reached out tentatively, to shake it, but found himself pulled in and embraced fiercely. They clung together awkwardly for several seconds, then parted gravely. Between man and boy there was not enough confidence for spoken words.

❖

Arthur Linden stood next to his son during the police interview. This time he did not attempt to pull any strings. Nor did he interrupt, except to endorse David's innocence in Sylvia's disappearance. For the next few hours the boy was pummelled mercilessly with probing questions. Afterwards, father and son walked slowly home to face their respective mothers.

Mary was poised for attack. Another tremendous row ensued, during which Ethel Linden called a taxi. The old woman pressed Arthur and David out of the house, insisting they drive smartly round to see Sylvia's parents.

In the Sharps' modest house David sat cowed, overwhelmed by shame. Even young Katherine looked wretched, but she came and sat next to him, and for that simple gesture of compassion he felt a wave of gratitude.

That afternoon, they hammered out a future for Sylvia's baby. On Tuesday morning Arthur and Ethel took David to the hospital to see his little daughter. They stood around the cot and gazed in wonder at the sweet girl, less than a week old. It was Ethel who picked her up.

❖

It was also on Tuesday morning that Tony, frustrated by the non-arrival of Greta, installed Sylvia in Hisper Cottage, a derelict smallholding perched on a treacherous cliff, several miles up the coast, which he had bought from a farmer who had no use for the precipitous, stony land.

Tony's ancient van bumped along a dusty track which teetered perilously close to the cliff edge. A rock fall had cut off the track in mid-air and Sylvia was just about to leap out of the passenger door before they all plummeted into the greedy green sea, when Tony swung the vehicle through an open gate.

Before them, listing slightly, with its back to the rising headland, stood Hisper Cottage. Sombre, lichen-covered, the stone house seemed to be crumbling back into the earth. Thistles barred the way to a peeling blue door and weeds clawed over the windowsills. Clinging to the back of the cottage, cowering from the relentless buffets of down-rushing westerlies and driving easterlies, a wizened tree cheated upwards, curling beneath broken gutters, sending exploring tendrils into dark spaces under missing slates.

Sylvia's fingers lingered on the cold sill as she peered through a filthy window. For a moment she had the uneasy feeling that she was offending someone's privacy, as if there was a reason why Tony's key failed to turn in the door. She sensed defensiveness about the place, a scenting, an animal rite of proprietorship.

But Tony's weight finally won the battle and the blue door reluctantly surrendered. Sylvia stepped gingerly across the threshold and saw – filth! Abandoned bits of a home had been left to decay. Dirt and damp rose from the stone-flagged floor.

Tony examined some black grainy deposits on a kitchen table.

'Mice!'

Liz rolled up her sleeves, flung open windows, handed Tony a dustpan and Sylvia some Vim. 'Nowt a bit of elbow won't shift.' She set to, as only a woman who has had five children knows how, booming out instructions. 'Fetch the ash pan. Take that rug outside. Fix up a line. Clean t'sink.' Work was lightened by her reckless renditions of Deanna Durban songs.

'Waltzing, waltzing, high in the clouds,

Only you and I in the clouds

Over aaaa moonbeam . . .'

As she slurred up to the top note, Sylvia winced and Tony ducked his head.

The cottage boasted few creature comforts. Ice-cold water gushed from a standpipe in the scullery. Waste flowed down a drain to the sea. There was no electricity, only candles and a tilley lamp.

But by lunchtime the kitchen was habitable and a single painted chair stood next to the rough wood table, now cleaned of mouse droppings. With its cracked sink and black range, this must, for the time being, suffice as Sylvia's home, because there had been a soot fall in the other downstairs room and the only bedroom upstairs was uninhabitable due to roof leaks. Her case was dragged in from the van and laid under the window. An old settee would have to double as a makeshift bed.

Sylvia tried hard not to notice the smell. She tried hard not to look in the corners and remember the thick cobwebs which she had just swept away. Webs meant spiders!

An old clock ticked on the mantelpiece beside a framed sepia photograph which was so filthy that she couldn't discern whether it was a portrait of a man or a woman. One indignant eye looked down on her accusingly, as she sat nervously on the settee.

'You'll be OK here, no?'

'Fine, thank you.' Sylvia raised a tight-lipped smiled as she looked at Tony's grimy face. She was close to tears.

'Where's the toilet?' she asked.

Dodging nettles, she opened the creaking shed door to find a hole in the ground. Apparently each morning the ash can had to be emptied into the sea and refilled from the cleaned grate.

What could she do but accept this dubious hospitality? These people were so kind. Running away meant hiding, and hiding meant being alone. The logic of that hit her even harder when Liz climbed into the van and Tony backed it down the lane.

'Tarrah . . .' Her hand fell and she sat down on the worn doorstep. Her insides were quaking. Leaning against the doorjamb, she welled up with helpless anxiety, an inner tremor which would be her constant companion for the next three years.

Time began to slow. Sitting still on the step, she watched the sun sink into the moors, realizing just how far away she was from other human beings. There was farmland either side, but the nearest dwelling looked miles away. Tony owned the field in front of her, which fell over the cliff. To the north a precarious path descended through tussocks of spiky grass to a small bay. Behind Hisper Cottage the land continued to tilt upwards as the cliffs curved in an arc towards an even higher headland. Above, the sky was a tumble of grey, full of squawking seagulls.

And the sea? An impossible, endless horizon.

Standing, she found she was stiff. The fire in the range was already dying. She shovelled on some coal, and suddenly saw her father, cutting the stuff from the coalface. Turning a piece in her hand, she let it blacken her fingers.

'He called me dirty,' she told the burnt kettle, as she tried to settle it into the embers. 'But I'm not.'

Nor was Sylvia dull. Her bright mind was both restless and fearful. In the absence of conversation, the chatterbox inside her head began to entertain itself by popping random questions.

Why does coal burn? It's a stone.

Lighting a candle, Sylvia asked the flame – Do bees sting because we steal wax from their babies' cradles?

'Oh, Hell! I'm talking to myself!'

On the first afternoon, deliberately trying to chase away spiders, mice and ghosts, she clattered around the cottage, speaking aloud anything that came into her head: songs, nursery rhymes, the hundred Bible texts she had learned at Sunday School. But too quickly, the definition between speech and thought blurred. Occasionally there seemed to be two parallel conversations, one rattling around her head, and another which echoed around the dirty walls.

Tragically, as she sought to fascinate herself, the vulnerable girl's ruminations began to stray along the genetically buckled pathways in her brain. Idle notions sometimes lost their way. Every time she poked the range, for example, she could hear her father singing, 'Home, home on the Range, where the deer and the antelope graze . . .'

❖

Time was so slow it solidified.

Night came, dark as blindness. Hour after sleepless hour, she stared at the flickering candle. Only when the sun rose did she manage to doze in safe daylight.

Despite the warm weather, Hisper Cottage felt damp and chilly. The range died. Blackened beast, it filled her with terrible awe; she couldn't relight it, so she ate her food raw and drank cold water. Then she just stopped eating.

It was Thursday before Tony returned. By then a gusty wind was hurling down from the moors, and she was shivering. The kindly Italian relit the range, played cards with her, then left her alone again.

Darkness seemed to amplify the fearful crash and suck of waves against the cliff below. Earlier that year the whole of the east coast of England had taken a terrific battering from freak storms; low coastal areas had flooded and huge cliffs had fallen. Remembering the pictures on the newsreels, Sylvia sat by the little window watching black clouds flee out to sea, and she began to wonder about the security of the land beneath the cottage. What if it began to slip?

Time smouldered in the range's cinders.

It squeaked under the roof tiles.

Time looked like the space between the stars.

By Saturday, when Tony's van tooted at the gate, Sylvia's floodgates burst.

❖

Liz Baxter held Sylvia's slender, shaking frame to her own vast bosom. This wasn't right, leaving a teenage lass all alone. The black lines under the girl's eyes were a worry, but – worse – she wasn't eating! For Liz, skinniness was a sin. Cooking was both her job and her joy. She put on several pounds every year and was proud of it. Her rolls of fat were a sign that she was surviving widowhood. This daft young girl might be heartbroken, but Liz could not let her fade away.

So the following evening, when she and Tony returned, Liz went to open the back of the van, and out bounded a large, boisterous golden retriever. He turned two daft circles, then leapt at Sylvia from a yard away.

'Eee! Look who's come to see you,' chimed Liz. 'Mustard, 'e's called, on account of 'is temperament. Chews everything to shreds.'

The dog pushed at Sylvia until she was forced to run her hands through his fluffy cream coat.

'He's huge. Who does he belong to?'

'Meself, I suppose. Some old bloke came into t'caf on 'is way to get 'im put down. 'E were only a pup. Sat with a bit of string around 'is neck, all quiet – as if 'e knew. What could a body do? Bugger's never been quiet since, mind. Broke almost every ornament I've got. And my landlady, she's sick to death of his noise. Will you look after Mustard for me, lass?'

Mustard cocked an ear.

❖

Liz and Tony left. Sylvia curled up on her settee and Mustard pulled his blanket along the floor until he could lay his head next to hers. The sea roared on, but she placed a hand in his warm coat and, at last, she slept.

Next morning they scrabbled down to the deserted beach together. The weather had relaxed, and the North Sea, in serene humour, gently tossed seaweed in shallow waves. Mustard bounded in and out of the water, chasing shrieking seagulls, every now and again shaking a glorious halo of sparkling droplets around his sodden body. Sylvia splashed behind him, the icy water painfully exhilarating around her ankles.

Eventually hunger pangs sent them clambering back to their new home and Sylvia, maternal instincts blossoming, gave Mustard a drink and a digestive biscuit, then ate the rest of the packet herself.

That afternoon she took Mustard to explore the south headland. It was a hard walk, through spiky grass and wild broom, and her body was still weak from childbirth. Panting, at times crawling, she reached a high rock. Fearful that the daft dog would leap out into infinity, she kept her hand firmly through his collar.

She stood tall, feeling the gentlest sea breeze against her ribs. From up here she could see further along the coastline: headlands layered, one behind the other, into the distance. The shimmering bay was blurred into the horizon by a summer haze. Below her, gulls circled against the cliffs, and

Sylvia leaned forwards, imagining the thrill of swooping over the listing moors, out into the seamless blue.

'A far cry from Newcastle, isn't it, bonny lad?' She sucked in the heady air. 'Look, Mustard, there's a ship, right out there. Where's it off to? France, Norway, Greenland? Will I ever go on a ship like that? Sail around the world? I'll take Alice with me; get her out of the coal dust. You can't come, silly animal. Oh, I wish Greta would get here. She said she would take me to New York.' She sighed and looked down at her new companion. 'Where is she, Mustard? Why hasn't she come?'

❖

Greta regained consciousness after a large blood transfusion, some strategic stitching and thirty-six hours' sleep. Pushing herself into wakefulness, she focused on a familiar face. Oh, God! Unhappily, she shut her eyes again. Her father moved in quickly to hold her close. The smell of his cologne turned her stomach.

'Alexandra. Alex darling. I'm so happy . . .' He hung his head. 'I know what you think, dear. Why you went away. I must explain.'

'Explain away, Father.'

'When you're better.' He grinned, teeth gleaming in his handsome face. 'Darling, where have you been all these years? We tried so desperately to find you. I thought . . . I thought you might be dead. Oh, Lord!' His expression could change in an instant, confusing the listener with lightning shards of sincerity. 'When the hospital called and said you were here, I couldn't believe it.'

Were those actually tears in his eyes? A wound which had

never fully healed was reopening inside Greta, but she pressed its ragged edges back together. Her priority was to protect herself. There was only one thing she needed from her father – an alibi.

'It puzzles me, Father – why you never notified the police. I was just a child. Yet I was never registered as missing, was I?'

Douglas Hythe fidgeted with the clipboard on the end of the bed. 'Temperature's normal, I see. They tell me you've broken some bones in your hand and that you . . . em . . . haemorrhaged. What happened, darling? An accident? Or maybe . . .' he adopted a misjudged air of confidentiality '. . . an abortion?'

Greta (Alexandra) laughed low and long.

'What did you tell everyone, Father, when I left?'

'That you were with your mother's family in Venice.'

'Good.'

❖

Reckoning.

Time for discordant truths. Douglas Hythe, charismatic performer and lonely composer, sat in the corner of a bar, nursing a cognac.

I can't feel guilt, he told himself. Who has the right to judge? But what can I tell Alexandra? That I did love her mother? That I miss Sophia's friendship – even today? My daughter – a raven-haired beauty now. The only bit of Sophia left on this earth. And that's where my judgment lies, I suppose. In her slender hands.

He sniffed the brandy until it tingled around the hairs in

his nose, then swallowed, to drown the lump in his throat. A series of fond reflections made him smile sadly. Sophia, his glorious queen of pathos: lofty, quarrelsome, brimming with passion, overflowing with danger and gaiety and all the things which turned a young man's head.

Alexandra, however, had been an unattractive baby who became a straight-backed little girl with challenging eyes and a large, expressive mouth, which generally stayed clamped shut. Opening a small pocket of insecurity, Douglas allowed himself to glimpse his love for her. He closed his eyes and touched it. It hurt so much he wanted to scream. Shame flooded in, a tidal wave of remorse. He had lost his daughter long before she ran away from him. He lost her the day he found he could no longer embrace her, when she was about ten years old.

The 'Revelation'. The epiphany. Whom could he blame? God? Mother Nature? Or Martin?

Brandy souring his stomach, the thought of his butler/companion made him nauseous. The boy had been a dancer in a cabaret show. Strictly back row. Handsome and gay. La la la. Handsome and gay. Douglas, revelling in his own growing stature as a concert pianist, had become vain to the point of kissing his own reflection, when Martin kissed him on the cheek. And suddenly, all of Douglas's confused childhood fantasies, all his adolescent insecurities, all his bouts of impotency – made sense.

An experiment, that's all it was. Not love. Just besotted anxiety. Douglas still adored his wife and daughter, yet the insanity of infatuation, the thrill of the unthinkably forbidden, titillated him until he lost all control. When he tried to reject his handsome young lover the desolation had been sweet torture. Reconciliations had always been – exquisite.

Now, no longer a youth, Martin's possessive jealousy had expanded into near madness. In the master and slave game, he whined and wept, but contrarily it was Douglas who felt the rein fixed to his back, fastening him to his own weakness. And every now and again, Martin yanked that rein.

Well, he would have to be disposed of. Douglas must clean up his act. Immediately.

❖

Dear Tony,

I pray to God that Sylvia found you. Unfortunately I was taken ill and rushed to hospital, so it will be some time before I am able to come to Scarborough as promised. Forgive me. Meanwhile, I know I have no right to ask you to care for Sylvia, but I don't know what else to do.

I have returned home to Halstone House. Yes, I am now staying with my father. He believes I was living in Italy, and I don't want him, or anyone else, to know about my life as Greta, or my relationship with you, so, although I am desperate to see you again, it would be best if you don't come here.

PLEASE don't tell Sylvia my real identity. If the police find her, it would be best if she describes me as a strange gypsy who helped her at a moment in time, and left. When the dust settles, I shall come and explain everything to her myself.

There is a way I can help you both. I'm afraid it entails a bit of dragging around. Enclosed is a docket

for 'Left Luggage' at Kings Cross Station. I've left a
suitcase there, containing a box. Key enclosed. Please
use the contents freely. It's the least I owe you both.
  I hope to see you very soon, dearest Tony.
  All my love to Liz.
  Greta

❖

Dear Mam, Dad and Katherine,
I am safe and well, staying with some nice people.
Please ask the police to stop looking for me, because
even if I am found I will refuse to come home until I
am ready. You didn't want me anyway.
  Someday soon I will come back for my baby girl.
How could you have given her to the Lindens? Tell
them that I WILL NEVER agree to ALICE being
adopted and I WILL NEVER sign any papers.
  My friends say I should ask you to forgive me, but I
don't feel sorry. Do you?
  Sylvia.

No 'love from', no address, just a blurred Glasgow franking
on the envelope.

Violet wept in her husband's arms at last. Katherine wept
on Hendo's hairy shoulder. He repeated the contents of the
letter to David, who wailed guilt into his sax. The police
scaled down the search, and baby Alice Sharp went home.

Baby Janice, named after the kind young nurse who cried
bitterly as the infant was carried out of the hospital, was
placed in an orphanage.

Typewriter eyes

moved nervously from left to right and back again.

'Your mamma was dying, my heart was breaking,' claimed Douglas Hythe. 'Perhaps I had some kind of break-down.' His tone was inappropriately lyrical. 'I was bitter, at life, at God. A man like me, a musician, has passions which . . . overwhelm.'

'Lust.' Alexandra sneered away his pathos.

'Something purer than that.'

'Did Mamma know? Did she?'

Typewriter eyes stopped.

'She only knew I loved her. Right to the end.'

'The end? Where was that love at the end? All I could hear was the rattle in her chest and you crashing away Elgar. It was me holding her hand, a little girl.'

She gathered her father's guilty inadequacies around her, as if, by luxuriating in reproach, she could shunt gypsy Greta Korda, husband killer, into an emotional siding.

'You've grown so beautiful.'

But Greta's criminal ugliness would not be so easily

shunted. It shuddered through the alter ego of Alexandra, rumbling behind her umbilicus, trembling across her chest, then lurching deep down into her groin, trickling through her bladder and along the inside of her legs. She was a killer. Only one ticket now, and that was to Hell.

'Have there been men in your life? Perhaps you understand now that love and body can be counter-melodic, even discordant?'

Flashing fairground lights. A vagina with a will of its own. Hands that could kill without thinking.

'And how do you live now, Father?'

'Alone. Lonely. No woman has ever been able to fill your mamma's place.' Douglas shook his silver hair, then gasped out, 'And no man.'

The composer looked over his left shoulder. He twisted his head so far that it seemed as if he was staring into another mysterious, alternative world. 'I felt sickened,' he admitted. 'I'd been weak, drawn into something wrong.' His shockingly sincere attention came back to his daughter. 'My punishment was losing you and your mother almost simultaneously.'

'And Martin?'

'Sacked.'

The typewriter shifted a line. Bing.

❖

Seven tedious hours on the train.

At Kings Cross, feeling like a spy on a mission, Tony Torricelli retrieved Greta's smart leather suitcase from Left Luggage. Strange, he thought, it's almost identical to Sylvia's.

Desperate for fresh air, he pushed himself through the

station bedlam. The hot city heaved. Acrid motor fumes from revving taxis hung poisonous in rising dust. At the entrance to the tube station, crowds jostled with futile aggression.

Tony felt claustrophobic, hungry and suspicious. Across the road was an unappetizing selection of greasy cafés. Food! Famished to the point of desperation, he loitered outside a 'new-fangled' Chinese restaurant. Poked his head inside. Nice smells. Should an Italian even consider eating Chinese food? Aloof as a lardy Adonis, Tony accepted a seat at an immaculately clean table and studied the menu.

An hour later he sat back contentedly, having enjoyed every mouthful, whatever it was. More relaxed now, he settled his elbows on the tablecloth and considered. He'd waited for Greta for three long weeks, hoping against hope that he would hear from her again, but – nothing. Could she be really seriously ill?

La mia Greta, he sighed to himself, she must be in her late twenties now. Tony pictured her as a teenager, winding her innocent affection around him like a garland of fragile daisies. Tony's very worst suspicion was that, in order to survive, she had sold her young body.

The case was heavy on his lap. He flicked open the catches. Easing up the lid, he flung a guilty glance over his shoulder, slid his hand furtively in, and pulled out – tangled silk. Startled, he slammed it shut. This was not the time and place to rifle through Greta's undergarments.

Wide eyes fixed on the case, he noticed on the bottom corner some elegantly embossed initials – S.R.

Either Greta had called herself by a third name, or this belonged to someone else.

Coincidentally, at that moment, Greta was only a couple of miles away, standing on the banks of the Serpentine, holding the hand of a very kind vet and enjoying a flutter of power as he studied her lips. Bright and honest, Samuel Phillips had an air of professional confidence which, despite his youth, made her feel safe and inappropriately light-hearted. His kindness was a novelty. For a few precious moments, she escaped into it.

'Flowers are lovely.'

'My pleasure.'

'And you've driven all the way back down here.'

'How did the hospital check-up go?'

'Fine. All mended.'

'You look fabulous.'

'Better than that first day?'

He kissed her cheek, lingeringly, as if he wanted to kiss her properly.

Not yet, lad, Greta thought. Not until your admiring eyes and wishful thinking have painted a new Alexandra; someone I can live with.

'Where are you staying?'

'Strand Palace. You?'

'Grosvenor. My grandfather – my nonno – sent me some money. Could I treat you to the theatre tonight?'

'If I buy supper.'

Greta kissed his cheek. It smelled clean.

❖

A servant knelt at his master's feet. Douglas stroked the younger man's oily head.

'I can't bear it,' Martin wept, toying with the musician's shoelaces. 'I've tried to stay away. Three whole weeks. But I miss you. I miss my home.'

'Don't you like the flat?' Douglas felt unbearably sad.

'FLAT! It's a backstreet cellar. How can you treat me like this? Hiding me away like some – mistress? After all these years.'

'There'll be someone else . . .'

With the grace of Nureyev, Martin leapt to his toes and, arms outstretched, pelted down the hall.

❖

Back in Scarborough, Tony laid Greta's case on the floor. Opening it reverently, he lifted out the lingerie, holding each piece up to the light, savouring its sheerness.

Then, as he ran his hands through blouses and slacks, he felt a hard box. Makeup? Fascinated, he hauled it out. But no. It was a cash box! Locked. He fumbled in his back pocket for the key from Greta's envelope. It fitted, turned. When Tony saw the huge pile of grimy notes a deep flush crept up his face. He picked up a five-pound note, then a suspender belt. Oh, Greta, he thought, what sin bought you this? He relocked the cash box and dropped the key back into his trouser pocket.

More urgently now, he riffled through the case and found some crackling paper charts. He twisted them around several times before realizing what they were. Two were covered in graphs monitoring the vital functions of Greta Korda and

Sylvia Sharp. The other two broke his heart. Alice Sharp and Baby Unnamed.

And then he noticed marks on some of the crumpled fabrics. Blood? Yes, old, brown blood. He held up the cash box. On one sharp corner, a smear of the stuff had dried and caked. Trapped in the metal seam were two short black hairs.

❖

Greta stroked her hand along the piano keys. Her father flinched.

'Been with that nice young vet again?'

'No questions, Father.'

'I thought you were staying up in town, to shop.'

'I prefer Italian shoes.'

'And Italian coffee, I dare say.'

Douglas Hythe sat on the chesterfield and crossed his legs. Greta shuddered to realize that, beneath his paisley dressing gown, he was naked. Cool, handsome and smiling as ever, he smelled old-mannish.

'Speaking of coffee . . .'

As Greta walked through Halstone House, she wondered what Sam might think of the balding carpet and the dried mud crusted on the hall floor. She touched the sagging curtains. 'I'm sorry, Mamma,' she said, 'about this. I ran away from it. From him. Even from you, from the memory of your illness. And now, Papa and me, we're tied together by two different Satans. You saw what I did, didn't you, Mamma?' She closed her eyes and tried to see Sophia's face. 'Are you watching over my baby, Mamma?'

Sadly, Greta opened the kitchen door. Then stopped.

Stared. There, with his neat little backside parked against the oven, arms crossed, confronting her in whole, ugly flesh, was the unspeakable monster of her nightmares.

'Alexandra. Darling. You've grown.'

Breath seemed to puff away from her. Her eyes, unable to tolerate his, slid down Martin's slender body and rested somewhere near his waistband. She could see it again, the contours of his rump, her father's nakedness.

Martin was playing the leading role in his own drama. He spread his arms wide, graceful as a swan.

'What's the matter, darling? Hoping I was dead and buried?'

'Oh, yes.' Courage came storming back. 'How did you get into this house?'

'How did I get in? With my key, dear.'

'Why, after all these years? Why torment him?'

'Perhaps torment gives him pleasure?'

'Go back to your gutter!' she hissed. 'To whatever slime you crawled out of.'

'Back? Where do you think I have lived all these years, Alexandra, my sweet?'

Truth was trickling through his malicious words. Greta's throat contracted.

'Your papa loves me. Always has.' Martin extended his foot, turning his arch inwards, pointing his foot. 'Poor baby, you ran away. He was so sad. Well – quite. For a while. But then there was just the two of us. Oh, terribly guilty, yes. But how could he hurt me? Such a good boy? Obedient. He needed comfort, and love.' Lips pursed, he blew a kiss heavenwards.

'Liar!' Spittle flew on the word.

Martin advanced on her. She backed away in revulsion.

'Let's turn the tables, Alexandra. Why have *you* come back? Why should I cower in a hovel; I, who adore him even more than he adores himself? How much do you love him, sweetheart? Enough to care for him when he is old? Enough to polish his shoes? Enough to massage his fingers when arthritis stops him from playing? Enough to dance for him? A monarch, my dear, only needs one queen.'

And the wretched ghoul, Martin, began swirling in a bizarre dance. He extended his right arm, leaned forward from his hips and stretched his leg into arabesque.

'Evil!' Greta spluttered. 'You're . . . you're a devil.' His dance steps undulated around her. The kitchen spun around him. 'You wrecked his life. Killed my mother!' The strong hands of Greta the trapeze artist grasped the table. She wanted to choke the life out of him. The urge was shockingly familiar.

'Ah!' Mocking, Martin swept his hand over his brow. 'How can you say such things? As if I would have hurt your mamma. She was magnificent.' Completely absorbed in his own screenplay, he eased his weight up on to the table, placing his rump right next to her fingers. Like a forties movie star, he crossed his legs and placed his hands coyly on his knees.

Appalled at the begging in her own voice, Greta whispered, 'Did she know?' The pain was unbearable. 'Did my mother know?'

For a split second she thought she saw compassion in his

eyes. Then he leapt up and flung himself towards the door, turning and delivering his last line over his shoulder.

'Probably.'

Once again the extraordinary tumult of history was repeating itself. She packed a bag. No goodbyes. Too much bitterness to bear. But this time she was older. This time she had her passport. And this time she understood. As she began her trek down the drive, she cast Samuel Phillips from her mind. The charming vet had been a pleasant diversion.

Now she needed her family. Her real family. The Marlettis.

❖

Martin stood like a suit of armour in the corner of the hall as Douglas flew past him. He heard the musician scrape away the piano stool. He heard a crashing chord, furious swearing, and he knew Douglas would be bent double over the keys, with his voluptuous mouth twisted and his fingers stretched into pounding hooks. When the discordant thunder began to tremble through Halstone House, Martin closed his eyes and began to sway.

❖

Two weeks later, in Italy, Nonno Marletti traced Alexandra's jaw with shaking, gnarled fingers. His long-lost princess, daughter of Sophia, had come home at last, to play with Venetian glass and Marletti jewels.

At times, the princess's crown would be weighty with the novelty of adoration. Perhaps, initially, her every waking thought would be of a growing daughter, but the image of that small face was always washed over with Dick's blood. So she learned to burn away the pictures by looking straight at the Mediterranean sun. And so, the woman who was Alexandra Hythe would distance herself from Greta Korda.

Venice had its own stink. The family had its own dirt. Time and truth could slip away on slow canals.

David

returned to Gosforth to be welcomed like a prisoner thrust back into society. Girls ignored him; boys hid smirks behind bitten fingernails. Hendo turned his back, but the eloquent Alan, with his undisputed talent for sarcasm and a recent grasp of communism, waved a vitriolic finger, accusing David of hiding, like a miserable, bourgeois prat, behind his parents' wealth, and of abusing then abandoning poor Sylvia.

David lashed back, 'You fancied her yourself. That's your problem, squirt.'

The squirt's small, bony fists belted him hard between his ribs. David, hurt and astounded, thumped back, and Hendo suddenly felt so incensed at the whole situation that he clouted both of them. Unfortunately, the big boy was not yet fully in control of his huge limbs. He stumbled and hit the pavement with his chin, biting a hole in his tongue which bled bucketfuls, causing a dinner lady to faint.

While he was being rushed to the General, David locked himself in a cubicle in the toilets and slid his forehead over the white tiles to relieve the pain under his skull. Alan shouted, 'Coward' over the partition, while a posse of jeering lads sat on the sinks listening to David vomit.

❖

The pain in Hendo's mouth kept him awake all night, his brain buzzing with rights and wrongs. As he cycled to school the following morning, his haversack was unusually heavy.

'Hey! Davy,' he whispered, with a new speech impediment caused by two knotty black stitches in his tongue, 'meet uz down the bank.' Over a school lunch of cheese pie and rice pudding with Delrosa, he repeated the message to Alan.

The Grammar School was a proudly symmetrical building, with internal quadrangles and a central nave which formed the entrance and hall. It was separated from the Great North Road by a formal sports field where, on rare warm June days, boys in cricket whites scattered the field or lounged around the pavilion.

Behind the building was a muddier playing field. At its far reaches was a hole in the fence. Should a lad dare risk a thousand lines of Chaucer, he could slip between the brambles and slither down a railway embankment.

David arrived first, skidding through the long grass, hanging on to twigs, avoiding nettles. He was infuriated to see Alan easing nimbly down behind him, but anger and awkwardness were suppressed by a low rumble in the seats of their pants.

'Buggeration!'

Scrambling behind flimsy hawthorns, they crouched in billows of grey vapour as an ancient black steam engine chugged past with a stern clanking of chains. David automatically counted the empty wagons. Thirteen would have meant bad luck.

'Gerra hodda this.' Hendo appeared above them and handed David his haversack. After wriggling down the slope on his backside, he extracted from his bag three part-full pop bottles. The sloshing liquid was amber and cloudy.

'Tizer Tornados. Latest thing in cocktails. Must be mixed in a jam pan in the middle of the night. Gin, a slug or two of amontillado, a dollop of Nan's cherry brandy, finish with Tizer. Liquid gold. A've got fags anall. Aboot time wuz had wuselves a bit of a party.'

David lit a Woodbine in the cup of his hand.

'Give uz a slug.' Alan grabbed his bottle. Lying on their backs, they took large mouthfuls of the nectar. As it hit the cheese pie in their bellies, each felt a sudden mellowing. Fags were passed, and they lay watching their smoke melt into the clouds. After a while Hendo sat up dizzily. He staggered down to the track and tried to walk along the metal rail, with his arms outstretched. As his ankles skidded away from him, he farted. David, in true camaraderie, farted back.

An hour later in the Biology Lab, Hendo picked up his dead frog and burped. The Science mistress glared.

David was gingerly examining his specimen, holding the blackened thing between his forefinger and thumb. Smiling widely at Hendo, he swung too far back on his stool. The stool tipped further and further. Lanky limbs flailing like a slack puppet, David threw out his arms to balance, and his dead creature flew in an arc through the formalin-scented air and landed noiselessly on Joyce's clever head.

As David's bones thudded on the floor, the superior girl

looked up. The whole class was giggling and pointing at her haystack of curls. Groping her head, she discovered the frog's rigid little limbs entangled in the frizz.

Chortles spluttered contagiously, hands slapped over mouths. Alan's laughter exploded down his nose, while poor David, helplessly prostrate, cursed very forbidden words.

Unfazed, Joyce simply dragged the frog out of her coiffure and, scalpel poised, defiantly slit open its slimy stomach.

Revulsion tipped the class into hysteria. Two girls rushed from their benches screaming, saucer-eyed in phoney dread, lest all the little froggy corpses leapt back to life.

Furious, the Science mistress whacked Alan across his blond head and advanced on David, who was lying incapable on the floor. But Hendo's burping deepened ominously. His giant shoulders began heaving, as cheese pie and Tizer tornados curdled, and he bolted outside with the hasty grace of an orangutan.

Fortunately, the poor teacher's sinusitis prevented her from detecting alcohol fumes. She regained control by kicking David until he got up, then slapping several sets of knuckles and giving detention to the whole class.

Three white-faced teenagers staggered home together, friends, as it were, reunited.

And yet an insidious thread of distrust remained. Competition entered the triangle. Schoolwork started getting tough and each of the three had his own reasons for craving success.

The clock

tocked towards four o'clock, as Sunday rain spat across the windows of Hisper Cottage. While Tony was fetching coal, Liz Baxter dropped her knitting needles and said, 'See how much weight e's lost? E's set on gettin' this fangled RISTORANTE goin' for Christmas, and e's tetchy as a cat. All this flamin' Italian stuff! Grave doubts. It's grave doubts I've got.' She poked a knitting needle between her plaits to scratch her scalp. 'I'm not even allowed to say Caf no more. Got to say RISTORANTE. With an "e" at the end. We've been closed for a fortnight while 'e paints purple grapes on t'walls.'

'What was that stuff he cooked tonight?'

'Sloppi ploppi.' Liz crunched defiantly on one of her home-baked biscuits. 'If Tony don't slow down a bit, he'll have a heart attack.'

Sylvia's smile, brittle as brandysnaps, crumbled. She stared at the fire, debating with her inner chatterbox the seduction of purple grapes and whether the Grapes of Wrath were poisonous. While her head was singing, '. . . he is tramping out the vintage . . .', Liz frowned over her clicking needles.

'You're set up nicely now. Do we need to come up so often?'

The hymn, with its holy, juicy imagery, stopped.

'Can't I come to Scarborough, and paint spaghetti?'

'No. If you get recognized, Tony'll be in trouble. We both would, pet.' Liz rolled up her knitting. 'When are you planning to go home, lass?'

Later, lying alone on the settee, Sylvia talked aloud, her voice bouncing off the freshly distempered walls.

'They'd put me straight back in St Hilda's. I'd never get Alice off the Lindens.'

Leaning on the mantelpiece, she complained to the wretchedly noisy clock, 'All these hours of waiting, and I'm still only fifteen!'

She touched the old sepia photograph, which had been rubbed clean to reveal a handsome, moustached soldier. 'I need a brave hero like you. We'll creep stealthily into Ethel Linden's house and steal my baby back. Dare we?'

She picked up the candle and surveyed the room. 'Could we bring Alice here, Mustard?'

During September, Tony had worked every night, repairing the roof of Hisper Cottage. Sylvia had helped, lugging planks, handing up slates, nails and elastoplasts. Once dry, the attic bedroom had been swept and a mattress laid on the floor. At the tiny eave window, rosy curtains now framed the sea. Unfortunately the stairs opened directly into the bedroom, so it was draughty and at night, when Sylvia lay resisting the vulnerability of sleep, she often felt sudden shiverings. Also, the crafty enemy Spotted Damp crept determinedly up the walls, so the rooms were only warm as long as the range beast roared.

'Money's the problem,' Sylvia explained to Mustard, who looked interested, but wasn't. 'Liz feeds us. Tony buys coal. They're so kind it's embarassing. How can I get a job? How long before people forget my face?'

On this late October evening, Sylvia felt even worse panic than usual, facing several days alone, sitting from dawn to darkness, counting minutes. Nights were worse, shivering in bed through relentless dark hours of wind-howling and sea-roaring, waiting for the dawn of another ticking-tocking day.

Ten to nine. Six hundred seconds to nine o'clock.

'Why,' Sylvia asked the deaf, mute, monochrome soldier, 'has that clock got Tempus Fugit written on its face? Tempus is Time. What does Fugit mean?' She pronounced Fug like bug, hug, tug. Putting her own face against the ticking face, she lined up her nose with the fulcrum of the two hands.

'You're getting louder, Tempus Fug. You talk too much and say nothing. I'm putting you in the lav with the incy-wincies. You can shiver your bloody tocks off.'

An hour later she relented, and brought the clock back in from the cold, needing the reassurance of its moving hands, hating it even more.

Now suffering severe postnatal depression, Sylvia was sliding down her own tunnel of hours into a fetish world of curious time chasms.

Nine!

Obedient to Tempus Fugit, she locked the door against burglars, pirates and bogeymen. Deciding to sleep on the settee, she hurried upstairs to collect her eiderdown. Pausing at the tiny attic window, she looked out at the black, swelling sea, which was fractured with massive, rolling breakers, and her over-stimulated imagination took her into the icy salt water, feeling its hard will pushing her thin body this way and that . . .

She clattered down the stairs and pulled Mustard close. Tocking filled the empty room. Wrapping the eiderdown around her legs, she stared at the fire's embers.

The candle guttered. Three hours vanished in sleep.

Tock.

Sylvia woke, shivering.

Tock.

Rising from the settee, she reached up, grasped the clock and dropped it on the hearth. Shards of glass danced. The tocking stopped.

As she crawled back towards the sofa, she thought she heard a voice (perhaps it was her own) chastise, *Temper, temper!*

She laughed then, loud, because no one could hear her; louder still, with a touch of moonlit hysteria.

'Oh, Tempers, tempus!' she said aloud, curling around the dog. 'Oh, fuggit, fuggerit, buggerit!'

The North Sea roared. The dog whined.

'Mustard, I'm going bonkers.'

❖

Sylvia dreamed she was clutching Alice, sprinting through a storm, chased by a voice which pressed hard into her back.

'The North Wind doth blow . . . !'

Alice's pink blanket flew away, leaving baby skin naked,

slicked with rain, but Sylvia was too terrified to stop. Again, overhead, the great bird came, whipping the air. But this time giant talons gripped Sylvia's shoulders. She was being yanked upwards; Hisper Cottage, the moors, the cliffs, were shrinking away, while the baby wriggled and kicked, slippery as a fish.

As merciless claws punctured Sylvia's skin and paralysed her muscles, Alice slipped into the tempest. With her little limbs outstretched, the baby plummeted down, down, spinning and turning, until she was just a pale falling star against the grey ocean.

The voice was still reciting, '. . . do then, poor thing?' as the baby hit the water.

❖

No wind. No wind at all. Just a gull scratching at the roof of Hisper Cottage.

Desperate for dawn light, Sylvia flung open the door. Mustard bounded out, disappearing into a day which was grey and unusually still.

Famished, Sylvia foraged in the larder. She had remembered Alice! She could eat! If she ever forgot her baby, food was the one luxury she could forfeit, but today, with maternal longing gnawing at her belly, she crammed bread into her face.

Later, nauseous on lemon curd, she walked down to the deserted shoreline and sat on a rock, watching the glassy slide of an eerily becalmed sea. A small flock of seagulls landed in the shallows, some standing, some sitting thoughtfully on the water. As though choreographed, they all turned to face inland, looking expectantly in the same direction – at Sylvia. Poor things, they were only waiting for a whiff of a breeze. But she picked up a handful of pebbles and hurled them, listening to each one plop, gratified when the gulls screeched, and wheeled away.

The busy voice in her head was reminding her of something she didn't want to think about. David would come home for Christmas, to find her baby, her Alice, at his gran's. Sylvia stared at the sea, emotionally paralysed, until a Bible text trickled through her misery.

Many waters cannot quench love, neither can the floods drown it.

She put her finger to her lips, tasted sea salt, bit nervously into her own flesh. Only when Mustard bounded towards her did Sylvia realize how much she was hurting herself.

❖

Twenty miles down the coast a cash box now rested on the seabed. Greta's suitcase, matching Sylvia's, was washed up in a tangle of seaweed in the mouth of a cave.

Under a floorboard in Tony's flat, wrapped in oilcloth, were the baby charts and almost two thousand oily pound notes. The Italian refused to spend a penny of Greta's dirt money.

❖

'I'm going daft!' Sylvia was pacing the floor like an imprisoned lioness, her orange mane crackling as her head whipped around in frustration, arms folded across her bony chest.

Tony was staring at the coals.

'We're just so busy,' Liz apologized. 'Can't cook ploppi fast enough.'

'It's November tomorrow. I've been here, all by myself, since June.' She wrote '5 MONTHS' in the condensation on the window.

'When I was your age,' Liz reminisced, 'I was . . . hmph . . . well, best not say what I was doin', but I suppose it was 'ealthy enough. Only natural that you miss people of your own age. Come on now, no need for tears.'

Liz turned her three double chins in Tony's direction, but he simply yawned, a great gasping affair followed by a snort. He got up to leave, hauling his braces over his shoulders.

'Why can't I come down to Scarborough?' Sylvia pleaded. 'I'd work in the café, earn my keep.'

Tony suddenly turned on Sylvia. 'Where, tell me, are the bars on this cage? If this not good enough,' he waved his arms around, eyes bulging with indignation, 'then go. Go! But not to Scarborough and not into my Ristorante. If you caught, what they accuse Tony of? Kidnap? Child – what it called – molestation? Eh? And Liz? Liz is accomplice.' He pulled on his jacket and opened the door. 'If you no wanna go home, you wait here for Greta come.'

'Greta's not coming, Tony, and you damn well know it.'

❖

It was five whole days before Tony returned. Puffing into Hisper Cottage on a gust of iced air, he threw a pile of books on to the scrubbed kitchen table.

'*L'ozio è il padre di tutti i vizi.* You miserable because you have nothing to do. So I bring you schoolwork. Yes?'

Sylvia began to laugh, but Tony's round olive face was deadly serious.

'*Si!*' He stabbed his finger, mimicking one of his own teachers, many years ago. 'This Mathematic book has questions in the back; you can do these. Here now is a book of Biology, with flowers and trees. Big one is Atlas. Red one, Dictionary – look. Here, of course, Shakespeare – I pick *Othello*. And this . . .' he waved a volume triumphantly, '. . . poetry. English ROMANTICS. Woman in library advise. This is how we proceed. You work, I check.'

'You can't mark my schoolwork, you're too busy. And you're Italian.' She was laughing again, relieved to have his company and his forgiveness.

'You think, in Italy, one and one make three? I ama very good MATHEMATICO! And even if I don't spell so good, I read your writing and I know if is . . . sensible. Here also are some paints. Maybe you will be famous artist!'

He put on the kettle and reached for the cocoa caddy.

Sylvia picked up the biology textbook. Leafing through it, she remembered, with sudden pride, the heady day she had been top of the class in a botany test – beating even David, the brainbox who had got her pregnant and then abandoned her.

She saw her own tragedy then; her useful brain locked in its lonely vigil on a Yorkshire cliff top. She wondered fleetingly about her sister, Katherine. Just at this moment, was she doing her homework on the dining-room table? Getting good marks? Pats on the head from Dad?

What about Alice? Would she be clever, like her father?

Would she some day hold her mother's ignorance in contempt?

Now Tony was reaching into his overcoat pocket, handing her an envelope. Sylvia opened the packet, seeing only graph paper. Geometry?

No. No! A familiar crackle between her fingers. It was Alice's baby chart!

'I get this in post,' Tony lied. 'No letter.'

Sylvia clutched the chart to her chest. The chatterbox in her head seemed unable to string a sentence together. Her eye fell on the red dictionary. She picked it up. The fat volume trembled in her hand, vibrating with a billion expressive possibilities. Yet the unschoolable part of her brain sparkled around a sensation which chains of words could never fetter.

She looked up. The soldier on the mantelpiece was watching. She flung the inadequate dictionary at his silly face. As he tipped and tumbled, Sylvia's whole body began twitching with unleashed rage. *Botany for Beginners* crashed against the wall, and slid behind the settee. The atlas broke Tony's cocoa mug. Byron and Shelley hit the hearth singeing Harold and Ozymandias as the tornado of Sylvia's frustration whipped around the room.

It was only when she finally saw Tony cowering, with his sleeve over his face, that a ping of guilt froze her. Turmoil fell in stinging stars, around her head, across her shoulders, dying as they touched the floor.

❖

The kind Italian tried to hold her.

'In the war, I am put in camp. My head screams to be free. For me, no choice. Different for you, Sylvie. You can go home.'

Tony felt the girl's body relax. Her odd mutterings stopped. He sighed, wiping his eyes with his spotted hanky. 'Meantime, you learn from these books, to keep you growing up. Right?'

She grabbed his hanky, and scrubbed her face, which was now pale, calm and honestly wretched.

Tony wrapped her thin coat around her shoulders and wound the scarf which Liz had knitted around her neck. 'Come.'

Pulling her gently through the door into the freezing night, he dug in his pocket and fumbled at something fastened on the gate. A strike of a match, a tiny flare, a spark in the darkness, and, with a sudden fizz, the gate lit up. Nervously, a Catherine wheel began to turn. It stuck for a second, and then whirled in a blinding, spinning light.

'Rockets next. And Rainbow Shower,' the Italian enthused, sorting through the box of fireworks.

He lit a sparkler and put it in her hand. As the sparks caught the glisten in her eyes, Tony could not know that Sylvia was seeing her dad, in the back garden in Gosforth.

❖

December winds shook the door, the fire smoked, water from the tap ran as liquid ice, and wild nights sent Sylvia cowering under her eiderdown. A tiny tilley lamp flickered by her lonely bedside while she listened to the windowpanes rattle. The clock had been repaired, after its 'accident', so Tempus Fugit fuggered on, ticking and tocking as noisily as ever.

Tony and Liz now only visited twice a week, but Sylvia was so desperately grateful for their company that she never complained again. Time was now spasmodic, moving along in fits and starts as she spent her days doing Maths equations and writing essays on odes until her eyes ached. The deeper she delved into literature, the more conscious she became of her own tumbling emotions. Deprived of conversation, she found herself memorizing Shelley's poignant outpourings and Shakespearean expletives, while Desdemona's muffled screams haunted her dreams.

The nightmares which ravaged her sleep inspired her to write terrifying chase stories, documenting the startling words spoken by utterly unimaginable characters. In safe daylight, on blank sugar paper, she tried to paint the disturbing images which walked with her for long mornings; then she would defeat them by burning the pictures on the range. But the thing she could not capture was the great bird she could never see, because it always attacked from behind, or above. Sitting at the window, she would watch the greedy seagulls, trying to draw their foraging eyes and open beaks. She didn't fear them. Their squawks had no language. But the giant dreambird, who flew in the darkness, pecked holes in the back of her head and pushed strange thoughts under her skull.

Because she kept forgetting to remember Alice, Sylvia hardly ate. Her breasts shrank away and her periods stopped. Her compulsion to escape Hisper Cottage was becoming fanatical, and yet perversely, with her nerves shredded from lack of sleep, she suffered palpitations at the very thought of being in a crowd. Several times she walked defiantly down the track towards the main road, fully intending to get on a bus, but when it approached, steamy with folk from Whitby, she found herself cowering in the hedge.

On 14 December Sylvia stood waving goodbye to her friends, clutching Liz's old raincoat to her chest. The winter air was razor-sharp and the moon hung like a sabre between rushing grey clouds. She latched the door and bolted it.

'Here, lad, give uz a cuddle.' She ran her hand through Mustard's golden coat. 'Thank God for Liz,' she sighed, picking up a very large red jumper with a darned sleeve. 'I'd rather wear her honest cast-offs than Greta's stolen stuff.' The dog yawned. She lifted the picture of the soldier. 'Were you brave, soldier? Courage is a funny thing, isn't it? Brave people don't need it. Only people like me do.'

❖

Violet Sharp held the Christmas card against her cheek. It sparkled with cheap glitter and was simply signed 'Sylvia'. Never had Santa looked so ugly.

In the window, the tree was already dropping needles.

❖

David's gloved hand clutched his exam results. They were excellent. He stuffed the paper in his haversack and cycled down Gosforth High Street feeling relieved. This report would go some way towards regaining his father's respect. Self-respect was more difficult, but guilt over Sylvia was now conveniently softened by a neat cushion of transferred blame. She'd been willing enough to do IT. She'd run away, leaving

poor little Alice behind. Now HE had to live with the consequences.

Carollers were singing 'Little Jesus, Sweetly Sleep'. It was
already dark; yellow light from the toyshop window spilled
across his gabardine and dripping cap.

David Linden, a schoolboy, was selecting a Christmas
present for his daughter.

❖

Tony cooked Christmas lunch on the range in Hisper Cottage.
He and Sylvia were alone, because Liz was with her daughters in York.

He was moved, as he stirred very English gravy, because
Sylvia had knitted him a huge scarf. Also, wrapped inside it,
was a painting of a seagull and a poem she had written herself. She seemed to have a talent for naive rhyme, and a feel
for the iambic sonnet. The words were light and humorous,
yet somehow deeply personal.

With flushed pleasure, he had watched the girl open his
present to her – a new grey skirt and baby-blue blouse. As she
twirled around the kitchen, he knew for certain that the
clothes she wore from the suitcase were not her own.

Liz had left gifts for Sylvia: Apple Blossom talc and a
packet which said 'OPEN LATER'. He knew that it contained
a new bra, two cup sizes smaller than the one Sylvia had
arrived in.

❖

On the first Saturday in January a plain girl with a red nose
and chapped lips alighted from the bus in Scarborough, hold-

ing a hanky against her face. Sylvia's hair was scrapped back into a scarf and her shoulders were hunched beneath Liz's enormous raincoat. Inside she shook like a jelly but, after half a year in solitude, her New Year's resolution was to defy Tony and spend just one day among people. In her pocket was the remainder of Greta's money.

Scarborough was abustle with January sales, the resident winter population pursuing bargains in Boyes Store. Breathing too fast with nameless anxiety, Sylvia nudged through thronged pavements to stare at gaudy shop windows. From a fish and chip shop came that familiar, mouth-watering smell. Unable to resist, she leaned against the counter and ordered chips with scrapings. Suddenly the penetrating warmth of the shop sent her heart soaring with blissful normality, shivers and snuffles almost forgotten.

Fingers licked clean of vinegar and grease, she headed for the chemist's.

'Nasty cough you've got there, pet. Linctus? Me mam swears by this one.' But Sylvia would not waste Greta's ten-bob notes on medicine.

Later that afternoon, back in Hisper Cottage, Sylvia held a red tress to her face and ran a strand through her mouth, enjoying the luxuriant, intimate taste for the last time. Then she hacked it off. As she tried to cut a fringe, the hair would not lie properly and it got shorter and shorter. In the end she was left with a curly crown which looked like a job a bad barber would have done on a lad for sixpence. Vanity abandoned, Sylvia felt only excitement. Dye ran down her face leaving trails of grey, but when she was finished her hair was as black as a proverbial heap of nutty slack.

Tony stood at the door with his mouth agape and a moist glaze over his big brown eyes. He was appalled. But relieved. Sylvia would never be recognized.

'I speak with Joe. He has shoe shop. I say you family. OK?'

Sylvia hugged the man who had reluctantly become her friend.

As the moon eclipsed the sun

on 30 June 1954, the sea blackened and an abrupt breeze skimmed across Sylvia's shoulders. She was standing on the cliff top, with only grazing sheep to hear her reciting her favourite poem.

'. . . Ocean of Time, whose waters of deep woe

Are brackish with human tears . . . Oh, fuggerit, what comes next?'

The mysterious day-gloom deepened. Between Shelley's lines slipped a voice, whispering a Bible text.

I will make darkness light before them, and crooked things straight.

Sylvia threw back her head and lifted her lonely voice towards the shifting planets. 'Mighty Lord! When you've finished playing with the moon, can you please straighten my crooked life? Will you show me the way to look after my baby, and work at the same time? Can you help me, God, to do the legal things to get Alice back? I've already missed her first birthday, you see . . .'

Sylvia forced herself to keep speaking aloud, hoping her

prayers would be more potent if offered audibly into the mystical moment.

'I'll be sixteen soon. Help me shift this puppy fat. When it's gone, I'll know that's your sign that I'm grown up. As soon as I'm thin, God, I'll go back for Alice. I promise.'

❖

Violet Sharp stood in the back field, her tired eyes fastened on the miracle in the sky, as she listened to children playing on the swings.

❖

Ethel Linden sat in her garden in Corbridge, beneath the great oak, watching the curve of the moon shift over the sun. She was upset. Lucy the spaniel had died and Mary was threatening to visit.

❖

David, Hendo, Alan and Katherine were among the noisy playground throng, flirting, gossiping, pretending interest in this 'significant' scientific phenomenon. A tiny scrap of the sun reappeared like a diamond in an engagement ring and Hendo looked slyly at Katherine's upturned face.

❖

Little Alice sat giggling on her grandad's knee. No one was looking, so he kissed his little treasure tenderly. She was chubby, with large round eyes and a top curl of dark, wispy hair.

Baby Jan sat blinking in a wooden high chair with a line of others, eating Marmite soldiers. She had finer features than Alice. Her nose was tiny and her rosebud mouth pouted.

❖

A few miles away, the child's namesake, Nurse Janice Kirkstone, quarelled with her husband Matthew yet again. Would he never understand her grief for her blighted ova? He called her yearning 'insanity', but he signed the forms anyway.

Janice cried all the way to the post box, while . . .

❖

. . . Greta, or rather Alexandra, was dancing in Venice.

Perishing

cold gusts buffeted the bus shelter where Hendo stood waiting. He hunched his wide shoulders and tucked his hands under his armpits. During the last two years his muscles had thickened across his chest and back; his jawline was already leathery with shaving and the thatch on his head had been hard-pruned against his skull.

He was really looking forward to the Tatler tonight, where he would watch cartoons with open-mouthed pleasure and, during Pathe News, neck his girlfriend with equally open-mouthed enthusiasm.

A rapid clicking of heels, and Katherine Sharp ran into his arms, warming his lips with hers.

'You'll never guess.' Curls flew about her excited face. 'We're buy'n a house! Down South Gosforth.'

'By . . . lad! Your dad's never looked back since he started with the wagons. How many's he got now? Three? Where there's muck, there's a posh new house.'

'When he left the pit, me mam went mad. Said we'd starve. Now she's swank'n about bay windows. The house is nearer dad's yard, but I'll have further to walk to school.' Katherine took Hendo's face in her cold hands. 'And no more tappy tappy on the wall for you and me.'

'Mebees another pretty lass'll move in next door.'

'Aye. And mebees I'll get meself a rich lad now.'

Hendo pressed his nose into her neck, feeling the rough wool coat beneath his palms, wishing he dared unbutton it and slip his hands inside. For a while they forgot everything, kissing greedily, until Katherine sighed and snuggled into his chest.

'It's weird. The thought of shift'n.'

'Like . . . ?'

'An adventure. Like I'm about to jump over a snake-infested canyon, and the snakes are all jealous lasses.'

'Who's been read'n too many comics?'

'Huh. Have you ever read a girl's comic? Yours might be full of spaceships and heroes. Ours are yawnable stories about school quarrels and new shoes. And bloody cake recipes.'

'Stop swear'n, bonny lass.'

'Good for the goose is good for the bloody gander. Wish I was a bloody lad. Wish I could go to bloody university, like you lot. Wish you weren't all bloody well leav'n me behind.'

'Divent start on.'

'Bloody architecture.'

Another kiss. 'Will you be faithful, pet?'

Katherine shook her curls. 'Definitely not. David wants to stop in Newcastle. Why don't you?'

'If Davy wants to do Medicine at King's, he'll have to get

good results. Nee chance of them accept'n me. Probably have to be London. Alan's off to Oxford.'

Alan Watson was now house captain and top in all of his three subjects. David was also a house captain, mostly because he was handsome and all the girls voted for him. Hendo was a prefect, wearing his short black gown with pride while fighting his subjects like a valiant soldier.

He looked across the top of Katherine's head, to a place where the future looked as bright as the stars.

'In a few years' time the Turrible Trio's all gonna be rich! Alan'll be richest, of course. Tricky bastard. Should've seen him in the Debat'n Society. Beetroot red, eyes popp'n oot. A was petrified. Voted with him just to stop him have'n heart failure. E's a rocket, that one, headed for the moon.'

'Rockets again. That's all lads think about. But it's me that's top of my year for Chemistry. A bloody lass. Mebees now that we're shift'n to a posh house, I'll become a rich scientist.'

'If you're gonna be rich, you'll have to stop bloody swear'n. Anyway, ambition's not about richness. It's about . . . dinnah . . .' Hendo hunted for the word to describe his own feelings, 'passion!'

'Lasses aren't allowed passion. They do teacher train'n.'

❖

Janice Kirkstone rushed to her doormat. It had 'Welcome' written on it – welcome to their new, pristine council flat. She tore open a large buff envelope and scanned the typewritten page, but anxiety was blurring the words.

'What?' Matthew asked, terrified.

'Yes.' Realization spread across her rounded face. 'Matthew! We've got her. Oh, I can't believe it! After so long. We can collect little Jan on Christmas Eve. I'm going to be a mam.' Then the floodgates really opened.

'Well, that's good then.' Matthew held his wife. He thought he should be very happy. Why had she never listened? Time and again he'd told her that children didn't matter to him. Baby Jan, whom they visited every Sunday, was sweet enough, especially now that she was toddling, but whatever this letter said, she wasn't really theirs.

❖

Violet wrote their new address on the back of all her Christmas cards – all except Sylvia's, which waited in a ribboned box, upstairs in an empty bedroom in the new house. On 20 December she wheeled the pushchair back to her old house to collect mail. The new tenant handed over a couple of envelopes. Nothing from Sylvia. Not even a card this year. It was a long, cold walk back to South Gosforth.

At teatime David popped his head around the back door. 'It's me, Mrs Sharp.'

'Howay in, love. Look, Alice, what's David got! Ooh! Chocolate drops. Taaa. Say Taaa. There's a good lass.'

David sat by Cuthbert's roaring fire and lifted the chubby little girl into his lap. It still felt strange, knowing that this warm, rounded, wet-kissing creature was his daughter. She never called him Dad – just 'Daydid'. Then of course there was Dandad and Danfar and Gommom and Nannan, not forgetting Tatwim.

Tatwim and Hendo came in on another flurry of chilly air,

faces polished with young lust and a couple of glasses of stolen sherry. Katherine smiled pertly at David and leaned forward to pick Alice from his lap, her full brassiere wobbling near his face.

'Hello, pet lamb. Kiss for Auntie Kath?'

'Watch your mouth!' hissed her mother.

'Why?' Katherine was getting really impatient with her mother's manipulations. 'When will you tell her the truth? Sooner or later the poor bairn will realize she's got all these grandparents, but no Mam and Dad.' She glared at David. 'Davy, why don't *you* say something? After all,' she hissed, 'she's your bairn. Someone has to sort it out. Face up to it, owa Sylvia's never going to.'

A silence as cold as the weather fell upon the room. Hendo, with his big soft heart, decided he didn't always like his girlfriend.

❖

In the shoe shop in Scarborough, Sylvia employed a plastic smile which momentarily disguised her hollow cheeks. Her lips, once smooth and wide, were puckered and dry. Back aching, feet throbbing, she dutifully lowered her lashes and inquired, 'Can I help?'

On the last Saturday of the January sales, patent leathers in one hand, suede boots in the other, feet aching beyond endurance, she faced the prospect of another evening on her feet helping Tony to serve pasta. Memories of Gosforth, her old home and friends were like mottled pictures in a closed book.

Yet another Christmas had passed. She'd bought Alice a

dolly in a satin carrycot, but never sent it. Even as she stood looking down at her customer's socks, she vowed to go back to Newcastle for her daughter's third birthday. For God's sake, she'd be almost eighteen by then. She could deliver the present by hand. Knock on the Lindens' front door. Wave the chart under her nose. Maybe . . . maybe it was almost time . . .

'Sorry! Oh yes, Madam, the buckle. Just a moment.' Wearily, she sat down on the back stairs, hacking at her recurring winter cough. The skin around her nose had dried and cracked with too much blowing. These days she always seemed to have a cold. In fact she rarely felt well. Tomorrow, Sunday, she anticipated with nausea, imagining one of Liz's willow-patterned plates burdened with a giant Yorkshire pud, awash with oily gravy.

Sylvia could never permit herself to be replete, in case she forgot Alice. To be plump was to look like a contented child. She had to convince them – David, the Lindens, her parents – that she was a sad, tortured woman. When she went back . . .

Meanwhile, self-punishment tormented every day of Sylvia's life. She continually chastised herself for failing to study hard enough, for not saving enough, not polishing her worn-out shoes, not cleaning the range. The climb towards adulthood was a cliff face cracked with fissures of self-deceit, and she kept slipping backwards.

She coughed again. Blew her nose. Liz was in York, at her eldest daughter Sally's. She was going to be late back, so Tony had asked Sylvia to help out in the Ristorante. In return, Liz had offered a couch to sleep on in Scarborough, so Mustard had been locked in Tony's flat for the day. Even if it meant dragging through another shift on her tired legs, the lonely girl was looking forward to some company and Tony's banter.

There were no other friends. Nor lovers. Seventeen and unkissed – since fourteen. When acquaintances began to exchange confidences, she quickly backed off. Her life was a lie. A false name and a fictitious history were conversational minefields, as were the constantly reappearing ginger roots. Even after all this time she still had difficulty answering to the name 'Nicoletta Torricelli'.

Hobbling down towards the Ristorante on stinging blisters, Sylvia coughed and coughed. It hurt. Phlegm rattled in her chest as she sucked in freezing air. This was a bad winter. The sea had been savage for days. While twisting currents in North Bay flung giant spumes into the air, South Bay cowered behind the harbour watching lines of rollers surging towards the Spa. It was so dark that the Castle, high up behind Foreshore, was lost in the night; yet jolly holiday lights along the Front still kept shining, reflected ironically in the furious, surging sea.

Hunger pangs gnawed at Sylvia's belly, but Tony's famed macaroni must not, NOT, be allowed to stay in her stomach.

And so, on this important night, two and a half years after arriving in Scarborough, despite her cheery, 'Hello!' as she pushed open the Ristorante door, Sylvia Sharp was already weak and ill. She weighed just over six stone.

And then, magically,

Greta was there, illuminating Tony's candlelit Ristorante as if someone had beamed her down from Venus. Her shoulders were wrapped in a cloud of grey musquash and her hair hung over it, glossy and groomed, a swathe of black silk. Her full lips, painted wanton red, smiled wickedly, and her eyes sparkled, diamond and sapphire. She hugged Tony, laughing at his surprise.

Stranded behind a table in the window, Sylvia stood transfixed. This was not the gypsy! This Greta was beautiful. And happy!

Two plates of cannelloni hovered in mid-air. Two diners looked up worriedly as the hands of their painfully thin waitress began to tremble. A pleasant-looking man was being introduced to Tony as 'a good friend, Samuel Phillips'.

Two laden plates landed clumsily, slopping red on the chequered cloth.

Sylvia walked crabwise around the edge of the room. A dagger of crystallized confusion knifed behind her eyes. So, things had changed for the gypsy! Mr Phillips was obviously the new, rich boyfriend. A couple. Matching. Polished like a pair of Sunday shoes.

'Dear Tony!' Greta was hugging the dumbfounded Italian. 'This place, it's wonderful.'

'Fin . . . *finalmente*! *Ben a . . . arrivati*,' he stammered.

Face averted, Sylvia edged into the kitchen, then watched the tableau through the porthole window in the door. Hugging herself tightly, rubbing her protruding ribs, she realized that Greta, this new glamorous creature, had simply not recognized her. Sophisticated women, of course, ignored waitresses, especially self-effacing, dark-haired, ugly ones.

Greta's mobile, carmine lips were moving like sexy kisses across her white teeth. Her dark skin glowed.

So, how was New York, Greta? Sylvia's bitter inner conversation threw up Geordie cusses and Othello oaths – Fie and fuck the fuggering strumpet!

Needing to cough, shoulders heaving, Sylvia sank her chapped hands into washing-up water. Greta's ruby smile swam in the greasy suds along with unwanted peas. Intense fury welled inside Sylvia as she wheezed over the sink. She wanted to hide, to run away from the horrendous injustice, to dash into the icy sea and punish herself for her own gullibility, for somehow, as she had shrunk away from life, the gypsy had conquered it, and was swollen with hideous, beautiful triumph.

Tony flung open the kitchen door bellowing, 'Nicoletta, come see who is here! And bring two plates of the "special". I go to cellar for wine.'

No, Sylvia thought, Nico(bloody)letta will not! Without drying her hands, she shrugged on her shabby winter coat

(Liz's daughter's cast-off) and slipped out into the yard. After the kitchen's bright light, the back alley was dark in the shadow of the huge, looming cliff. Only a timid gas lamp glossed damp cobbles.

She sprinted to the end of the alley and then out to the Foreshore where the tide, even within the arms of the harbour, was slapping hard. A bitter wind blustered into Sylvia's face, tightening ribbons of tension around her forehead, throat and ribcage. She coughed hard. Pain stabbed her chest and her eyes watered with salt spray. She walked briskly, hands deep in pockets, shoes clicking on the pavement, unhappiness lumped in her throat. Bent low into the wind, she couldn't walk fast enough. Greta's painted smile seemed to mock her hunched back, as tears blew in long streaks across Sylvia's cheekbones, into stained hair. How could a filthy gypsy turn up, after these tortured, lonely years, looking like a film star?

With her black hair flying around her head, Sylvia shouted obscenities into the icy gusts blowing in from the sea. On and on she stomped, until she became aware of the pain in her feet. Blisters and chilblains stung and twitched. She leaned against a wall and punched clenched fists against cold, old stone. And, as she hid her face, a voice at the back of her head screeched,

Arise, black vengeance, from the hollow hell! And peck off her fuggering nose . . .

Sylvia turned sharply, knowing, before she looked, that she was alone.

A most unlikely compulsion overwhelmed her. To get to Hisper Cottage. The very place she hated for its solitude, its reluctant hospitality. She touched the cold metal key in her pocket, ducked her head again and dragged up the hill.

Clouds of frost, fine as fairy dust, were blowing across the town. Pinpricks of ice stung her cheeks and the hollow of her neck. Shivering, breathless, she stood at the bus stop, balancing on one painful foot at a time, coughing infected mist into icy air.

Forty minutes later she was frozen stiff. It had started to snow, flakes laying on her bare head, tickling her nose until she sneezed, again and again. Two men had joined her at the stop. Could they hear her teeth chattering? Her bones rattling? The men slapped arms across bodies. Sylvia did the same, her gloveless fists curled into her sleeves. At last, two headlights appeared in falling whiteness and a charabanc pulled up, spilling yellow warmth across her ashen face.

During the treacherous journey, she never warmed up.

As she got out of the bus, the cold stung her eyes, making them water. The heavy vehicle lumbered cautiously away, taking all light with it. Alone in the darkness, Sylvia was enveloped in a cloud of spinning ice crystals.

A telegraph pole, black against the whorling sky, marked the track which led to Hisper Cottage. She laid her ungloved hand on the wooden pole and coughed. When she finally caught her breath, she pushed on. As she trudged up the long track, frozen mud crunched in the potholes beneath her feet. Her legs felt too weak to correct her balance, so she kept clinging to bits of prickly hedge. Her hands were numb – cuts and grazes, from twigs snapping in her fists, went unnoticed. Gusts of arctic, snow-laden air blew under her coat and around her tiny waist, blanking her vision as flakes settled on her eyelashes. Shivering from the core, she coughed again, and this time the girl's bladder contracted. She began to wet herself, drip becoming flow, flow becoming shameful release as urine warmed a trail down her legs, into her nylon stockings and shoes.

Weeping now, she stumbled towards Hisper Cottage. No welcoming glow from the windows, no Mustard to leap at her. She wondered bitterly if tonight her fickle dog would cuddle into Greta.

Numb fingers fumbled with the key. The frozen lock refused to turn. Damn this place, she thought, it's never wanted me. And with that bitter thought, the door of Hisper Cottage swung open and Sylvia fell thankfully into the dark interior.

Fastening out the night, she kicked off her shoes, pulled down her sodden underwear, then fumbled on the mantelpiece for the candle and matchbox. Even the tiny flare was a comfort. In flickering candlelight, she found the paraffin lamp and lit it. Coughing, her whole body aching so that her limbs moved in slow motion, she pushed a knot of newspaper into the range. Bending to grasp the coal scuttle, her arms were too weak to lift it higher than her shins, so she lit the newspaper and held her hands up to it, hypnotized by the rapid flame which grew into a blaze, leaving nothing but crumpled ash as it died. Pinpricks of feeling returned to her stiffened fingers, then the warmth was gone, her bones even more painful for having been warmed for an instant. She tried the coal scuttle again, but the effort just seemed too much. A deep pain in her chest and a feverish ache in her joints were overtaken by another, more destructive pain. Self-pity. She knelt on all fours and began to whine.

With a tremendous crash, the front door blew open, slamming against the wall. Sylvia screamed. A blast of air cut into the room, blue-white flakes billowing like the skirt of the Snow Queen.

The candle blew out.

As Sylvia staggered to the door, her hip hit the table. A jug tipped and rolled. It clattered against the tilley lamp, which also fell, and both crashed on the floor. Sylvia managed to bolt the door, but the lamp had spilled paraffin on the corner of a rag rug. Escaping from its broken glass tube, the tiny flame licked along the trail of paraffin and the matted fabric flared instantaneously.

In that second, Sylvia considered letting Hisper Cottage burn, just to warm herself.

A sliver of Time slipped. Flicker became flame, and suddenly the room lit up with golden, smoky crackles of fire. Sylvia threw herself towards the tap, filled a saucepan with freezing water and hurled it. Then another, and another, strength finding her arms, then seeping away again, when she finally sat in ashy darkness. The small blaze was out. Another fit of coughing shook the breath from her scrawny body. Blindly she groped for the stairs and crawled up into the attic bedroom.

Damp pillow. Shivering eiderdown.

Her feet were an agony of cold. The cough choked in her throat and tightened painfully across her chest. Frail and frozen, her body alternately clenched and trembled.

As night bore down, a film of sweat seeped from her shivering pores. She could hear a weird noise. A wet, burbling sound, in time with her breathing. Her lips were dry, her tongue leaden in her throat. The frigid air hurt her heart too much. It wasn't worth trying to breathe it.

A draught lifted the curtains. Her fever heard the ghosts of Wordsworth and Shelley chanting unlaced lines . . . *breath of night, like death did flow . . . low breathings coming after me . . .*

Sylvia tried to pray, but her inner voice was already silenced. Shadows hovered around the bed, white faces drifting through the darkness, nodding grimly.

❖

The North Wind became a tempest, thrusting at the North Sea until its rollers roared. Leaden clouds charged across the rampant waves. Beneath the sleety wind, frost, the silent creeper, cut deep into the riven moors, its spiteful, icy fingers digging into soil, stone and cleft, tracing fabulous patterns across windows, crawling under doors. It glittered on the stone-flagged floor of Hisper Cottage. It froze the puddle around the burned clippy mat and stiffened the curtains at the window.

Sylvia slipped from consciousness. Claws of fever clutched at her hungry body, dragging it down and down until her functions crazed and her lungs flooded. Death knocked at Hisper Cottage door once again.

Samuel Phillips

stared into the burgundy depths of his wine, then slowly sipped. The initial bubble of banter had burst. Alexandra and Tony were sitting in reflective silence, and Sam felt like a spectator, utterly sidelined. What was the relationship between these two, he wondered resentfully. Was it his imagination, or did the conversation have invisible edges and depths? Rolling the dark liquid across his tongue, Sam was astonished to witness the artistry in Alexandra's evasions, her skilful deployment of vagueness, shuffling names and dates just enough to cover gaps. Uncomfortably suspicious of his own gullibility, he recognized, in Tony Torricelli's discomfiture, another intelligent brain frustrated by inconsistencies.

What power does she have over men, he thought, this woman who continually vanishes then reappears like a magician's assistant? Is it her elusiveness which makes her so desirable? That mouth which only ever kisses like the stroke of duckdown, which seduces me every time?

She lived in Italy, of course, which didn't make for easy romance, so Samuel's infatuation had been fed on spasmodic doses of glamorous tantalization, oases of romance in a desert of fleeing months. A spring lunch in Kensington, an autumn supper in Soho.

There had even been a deliciously titillating Parisian tryst. Oh, Sam's anticipation had been lustfully sweet, as he planned warming her Latin blood with the fire she inspired in his fingertips. But – Alexandra had her own style: flirting under the Tour, arm-clinging up the Champs, playful chasing beneath the Ponts. Each time his blood began pumping and plumping the temptress wriggled prettily from his grasp. Having taken him to the city of lovers, she held him at a distance with the skill of a nun. Then she fled back to bloody Venice again.

A few postcards. The odd telephone call.

Realizing that she was never going to invite him to her family home in Wiltshire, Sam had invited her to his. He had no idea why she had accepted and now, seeing her with Torricelli, he was beginning to suspect an ulterior motive.

I'm like a limp garment, he thought, left hanging in the wardrobe, month after month, just needing a quick press before moulding to her curves again. And, like that dress, I could be discarded tomorrow.

On the way up the country, cosy in the Super Minx, Alexandra had talked enthusiastically, but instead of permitting him to glimpse the woman behind the gloss, Sam now knew a great deal about Venetian palaces, Italian glass, Italian wine, Italian food and Italian politics; nothing at all about her life before Venice, her childhood, or even her schooling. Even the most casual reference to her mother had seemed to cause Alexandra such staggering heartache that he had backed off.

So Sam knew the taste of her lipstick but not of her skin. In lust, if not quite in love, he sighed at his empty glass. Who was this Italian? Why did he keep calling her Greta? Who were these girls Sylvia and Nicoletta? Were they all related? Italian cousins? No, Sam knew instinctively that the relationship between them was not familial; there was too much nervousness in it.

They were talking about that painfully thin waitress who had run off in a huff.

'I understand, Tony,' Alexandra was conceding stiffly. 'She hates me. But there were circumstances, I became ill . . . em – Sam darling,' her eyes flirted, 'would you mind checking into the hotel? It's late. Tony and I have so much catching up to do. I'll join you later. You don't mind, darling, do you?'

Of course he bloody minded. She wanted him out of the way so she could have a secret conversation with the middle-aged, pasta-boiling Eytie! But decency was Sam's middle name. What right had he to mind? He was neither her husband nor fiancé, not even her lover.

He rose and shook Tony's hand. Putting his palms on Alexandra's shoulders, he asked, 'I'm confused. Talk to Tony tonight. Talk to me tomorrow. Please?'

'Fine.'

He didn't trust her bright smile.

❖

When Samuel had gone, Greta moved to sit beside Tony. He put his arm through hers and for a while they were quiet.

166

'What about your daughter, Greta?'

'Wherever she is, she's better off than she would have been with me. I expect she was fostered.' When Greta thought about her child she conveniently imagined her in the arms of a loving, grateful family, a doughy substitute mother with a soft lap and ample breasts, and a hardworking, smiley father.

Tony replied sharply, 'This a selfish fantasy, dreamed for your conscience. Your baby, she is in an orphanage.'

Greta flushed deeply, catapulted into horrific, Dickensian images of dark corridors and frightened children, of grimy cot sheets and unchanged nappies. Urine. Smells. Two and a half years!

'You no read the papers?'

'I was in hospital, unconscious . . .'

Tony rose and opened a drawer. The newspaper had yellowed. As Greta devoured the article next to Sylvia's picture, panic rose in her breast. One child gone to live with some old crone, the other in an orphanage! Forgotten, unwanted, unloved.

GUILTY!

She grabbed the paper and rattled through it, searching for mention of Dick. Tony pulled the pages away from her and folded her in his arms. The odour from his armpits was as rank as her crimes.

'Why didn't Sylvia go home? She only planned to run away for a few weeks.'

'Too young. Weak. Afraid. Obstinate.'

'I never imagined . . .'

'Waiting for you. You no come back. Why, Greta?'

In the darkened room above the Ristorante Greta began,

haltingly, to unburden herself, laying before her devoted friend one millstone after another: her sordid life as a gypsy, Dick's cruelty, the torture she had endured during her labour and the agonizing decision to leave her child. Then came the hard part. She described the 'accident' in the caravan, calling Dick's inert body 'unconscious', explaining that, in panic, she had to run from the consequences of her actions. But Tony remembered the blood on the box.

'You kill him?'

An almost imperceptible nod.

They were quiet again for a long time.

'Tony, I'll tell Sam some of this. But not what happened with Dick. He would never condone . . .'

'Murder?'

'Don't say it like that! Self-defence. He raped me like an animal. You can't imagine the pain, the humiliation. And I almost died myself . . .'

'But,' Tony shook his head, 'never will a man like Sam understand.'

Greta lay back against Tony's arm and closed her eyes. 'Jesus Christ,' she murmured, 'I'll go to Hell.'

'We go together.'

❖

An hour later, in his van, Tony sat licking his heavy moustache, enjoying the blunt abrasion against his tongue. Irrational jealousy tortured him. Greta had just disappeared through the revolving doors of the hotel, presumably to fall into the arms of Samuel Phillips and weep over his pyjama top. Did they share a bedroom? A bed? Make love? Missionary position or something more interesting?

'Sheet!' he hissed between his teeth, slamming his hand on the driving wheel. He couldn't understand himself. 'Do I hate as a father hates to think of his daughter defiled? No. I am not Papa. But I love her as my child.' He was chewing at his lips. 'No. Not as my child. What am I, that I do not love as a man should? I have no one . . .'

With a sudden, violent jolt Tony remembered Sylvia. He understood the depth of her anger towards Greta. Proud girl, he could picture her sitting shivering on Liz's doorstep. But by now Liz should have returned and the teenager would be tucked up on her couch. Poor kid. She hadn't been well either. Perhaps he should just pop around and talk to 'cousin Nicoletta' for a while.

Five to eleven. Late. Never mind, he needed to do something clean, to wipe the taste of jealousy from his lips.

❖

Samuel was waiting in the lobby. He took Greta's hand and led her to his own room.

'Are you Alexandra or Greta?'

'Both. Neither.'

'Do you trust me?'

'Yes.'

'Whatever you can tell Tony, you can tell me. Start at the beginning.'

The beginning? Perhaps the beginning would be enough to sate Sam's curiosity.

❖

Liz opened the door in her dressing gown.

'Where's Sylvia?' she demanded. 'I thought she was sleeping 'ere tonight. I must have dozed off. That nice chap was on the radio . . .'

Tony's jaw dropped, his eyes widened with alarm.

They always run away, he thought wildly. He turned and rushed to the van, but Liz was behind him, holding the door so he couldn't close it.

'Where is she, Tony? What's happened?'

'Greta came back! Sylvia ran out. I . . . I not know.'

Liz clambered in. 'Greta? Mercy me! But where's Sylvia? Start that bloody motor. Where have you tried? God, you're a silly old bugger!'

As they drove through the town, Liz pressed her nose to the window, scanning every shop doorway, every stone doorstep. 'She's got no friends. Either she's huddled in a corner somewhere, or gone back to t'cottage. It's bloody freezin. And she's poorly.'

Tony winced at his own ignorance. 'She upset at me, for fussing Greta. I thought she come to you.'

'I've left t'door open, so she can get in. Surely she'll not stay out in this. Glory on us, snow's layin fast!'

The frosty wind was growing wild and ice flakes danced frantically across the van's windscreen.

'She go to cottage. We check.' Every frustrated paternal bone in Tony's body was wracked with premonition.

'Watch out!' Liz shrieked as the van slithered sideways down Columbus Ravine. The roads were treacherous. At

Peasholm Park, Tony tried seven times to get the vehicle up on to the Burniston Road, but each time they came to a slithering halt, his knuckles white on the steering wheel.

'What'll we do? What'll we do?' demanded Liz, who was still in her slippers. 'Pray God, she's not tryin' to walk it. I'll not rest until I know she's safe and warm.'

Anxiety fluttered in Tony's guts. How many young girls would run out of his life? What did it matter if they were substitute daughters, mothers or lovers? What did any of it really matter? Caring was caring. He would tell Greta that tomorrow.

He never did manage to get the van out of Scarborough that night. It was after one in the morning when Tony asked the hotel porter to fetch Mr Samuel Phillips. He needed male help and he didn't dare ask the police. Sam came down alone and within minutes he was duffled up and revving his own motor. The substantial car was heavier than the van and had better tyres.

The roads were now completely deserted and white sheet-frosted. The wind felt like an avalanche. Sam took a run at the first gradient and they landed sideways on at the top. Progress from there was slow; at each small slope the car slid and scrambled, but Sam pressed on. Tony swore in Italian throughout, while Liz scolded, 'Stop yer daft prattle, it's twistin my nerves.' She was scared, not just for Sylvia's life, but for her own.

When they finally reached the lane to Hisper Cottage, the wind was rocking the car. Sam looked at his watch.

'Twenty past two. She'll get a bit of a shock at this unearthly hour.'

Hisper Cottage cowered in darkness, as icy blasts buffeted the cliff below and hurled sheets of snow across black, twisted gorse. Sam and Tony bent double as they braved the stinging onslaught. Liz, beslippered, arms folded across her considerable chest, hands tucked into armpits, remained shivering in the car, feeling the vehicle lift and shudder in the perishing gusts.

Tony's key turned in the lock, but the door, obstinate as ever, refused to yield. He knocked and shouted, while Sam banged his palm against the frost-crazed window. Prickles of icy air penetrated coats, jumpers, vests. There was no movement inside the cottage.

Tony turned to the sea. 'She dead on road. I know it. Or in there . . .' He could hear the thundering waves roaring beneath him. Again, he felt a terrible sense of déjà vu.

Sam hurled a pebble at the upstairs window. 'Look, Torricelli, we'll not get back to Scarborough now. We'll have to get in somehow, bed down till the road is safe. Wherever Sylvia is, she's probably warmer than us right now.'

They used their combined weight against the door, wrenching the bolt from its fixings, and the two tumbled into the welcome blackness of Hisper Cottage.

'Silvie! Halloo,' called Tony, hopefully.

Sam's lighter flared. Both downstairs rooms were empty.

While Tony went back to help Liz, Sam fumbled up the staircase, feeling his way in pitch darkness. A sickening, familiar sound was drawing him. Animal. Rattling. Gurgling. His tiny lighter flame failed, but Sam walked blindly, until something on the floor, perhaps a book, tripped him, and he stumbled, falling awkwardly towards the bed. The human body, the unexpected, waxen warmth, the harsh rasping breath against his cold face, made him shout out.

Tony was behind him. 'What? WHAT?'

Sam ran his hands over the curled form beneath the covers.

❖

Greta turned over and looked at the clock. Ten past four. She reached out, questioning the cold indentation on the pillow next to hers.

Three hours ago Sam had made love to her for the first time. It had been wonderful. Cleansing. She languished indulgently in the memory of his body, muscular against hers, healing the scars, kissing away the badness; then the bliss as he had entered, keeping her hovering at that gateway to ecstasy, pushing so gently that her reluctant muscles melted. She had accepted Sam wholly and discovered that passion could overflow with generosity and sincerity.

Where was he? She needed to try it again.

Doing the best

she could, Liz followed pasta sauce recipes while Greta laid tables. For three days Tony had stayed at the hospital watching Sylvia's undernourished body struggle to cling to life.

❖

'Hold steady now.' The kind vet injected a cat's flank. He was thinking about the young girl down in Scarborough, confessing a tingle of pride in the knowledge that if she survived it was largely due to his speedy, professional action. He gave the skinny little puss a quick cuddle and passed her back to an equally skinny old lady.

Sam prayed that Sylvia would survive, that he had truly done his best, that the doctors would care enough, that nature would do the gracious thing and allow her a 'second shot'. He also prayed for his Alexandra who was locked in a deep sulk of self-reproach.

Now that Sam knew more about Alexandra's history, he understood how her own distorted childhood had shaped her. But did all that really excuse her for deserting a vulnerable young girl? How could she be so ruthless, this woman with one beautiful face and two separate identities?

Sam recalled his horror as he had wrapped Sylvia in a blanket and lifted her featherlight frame out of Hisper Cottage. As the nurses shooed him away he had glimpsed her ribcage, contoured in alabaster skin so thin, blue veins so close to the surface, that she might have been carved from Italian marble. Needlessly, tragically ill – and no one had realized.

And now a new problem. Because of lies.

Sylvia's parents had not been notified. They had no idea that their daughter lay fighting for her life. In his haste to have Sylvia admitted to hospital, Torricelli had given her name as Nicoletta, claiming to be her next of kin. An urgent, blameless decision, yet one which was impossible to reverse without dreadful repercussions.

If the police found out, and if, Heaven forbid, the girl died, Tony, Alexandra, Liz could all be accused of kidnap, neglect, even manslaughter! Or she could die without anyone ever knowing her real identity, so the truth might lie on his own shoulders for ever. What a situation! So ethically wrong that he felt a rush of blood to his head at the thought of the moral crime he was endorsing.

The telephone jangled and he was summoned back out into the snow. At the wheel of the car, slipping down an ice-crunched lane, he struggled to sort through the moral mayhem in his brain.

If the Lord chose to spare the girl's life it was for a reason. If he, Samuel Phillips, had been instrumental in saving that life, then he now had new responsibilities. To her parents, to her child, to Sylvia herself. He would never be comfortable sitting on the fence.

As for Alexandra, he was determined to persuade her to rescue her own baby from the orphanage. But with that decision came a harder one. Could he ever take Alexandra's child as his own?

❖

'Tony?'

Sylvia felt a warm, plump hand holding hers. Through a thick mist she tried to focus on her friend's face. 'Hospital . . . ? What's the matter with me? Drink . . .'

'Nurse . . . someone, come quick. She awake . . .' Tony held a cup to her lips. Sylvia sipped, then slunk back into slumber again.

❖

'What's it called?' Hendo was thoroughly disgruntled.

'A Vincent ruddy Rapide.'

'Vury nice. Al reet for some. Buses for us, kiddo, a brand-new posh motorbike for Davy boy. Lucky bastard. Wouldn't be so bad if his dad had bought him a car – we could of all gorrin it.'

'The lasses'll be daft for him now,' complained Alan. 'Keep an eye on Katherine, she's . . . well, rather flirtatious.'

'RAAATHER flirtatious. Spit it out! Tell this stupid, besotted bugger that she'd sell her bloody soul, never mind her body, fer a thrill on the back of Davy's new bike!'

Hendo kicked at the wet cobbles. Silence fell between two

friends. Uppermost in each mind was envy of David. A best friend, a mutual enemy.

'Howay!'

'Where?'

'Down the Jubilee, for a black and tan.'

❖

Drizzle muted stone, sea and sand into a dreary, monochromatic mess, yet inside Hisper Cottage it was warm and cheerful. Happiness bubbled in Greta like spring water cascading from the moors.

Sylvia was recovering.

No wonder she'd become ill. The girl was a stick. Why on earth hadn't Tony used the suitcase cash? Life could have been so much easier. But now Greta was back, and Greta had plans. She had been shopping, buying furniture, linoleum and rugs. Money cured all. Maybe even scarred lungs.

During her pampered sojourn in Venice, Nonno had arranged a large, regular income for his princess. The suitcase money was a thick icing on an already scrumptious cake. After years of gypsy poverty Greta now intended to revel in her bounty.

Happily exhausted, she poured water from a shiny new kettle over fragrant tea leaves in a blue china pot.

Tomorrow workmen were coming to dig a septic tank into the garden, so the primitive ash pan would go. Hisper Cottage would be a home if it bloody well killed her. Part one of THE PLAN. Consciously or unconsciously, Greta was nesting.

'Not going back over Italy, lass? Stopping here? Well I

never!' Liz was delighted. 'But why not get a nice little house down in t' town?'

'I like it here. On this cliff top, with the hills behind and a clean wind off the sea. I crave freedom, Liz. Too many years with a dominant husband, now a suffocating family. A woman of my age should be allowed to live by her own rules. And I want the chance to make things right, do something for Tony, helping him with the business perhaps. Also for Sylvia. I want to look after her.'

'And if you do all that, young Sam might be impressed?'

'Am I that transparent?'

'Oh aye.'

❖

David felt like a clumsy spaceman in his Barber suit. He pulled the leather helmet over his ears and dragged on huge gauntlets. Then he took the gloves off again. Until he was used to the controls it was better to be able to feel what he was doing, even if his hands froze.

The silver machine gleamed, its 1000cc engine ready to zoom.

If David himself wasn't quite so ready to zoom, his father certainly was. Linden Senior was perched on the pillion, arms around his son's waist, eagerly urging the lad out on to the open road.

'Toe it. Slip into gear gently. Open the throttle. Here we go. Woo!' Arthur Linden hadn't enjoyed anything so much since his son's first train set.

David felt peculiar in his father's embrace, but as the bike responded to his tentative wrist and picked up speed, a fearful exhilaration awoke in him. He leaned to his left, taking the pretty vehicle around into Salters Road, opening the throttle to a roar.

❖

'Surprise!'

After so many weeks languishing in a hospital bed, Sylvia felt intense pleasure at being outside in the open air. But – were they . . .

daffodils?

Outside Hisper Cottage, hundreds of luminous, yellow nodding heads were dancing in frenzied profusion under the windows, along the path, in clumps by the gate. A newly painted gate. Red as lipstick.

'More surprises to come. Welcome home.' Greta threw those long muscular arms about her, but Sylvia felt too weak and suspicious to respond. Mustard bounded through the fragile flowers, his coat collecting yellow pollen. He jumped up at Sylvia, pink tongue lapping.

The cottage door stood open. She stepped over the threshold and stopped. Four faces watched hers: Greta breathless, Tony proud, Liz thankful, Sam unsure.

'It's . . . it's . . . really nice.'

But she was crying inside. Greta had stolen Hisper Cottage! The only home she could offer Alice.

All essence of Sylvia had been swept away. The sofa on which she used to sleep, gone. The clippy mat with burn marks from popping coal, gone. The painted chair, the table, the photo of the soldier, all gone. In their places, Mod Cons.

But old Tempus Fugit was still tocking. Samuel Phillips

179

laid a hand on her shoulder. The warmth of his palm was soothing.

'And in the refrigerator,' Tony proudly blustered, his large head ducking in and out of a white appliance, ANTONIO'S HOMEMADE ITALIAN ICE CREAM!'

'Coffee cake for tea,' added Liz, her kind face flushed with eagerness. 'Got to fatten you up, lass. That's old Liz's job.'

They would make her eat! She would forget Alice! Sylvia's nausea increased when faithless Mustard nosed Greta's fingers.

'You must be tired,' fussed Sam. 'Up to bed. Good girl.'

Sylvia sought dignified words of thanks. 'Everything looks . . . clean, new, lovely. I'm so glad to be home. Thank you. Everybody.'

That was sufficient encouragement for Greta. She thumped up the stairs while Sylvia followed slowly, already resentful of what she would find at the top. Must she now share her bedroom with the gypsy?

'I've hung this curtain to separate the room. We've put in another window. You might like the one overlooking the sea. And look here. A sink. Hot water from the range rises into a tank. I'm planning to have a complete bathroom built downstairs.'

❖

The Minx almost drove itself back to Fontbury while Sam's conscience fought an internal war. As he crossed his own threshold, he made his decision.

He lifted the telephone.

'I have information about a missing girl, Sylvia Sharp.'

'Hold, please.'

A pause, then an overly friendly voice.

'Good afternoon. DI Howard speaking. What's this about Sylvia Sharp?'

Sam hesitated.

'I suppose you want to remain anonymous. But any information could bring much comfort to her family . . . or would it?'

'Yes.'

'She's alive and well, then?'

'Oh yes, alive. Not . . . well. Not really. Getting better though.'

'Where is she?'

'Em . . .'

'Ill, you say. Did someone hurt her?'

'No. She's been torturing herself about leaving the child. Have these Linden people fostered her baby formally? If I can persuade her to come home, can Sylvia ever have her baby back?'

'Depends. What do you know about this gypsy woman?'

Sam dropped the phone.

❖

'This is the way the ladies ride, nym, nym, nym,

   This is the way the gentlemen ride, trot, trot, trot,

   And this is the way the hunters ride, a gallop, a gallop, a gallop,

   Wheee . . .'

Matthew Kirkstone jostled baby Jan up and down on the end of his leg. Her squeals were music to Janice's ears. Matt was trying so hard. Early days, of course, and the poor mite's spontaneous bellows were disarming, but when she was charming, oh, she melted the heart. To Janice, little Jan's smiles were pure joy, and the accidents, well, that's what you had to expect.

The nurse gathered up her very own wriggly bundle of daughter and hugged her. Singing in a silly bass voice, she said, 'What's the time? It's time for . . .'

'Tea,' piped up the baby.

'And what does babba want? Eggy eggy. Yum, yum, tank oo, Mum.'

Matthew picked up his paper and flicked it irritably. His wife had turned into a moron.

'White horses

right across the horizon,' said Sam, hitching himself up on the stone wall outside Hisper Cottage. It was almost June, the weather had been good, and he was relieved to see Sylvia looking very much better. Squinting into an early summer sun, he said, 'I could watch the sea for ever.'

'No, you couldn't,' replied Sylvia.

'Well, not literally for ever.'

'Not for five minutes. It's hypnotic. Impossible to watch without your mind slipping away.'

'Is that what's been happening to you?'

'Probably.' Her neat nostrils flared. 'My stomach still keeps churning.'

'Like feeling excited?'

'Like being chased by Neptune with his bloody trident. Bad nerves, that's what Mam would call it.'

'Did your mam have bad nerves?'

'She spent a lot of time on the lav.'

Sam laughed. 'Tell me about her.'

Sylvia folded her arms. She began clucking her tongue,

with her lips pursed. Ah, thought Sam, so this was the irritating habit which Greta complained kept her awake at night.

Tuttuttuttutt.

Sam listened patiently.

'Washerwoman,' said Sylvia suddenly. 'Mam washed everything in sight. Clothes, plates, cooker, skirting boards. But I got dirty and she couldn't scrub me clean.'

'Oh, lass.' Sam took her hand and stroked his thumb across her papery skin. 'You just fell in love too young.'

'Did I?'

'And I'm sure you miss your mam dreadfully.'

'Not really. I miss me, though.'

'Ah.'

'I've lost Sylvia somewhere.'

'Because . . . Nicoletta isn't real?'

'Because nothing is real. I'm living inside a story. I'm two people, neither one nor the other. Greta is also Alexandra, but she's a better actress than me.'

The sun erupted through the clouds and Sylvia's leaden jaw lifted, as if she were a puppet and someone had pulled her eyebrow strings. Sam found himself pinned by pale, bright eyes.

'What does the sea sounds like?' she asked, with a sudden flirtatious sparkle. 'Close your eyes and really listen.'

Sam obeyed, and concentrated on the sound. It wasn't quite what he expected. There was no crashing or sobbing. It was more like . . .

Sylvia gabbled, 'Imagine God is building a new organ for Heaven. He picks up the first long, hollow pipe and tests it by blowing down it, as hard as he can. All of God's breath echoes down the pipe, ringing on and on. That's what the sea sounds like. The noise isn't just made in the bay, it comes from over the whole world.'

'Does it frighten you?'

'It should frighten everyone.'

'What a remarkable young woman you are.'

'A woman?' Abruptly the pale eyes puddled.

Her mood changes so suddenly, thought Sam. She's still very fragile.

'Yes. You're a lovely young woman called Sylvia Sharp, not Nicoletta, and I believe your story will end happily ever after.' He glanced down, noticing the fast heartbeat in her neck. 'In this lonely place, growing up must have been like climbing a mountain. Every day the peak has seemed further away, until the climb, I suspect, became more important than the mountain itself. But now, here you are, standing right on the peak.' Gently, he lifted her chin, turning her pale face to the sun's kind rays. 'You can go home now. It's time, love.'

Sylvia leapt up and dashed away down the path. Sam waited for a moment, then followed her. She was standing in a circle of gorse. As he touched her shoulder, she jumped, then shivered.

'What's the matter?' He tried to uncurl her fingers, which were gripping the prickly gorse, seemingly without feeling the barbs drawing blood.

'Time. Temper temper fuggerit . . .' Sylvia began talking so rapidly that Sam lost most of her words. Something to do with minutes and seagulls.

Gently, Sam pulled her towards his chest. It never occurred to him that he shouldn't. Looking over her shoulder, towards the cottage where Alexandra waited for him, he patted Sylvia's back, just as he would a young colt, unaware that his touch was surging through the young girl's jumper to skin, skin to blood, blood to organ, hotter than any truth and almost potent enough to silence Time itself.

'Come back inside, love. I want to talk to you and Alexandra together.'

❖

'I've been doing a bit of sleuthing, in Newcastle. Your baby, Alexandra, has been fostered by a good family, as you hoped.' Sam spoke compassionately. 'Apparently, she was in an orphanage, but a young couple now look after her. That's all I know. The rest is up to you to discover. You are still legally her parent.'

Greta was sitting very straight, her strong body tense against Sam's, her eyes lowered and her fingers tightly laced through his.

Sylvia watched their entwined knuckles for a while, then looked down at Mustard. She stroked his warm, blond chest and kissed his head.

'What about Alice?' Greta asked. As if she cared!

But Sylvia's bitterness dissolved when Sam released Greta's hand and came to sit beside her. She could feel his breath on her face, see the dark pores of his shaved chin and his tiny scar. The closeness of his smile made her feel as if somewhere in the universe, promises could be kept. Again, she fell towards his chest, knowing that Greta was watching.

'I'll take you.'

'What?'

'Home. Next week, if you like. To see Alice.'

Invisible feathers fluttered across her vision and her head filled with throbbing tocks. 'I can't fight the Lindens!' she panicked.

'Listen, love. I've been checking.' Sam put his arm around her shaking shoulders. 'Hold steady. Take a breath. Alice is not with the Lindens.'

'Not? Where is she? Where's my baby?'

The tocking was hellish, hammering all hope out of her head. Alice slid away, beyond Sylvia's grasp, through the doors of the baker's oven, into an unreachable world as blankly blue as Heaven.

Greta, actress, was suddenly at Sylvia's side, her face all dark concern. 'Where is her baby, Sam?'

'She's with Sylvia's parents. Has been all along.'

'Mam and Dad kept Alice?'

Tickling furiously in her ears, came a voice, saying *Oh, Tempus! You fuggering Iago.*

❖

David was shouting, returning his mother's volume, decibel for decibel.

'If I don't get a place in King's, I'm not going anywhere else. I can't leave Alice. You don't care about her at all, do you, Mother? You'd send me to Timbuktu if you had to.'

'I want to be proud of you.'

'So I've got to be a doctor? What if I lose Alice?'

'Your grandmother keeps a grip on the child – with her money.'

David would not hear a word against his gran. 'The same

money you spend on your daft hats. You never earned any yourself. And Dad and I are just things to be ... shaped up ... pummelled and carved until we suit you. But you make us all ugly. Hideous.'

'Your father was always hideous.' Mary stormed past him, heading for the stairs and another perfumed bath.

David looked down at his father, who had his head in his hands on the formica table.

'Dad, I'm eighteen. Alice is my child, not Gran's, certainly not Cuthbert Sharp's. I ought to look after her.'

'You're just a lad.'

'Old enough to be called up and killed if this Suez thing boils up. Look, I know how badly you want me to go to university. But if I leave Newcastle, the Sharps will become Alice's parents. Kath already has to pretend to be Alice's sister. I must stay close. If I don't get into King's, I'll get a job.'

'You're a bigger man than me, son.'

❖

'Piss'n down again! Every Friday night, bloody pisses down. It's supposed to be summer.'

'Push off, Hendo.' Alan was on detention duty, presiding over several teenagers who sat mutely attempting to translate Chaucer. Hendo, huge in the class doorway, was picking at a chocolate stain on his black gown. Alan nudged him out into the corridor. 'You're disturbing my victims.'

'That little lass out of the fourth year is always in detention when you're on duty. You're on to a good thing there, bonny lad.'

'I prefer mine older and more intelligent. What will you

do tonight? You can't take Katherine out in this rain. She's getting used to better things.'

'Oh aye. Heaven'll piss on me the neet,' Hendo grumbled, 'and the morra, Kath slings her leg over Davy's bike, and zooms off to Corbridge. She's supposed to be my lass, but that bastard sees more of her than me! Yer bugger, a think a'm in one of them bloody triangles!'

❖

A pear-shaped woman, wearing a spotless apron and a Gilbert and Sullivan smile, placed a silver tea tray next to Ethel Linden.

'Thank you, Daphne.' As the char waddled back to the kitchen, Ethel winked conspirationally at her guest.

'Daft Daphne. Heart of gold.' She poured Violet Sharp a cup of tea and offered a slice of lemon drizzle cake. 'The wind's blown the rain away. We could take Alice for a walk.'

Watery sunbeams played on a Chinese rug where Alice sat cross-legged, her soft black ringlets jumping about her dimpled cheeks as she tried to pull the arms off a china doll.

The house in Corbridge smelled of baking and lavender polish. Violet leaned back into a feather-stuffed armchair and admired the long windows, heavily draped with Wedgwood-blue velvet, which framed an even bluer sky. Clean white clouds were tumbling in front of the wind. The branches of two ancient elm trees swished, leaves sparkling as the sun refracted through raindrops. In the centre of the lawn a great oak danced its legless dance; the swing which hung from one sturdy branch tossed emptily.

Contentment washed over Violet. No wonder Alice loved holidays in her second home.

'We are doing our best by her, aren't we?' she asked Ethel.

These two women liked each other; not with a comfortable gossipy affection, but with a hesitant relationship based on respect, laced with a bittersweet tot of envy.

'She'll never be short of love. Nor much else. Not with you and me watching out for her. Yes, we're doing it right. These visits are the highlight of my life, Violet. There's nothing much else now. My boy is tied up and lashed to a railing by his blasted wife.' She raised her veiny legs to rest them on a pouffe, smiling indulgently at Alice. 'Dear little soul. Oh, how much these young people have lost. I blame Bloody Mary, you know.' Ethel's crinkled lips pursed as she gazed across the lawn.

Violet nodded. 'David and his dad come round owa house regular, on that motorbike. You should see Alice's little face light up, all smiles and kisses. Actually there is something . . .'

'Your man seems to think quite a lot of his grandchild too,' Ethel interrupted.

'He's a great soft dumpling were owa Alice is concerned. Like he used to be with the girls, but now he's – more, somehow. He still won't talk about Sylvia, though. He's sorry, you know. Just can't say it. Only I do worry. We need to sort something out, now that she's chattering so much.'

A pause. Both women were equally aware of the problem. Too soon Alice would start asking questions. David was not in a position to be a proper father and Cuthbert Sharp seemed to be taking his granddaughter as a third daughter.

As Violet tried to order her thoughts, Alice climbed on to

her lap. The bairn was as bright as a button and it paid to watch what you said. Doing her best to control her wriggly charge, Violet ploughed on with the second thing she had determined to say.

'While we are on our own – I've tried to say this a few times – that I'm sorry.' Alice was doing her best to push her brick into Violet's mouth. 'OOH. No, my pet.' She lifted the child back on to the carpet, and Alice wandered across to give her prize to her great-grandmother, who took it with dignity.

Violet continued anxiously, 'This house would've been a smashing place for Alice to grow up. But it just didn't seem right. It was your kindness what showed us up, right and proper. Made me see sense. I've got a lot to thank you for. Not just the money.'

'We can both have a role in Alice's life.' Ethel planted a kiss on the child's forehead and pressed a piece of cake into her hand. 'There's a good girl.'

Dear little Alice walked over to her dolly and, squashing the cake crumbs into a soggy mass, crushed it into the china face. Ethel only smiled, knowing Daphne would clear up the mess. 'Women, I've found, are not generally good at sharing, but somehow you and I have managed it, with the help of young Katherine, bless her. When Sylvia comes back, I hope she'll be glad.'

Violet's cup shook slightly in its saucer. 'You heard about that anonymous phone call? Ee, Ethel. Dare I hope?'

'You must.'

Violet closed her eyes.

'Ah, here are the youngsters.' Ethel rocked herself out of her chair. 'Did you get caught in the shower?'

Black hair dripping, David threw his jacket over a chair and Katherine, fresh-faced and anything but innocent, threw hers on top. Sylvia's sister certainly had her feet well and truly under the Twin Elms table. Violet worried that she seemed too comfortable in this substantial country house with its cumbersome old furniture.

There had never been any need for a nanny in Corbridge. Sylvia's sister had always accompanied her baby niece on holiday weekends, expertly administering bottles and changing nappies, yet leaving the old woman with plenty of time to enjoy little Alice. It had been a good arrangement. Katherine had earned pocket money and the baby had been secure. As Alice had grown into a toddler, the teenager's bouncy energy had become essential in keeping up with the two-and-a-half-year-old's demands. Katherine had been another mother to Alice and she loved her as much as any of them.

She's a good lass, thought Violet. Warm and giving. But I sometimes wonder if my second daughter has an ulterior motive for fussing over old Mrs Linden.

'What time's the bus, Mam?'

'Ee, look! Ten to! Must dash. I'll meet you at the bus station tomorrow afternoon, Kath. Mind you keep her reins on. Bye-bye, pet lamb. Give Grandma a kiss.'

Walking down the drive, Violet waved to the tableau at the front door. So, she thought, David is staying over too. No harm, I suppose.

There would, however, be great harm. And just one week later.

The Tyne Bridge

was being painted jade-green. Four men slung in a basket, hundreds of feet in the sky, were slapping paintbrushes against knobbly girders.

Don't fall!

In the back seat of Sam's Hillman, Sylvia sat with her hands locked into Mustard's coat, her whole body taut as stretched elastic. A tangle of sentences threaded through her head, shuffling into speeches, entrance lines, exit lines.

Flexing her toes in her new shoes, she smoothed the creases in her pencil skirt and stared at Sam's broad shoulders, drawing on all his precious words of flattery. Had such a wonderful man really called her brave, patient and beautiful?

❖

Euphoric, heroic, Samuel Phillips drove into Newcastle positively tingling with misguided confidence. On this significant Sunday, 5 June, the city looked clean and hopeful, its colours vibrant against the washed sky.

'Glorious day for a homecoming!'

During the journey his attempts at conversation had been answered in monosyllables, his two passengers displaying diametric signs of nervousness, Greta's face closed, Sylvia's all atwitch. As he drove down Northumberland Street, he warned Sylvia again that her parents might react strangely at first.

'They'll be shocked. Probably say all the wrong things. Give them a chance. I wish we'd been able to write and warn them.'

Greta snapped, 'They'd have told the police. Sylvia would have been descended on with a million questions and I'd have been welcomed with handcuffs.'

Sam patted Greta's knee. 'Darling, I really admire you for coming today.'

I don't, thought Greta, painting her lips. The girl had crucified herself. Who would her parents blame? Themselves? Of course not. They would point at the kidnapping gypsy. Despite her blithe promise to Sam, Greta had absolutely no intention of facing them.

From the back seat, Sylvia suddenly blurted, 'I was a broken doll. They kept the new one.'

Greta smiled slowly at the road ahead. Sam might think this was a prodigal returning. She knew better. Sylvia wasn't coming home, she was just coming to get Alice.

They were motoring past the Maternity Hospital on the right and the dewy Town Moor to the left. With a deep surge of horror, Greta stared down at her carmine lipstick, pushing the penile wax up and down in its tube.

'Here, Sylvia.' She handed the lipstick backwards. 'The redder the lipstick, the bolder the woman.'

'Which way?' asked Sam.

Sylvia gave fluttery directions through Gosforth.

'Alice will love Hisper Cottage and the seaside,' encouraged Greta. 'Tony and Liz will fuss her. Mustard too. We'll all help. Tell them that. How can they argue? Stop!' she commanded. 'For Heaven's sake, Sam, don't park right outside the house. Give Sylvia chance to compose herself.'

So they sat for a while in silence. Sam rubbed his neck. Sylvia blew her nose and stared at the house. Greta fidgeted, alert as a bird.

A gang of children in homeknit jumpers played hopscotch on the drying path. A pensioner knelt on a bit of old mat, trowelling weeds from his borders. Two teenage lads were perched on a wall, smoking.

❖

'Bloody Linden.' Alan was fuming. 'How long's it been going on?'

'Divent rightly know. Divent care a bugger. Spoilt bastard always gets what he wants. Katherine Gobby Sharp won't be any more faithful to him than she was to me.'

'I hate him.'

'Mind, if a'm honest, a guessed,' Hendo confessed. 'All them weekends up in Corbridge. And lately she's been, well, frigid. Bloody block of ice, to be truthful.'

Alan stamped out his cigarette. 'I'll turn his ugly mush inside out. That's after I've kicked a dent in his bloody Vincent.'

'Everything looks so small,' whispered Sylvia.

Greta opened the car door. 'Take your time. I'll have a peep in the back street. See if Alice is playing outside. Can I get through that alley? While you go to the front door, I'll keep watch. Just in case.'

'Don't be ridiculous,' snapped Sam. 'We can do without cops and robbers tactics.'

But Sylvia said, 'Thanks, Greta. Turn right; count seven houses along.'

As Greta strode off, Sylvia walked towards the door. It had been painted maroon; the obscured oval glass was dark and ambiguous. As she reached for the knocker, Sam put his hand over hers. His hefty knock echoed through the house.

No reply. They knocked again. Nothing.

Answer. ANSWER! Sylvia began trembling. Were they hiding Alice? The door was refusing her. Staying closed. Saying, no, go away, you're not wanted. As she picked at the scab of rejection, part of her was glad, relieved.

Sam put his arm around her thin shoulders, drew her back to the car, then went to talk to the two smoking lads. One was very tall and swarthy. The smaller one stood behind him, keen-eyed.

'Do you happen to know when Mrs Sharp will be back?'

'They've shifted. Down South Gosforth.'

'Oh! Crikey! Could you give me the address?'

'Nee bother.'

❖

While Hendo gave directions, Alan found himself drawn towards the girl in the car, who was staring at him over a hanky. His casual, flirting saunter began to quicken. She had short dark hair and no tits. But in two more paces Alan recognized her wide, beautiful, water-coloured eyes.

❖

David flew round corners, air pummelling his face, flies sticking to his greatcoat. The bike between his legs throbbed and his balls tingled.

He could see a light at the end of his tunnel. A few years away, but there for the taking. Wife and daughter. Katherine and Alice. A job. A cosy little house. Money in the bank. Life could be very, very good.

Except for his mother. Was it rat poison that contained arsenic?

❖

Hendo was running for his pushbike. Alan was trying to keep up, shouting, 'She wouldn't speak, but it was definitely her!'

'Me mam said there'd been a tip-off! Howay. Gerron the back!'

The big lad pedalled, standing up, while the lighter one sat on the saddle with his legs flying loose.

❖

There was a rag and bone man in the street. The horse stood patiently, her cart laden with soiled clothes, old books and a rusty mangle.

Sam was checking the address. Sylvia cowered against the leather upholstery.

'I'll cover the back again.' Greta strutted off, her French pleat bouncing and loosening as she turned the corner.

Sam helped Sylvia out of the car and drew her behind the cart, taking her face in his hands. 'Sylvia Sharp, I'm proud to know you.' He kissed her forehead. Buoyed by the warm trace left by his lips, still grasping his hand, slowly but purposefully, she edged along the side of the cart.

'Ready?'

She nodded. The heavy-footed horse stamped.

'NO! Wait!' she hissed, backing and standing on Sam's toe. 'Look!'

A motorbike had roared up to the kerb. Its rider dismounted and removed his leather helmet. Sylvia retreated into Sam's jacket.

'David,' she mumbled, trying to hide her face in her new friend's shoulder. Her heart was leaping with a dreadful clang of hope. She had seen enough to know that David's hair was just as black, his nose just as high, but he was even taller. He had the body of a man, but also the familiar face of the boy she used to kiss with greedy adoration. Every fibre of her body pricking with remembered passion, she tried to control her breathing in readiness to speak to the lad who had so scarred her life. But, as she composed herself, she heard a knock, followed by her mother's voice. Then a smaller voice floated over the road.

'Daydid! Tweeties for me? Ooh, ta!'

Gently, Sam turned Sylvia around. She saw David take the hand of a little girl in a lilac smocked frock. The child had hair as dark as his. It fell in ringlets, held away from her wide forehead by a large white bow. She was utterly beautiful. So beautiful that in one unthinking second, those words – 'dirty', 'whore', 'bastard' – drowned in their own ignorance, and the twisted icicle of shame inside Sylvia melted.

David did not go into the house. He was fussing and consoling Alice, who had dropped jelly babies on the ground. Out of the door emerged a young woman wearing a huge skirt pinched tightly at the waist. Katherine lifted her face to David's. As Sylvia blinked away tears, her old boyfriend bent down to kiss her sister full on the lips. Then he picked up little Alice and took Katherine's hand. Together they sauntered up the street towards the park.

The rag and bone man slapped leather across the horse's rump and the cart pulled away from the kerb, leaving Sylvia and Sam exposed.

A pair of pigeons swooped down to fight over the dirty sweets.

❖

Greta could see nothing because the back street was blocked by a large coal lorry. She returned to the corner just in time to witness – the KISS.

They began walking towards her, the couple and their small girl. She was about three years old. Big eyes and a mass of dark curly hair. Greta's heart began to pound as she searched the small face. The youngsters were swinging the child between them. 'One, two, three, wheeeee . . .' and the little one was stretching her body, thrusting her feet forward, squealing with delight as she flew through the air.

My baby.

They passed her. She could have reached out and touched the child. Tearing her eyes away, Greta glanced up at Sylvia and witnessed a torrent of jealous fury flowing from the girl's red-rimmed eyes. Sam's hands had slipped under Sylvia's shoulders as her knees buckled. Something was badly wrong.

And Greta knew that there would be no happy reunion. Sylvia would never knock on that door. The child called Alice was lost to them.

No.

In that moment, Greta, born Alexandra Hythe, shed all control. The passions inherited from both her mother and her father, the drama, the emotional cascades, the pathos and fury, the singular focus of will, all rose up and unleashed in her a ferocious, jealous yearning. Her body, freed of all logical responsibility, became a puppet of impulse. And

Alice's life story

now splintered into a dozen horrifying dramas.

❖

Hendo and Alan reached the street just in time to see a woman in high heels sprinting behind David and Katherine. Later, they would decide that she looked like Jane Russell, that her strength was at odds with her beauty, that her actions were so insane that it was like a scene from a movie. They saw her tip wide shoulders to elbow David aside. Katherine yelped and lifted Alice protectively. But in an outrageously violent action, the woman attempted to wrestle the child free. Alice clung to Katherine, terrified.

'Get off!' David was shouting impotently, scrabbling to pull the woman away. But she kicked one muscular leg backwards, digging a sharp heel into David's soft inner thigh.

Pushing Katherine heavily in the chest, the dreadful woman managed to tug Alice out of Katherine's arms. The teenager fell backwards, screaming as her coccyx hit the pavement. David, matching the woman's violence, jumped on her back, slung his arm around her neck and punched her in the kidneys. To defend herself, Jane Russell had to drop Alice.

The little girl started to run, crying, towards her home, her podgy legs toddling too slowly, her large white bow flopping.

'Get the bairn!' shouted Hendo to Alan. But they were on the wrong side of the road and had to dodge cars to cross.

David threw off the woman and went to catch his daughter, but Insane Jane caught him by the collar. She was amazingly strong. Manly. She turned David around and slammed her fist into his face. Then she sprinted after Alice and gathered her up, without losing pace.

Hendo and Alan chased her, but Jane Russell – Greta – was flying.

In this single, life-changing moment, the passions of Sylvia and Greta gelled. The younger girl unlocked her legs and pelted towards the car. Déjà vu. The Lagonda. She was at the door. Opened it. Opened her arms.

❖

Poor Sam stood stock still, stunned, one arm across his stomach and the other across his mouth. What he was seeing could never be real. Too late he realized that he had left his key in the ignition. Greta had already thrust Alice into Sylvia's arms and was at the wheel. The tyres threw dust into the air and his car screeched off.

Shouts and anguished screams rent the air.

Two lads were running towards the house. The smokers.

'The bike, Davy, get yer bloody Vincent,' the tall one bellowed.

He and David leapt on the motorbike and tore down the

road in pursuit of two utterly deranged women who had just turned the vet's respectable life upside down.

Sam became aware of eerie wails. A woman, presumably Sylvia's mother, stood howling on the pavement, while the young girl hurled obscenities down the road.

Then, like the final vehicle in a Keystone Cops' chase, out of the back street trundled a filthy lorry, with a ginger-haired man bent over the wheel. The blond lad ran into the road waving his arms. Sam watched Alan drag open the lorry door and leap in, pointing, shouting. A crash of gears, the lorry accelerated, the driver's ginger head straining forwards.

One of the side gate-panels was loose, flapping danger-ously as the vehicle swung around the corner. Something propelled Sam's legs. They pounded like pistons on tarmac as he sprinted with every ounce of strength towards the acceler-ating vehicle. It almost escaped him, but he pushed himself even harder and with a tremendous lunge he managed to jump up and grasp the tailgate. His feet still floundered against the rushing road but with a couple of bounces, body swinging crazily, Sam managed to hitch a foot around the side of the tailgate and with a final thrust, he vaulted into the back. Sugary black coal dust danced around him as he was bumped about in the bottom of the empty lorry.

Fighting to catch his breath, Sam's insides turned to jelly. Christ! What was he doing? His hands flailed for something to hang on to. They were black.

'It's all right! It's all right, pet!'

It wasn't.

Sylvia was trying to control Alice's struggling limbs and calm her bellowing. Aware of the infant's skin, her smell, her breath, her wet tears, her kicking shoes, Sylvia felt a thrill of pleasure and fear.

Round corners Greta skidded, past shops and churches, up streets, down avenues.

'Which way, Sylvia?'

'Ouch – up left, that's it, now up that lane on the right, oh shit . . . NO!'

Greta had swung the car into a very narrow back lane, walled high on both sides by enclosed yards. It was not a short cut, it was a dead end. Rearing ahead was a stout railing and, behind that, a steep railway embankment. Greta slammed on the brakes and screeched to a halt. Alice slid from Sylvia's lap to the floor.

Behind them came the roar of a motorbike. A skid. Rubber shrieking against tarmac. One deep, hard thud. Sylvia was bending to Alice as she felt the impact of the bike in her back, then her head whiplashed forwards and hit the dashboard.

With a dreadful thwack a flying human body hit the soft top of the Hillman. It flailed over the windscreen, then bounced heavily off the bonnet and catapulted on to the road, rolling over and over, one foot dragging obscenely, out of sync with the rest. Hendo's lanky frame finally came to a halt when his head smashed with an ugly crack against the iron bars of the railing.

Greta leapt out of the car. The bike lay mangled on the road. Its wheels were still spinning and trapped beneath it lay David Linden.

An eerie stillness settled on the street. Tragedy lay quietly in each corner.

Then came the roar of the great black lorry. Unable to manoeuvre into the narrow space, Cuthbert Sharp used his vehicle to block it. Before he had jerked on the hand brake, Sam was out of the back and running to where David lay trapped in a tangle of twisted spokes and chromium handlebars.

Straining his arm muscles, Sam pulled the bike off the young man and knelt beside him, swiftly assessing bodily damage, knowing too much about the pain and the time it would take to heal. The injured lad trembling beneath his fingers was the love of Sylvia's life. Sam wiped the coal dust from his palms and worked skilfully.

Alan had leapt from the lorry and pushed past Greta to get to Hendo who lay as still as death, skull pressed hard against the railing. Terrified, Alan began to shake. Between his feet a trickle of blood meandered across the pavement from beneath his friend's down-turned face. A splintered pinky-white bone protruded out of Hendo's shredded trouser leg.

As Alan hesitated, the mad kidnapping woman came and knelt by Hendo's head.

❖

Sylvia's father yanked open the door of the car. With the same strong, square hand which once smacked her bottom, he pushed her roughly in the face. As Sylvia's neck snapped backwards, Alice leapt like a chimp towards her grandad's chest, and he collected her up, kissing the baby with big wet lips.

Sylvia watched those lips, which were now hurling abuse at her. Dazed by the blow to her head, the jarring whiplash, the shock of blood washing over the road, it took some seconds to realize that her father did not recognize her. Yet, with absurdly feminine tenderness, Cuthbert was caressing his grandchild. Her baby. Her Alice.

All emotion was blotted out by a pain which seared between her neck and forehead. The dreambird's beak was pecking through her skull. As Cuthbert crooned and walked his baby to safety, very, very slowly, Sylvia slid from the car and inched backwards. Behind the wheels she saw a young man lying quietly on his side, one amber eye wide open, expressionless.

David. Oh, David.

Someone was shouting. At her. Ambulance. Nine nine nine. GO!

Greta was shouting too. 'Dear God! Sam! Here. Help me. He's dying.'

The back lane was a corridor of high walls. A couple of gates opened; some women edged nervously out. Sylvia began to run, past her father's lorry, out into the road. She was stumbling along as fast as she could, but Alan overtook her, shouting to the women, asking where the nearest phone box was. For no reason at all she followed him, but when Alan turned left, Sylvia turned right, her feet clipping along the pavement with a will of their own. The scene behind her was a nightmare of impossibility, unbearable. On and on she flew, past nosy folk charging in the opposite direction, past a corner shop, a post box, over a bridge, tiny drops of blood catching the breeze.

By the time the ambulance arrived, David had mercifully lost consciousness. Where the heavy bike had landed on his right leg he would later discover that both fibula and tibia were badly broken. His handsome face was still just as handsome on the left side, but the flesh which covered right cheekbone and jawbone had torn away, as his face had skidded along the road.

Hendo was in a long dark tunnel.

Coats were laid over the boys. Crowds gathered; children were shooed back behind doors. Cuthbert took Alice into the cab of the lorry. He had to move his vehicle when the ambulance arrived, but he parked on the opposite side of the road, where he could watch compassionate hands working on David and Hendo, trying to stem the blood which was seeping through bandages, and dripping under stretchers.

What should he do? He had to protect Alice, yet he couldn't leave. So he just sat there, letting his granddaughter play with the steering wheel, watching the dreadful scene through bulging eyes.

At last the ambulance bell clanged, loud and urgent, as it pulled out of the lane with its two precious burdens.

The bell was Cuthbert's klaxon. He shot out of the lorry and lifted Alice down. Young Alan was walking towards him. 'Get the bairn home! Keep her safe.' He thrust his treasure into the lad's arms, then stormed back up the lane.

The woman was leaning against the dented car, her smart suit splattered red. With a fist of iron, Cuthbert grabbed her arm and pulled her face close.

Never had a man been so near killing a woman in broad daylight with a host of witnesses. But, as he raised his hand to her, a pair of wiry arms began tugging at his elbow, a voice bellowing into his ear. It was Alan. The stupid lad had not taken Alice home! He'd left the toddler to cower, wide-eyed, against the wall, and he was yelling, 'It was Sylvia, Mr Sharp! Sylvia in the car. She's run off!'

Strength ebbed from Cuthbert's fingers. His lips went slack. 'Sylvia?'

The madwoman was rubbing her shoulder. She was tall. Not scared of him, not humbled or sorry at all. She was dark and dangerous and crazy, and she fronted up to Cuthbert, hissing, 'Yes, it was Sylvia. And if you want to see her again, you'd better keep this between ourselves.'

He felt a pressure in his chest. Whipping his head round, he searched the mob of voyeurs for the young woman from whose arms he had hauled Alice. 'No,' Cuthbert said. 'No.'

The man who had hitched a ride in his wagon shouted, 'Sylvia! Where is she?' And he jogged off down the lane.

Cuthbert turned on Greta, spluttering, 'What bollocks is this?'

Alan carried Alice towards them, saying, 'It was Sylvia.' Then the traumatized lad swore on a snake hiss, in the madwoman's face. 'You should be fucking HUNG!'

But she shook her head. 'An accident. The bike hit my car. Going too fast.'

'Liar! Kidnapping bitch!'

'If you hold your tongues, I'll bring Sylvia back to you. Give me a chance,' she whispered urgently. 'Just don't speak to the police, Mr Sharp. Get away, now, with Alice. I'll come to your house as soon as I can.'

Alan, puce with rage, but quicker-witted than Cuthbert, said, 'Give her an hour. For Sylvia's sake. Come on.'

But Cuthbert was too maddened and confused to move.

'Sylvia is fragile. She'll be terrified of all this,' Greta warned, eyes flashing. 'It might be your last chance to see her again.'

The poor coalman, silenced by a million whirling emotions, threw a murrey scowl at the bitch who had caused this mayhem, then turned and followed Alan, pushing people out of his way. As he revved the lorry, a long black police car turned the corner, parting the crowd.

'HELLO, OFFICER!' said Greta, summonsing sudden tears. 'Thank God you're here. I can't understand how it happened . . . Oh! Those poor boys! Wretched motorbikes!'

❖

At an upper window overlooking yards, an elderly man was peering through his aspidistra, cursing himself because he hadn't found his Brownie camera fast enough. He was the only person who had actually seen the crash, then the ginger bloke pulling a child out of the car.

After many years of profound deafness the old man could only speak in distorted, elongated vowels. A policeman knocked his door, asking if he had seen the accident. But the ignorant copper, not understanding the old man's impediment, was rudely impatient, treating him like a stupid kid.

'Their loss,' the witness muttered bitterly.

When the kidnapping madwoman, bloodied and haggard, knocked on the Sharps' door, they did not invite her in, even although Alan had already taken Alice to safety.

So Greta stood on the doorstep, and told Sylvia's parents that she was the woman their daughter had run away with. She talked slowly, precisely, in a posh accent, giving only excerpts of a long story. Cuthbert and Violet listened in silence until Greta said, 'But Alice is my baby.'

❖

Along the edge of the Town Moor ran a line of fabulous detached mansions of individual design, with high walls, private gardens and upper views of grazing cows and city towers.

For a while Sylvia simply stood, breathless and dizzy, staring at these signatures of wealth. Nothing in her mind would stay still. She remembered fighting to hold on to Alice, feeling the softest skin, the resistance of strong little arms as they pushed against her chest, feeling the impact of tiny, kicking leather shoes. Then blood. A lot of blood. On the pavement . . . on someone's hand . . .

No!

Her heart was ticking too fast; it wouldn't seem to tock. She laid her hand across her breast and tried to control it.

Smart new shoes dragged. Ankles twisted and slipped. Shock, combined with the blow to her head, fuzzed her thoughts. She was so weary that her legs were trembling.

Finally, she fell, and let her clothes soak up the earthy wetness from the long grass.

A woman in one of the houses spotted her but, by the time the police arrived, Sylvia had roused herself and moved on.

❖

'It's not true. Can't be!' Violet was rolling maniacally around the settee.

'On my life, that bloody posh cow'll never set a hand on my bairn again.'

'What can we do?'

'Ethel'll keep Alice safe. They'll be on a train tonight.'

Cuthbert sank wearily on to the settee. Violet's head was shaking in spasms, as if denial could erase the facts. Katherine sat in the corner watching them.

'But Sylvia! Where's owa Sylvia?' Violet wept. 'Why didn't you notice, you stupid bugger?'

'It didn't look like owa Sylvia.' Cuthbert had been driving the streets for hours, looking for his daughter.

'She's been very poorly. So that madwoman said.'

Katherine sprang to her feet. 'Who cares?' she screamed. 'She can die and go to Hell and stop there! Don't you realize what she's done? Hendo might have brain damage. End up in an asylum. And David! His face! His legs! She causes all this, then runs away! Again!'

'My fault she ran off in the first place,' shouted Cuthbert, punching his thumb into his chest. 'My fault Alice has no mother. Me the bairn'll blame, when she grows.'

'And who will Alice blame if her dad dies? David could be bleeding to death while you're bellowing.'

'You've a bit to answer for yourself, girl. Slobber'n over the lad in broad daylight! You're a crafty minx. Is it old Ethel's money you're after? Or gett'n one up on your sister?'

'David and me love each other. We're going to get married and take Alice to live in America.'

'Over my dead body!'

'You can't stop . . .'

'Shut up, shut up, both of you!' screamed Violet. 'How can you talk of take'n Alice anywhere? She's Sylvia's bairn in case you both forgot.'

'No, Mam. You're wrong. Alice belongs to thems what love her.'

❖

In the hospital waiting room Hendo's parents held hands.

David's parents did not.

Hendo's parents prayed. Arthur Linden prayed too.

Mary Linden stamped around, demanding information, shouting at nurses, berating the doctors, berating her husband for buying David the motorbike in the first place and for no logical reason at all, venomously tongue-lashing her mother-in-law.

❖

Alan wiped Alice's nose and popped another jelly baby into her mouth. They were on the bus to Corbridge. Ethel Linden had been astonishingly calm on the telephone. Her grandson was gravely injured and, although she was deeply distressed, her first responsibility was to protect Alice from this mad-woman.

The Tyne valley slid by, but all Alan could see was Hendo's torn trouser leg and the gory mess of David's face when the ambulance crew turned him over.

His conscience was brimming. He had agreed to say nothing to the police about the madwoman's attempt at kidnapping Alice – at least until Sylvia could be found. But his intelligence told him that this was no white lie, it was black and dangerous. Moralist, idealist, Alan felt his forced dishonesty as hard as a nail in his boot.

❖

This particular allotment was manicured. A pretty garden of vegetables, cherished by a man who perhaps enjoyed his hobby more than his home. Between each hoed patch ran a velvety grass strip. Great rhubarb leaves shaded tilled earth. Rows of potato plants lay in humped lines and lime-green seedlings pressed upwards through the soil.

From the bushes Sylvia watched the gardener's loving labour. Then, when he departed, sore back laden with produce, she slipped into his shed, lay back on his old deckchair and finally allowed concussion to draw her into sleep.

❖

Poker in hand, Samuel Phillips, a man known for his calm, rational demeanour, bellowed, 'You swapped the babies?' He crunched at the coals like a soldier on bayonet practice.

'Not swapped. Not exactly.' Greta was huddled in an armchair in Sam's home in Fontbury.

'How could you do such an appalling thing?'

'Give me a chance to explain.'

'But will I believe you? You are such an accomplished liar, Alexandra, or should I call you Greta, or Gloria, or Lady Godiva? Lies just slide off your tongue, quick as spit. And I'm left nodding like a feeble moron, up to my teeth in trouble – and I hate it! I HATE IT!'

'I've had to survive on lies since I was a kid,' Greta retorted. 'But I couldn't lie to myself. I knew I wasn't a fit mother . . .'

'Damned right!' He stared at her, trying to see who she was, this double-faced, feline creature whom he both loved and despised. 'What did you hope to gain?'

She drew a breath.

'Mrs Sharp talked about Sylvia's baby going to this baker and his wife. It sounded such a good, healthy life – so . . . safe. If Dick had ever laid hands on her . . .

'As we were leaving the hospital I went back. Picked up my baby. My own daughter, so tiny, helpless. Where could I take her? Yet how could I leave her?

'They were alike. Both pretty as dark-haired cherubs. Sylvia and I had removed their tags. So I just left it to fate by . . .'

'By?'

'Putting them in the same cot.'

'The same cot? How bloody irresponsible!'

'Yes. And desperate. And a little mad. But Alice is mine, Sam. I know it.'

'You don't.'

'I saw that mass of ringlets, little legs swinging through the air, and I saw myself. I saw my mother. She's mine.'

'So you thought that gave you the right to grab her? God save me!'

'I can't remember deciding to do it. Oh, Sam . . .' she jumped up and clutched his arm, '. . . what should I do?'

He pulled abruptly away. 'Jesus. Don't ask me.'

'Sylvia will take her back to Scarborough. Hisper Cottage. It could be a home for all of us. Sylvia need never know. We could share Alice.'

Sam exploded.

'Manipulator! You're so steeped in lies you'll drown us all. Lies cost lives. Haven't you learned that yet?'

Oh, how right you were, Sam. How prophetically right.

❖

Tony sat staring into an empty grate, fumbling with his rosary and mumbling to himself.

'So it happens. I always know bad to come of it.' His ear burned where the Ristorante telephone had been pressed to it. Sam had painted such an appalling picture. 'Young men hurt. Maybe dying. Sylvia run off. Greta done such a bad thing. My blame. I search my heart. I know. Foolish man. Should have sent little Sylvie straight back home. Baby is there for her all this time. Terrible thing I do. Now all there is . . . to wait. To pray. Make Sylvia safe, sweet Mother. Make her safe. And forgive my passionate Greta.'

Downstairs Liz was letting herself in, shouting up the stairwell, 'Any news? I'm bustin to know 'ow it went.'

The Italian shoved his rosary back in his pocket.

Where?

Sylvia woke with a start, engulfed in a shiver. A lumpy bruise blazed magenta on her forehead and streaks of dried blood criss-crossed her face.

In the confined space she struggled out of the deckchair, knocking plant pots from a shelf, spilling compost across the wooden floor. She crouched to pick up a fragment of red terracotta. Bill and Ben . . . She shivered again and crossed her legs, wondering if she was in one of her desperate toilet dreams.

Wake up!

Teeth chattering, she pulled the brown cardigan around her and retracted her hands into the knitted sleeves.

Cardigan? She looked at it. A horrible, thread-snagged old thing. Where had it come from? Ugly or not, it swamped her jacket and she was glad of its warmth.

Cautiously, she peered out of the door and stepped into a morning which smelled of dewy earth. Dawn was kissing cabbage leaves with a sparkle of gold; starlings fluttered away; a blackbird chirruped.

There was no one around, so in a space behind the shed, she dropped her pants, sure she was wetting the bed, but unable to stop.

Wake up! Was she awake?

Her stockings were ripped to shreds. As she rolled them off and pushed them into her jacket pocket, her fingers found her purse. Three pound notes, two florins, a few pennies. She pictured the big silver cash register in the shoe shop. Fast as a dying man watches his memories, Sylvia scanned her Scarborough life. Rushing behind, swifter than a single tick, clustered horrific images of yesterday. With equally rapid efficiency, her mind transferred the pictures to sugar paper and stuffed them into the daydreamed range.

Floating down from the endless sky came a soporific veil of denial.

In the distance, where several paths met, was a tap and water butt. Dew soaked Sylvia's bare legs, as she stepped through the vegetables, like a child in a ballet lesson. Sliding her fingers into the metal tank, she cupped her hands and splashed cool water into her eyes, letting the sensuous flow trickle down her chin and into her bra. She twisted the tap and sucked icy water into her mouth.

The sun was warmer now. On a bench, in the middle of the allotments, Sylvia sat watching a spider build its web between two bean tendrils.

Tick. Tick. Squeak. Tick. Tick. Squeak.

A man was approaching on a rusty bike.

Sylvia rose on to her toes and fled.

❖

'It's like talking to the back of a bus!'

Monday morning. Liz was following Tony around the Ristorante tables, nagging at his back.

'Why you shouting like bloody fishwife?'

'We've got to go look for 'er.' Her bag was ready at the door.

'No.' There was tomato sauce in Tony's moustache. 'She come back here. This is her safe home now. Be wise, cranky old woman. Sylvie could be in London by this time. Or France. Or bloody Venezia with my bloody fat cousins. Or taking tea with Pope. What good is there? We wait. This is all we can do.'

'If you are not going, I am!'

'Please-a your bloody self.'

She untied her apron, hauled it over her head and threw it at him.

❖

Cuthbert Sharp had scoured the streets of Jesmond till past midnight looking for Sylvia. Eventually he fell into bed, tossing over and over, with his daughter's strangely thin face before his sleepless eyes and Alice's cries in his ears.

At dawn Violet shook him.

'She's mad, isn't she? This Hythe woman?'

'As a box of frogs.'

'We should tell the police. Her and that vet could've lured Sylvia into some kind of cult. Me poor lass. Brainwashed!'

'All this tripe about muddle'n up babies – makes nee sense, nee sense at all.'

'And she says owa Sylvia doesn't know?'

'Aye.'

'She kidnapped Sylvia and she now wants Alice anall. What for?' Violet gripped the eiderdown and whispered, 'Witchcraft?'

'Bloody hell, woman!' Cuthbert sat on the edge of the bed, chewing his coaly fingernails. 'Divent make bad worse. This is nowt to do with the occult; it's to do with money.'

'A ransom?'

'Na. Opposite. She said her family was rich. They would fight us for owa Alice. She was blether'n about Italy and swank'n that her dad was dead famous. Piana player or summut.'

'She's in cuckooland.'

'She's hard as flint. Two young lads smashed up, near dead – all she could think about was shut'n my gob.'

'Will she keep her promise, Cuth? Bring Sylvia home?' Violet started to cry complicated, pessimistic tears.

'Hush, hush.'

'If we go to the police, and if the woman's arrested, she'll tell them the cock-and-bull story about being Alice's mam. Wharrif they believe it? They might take the bairn away from us.'

'Owa my dead body!'

'But you said she's got papers from the hospital.'

'Proves nowt. We'll be cleverer than she expects. Ethel's not daft. She'll be in Scotland by now. We'll give that mad Hythe woman a couple of days to bring owa Sylvia back.'

'And then what?'

'A'll morder the bitch.'

'Cuthbert!'

'A kna. But we've got a fight on owa hands, lass. Mind, it's the Lindens' fight anall.'

'Poor David. OH, MY GOD!' Violet jumped up. 'What if David's already told the police . . . ? Or Hendo?'

'Bloody hell!'

Cuthbert scrabbled into his trousers. He ran to the telephone box on the corner. Grappling with the telephone directory which hung from a string, he searched for the number of the Royal Victoria Infirmary.

Four pennies in the slot. Press button A.

'How is David Linden? Would he be up to having visitors this afternoon? Just for a bit chat?'

The nurse was firm. 'Far too soon for the lad to see anyone but his parents. Actually it'll be a while before he chats to anyone.'

'Why's that?'

'The nature of his injuries. I'm not at liberty . . .'

'Oh, that's turrible. Turrible,' said Cuthbert. 'And what about young Henderson?'

'I'm afraid . . .'

His next phone call was to the home of Arthur and Mary Linden, who had just returned from a night vigil at the hospital.

Two hours later the Lindens entered the Sharp house, stiff-lipped and stiff-backed. Mary sat on the very edge of their settee, as if fleas would bite her bum.

'His beautiful face is MUTILATED! Stitched up like a handbag.'

'No eye injury. Thankfully.' Arthur moderated.

'Leg broken in four places. He'll limp for ever.' Mary.

'Ribs should heal quickly.' Arthur.

With his own form of stout dignity Cuthbert took the floor, backside to his hearth, feet apart. Violet, poised gracefully in her own home, felt a flutter of pride at her husband's calm articulation as he delivered his story about the madwoman and her claims. She herself felt calmer, wiser, more in control, less tempted to weep, even alertly powerful, when Alice's other grandparents looked utterly dumbfounded.

'She's a liar, of course. Totally loopy,' Cuthbert finished.

'What's the name again?' Arthur asked.

'Hythe. Sandra or summut.' Cuthbert frowned. 'Trouble is, if this posh witch starts shout'n 'er mouth off about being Alice's mother, the papers'll have a bloody party. Mebees they'll write that your lad's a hero fer hadd'n after the madwoman. But oot it'll all come – how you covered up for 'im. Sorry, missus.' He stared bluntly at Mary Linden. 'Needs to be said.'

But Mary only lifted her haughty shoulders in a dismissive shrug.

Violet, loathing her, managed to say, 'I've been pray'n for him. And poor Hendo . . .'

Mary threw in, with a ton of implicit blame, 'Terrence will be a cabbage!'

'Still unconscious,' said Arthur.

'Truth is,' said Cuthbert, with rare humility, 'it's all OWA fault. YOUS! WUS! Fer what we all did three years ago. Now don't interrupt, missus.' He raised his voice against Mary's indignation. 'What say Hendo – dies? We'll all be guilty! Shamed! We needs be careful. Mind wor tongues for a bit.'

Violet felt a wash of gratitude towards Arthur Linden

when he said, with unexpected compassion, 'You want us to wait, because it might be your only chance of getting Sylvia back. I don't blame you. She's Alice's mother. We mustn't let her slip away from us again. Also – I fear – we must find out the truth about this swapping claim. So, what are we up against? Who is this rich and famous family?'

'Italian royalty or summut. And this piana player called Hythe.'

'Douglas Hythe, it must be!' piped up Mary, who hated music but liked gossip columns. 'Wife was Sophia Marletti. Actress. In *Sweet Reversal*.'

'So the papers would have a field day,' mused Arthur.

'Damn,' said Mary.

'And Hellfire,' added Cuthbert.

Arthur leaned forward. 'People from theatrical backgrounds are often deeply troubled. Swapping babies, snatching Alice, the woman is irrational. If the authorities found out about her antics, she'd never get custody of a child. I'd like to know why this "rich" woman was living as a gypsy. We should do a little investigating ourselves.'

Violet nodded to every word Arthur said.

'Aye,' Cuthbert was also agreeing. 'My theory is that she got herself up the spout with some politician. We cannut let a woman like that take owa Alice away. Why, man, it would kill your David. And Ethel. We must find owa Sylvia. She's the bairn's real mam. Then there can be no argument.'

'You're convinced it was Sylvia?'

'Well, young Alan says the vet and the lass called at owa old house. Apparently the lass was weep'n. He was sure it was owa Sylvia. That's why they followed.'

Violet endured a fresh rush of silent pain, followed by a sudden plummet of quiescence. Cold prickled up her arms. Outwardly as calm as a deep, ice-covered lake, she picked up the cooling teapot and walked out of the room. But she didn't go to the kitchen. She opened the front door and stared out across the road.

Proud, blinkered men, Violet thought – blind warriors who can't see past their noses. There's another truth. A terrible, terrible worry. Somewhere out there – who knows where – is another little girl. Nearly three. What's she called? Who tucks her into bed?

❖

Mary Linden was vexed. Why should she give a damn about Sylvia? Why should she sit in this spartan room, taking tea from an ignorant woman who didn't even have china cups?

Because, she realized, the hurt done to David's poor young body gave her pain – inside. It felt unexpectedly horrible. Someone must pay. Who? She would get to the truth if it killed her. And, by God, when it came to ruthlessness, she could teach this Hythe woman a lesson or two.

'I suggest,' she said haughtily, 'that we locate Mr Douglas Hythe – speak to him about his daughter. She might have a history of mental illness.'

Two grandfathers looked at her, aghast.

'Oh, for God's sake,' she exploded, 'he's just a man with clever fingers and a big head.'

But privately Mary smirked, understanding why both Arthur and Cuthbert were reeling. A third grandfather, especially one who was rich and famous, was one grandfather too many.

They tried, these two men, in a pincer of masculine wills, to forbid Mary from contacting Douglas Hythe.

But, of course, Mary would.

❖

Sylvia wandered down Gosforth High Street, her head so muzzy that the familiar town was edged with rainbows, as if she was looking through a prism. Across the road were the Assembly Rooms, the pet shop, the butcher, the Toddle In Café. Passing Woolworth's, she caught sight of her reflection.

Was someone else walking through her life?

An ironmonger's came in and out of focus. Traffic swerved around her.

Trees in Central Park had unfurled emerald leaves; immaculate flower borders were massed with roses. She reached out and touched a pale lemon petal.

Loved me. Loved me not.

She could see David, lying on the tarmac, under the wheels. Was he dead?

The roses were crumbling, yellow and pink confetti falling around her feet, as she grasped a barbed stem and welcomed the piercing pain.

On the tennis courts four girls were leaping around in short white skirts. Sylvia pressed her face against the metal mesh wall, grinding her cheek into the wire until she could taste rust on her lips.

Tempus bounced with the ball. Tick, tock.

The girls stopped playing. They were looking at her. Sylvia

backed away, gliding on mercurious feet over peculiarly poignant lawns.

In her right hand she felt the weight of an invisible tennis racket. As memories pinged before her eyes like dancing fireflies, one by one she swatted them, extinguishing their glory.

Katherine playing in the sandpit. SWAT!

Her mam's picnic basket. SWAT!

Ham and pease pudding sandwiches. SWAT!

Crushing daisies, she lay down on her side and watched a thrush hopping through a hedge. Suddenly the familiar dreambird was fluttering inside her belly, its feathers tickling her ribs, her breasts, between her legs. David's face was over hers, his lips hot and lustful.

She was up, stumbling through the park gates. Down St Nicholas Avenue she staggered, and into South Gosforth railway station, where a voice was announcing a train to the coast.

❖

'Still no sign your end, Tony?' shouted Sam down the telephone. A queue of trembling animals lined his waiting room. 'Greta's going down to Newcastle to carry on searching. No. Police aren't doing much. Yes, you should stay in Scarborough. What? Liz coming? What time is her train due? Greta can meet her. Personally I think Sylvia will make her way back to you. She's emotionally shattered. Yes, I know. I feel the same.'

❖

At Tynemouth a sea fret saturated the air. The ruined castle was an eerie shadow, a 'wet on wet' water mark soaked into white paper. Sylvia wandered along North Pier, feeling it huge and solid beneath her feet, as it curved dimly ahead, fading into opaque mist. Above, floating in the silken sky, was the pulsating beam of the lighthouse. Flash. Tick. Tick. Flash.

The Tyne, on the sheltered side of the pier, was tranquil. Far below little boats knocked together, huddled against the vast stone barrier. But on the seaward side deep water, grey as lead, heaved.

Close, yet invisible, a ship sounded its hollow foghorn.

Sylvia reached the end of the pier. Mist swirled between herself and the town. Cocooned in white vapour, she leaned against the wall of the lighthouse and looked up its rearing length to the flashing light in the sky. Dizzy, she closed her eyes and listened to the familiar sea; God's breath, piping under and over the waves. And she remembered a dark night in Hisper Cottage, being very, very, cold.

❖

David's lips wouldn't move. Imprisoned in claustrophobia, he cried. His father's face hovered over him, wiping tears he couldn't reach. His mother was holding his hand. She looked old.

He tried to cough, and heard himself choking. Pain coursed through his body, but he desperately needed to ask . . .

Mercifully, his dad understood. 'Don't worry, lad, Alice is safe. We'll look after her. Now, go back to sleep.'

Little Alice was naughty for Ethel, running out of her reach and crying that she wanted to go home. The old woman was not used to dealing with her great-granddaughter alone, but that would soon be remedied. A hired nanny named Clara Blake, who carried excellent references from a family in Glasgow, was joining them for a wee holiday.

Ethel had been reassured that David would mend, although his face would be scarred. Meanwhile (wonder of wonders), Bloody Mary seemed to be making a half-decent hash of playing mother – for a change!

❖

God's pipe was very loud, this close to the huge North Sea, which pressed omnipotently against the pier, pushing, pushing, pushing again. Huddled against the lighthouse, hair plastered to her bent head, Sylvia trembled like a lost dog.

Eventually, she roused herself and walked again, not knowing where she was going or why. The firefly memories were back, trying to sting her eyes, but she drew her hood of denial even more tightly around her head, sacrificing all anxieties to comforting aimlessness.

Down on the beach the soft sand made her walk like a drunk. Eyes fixed on tipping rollers, she staggered towards the sea. Suddenly a brilliant, joyous picture rose before her. Herself. A miniature Sylvia paddling with her best friend Dothy, their tiny toes icy in white running foam. They were wearing matching costumes, Sylvia's baby-blue, Dothy's baby-pink. The cotton was scrunched with elastic into little squares, clinging, wet and gritty, sand trapped scratchily in the crotch.

Seventeen-year-old Sylvia took off her shoes and watched wavelets curl around her ankles. She looked up. Dothy was still there. The serious, beautiful elfin child was carefully filling a small tin pail with seawater.

'Dothy!' shouted Sylvia. 'Oh, Dothy . . .'

The little girl ran out of the waves, sploshing her bucket, digging her toes into the sand to help balance.

'Careful! Wait for me . . .' Sylvia lurched towards the child, whose swimming costume was as pink as fairyland.

❖

Greta was furious that Liz had brought Mustard.

'If anybody can find Sylvia this dog will,' insisted Liz.

So they took him to Jesmond, to the scene of the accident. Both women put their hands over their mouths as they looked at the brown stains on the road. The daft dog, however, peed up a wall and wagged his tail.

'Where did she go, lad?'

Mustard, enjoying the attention, chased his tail.

'This isn't the slightest use,' snapped Greta.

'Right,' said Liz firmly, 'we'll ask the police if they've heard owt.'

'I don't think so!'

'What sort of woman have you growed into, Greta? They'll expect you to be worried about your friend.'

'I gave my name as Alexandra Hythe.'

'Oh, the posh one.'

'The true one. What if Sylvia's father's told them about . . .'

'You'll just have to risk it, because our friend is ill, and lost, and cold. And it's your fault!'

'Shit.'

'Shovelfuls.'

❖

As they climbed back into Sam's battered Hillman, the old man behind the aspidistra turned the wheel on his hearing aid. In his other hand he was cradling his Brownie. He wound on the film and wrapped it in a paisley handkerchief.

He smiled. The young, he thought, ignore the old at their peril.

❖

'DI Howard?' A young police officer stuck his head around the Inspector's door. 'Accident yesterday. Jesmond. That lass who ran off. A couple of her friends are here, asking.'

'Who?'

'The driver. Miss Hythe, and some other biddy.'

When Howard saw the tall, elegant woman again, he played with his tie and rolled backwards on his heels. Sexy, he thought. Bloody Amazonian.

'Ah, the lady with the dented Hillman.'

'How are the boys, Inspector?' the beauty fluttered. 'I'm so worried.'

'One lad's a bag of broken bones, and the other's still unconscious.' Howard watched the woman shudder and gave

229

her seven out of ten for sincerity. Maybe six. 'Nasty smash. You were stationary, I understand.'

'I was. They came up so fast.'

'Perhaps you braked a bit too sharp?'

'It all happened so quickly . . .'

'Nicoletta. Any sign? We need her statement.'

'No. We were hoping you'd have found her.'

'Afraid not. But,' he confided, meeting Greta's riveting blue gaze, 'a young woman matching your description was seen on the Town Moor – lying in the cowpats. Another possible sighting in Central Park this morning. A girl vandalizing a rose bed. Is she mentally unstable, this lass?'

'No!' The older woman vigorously shook her jowls. 'Can't be her. But if it is, although it can't be, and I'm sure it's not, but if it is, you must find her quick!'

Hythe was smoother. Smooth, Howard thought, as her nylons.

'It's possible she's concussed.'

'That is a concern,' he agreed. 'Unfortunately there has been another occurrence, down at the coast. Incident with a child. Mother panicked. Same description – skinny young woman, very dark hair; a bit absent. It's a pity you couldn't give us more information. She definitely has no friends and family in Newcastle?'

'I don't know.'

Greta then repeated her utter fabrication that Nicoletta was a hitchhiker who she had picked up outside Doncaster. She apologized very prettily.

'I'm afraid I'm not much help.'

No, you are not, lady. Her gaze, full of serene sorrow,

stirred something in Howard. His body stilled, while his intellect began to probe his intuition. The raven beauty was lying, but it was not logic which was jarring him, it was something on the other side of his brain, something more profound, a flash of notion and prenotion, and it was surprisingly personal.

To cover his inner shudder, Howard turned to the older woman with her silver coronet of plaits. 'And your connection is . . . ?'

'I'm just with her,' the old biddy replied, hitching her thumb. She began fanning her face menopausally. 'Hot,' she mumbled, and wobbled hurriedly out of the station.

'Fear not.' Howard grinned at the beautiful woman before him. 'We'll find young Nicoletta soon. Where can I contact you?'

'We haven't found anywhere to stay yet. But I'll telephone the station every couple of hours.' She turned to leave. 'Thank you, Inspector.'

As she walked away, the Inspector inspected – high, rounded backside, stocking seams dividing unusually tight calf muscles.

Thank you, my dear.

❖

Matthew Kirkstone came home from work unusually early. Baby Jan was ready for bed.

'Where's Daddy's girl? Been good for Mammy the day? Got a cuddle?'

The reluctant father lifted his surrogate daughter on to his lap. She was sticky around the mouth, but her trusting eyes pierced him. He smiled and stroked her long silky hair. Her little frilly knickers brushed his arm and he cupped his hand around one chubby knee, enjoying the feel of her soft skin.

Janice watched from the kitchen door, wishing her husband still enjoyed cuddling his wife.

❖

A hard wind was whipping in and out of the caves which tunnelled beneath the road. Sylvia curled into a shelter, pulling her knees up into the cardigan.

Why had Dothy run away?

She looked at the line of hotels, then back at the sea. All she wanted was to be safe and alone, in Hisper Cottage.

When she realized how hard she was crying, she dropped her head to her knees, to hide her face. Curled tight as a hedgehog, she started to rock; bang, bang with her spine against the wooden shelter. The rocking and knocking had a rhythm. Tock tock.

With the rhythm came a number. Over and over again the number rocked. A number she had memorized and used often.

A young couple walked past her. They stared, and walked faster. Sylvia stood up. The number was insistent. She ran then, sprinting up and down streets, until she stood, breathless, in front of a red telephone box.

Four pennies in the slot, dial the number and press button A.

With a clatter the coins fell.

'Tony. Oh, Tony.'

❖

Forty minutes later Greta also put four pennies in the slot, dialled and pressed button A.

Sam's voice was high with relief. 'She called Tony!'

Greta felt a dull trembling inside. 'Tynemouth, you say?'

She drove with her jaw set tight, desperate to get to Sylvia before the police.

Liz read the map. 'Upover.' She pointed right. 'Downover.'

In Whitley Bay they followed the coast road as it curved around the cliff tops, through Cullercoats and into Tynemouth. There they left the car and walked. And walked. And walked. Along the top and back again. Out to the pier, under the Castle, until the sun went down, leaving the town grey and the sand dull as mud. Mustard dragged on his leash, his coat parting in the cold wind.

'She came to t'sea,' Liz reasoned, 'so she'll stay by t'sea. Reminds her of home. Well, that's what I think.'

Greta shrugged helplessly and stared at the wide horizon, where night clouds were rolling in.

Nestled in an outcrop of rocks was a seawater bathing pool. Greta crossed the road and headed towards it. Tottering behind her, Liz had also spotted the silhouette of a hunched figure sitting with feet dangling in the water. Mustard began to pull, choking on his collar. As they reached the railing Liz let go of the leash and the dog bolted, ducking and swerving until he bounded towards the lonely profile. His barking broke the spell. Liz shouted. Greta ran, but Mustard had surprised his quarry and Sylvia fell, shocked, into the water.

Liz screamed. Greta flung off her shoes, but as Sylvia sank without even a struggle, Mustard jumped in on top of her.

Yelling curses, Greta stripped off her skirt. Three passers-by hung gawping against the railing, watching the woman dive into the freezing water in her knickers. Seconds later she emerged, dragging a prostrate body behind her with one arm, fighting off a crazed dog with the other.

When all three finally stood dripping, spluttering and shivering on cold concrete, Liz threw her flap-winged arms around Sylvia.

'Poor lamb! What you bin doin with yourself?'

Sylvia clung tightly, but her eyes were vacant.

❖

When Sylvia faltered up Sam's garden path in Fontbury, she was wearing only Liz's voluminous coat. The vet's protective instincts surged, and he hugged her, but Greta's glare made him feel like a dirty old man.

The traumatized girl seemed unable, or unwilling, to speak. Sam considered taking her to the local hospital, but the doctor inside him wanted to heal her himself. He examined the bruise on her head and dressed the tiny cut which had bled disproportionately, then handed her to Liz, who took Sylvia upstairs, pulled a nightie over her head and tucked her into a warm bed.

Downstairs Sam picked up the phone, but Greta grabbed it from him.

'Don't tell the police, Sam. Think it through. She's upset,

confused and exhausted. She wasn't right even before we brought her back to Newcastle.'

He hesitated. 'Was it my fault, for bringing her home?'

'We both know this is all my fault. Before we tell anyone anything, let's try to understand her feelings. That policeman, Howard, told me he wanted her statement about the accident. What if she gets confused and admits . . . that she is the missing Sylvia Sharp? It will be like a bomb exploding. Is she well enough to face all that?'

Sam stroked his scar, watching her long fingers twitch the curtain, a cushion, the teaspoon in his saucer.

'You're very crafty, Alexandra.'

'You think I'm only worried for myself? What about Tony and Liz?' Greta flattened her palms to him, pleading. 'We must protect them too. And Howard said there was an "incident" with a child. Sylvia could even be charged.'

Liz came into the room, adding, 'My worry is that they'll hurt her up 'ere,' she tapped her head, 'even more. Greta's right. If they push her much further, she could go over t'top. Then they'll stick her in a mental hospital.'

With a frustrated humph, Sam folded his arms.

Liz did exactly the same – humph and fold. 'I've been in one of them places. No better than a prison. And nowadays they do expuriments with electricity on people's brains. On this occasion, 'appen your honesty may be her ruination. What she really needs is good old-fashioned love.'

Sadly, all three would remember this conversation with crucifying irony.

As Liz stared him out, Sam dropped his stance and stomped out of the room.

'Eh, lass, we've upset him now! 'E'll not get over this.'

'Oh, he will.' Greta felt calmer than she should. Sam was wonderful, but her baby was more important than any man could ever be.

'What shall we do about Sylvia's parents, Liz? We mustn't upset the poor girl even more, but I must keep my promise to the Sharps.'

'Question is, will a cuddle from her mam bring Sylvia back to her senses, or will it make her worse?'

'A mother's cuddle? Oh, Liz, I wish I could remember what that felt like.'

❖

Sam's home had been invaded by irrational, manipulative women. He pulled down the ripped hood of the car and drove out into darkness. The road rose swiftly out of the town and into silent hills where the Hillman's headlights swooped, as did his thoughts, around dangerous curves.

On a bare crest he pulled off the road. The headlamps died and blessed peace enveloped the dented Hillman and its driver.

On this clear, starry night he lay back in his seat and stared up at the endless dome of Heaven.

I'm infatuated by Alexandra, he confessed to the Plough, yet I don't even like her. She's been a mystery to solve, a titillating chase. Her body takes me to sexual heaven; but my heart stays earthbound, waiting for a purer kind of love.

To the moon, he acknowledged, I play God, convinced I have the power of healing at my vain disposal. I've languished in young Sylvia's grateful smile, watching her pale, sad eyes slowly brighten, and I've slapped my own back. Well done, Samuel.

Well done? Pompously assuming I could reunite her with her child? How shallow, blind and stupid. I should have left well enough alone. Sylvia could have had other babies. Other boyfriends. Now the poor lass has lost everything, even her senses.

Oh, Jesus. What if one of these young lads dies? I'll be a murderer, because I set it all up.

Staring at stars, his eyes were burning. He blinked until they were wet. Wallowing in remorse, he weighed the dreadful consequences of his actions, and, fleetingly, his stomach churned with the hideous lure of suicide.

❖

The grandmother clock chimed, bong, bong. Tears trickled over Sylvia's nose into the pillow, as she listened to Sam and Greta quarrelling downstairs. The sedative was dragging her towards sleep, but anxiety kept surging over crests and plummeting her down into fearful dreamings. As the clock continued its pendulous tocking, the bird came back.

This time he was so gentle that she could neither hear nor see him. She just felt his presence, and she dreamed the surprising emotion of love, for a creature who knew her so well that he understood something very important. Temper Fuggerit had to be stopped.

The bird carried her on a howling wind, across the raging sea and back into Hisper Cottage, where Dothy was kneeling, like Cinderella, before a dead fire, clutching the photograph of the soldier.

Bad time, said the worried child, pointing up at Fuggerit.

Sylvia lifted the clock from the mantelpiece and looked at its face. The hands bent, drooped, fell to the floor. They began to wriggle around her ankles, like worms.

Dinner for birdie! giggled Dothy. *Let them out.*

But when she pulled the door open, Sylvia's mother and Mary Linden were outside, throwing shoes, shouting, 'Tick! tick!'

Leave us alone! cried Dothy, slamming the door.

Inside the cottage the worms were multiplying, until the floor was crawling with them, like black spaghetti in bloody tomato sauce, which kept rising, a dangerous red tide creeping up Dothy's chest, slime slipping over her narrow shoulders, closing over her face.

Scream! Try harder. Scream!

Dothy vanished.

Sylvia felt strong arms holding her. A familiar voice, and a solid, naked chest to lean on. Sam's nipple was close to her lips. She wanted to bite it.

Two photographs

lay side by side on the Sub Editor's desk. One was a professional portrait of a luscious, dark-haired woman with lips as
ripe as blackberries – Sophia Marletti. The other was rather
more aspidistra than anything else. 'Crap shot. Let's see
the rest, Roger.' The young reporter, newly recruited to the
Evening Chronicle, handed him the pack of photographs.

'The old bugger selling this lot is deaf and can't speak
properly, so he wrote it down. Said it wasn't just an accident,
it was a chase. The car was cornered by Sharp's wagon. My
mate got a look at the report. Driver was a woman called
Hythe. I sussed out old Sharp. He'd say nowt, surly bastard.
So I hung around the RVI, introduced myself to Linden's
mam. Bitch! Gob like bloody Tynemouth. Whacks me with
her brolly, but then . . . sinks her pointy little nails in my arm
and starts asking her own questions.'

'About?'

'Concert pianist. Douglas Hythe. Said she wanted him to
play at some charity bash. That's how I started slotting
together this little jigsaw.'

'You've got the corners and straight edges. Now get the full picture. Keep working on the Linden woman.'

'That vicious baggage?'

'She's probably sexually frustrated. You're a fisherman. Go tickle the old trout.'

❖

On Tuesday afternoon Greta tried reading to Sylvia, but the girl wasn't listening. Sleep kept drifting across her creamy brow as Sam's sedative relaxed her.

All morning they had watched her weep, an impossible deluge flooding from her emaciated frame. To Greta, who despised tears, the sheer physicality of Sylvia's sobbing was disturbing. Nor did she risk embracing the girl, partly because she had noticed the ferocity in Sylvia's clutches, but mostly because she simply didn't want to. She was having difficulty suppressing surges of jealous spite when Sam stroked Sylvia's bony shoulder and Liz's fingers laced through her dyed hair. Greta, isolated for most of her life, remained defensively comfortable with her exclusion.

I'll go soon, she thought. Back to Italy. Away from the mess and the weakness and the sickly pandering. And as soon as I've gone Sam will want me again. Just as he always has. But when I go, I'll take my baby with me.

Lost in her own wishful, sun-kissed, Italian ending, she laid down the magazine.

Sylvia roused. Through pale, puzzled eyes she stared, as if seeking, in Greta, the answer to a riddle. Pursing her lips, she began clucking her tongue.

'Tuttuttuttuttit's passions will rock thee

As storms rock the ravens on high . . .'

'Pardon?'

'Bright reason will mock thee . . .' Sylvia mumbled, closing her eyes again, drawn by the sedative into a world of words which Greta could never imagine.

❖

Lipstick, rouge, a fluff of a hairbrush, and Katherine Sharp was ready for hospital visiting. Full of self-importance borrowed from her association with such a drama, she clattered down the hospital corridor in her new high heels.

She wasn't the only one dressed for the occasion. In front of her Katherine spotted a fuchsia hat; beneath it, Mary Linden's perm and her haughty little nose. Damn.

So the young girl put her new love on hold and went to find her old one. But in Hendo's ward a nurse warned her, 'He's still unconscious. Are you his girl?'

She nodded without conscience. The nurse took her to a little glass window in a door. Katherine saw the curves of Hendo's parents' backs, his mam bent as if she was in chapel, his dad with his brow heavy on his forearms, near his boy's knees. Hendo's head was bandaged with a halo of white. His face was yellow as scrambled egg.

And suddenly it was all real. Death was real. The hospital smell was a reek of real sickness. Sylvia – bloody Sylvia was real. Change and consequence were inevitable and cruel.

Trembling, she returned to the entrance, found a quiet corner and lit a cigarette.

Katherine was growing up. She wasn't sure what she was growing into. Adulthood was sliding its unpredictable layers over her naiveté and the hours she spent looking in the mirror only ever gave her half of the picture. What went on inside, those thoughts and emotions mysteriously beyond her control, were coloured and shaped, not only by her own character, but by the invisible hand of Sylvia. Every relationship she had, with her mother, her father, David, Alice, was clouded by her sister's dominant, tragic shadow. And Katherine resented it so bitterly that she could have chewed trees.

Her second Woodbine was lit by another smoker, a nice-looking lad called Roger. His idle chat calmed her and she felt very important when she told him she was David Linden's girlfriend.

By the time Mary's fuchsia hat wobbled out of the main entrance, Katherine was ready. She returned to the ward and approached David's bed. Her boyfriend was lying very still, the blankets caged to protect his damaged frame. A large dressing covered half of his face.

Taking his hand, she bent low and kissed it gently. 'Is it bad, pet?'

The boy's strapped chest heaved.

'I wish I could kiss you better. Every bit that hurts.'

David stared, as if her remark was childish and trite in the face of his dreadful suffering. Katherine shrank, unsure of herself.

Out of the corner of his mouth he wheezed, 'Hendo? Truth. Tell meee . . .' Saliva dribbled down his chin.

'Still unconscious. Truth? He looks shite.'

'Say . . . sorry . . .'

'Sorry? Oh, pet! It was an accident.' She avoided his bloodshot eye. 'Actually, it's all Sylvia's fault. Everything.'

Her lad's white knuckles retracted from her caress. An unmanly moistness glistened against David's long eyelashes. Fury shot through Katherine like shrapnel.

Rising lightly, she forced her lipstick into a smile. 'Tell you what,' she teased, winking, 'if Hendo's playing Sleeping Beauty I'd best nip along and see if I can wake him with a kiss!'

David lowered his sleepy eyelids. But Katherine hadn't finished.

'Dad says to tell you . . .' Her voice hardened. 'Now listen, David, because this is important. The woman that tried to snatch Alice has also got owa Sylvia. She says if we ever want to see her again, we've got to keep quiet. Not tell the police what she did. So that gives you a hard choice, pet. Alice safe, or Sylvia back. I know what I want to do.'

David was alert now, trying to hoist himself up.

'Shall we tell the police, David? You and me? Shall we tell them all these secrets? Or do you want Sylvia back?'

Once she had asked the question, she didn't want to hear the answer, so she blew him a kiss and strode away.

'Oh, David,' she muttered under her breath, 'who's going to tell you the rest?'

Katherine really had no intention of kissing Hendo. She had already seen his death sleep and the only fairytale left was her own, although even the pages of that book were torn and blotchy.

❖

Janice picked up the *Chronicle*, desperate, as always, to read something exciting in her horoscope. But instead of discovering what the stars had in store, she saw a glimpse of the living past and the dying future, hiding behind an aspidistra.

Against two photographs, the newspaper asked, 'Is this reckless driver Alexandra Hythe, daughter of Screen Queen Sophia?'

No, thought Janice, that is Greta Korda.

❖

In Pink Lane, where prostitutes in polka dots hovered on corners, someone else was reading a gutter-stained copy of the *Chronicle*. Someone who also recognized Greta

❖

who was, at that moment, washing a lettuce with a face as sour as vinegar.

'She's not said a word all day,' whispered Liz urgently. 'Don't know if it's illness or obstinacy. Let's hope her parents can help.'

'They should take responsibility for her now.'

'Sam's turribly protective. I'm not sure it's healthy.'

'Neither am I, Liz. Neither am I.'

'His fussin's making her worse. I think on my own girls. Widows and nurses – each one's had a turrible tragedy. Ruddy, bloody war. But brave lasses, all.'

'They take after you. Your own life hasn't been easy. Nor mine, for that matter. But Sylvia's sensitive. I am sorry for her. I just wish Sam was more sorry for me. He can't comprehend that I miss my baby just as much.'

'He sees you as strong. Men like strong women.'

The connecting door from the surgery slammed.

'Sorry I'm late,' called Sam, picking up the *Chronicle* from under the grandmother clock. He reset the pendulum, then walked straight past the kitchen and into the sitting room, where Sylvia was staring vacantly out of the window. He stroked her head and she closed her eyes like a soothed cat.

❖

It was a sultry, sulky evening. They ate with the windows open. Clanking cutlery jarred everyone's nerves, and the salad wilted.

Sylvia, awake but nauseous, rolled a piece of ham around her mouth, unable to swallow. Her friends chewed and pretended not to notice when she spat it out. Suddenly the words in her head were so important that she had to speak them.

'You never even said sorry.'

Liz jumped. Sam looked up. Greta froze. Sylvia heard her own voice, clear and strong, two tones lower than usual, very adult and womanly.

Greta started gathering plates. Sylvia's eyes followed her.

'You tricked me. Left me by myself, on that train. You said we could go to New York. But you never came back. And you never said sorry.'

Greta dipped her head so that her hair fell over her face.

'New York?' Sam laughed with artificial buoyancy. 'Would you really like to go there, Sylvia?'

Liz reached for her hand. 'Greta sent you to Tony and me. The best she could do – at the time. And we looked after you.'

'Who is she, Liz? Maybe she isn't either Greta or Alexandra. Maybe she's no one at all.'

The woman with old Rome in her blood and gypsy grime

under her skin lifted her eyes. Glacial blue glittered behind black threads. 'SHE's the cat's mother.'

'Maybe she is.' Sylvia stared her out. 'Maybe that's all she is.'

The back door was open. Greta walked out of it.

❖

Liz watched Greta's long, strong legs striding across the lawn and was glad to see both Sam and Mustard running after her.

'Oh, Sylvia lass, she saved your life last night.'

But as she turned around, she saw that the girl Tony called Nicoletta was holding her salad plate high on her fingertips, just as he had taught her. Transfixed, Liz watched the tall, gangly young woman walk out into the hall, but instead of going to the kitchen, Sylvia stood in front of the antique time-piece, which had once belonged to Sam's own grandmother. The plate lifted, inch by inch, tilting slightly. And then she hurled it. Fine china smashed into the innocent glass face of the old clock, shattering it. Lettuce and cucumber lay lime-green and guilty on the polished floor.

'Feel better now?' Liz felt cold, like a mother who suddenly sees the darkest side of her child's nature.

'No.'

❖

The hills had turned violet. Greta sat on a fallen tree trunk, watching Mustard dashing through the ripe corn.

Sam was slapping away a halo of midges. 'We all get confused about this Greta, Alexandra thing,' he said. 'She's just overwrought.'

'She's also right. I am no one at all. Maybe that's how I like it. In Italy I'm Nonno's princess. They suffocate me. I need freedom.'

'And the absolute freedom is obscurity?'

'Of course.'

'You'd better look at this.' Sam handed her the *Chronicle*, then leaned against his favourite gate and stared sadly at the rippling field.

Greta's fingers clutched the newspaper. It wasn't her own aspidistra framed photograph which shocked her, nor the fact that the name Alexandra Hythe was linked with the road accident in which two boys had been badly injured. It was the black and white face of her mother, a photograph which she'd never seen before, of Sophia's beautiful, benevolent eyes, which cut through Greta's layers of guilt, defence and passion. The scab which covered her heart began to bleed.

Sam was talking about Sylvia, but Greta wanted to slink back into her own childhood, and change it.

'Depressive illness,' he was saying, 'exaggerates all emotions . . .'

'My mother loved me,' Greta interrupted.

'What?'

'Utterly and entirely. That's how I want to love my daughter. Just the same way. I want that chance. I have as much right to give and take love as anyone else.'

'But you can't just take love. That's your problem. You tried to snatch a child away from people who have loved her since she was days old. It was unforgivable.'

'But she's my daughter, and I have more right than anyone else . . .'

247

'You have no right! You left that child without looking back.' Sam ran his fingers through his hair. 'Tell you what. Let's go to the police tomorrow, with the truth. They can test your blood groups. It could all be solved.'

'No!'

Wrongly, he read cowardice into the stubborn turn of her head.

'Yes! For everyone's sake. Confess. Sort it out.'

'I can't. Trust me, Sam, there are reasons.'

'None that are good enough!'

Greta's gaze fell from the purple sculptured horizon to the clover at her feet. Was it time to tell Sam her darkest secret? TELL HIM! TELL HIM!

'You're a lost cause, Alexandra. Gutless and selfish. You have no compassion, no conscience!'

Echoes of his outburst sang away into the hills.

'You call me Alexandra, but the woman you met in Kings Cross was Greta – a woman whose life was full of abuse and deprivation. Sam – I can't go to the police because Greta Korda did something bad . . .'

'I DON'T WANT TO HEAR THIS!'

'FINE!' Her lips tightened around her guilt. There was a sting in her eyes which she hated. 'You overflow with sympathy for Sylvia. But I've longed for my child too. Endless months and years. I'm no different from her; I just carry the pain in my own way.' Her voice cracked. 'Alexandra wanders cities with a swagger and a smile, but inside Greta is watching. Nannies pushing prams in Hyde Park. Little girls chasing the pigeons in St Mark's Square, or trying on tiny dresses in Paris. Oh, Sam, Alice is mine. I knew it as soon as I saw her.

Three years ago I had nothing to offer a daughter. Now I have.'

'Money? Nice little cheques from Italy? Does that qualify you to be a decent parent? What about the child's feelings? What about young Sylvia's?'

'Sylvia can have other babies!'

'*You* can have other babies!'

'Oh yes? I'm thirty. Who'd want to marry me now? Not you, Samuel Phillips, that's for certain. Hardly the amorous suitor these days, are you? Alexandra didn't quite live up to expectations.' Bitterness stung like nettles. 'You need someone as boringly virtuous as yourself. Don't worry about me; I'll look for another bastard like Dick. That's all I deserve.'

'Miss the dirt under your fingernails, do you?' He stood before her, pointing. 'You'll never make a decent man a decent wife!'

'A decent man's never asked me.' She slapped away his finger. 'It's ME who's the dirt under YOUR fingernails. The Filthy Gypsy. That's what you see when you close your eyes, isn't it? That's what you smell. I let you taste the filth in your own mind.'

In that moment Sam was as near hitting a woman as he would ever be. Not because of the insult, but because it was the truth. He vaulted over the gate and strode out into the lane.

Greta sat shaking, breathless with the havoc in her heart. The intensity of her emotions was shocking. She had an overwhelming compulsion to fly after Sam and dig her fingers into his stubborn shoulders, to kiss his face until he kissed back. That beast called LOVE, soiled and confused, contrary and spiteful, came crawling out of the darkness. Perversely, in the very instant she finally lost him, Greta understood what it was to love a man.

Stupid, stupid bitch, she swore at herself. You could have settled down in this lovely country town, cooked and cleaned and planted vegetables. Made friends. Made babies. Decent? I am decent. Underneath . . .

She took to her feet and sprinted until she caught up with him and grasped his arm.

'Sam! Forgive me. You're the most honestly good man that ever walked this Earth. Listen . . . please.'

He stood stock still, staring straight ahead into a tunnel of arching trees.

'I've always been afraid of men's love. My childhood, my father . . . who knows why?' She faltered over unrehearsed sentences. 'But you're the only man in the world who makes me feel – whole. I'll change. Teach me. Help me to learn – integrity. I'm so ashamed. Slates don't get wiped clean, I know. But I want a better future. A good clean future. With you.'

'You don't fool me, Alexandra. What you really want is a respectable father figure so that you can offer Alice a perfect family, complete with money, security and background. Well, I won't be used!'

'No! I promise! I love you. With or without Alice. We could have another child. Yours and mine. Oh, Sam, please.' What was the biggest, most convincing gesture she could make? 'Sam. If I give up any claim to Alice. Leave Sylvia to bring up my baby . . .'

'Yes?'

'. . . would you marry me, Sam?'

'You'd use your child as currency for a bridal veil? Oh, Alexandra.'

❖

By Wednesday morning Violet Sharp's eyes were raw. She had forgotten to pencil on her eyebrows, so the sockets were framed by thin, shiny skin. Her cheeks were sunken, jowls hanging in little puffs on either side of her trembling chin.

She answered the door nervously, to be confronted by a woman with silver plaits wrapped around her head.

'I'm Sylvia's friend, Mrs Sharp. Is your 'usband at 'ome?'

Cramps rumbled in Violet's colon.

'I'm called Liz, and I'm straight as a pencil. You and me needs to 'ave a chat.'

Leaden with dread and hope, Violet looked towards the car, where Alexandra Hythe sat stiffly at the wheel.

'Have you found Sylvia?'

'YES.'

Violet gasped.

'But she's poorly. Shock. Poor lamb's all of a do. Best if her mam comes first. Dad might – say things wrong,' Liz faltered. 'I've got bairns of my own, and grandbairns. You and me, we 'ave to trust each other, because if we can't get Sylvia better she might have a breakdown.'

Violet rushed down the path in her slippers, then stopped and ran back again. 'Me bag!'

She hesitated for a moment before getting into a car. The madwoman was at the wheel. The one who swapped babies and kidnapped girls. But Violet was never short of courage, so she climbed in, slammed the door and glared at Greta's back.

The dented Hillman shot off. Strange noises vibrated through the chassis because a chunk of the exhaust had fallen off. The ripped hood was fastened down with string, so gusts of air buffeted the women, rendering conversation impossible. Violet's fine hair whipped into her eyes and her ears began to ache, but she bore the discomfort proudly, a million questions rushing through her head.

Outside Stannington, the madwoman suddenly stopped the car and turned an icy stare on her.

'There must be no questions about where Sylvia has been. And you must say nothing about my conversation with your husband. Do you agree, Mrs Sharp?'

'Why?'

'If you don't promise, I'll drive you straight back home.'

'Does she know you muddled up the babies?'

'No. I may never tell her.'

'Well, Alice has Sylvia's nose and David's hair and Katherine's mischief. She's owa baby. So put that in your pipe and smoke it.'

'Will you promise me, Mrs Sharp?'

'Is she, has she been . . . a prostitute?' Violet tensed her shoulders bravely.

The older woman scowled. 'She's a good lass. Never looked twice at a lad in all these years. Fat lot of good it did 'er.'

The madwoman with glacier eyes said, 'The shock of

seeing David with her sister . . . she just won't talk about it. In fact she won't talk about anything. Mrs Sharp, Sylvia is very, very upset – too vulnerable for any more shocks.'

'How convenient.' Violet knew folk always underestimated her intelligence.

❖

Hendo was only alive in his head. His mam's worried face swam before him. He needed to breathe and her wet cheeks were pressed against his nose. Air! He needed air. His mouth felt dry, his tongue paralysed. Grunt grunt. Let me breathe. Grunt. Let me sit up.

Already exhausted, his head went back to sleep.

❖

Violet made no attempt to take her daughter's hand. Nor did she fall into the trap of smiling. Humbled, she stood several feet away from her dear, lost daughter, trying simply to meet her eyes, hoping that love and sorrow, gladness and humility could all be exchanged in a tender look.

But Sylvia would not return her earnest gaze.

Her daughter had changed beyond recognition. She stood staring out of the window, with her arms folded protectively over her breastless chest. During those silent seconds Violet battled to come to terms with her daughter's shocking appearance. No part of Sylvia looked right. She had grown very tall and her limbs were like a bag of sticks. Her hair was black as Hell's chimney, unhealthily dry and wispy. Out of her waxen face her pale eyes seemed to bulge, glassy, unfocused. The madwoman was right, Sylvia was ill.

The longer Violet stared, the further away her daughter seemed. And yet the love she felt for her firstborn daughter surfaced with a breadth and depth which overwhelmed her.

'Sylvia pet,' she began gently, 'they say you've been badly.' She reached out an arm, then withdrew it. 'They say not to ask you things . . .' Violet's nose was dripping; she fumbled for a hanky. 'It's understandable you're a bit shook up. It was a turrible accident. A shock. But David's gonna be all right. Everything's gonna be fine now. Dad and me and Kath and David, we've looked after Alice – for you. Just wait'n for you to come home.'

With still no shift in Sylvia's countenance Violet faltered and began again. 'Let's get you better, love. Get some roses back in them cheeks. Lord, lass, what have you done with your hair?' A sudden thought hit Violet. She fished in her handbag and brought out an old, dog-eared photograph. It was a hand-tinted monochrome of a little girl with long amber pigtails.

She walked towards her daughter's angular shoulder, and offered the picture. 'I carry this with uz all the time. To keep you close.'

Sylvia's long, bony fingers took the photograph.

'Look,' said Violet gently, 'that's owa old front room. You've got your party dress on. It was your birthday.'

'You gave Dothy a magic colouring book.'

'Oh!' Violet was startled at the depth of Sylvia's voice. 'I did. You said you wouldn't wear that dress unless Dothy had a present.'

Perhaps, thought Violet, with a jerk of intuition, I'm the only person who really accepted Dothy. Invisible or not, she was Sylvia's closest friend for most of her childhood. I must try to understand my lass again.

'You've got another birthday soon, love. Eighteen. All grown up.'

Sylvia's pale eyes, frilled with spiky, black, mascaraed lashes, finally met her mother's. Violet let her own warmth, painfully burdened with emotion, flow towards her daughter. Gently, she reached out.

❖

Sam, Greta and Liz stood huddled in the hall beside the crack-faced clock. Glances darted uncomfortably between the worried trio as they listened at the door. Mustard's ears twitched. They all heard it. A yelp, as a dog yelps when it is accidentally trodden on. Sam rushed into the room.

Violet and Sylvia were locked in an embrace and Sylvia was stroking her mother's greying perm.

❖

Mary Linden made her telephone call to Douglas Hythe. The gratitude in the great musician's voice was extremely rewarding, as was the silence when she told him he might have a grandchild. There was power in that silence, and Mary savoured a youthful rush of exhilaration in the pit of her stomach. This was going to be exciting.

❖

'You did what?' bellowed Cuthbert. 'Went all the bloody way to bloody Fontbury with two bloody madwomen and went to see owa Sylvia all by yer bloody self?'

'Ask yourself why. Look at you – all puffed up. What use would you have been around a sick lass? And have nee doubt, Cuth, owa Sylvia's in a bad way.'

'What d'you mean?'

'She's gone like a skeleton, like summut out of a concentration camp – nearly dead. Ye gods and little fishes! That's what you and me have done to owa daughter, Cuth.'

'You went behind me back!' he blustered. 'Are you gonna tell uz what she said?'

'Nowt. That's the point. She just stood there like a statue. Smiled at the vet as if he was God.' Violet rubbed her arm. How crafty Sylvia had been. How swiftly her eyes had changed. 'Ee, Cuth, I think she's gone a bit . . . mental.'

'Batty? Is that why she ran off?'

'Summut's turned her.'

'That bloody veterinary got her in his clutches, and that fuck'n gypo woman . . .'

'Hold your foul language! Your gob's got enough to answer for already.'

'Why did you go up there, without me?' asked Cuthbert helplessly.

'You'd've made bad worse.'

'She can't stop with perverts.'

'They're not perverts. The posh gypsy's certainly nutty as a fruitcake, but the other woman, Liz, is kind enough. Her and the vet's just worried to death about Sylvia.'

'When's she come'n home?'

'This isn't Sylvia's home. That's half the problem.'

'Are her and that vet have'n sex?'

'How am I supposed to know?' Violet shouted at him

because she had been wondering the same thing herself. 'Whatever's going on, Sylvia's gonna have to stop there till we sort out this mess with Katherine and young David.'

'Aye,' conceded Cuthbert. 'And if Sylvia's gone loony, best keep her away from owa bairn.'

Violet groaned. Cuthbert's love for Alice was blind beyond logic.

'But Cuth, she's not owa bairn!'

'She's not that bloody gypsy's!'

'No! Alice *has* a mam and dad, whether you like it or not. And we've gorra get owa Sylvia better so she can look after Alice.'

'But what if the mad bitch tries to grab the bairn again?'

'When the vet bloke ran uz home, he said that she'd admitted to him that it wasn't true. None of it. Mind, I don't see how she'd be so certain one day, then change her mind the very next.'

'Well, she was a gypo one day and Sandra the bloody Rich the next! Best telephone Ethel. Tell her to keep owa bairn safe until that madwoman is reet out of the road.'

❖

Violet sat at her dressing table and slid off her cardigan. A pinch. Just a little pinch and such a big bruise. Had Sylvia's claw grip been the result of overwhelming emotion? Or something much more horrible?

❖

Liz stood solemnly in front of Sam, who was reading Thursday morning's *Journal*.

'Greta's packing. She's runnin away again. It's got to be a habit, and I don't like it.'

'We've agreed to finish.' He shook the paper and slapped the page straight.

'Who agreed?'

'That's private.'

'So you've dumped Greta while you slaver over Sylvia, because you think t'younger lass is all frail and needs lookin' after. Samuel Phillips, for an intelligent bloke, you're thick as shit.'

'What?'

'Greta needs more love than anybody. You pander to Sylvia, yet you don't allow Greta any feelins at all. Or any . . .' she searched for the word, 'fragileness.'

'Fragility.' Sam sneered sarcastically, as if Greta was the least fragile being he knew. 'She is a cheat, a liar and utterly ruthless. I simply don't understand her.'

'You don't understand passion.'

'Of course I do.'

'Not Greta's type of passion. You don't understand the way she loves.'

'No, I don't.'

'Did she cry when you told her to go?'

'No.'

'No, she wouldn't.'

Sam put down the paper and closed his eyes. 'She's hard. I've always known that. Perhaps I even used to find that toughness attractive. But not any more. I'm sorry, Liz, but I can't respect her. That's an end to it.'

'Well, I respect her. She doesn't weep like Sylvia, but that's no measure of how she feels. You might be a good man, Sam, but in comparison to Greta, you're as shallow as a saucer.' She stomped into the kitchen.

A while later Sam came to lean against the cooker.

'Liz,' he was subdued, thoughtful, 'I know you and Tony love Alexandra. Why?'

'She's brave.'

'It's not brave to keep dodging everything.'

'She learned bad lessons too young. To survive, she always had to run away and hide. Been doin it since she was twelve.' Liz put down her towel and twirled her fingers in the bowl of water. 'She was just a bairn when she landed on Tony's doorstep with nowt but a spare pair of knickers. Some wretched, horrible fury was locked in 'er little heart, but she held her head high and her mouth clamped shut.'

'It was to do with her father. She told me.'

'Maybe you know more than me. But I remember how she hung on to me, not cryin, but wantin to.'

'Yesterday, when she saw the picture of her mother, she was more upset than I've ever seen her.'

'Did she tell you that she'd nursed her mam, all by herself, to death's door and beyond?'

'No.'

'Sores and nappies and pain, she'd dealt with the lot. My lasses were still babies at twelve. Sally, my eldest, she's a fine nurse now, but she wouldn't have been able to do what that lass did for her mam. When Tony brought Greta to me, all she had in her school satchel was a picture of Sophia, a tiny knitted teddy, and a wallet. Fair broke my heart, that wallet.'

'She stole her father's money.'

'Not that kind of wallet. This was Sophia's. Tied with ribbon. On t'front, written all beautifully, it said, "OUR DAUGHTER, ALEXANDRA BEATRICE HYTHE" and inside was 'er birth certificate and some baby photographs. A picture of a dog. Kiddy paintings.' Liz got out her hanky. 'But it was the letters. Dear Mummy letters, in baby writing, all up and down and words the wrong way round. And silly poems that her mam wrote. Oh dear.' Liz blew her nose. 'And on t'top was an envelope. She wouldn't let me touch it. But she opened it and let me look. It was full of black hair.'

Sam rubbed his brow. 'I can feel desperately sorry for her, as a child. But as an adult, she seems to have no integrity at all.'

'And how do you suppose that might have happened?'

'Circus life, I suppose.'

'She left us when she was a bairn and didn't join the circus until she was seventeen. How the hell do you think she lived between?'

The next morning Sam drove Liz and Greta to Newcastle Central Station, where he stood, with his hands tucked into his armpits, watching the train curve away over the High Level Bridge.

❖

Mary Linden patted powder over her small nose. She smoothed on leather gloves, slipped into a camel swing jacket and checked her face. Mirror, mirror on the wall? It complimented her today. A halo of blonde curls, angelic blue eye shadow, pearls around her throat – she looked positively adorable. The blatant admiration of the young reporter had done wonders for her mood. Pressing her little finger against the corner of her cupid's bow lips, she had no idea that some lipstick had bled upwards into her wrinkles. Vanity forbade spectacles.

Mystery solving, she said to herself, suits me.

Mary arrived at the restaurant before Hythe. As she waited, beautifully poised, at the table, she was extremely gratified to nod her head slightly at the Man from Pearl, who called for his money every week and was presently dining with a woman who was not his wife. The insurance salesman had always flirted with her. Now, when he saw that Mary dined with CELEBRITIES, he would understand why she had always looked down her neat nose at him. And if Arthur found out about her tryst? So what?

When Hythe finally made his entrance, the brilliance of his smile and his dashing charisma stopped Pearl's fork midmouthful. Glamour sat comfortably on the musician's dark-suited shoulders; he courted audiences instinctively. Mary extended her hand. Douglas took it and bowed slightly. The dated gesture did not go unnoticed. In Newcastle people did not do things like that. Never had. Never would.

Eye to eye contact was something Mary rarely enjoyed or employed, unless she was extremely angry; but on this occasion she met Douglas Hythe's gaze boldly. They rushed through essential preliminaries with exaggerated aplomb, both eager to get down to the business of exchanging information. Although they shared a taste for direct speech they were also both masters of pretence.

Mary was playing the role of grief-stricken mother. But all the while she was thinking – what beautiful eyes he has, they cut straight through me, and it's delicious, as if he's daring to look under my skin. Or maybe under my clothes. We're using each other, deliberately. We've already abandoned any pretence of middle-class morals. Although we haven't said the words, we are both admitting that our families infuriate and disappoint us. I like him. I really like him.

Just as Mary had recently discovered the strange, clutching power of her maternal feelings for David, something in her hormones also made her emotionally vulnerable to Douglas Hythe. He asked his questions so humbly, and his directness made her feel – what was it? SEXY. Oh dear.

By the time she sipped her coffee she was already infatuated with the fantasy which was Douglas Hythe, but as he rose to leave and kissed her cheek, she sighed. There might be luscious titillation in this new-found, not very secret liaison – but it could never be sexually fulfilling. Not with her varicose veins.

❖

Hythe was indeed a fantasy. In his manipulative way he had rather enjoyed playing old-fashioned court to a gullible, middle-aged woman. And the outcome was so satisfactory! He left the restaurant feeling uplifted with truths. Now he knew it all. A grandfather, his heart laughed, I am a flaming grandfather! With grossly unpaternal glee he revelled in the knowledge of his daughter's mistakes and secrets. So much for her moralistic judgmentalism!

A baby! To a gypsy. Nonno Marletti would positively seethe! And Alexandra had actually tried to swap the child with someone else's, then abandoned it! Surely she would never dare look down her nose at her own father again.

Things to do. He checked into his hotel and demanded a telephone.

At four p.m. Douglas Hythe took a taxi to the offices of the *Evening Chronicle* and after reading back copies from three years ago, was rewarded with a plethora of information about young Sylvia and her 'gypsy' friend. The start point for his search was contained in a single paragraph.

'A second baby was left behind on the same night by a gypsy from the travelling fair. Pictured above is Janice Kirkstone, the young nurse who discovered the empty beds.'

Next stop, the Maternity Hospital.

It should have taken him longer, but where scandal lurks, tongues wag. Douglas found his informant in the rather stocky shape of a midwife called Ada Parks. He turned up his charisma to full force, spreading his charm over Ada in a blush of flattery. His efforts were well rewarded.

By the following day, Douglas knew the whereabouts of both babies. A few door knocks in Kenton and it had been astonishingly easy to locate Janice Kirkstone. All he had to do now was to determine which child was his granddaughter.

The door of the Kirkstones' council flat was opened by a plain young woman in a frilly apron. For an instant Douglas could not look the woman in the face because behind her legs a small, dark-haired girl was pushing a doll's pram up and down the hall. Realizing suddenly that the nurse might think he was eying her ankles, he smiled and spoke so, so sincerely.

'I have some very distressing news for you, my dear. But if you hear me out, I think I may be able to help you.'

It was Friday afternoon and Arthur hovered impatiently in the tiled hallway of their home, watching his wife try on hats. Hospital visiting had become a ritual and she was running out of felt concoctions. It saddened him to think that Mary was a nightly form of entertainment in sick beds and the hospital canteen.

When the telephone jangled Mary grabbed it. Because they were so late Arthur went meekly to wait in the car, so he did not see the flutter of his wife's curled eyelashes as she listened to Douglas Hythe's news. Nor did he notice, as he drove to the hospital, Mary biting off her peach lipstick.

❖

Janice Kirkstone should have put baby Jan to bed. She should have cooked her husband's tea, ironed his shirts. Instead she rocked in her chair, cradling her sleepy child, daydreaming about a blindfolded knife-thrower and a foolhardy assistant fastened to his spinning target. The scenario kept changing, people swapping roles: Matthew, showing off, twirling blades, the horrible, horrible Mr Hythe, blindfolded and screaming. Then she stood by the wheel herself, and spun it faster and faster while a gypsy woman dressed in sequins begged to be freed from her lashings.

But the gypsy wasn't a gypsy at all. Little Jan's legal mother was certainly the woman in the paper, Alexandra Hythe. Worse still, Jan's grandmother was the fabulous, dead, Sophia Marletti. Janice gazed down at the toddler's sweet sleeping face. Dark lashes made sweeping crescents on pale cheeks and her rosebud mouth puckered around a pink dummy. Would she grow into a great beauty?

Janice had answered Hythe well, parrying the man's aggressive questions with her own, replying in vague mutters, 'Don't know, can't be sure, can't remember.'

Three years ago. Despite her feigned, dim-witted denials, she had the clearest memory of walking into that empty side ward and finding

❖

both babies, nose to nose, in the same cot. They were surprisingly alike, both much too beautiful to have been abandoned by the feckless mothers whose beds were empty.

While nurses scurried and searched, Janice lifted one of the babies. Under the blanket was a tiny knitted teddy bear, a clumsy, gaudy thing, with black, accusing eyes. Her anger at the shiftless mothers melted into poignancy. Were these the stitches of the broken teenager or the beaten gypsy? She slid it into her pocket.

When Sister defiantly slapped new labels on separate cots, Janice kept quiet, although the teddy bear in her pocket could have told his own story.

She fed and changed each infant in turn, her own needy heart flowing towards these abandoned babies; she would willingly have taken either home with her.

Then the teenager's family muscled in. An elderly woman lifted one baby, Janice gently picked up the other.

❖

Now, wrestling with her holy conscience, the Devil kept winning. How could she arm herself for the moment when the authorities came knocking? Or would they? Was there some devious reason for Hythe's seedy, con-man approach? His final advice to 'urgently test her memory' was blatantly a threat.

Blinded by flying knives, she failed to hear the door slam. Only when he was standing in front of her with his fists planted on his hips did she acknowledge her husband. Even then, Janice ignored his hungry ranting. She lifted her child closer to her breast, and said, 'If you want to keep our baby, Matt, you'll have to speak to me with a bit more respect, because it's happened, you see. They want her back. And only I can stop them.'

'WHAT?'

'Seems that our little lass has a very rich grandfather. And I've been thinking that I don't much like my marriage. That I don't much like me in it. But by God, I love this bairn and so do you. If we want to keep her, we've got to fight this together. Now, put the kettle on and make a brew.'

'But I'm famished.'

'What's more important, your baby or your belly?'

For the first time in their marriage Matthew put a match under the kettle and searched for the tea caddy.

Janice put knives aside and firmed up her plan. The key to keeping Jan was CONFUSION. How could they give the child to anyone, unless they were quite sure who had given birth to her?

❖

'Get the door, Vi!' Cuthbert's back was aching with heaving coal and he sat in his tired chair with his tired head in his tired hands.

Violet was nervously pushing her hair into place as she ushered an impeccably dressed man into their front room. A bloke with a smile to cut glass. Who?

Rousing himself, Cuthbert shook his hand, then withdrew it quickly when the bloke introduced himself as the father of the madwoman Alexandra Hythe! Bloody nerve! Uninvited, the charmer made himself comfortable on their settee. Already the coalman wanted to punch him.

Proud, defensive, Cuthbert set his feet wide on his hearth rug. 'She's owa bairn. Your daughter's admitted she lied.'

'I don't think she did, Mr Sharp.'

'Think owt you like.'

'Come now. We can do better than this. We have a mutual problem. Two babies left in a hospital with no form of identification. Which is which? I gather Alice isn't here?'

'She's out the bloody way! Till yous lot bugger off.'

'I was simply wondering if some likeness would be apparent.'

'She's the double of owa Katherine!' Violet chimed in.

Hythe nodded sagely. 'I've just seen the other baby. I'm fairly sure I can see my late wife in her.'

'The other bairn?' Cuthbert was incredulous. 'Why, man, that'll be YOUR one then.'

'Perhaps. But I've been doing some research. Apparently the only person who could distinguish one from the other was a nurse called Janice. Now this young woman, very surprisingly, is fostering the other child – has been for some time. Make no mistake; she will fight to keep her. I've questioned her at length. No good. She pretends ignorance. Clever move, don't you think? How can I claim my grandchild when I cannot prove that she is mine? She may even be your grand-child, Mr Sharp. Surely we must find out.'

'What's she like,' Violet was asking eagerly, 'this other little girl? Does she live in a nice place? Is this Janice a good mam?'

'Child is dark-haired, like Alexandra and her family. Her face is quite fine, I suppose. Small features, blue eyes. They live in a flat, council, clean. Janice clearly adores the child.'

Cuthbert was thinking like a man, combatively. 'Hus-band?'

'I get the impression he is somewhat belligerent.'

While Violet poured two thimbles of sherry, Cuthbert frowned into his bushy red eyebrows. If this other baby was proved to be the gypsy's bairn then it would all be over and done with. The madwoman could do her kidnapping act else-where. Hythe seemed crafty and powerful: a fearful enemy, a useful ally.

'Mebees we should go see these people. But for God's sake leave that batty daughter of yours out of it. We can do with-out her dramatics.'

'Agreed. Alexandra can be told when we're sure of the facts.'

Cuthbert felt a wave of irritation when Violet sat next to the posh bloke. Their elbows were touching as she said, 'My lass, she's having a – a breakdown, or some such thing.'

'Then we mustn't upset her.' Hythe turned his glittering smile on her. 'We'll sort this out between us. Perhaps by tomorrow the Kirkstone woman will have cleared her head.'

'We'll have to tell the Lindens,' worried Violet.

Cuthbert sniggered. 'I suppose one of them already knows?'

'A charming woman, Mary.'

❖

Unaware of her father's manoeuvres, Greta was sitting on North Bay beach in Scarborough. It was twilight. She let cool sand trickle through her fingers. The weight of Tony's hand on her shoulder made her want to cry, but she couldn't.

'Go back to Italy.'

'Not yet. I can't face Nonno's questions. And I'm not ready to leave Alice. She's my daughter, Tony. How can I walk away? Perhaps if Sam and I had settled down – maybe I could have had another child. But Sam despises me, with good reason. And now I may never be a mother.'

'Like for me.' Tony shook his large head. 'It is a great sadness not to have children. Maybe this time next year you will be married to an Italian count.'

'You've been reading Liz's romances again.'

'What about this other child – born to your name?'

Greta rubbed her chin on Tony's hand. 'If she isn't mine, she's best left where she is. Oh, Tony, Alice looked so like my mother.'

'Sylvie,' asked Tony carefully, 'she know infanzia muddled up?'

'No. She's too sore and vulnerable. There's an anger inside of her. It seems to have taken her into a dark, secret corner. She only comes out to blame me.'

'Blame is too hot for holding.' Tony shook his head.

'Sylvie will see Alice now? This deceit is bad. When truth comes out . . .'

'I don't think it will. The Sharps are still convinced Sylvia is Alice's mother. What can I do? Sam tried to make me promise not to fight them. So Sylvia may always believe Alice is hers.'

'More pain to come. I feel it.' He stood up and brushed sand from his drooping backside.

'Tony, can I stay here for now? I've been wondering,' she enthused suddenly, 'about Hisper Cottage and the land. It's a proposition, a business project for both of us. What about making it into a holiday site?'

'Caravans! Ona my field?' Tony was outraged. 'With lavatory blocks. Eugh! Never!'

'Not caravans. Little bungalows, like cottages. Pretty miniature houses painted in pastel colours, pink and yellow. Fully plumbed, with kitchens and bathrooms. Lawned gardens and a proper path down to the beach. A shop with milk and papers, sweets for the kids. It could be charming. I've got money . . .'

'Stolen?'

'It was as much my money as Dick's. I was his wife.'

'And Sylvia? Hisper Cottage is her home also, Greta.'

'Sylvia can be manager. A job. Don't you see? She can bring Alice, live and work for herself, still playing mother in Hisper Cottage.'

'Mothering your child?' He grieved at her desperation.

'Sylvia would be happy. That's what matters. Isn't it, Tony?'

He strode down to the tideline and let shallow foam curl

around his hairy toes, savouring the chill which tingled up his legs and into his groin.

Would he ever be able to come to terms with his feelings for this woman? All respect had dissolved, and yet there it remained, private and solid as ever. A love which was without label. A love which transcended sex, and blood. A very strange love indeed.

❖

Alone in her room in Fontbury, Sylvia opened the window and leaned on the sill, watching the sunset with an extraordinary surge of happiness. She felt fine. Soon Alice would be hers again, wonderful Sam was only feet away and Greta had gone.

As she stared at the glossed clouds, contemplating joy, a voice spoke behind her. Its tone was light and high, yet strongly masculine.

Hail to thee, blithe spirit!

Sylvia whipped around. All she could see was her own dark reflection in a mirror, silhouetted by the fiery, falling sky.

Bird thou never wert . . . ? Ha!

Ghostly singing filled the room.

. . . all a green willow,
I, said the sparrow,
with my bow and arrow,
Tock. Tock.

A phalanx of grandparents

mounted the stairs. Douglas Hythe was the polished spearhead. Behind him marched Arthur Linden and Cuthbert Sharp. Bringing up the rear, their wives – Violet, clutching a package, and Mary, who had chosen for the occasion an extravagant turquoise hat with trailing peacock feathers.

Oh, Mary, didn't you know how unlucky the big feather eyes are?

Round and round the stairs spiralled. As they passed the second floor Mary scowled at a woman in curlers. On the third floor, Matthew Kirkstone answered his door in rolled-up shirtsleeves. He folded his muscular forearms across his chest. Lean, young and strong, he stood firm in his doorway, ready to protect his lair.

'What's this? Pensioners' bus trip?'

Mary hated him immediately, and decided to win, even if she was disinterested in the prize.

'Droll,' smiled her hero Douglas. 'My name is . . .'

'I know who you are. Come back to bully my missus

again? Well, I don't scare so easily. I'd thank you to leave. That's polite for bugger off.'

'Mr Kirkstone,' Douglas attempted civility, 'this is an unusual and painful situation for us all. It must be resolved legally. The child you have been looking after is either my granddaughter . . .'

'. . . or ours,' piped up Violet.

The woman in curlers came to the bottom of the stairs. 'All right up there, Matthew?'

'Aye, Jess. Just Jehovah's Witnesses. I'll get rid.'

So the potential witness called Jess slammed her door, which, for Mary, was just as well.

In her position at the rear, Mary was thoroughly enjoying herself. This scene had been composed and directed by her. She felt proud and powerful, like a queen with three knights striding before her, preparing her way. The masterful, musical voice of Douglas Hythe was challenging the enemy in lyrical allegro.

'The child belongs to one of our families. I strongly suspect your dear wife knows which. These good people need answers and we have come to ask her again what she remembers.'

'Bollocks. You've come to take the bairn away. And you'll not. Not even over my dead body, cos my missus is Jan's mam now, and she'll never give her up. Now clear off before I call the police.'

'Perhaps we can help her remember.' Douglas drew out his wallet.

I wonder how much is in it, thought Mary.

'You think I'd sell our Jan like a china doll? She's flesh and blood – and she's ours.'

'But the law . . .'

'Sod the law. Anyhow, grandparents have no rights over kids.'

Mary's boringly good knight Sir Arthur intervened.

'We simply want to ask if, in all compassion, she can help us – understand. It's terribly upsetting. The child we love may not be ours. The little girl who lives with you may, in fact, be our real granddaughter. And you must be aware that you have no permanent claim to the child.'

'Aye,' Cuthbert Sharp put in his two penneth. 'And her real mam does have rights, whether that's my lass or his.'

'So where are these two women you call mothers,' demanded Matthew Kirkstone, 'while their mammies and daddies do their dirty work? A right pair! Buggering off while their babies' cords stumps were still bleeding. Prossies, are they? Pink Lane Tarts? What magistrate would take Jan out of a decent family and give her over to a whore?'

A giggle bubbled up inside Mary, making her peacock feathers twitch. Kirkstone turned on her.

'Hit your funny bone, did I, dear?'

But Queen Mary met his gaze with her pert little nose up. She elbowed past Arthur to take her place at the front.

'Tarts they may be – no, Arthur, don't try to shush me – but your wife's little secret is just as dirty as theirs.' Impressed with herself for thinking of this, she continued, 'She's trying to trick us. We'll take her to court. Mr Hythe is famous. Your wife has stolen his granddaughter.'

Kirkstone sneered. 'You lot don't want the courts. I know your type. Plant flowers in your own shit.'

'Oh!' Mary looked back to Sir Douglas for support and her feathers hit Matthew over the nose. 'The man's an ignoramus.'

'Up *your* amus!' answered Kirkstone. He tried to slam the door but Cuthbert Sharp leaned heavily on it.

'Na,' said the earthy knight of the pit head. 'We demand to see the little'un.'

'We'll not hurt her.' Violet knit her sincere, pencilled brows.

'For the last time, fuck off!'

Douglas pulled himself erect. 'Such offensive language is—'

'Fuck off, I said, you pompous prat!'

Mary was incensed. How dare this common young man insult the world-famous, cultured, charming personage of Douglas Hythe (the knight whose image now charged all her sexual fantasies)? She shook her fist in Kirkstone's face. 'Watch your filthy tongue, boy!'

'Boy?' Matthew curled his fingers around her gloved knuckles. 'What, old lady? Gonna smack me? Be warned, missus. I am no dirty, ignorant Geordie miner. Not your average, coal-humping caveman.'

❖

Caveman. Violet groaned, knowing this innocent word would cause mayhem. To any man who had worked down a mine, 'caveman' was the ultimate insult, usually levelled by white collar workers or clean-mittened southerners who struggled

275

to lift a scuttle. She watched her husband's temper rise from his boots to his eyeballs, her own stomach contracting in fear.

Thick neck bulging, Cuthbert pushed his nose into the younger man's face. 'You're look'n at one of those coal humpers, and if a can swing a bag of slack owa me shoulder, a can show a pup like you what's for.'

Matthew Kirkstone didn't flinch from Cuthbert's flying spittle. 'Who you trying to scare, teddy bear?' He shoved Cuthbert away like a boy in a playground.

Just then, from inside the flat, little Jan shouted, 'DADDA!'

Cuthbert set his jaw. 'You'll not stop us seeing that bairn. She's ours, not yours.' He lifted his elbow and tried to shoulder the younger man aside.

'Bastard,' swore Kirkstone, and he slung his arm around Cuthbert's neck, choking him, pulling him backwards, trying to throw him out. But the furious coalman had crafty, stocky strength. Like a gorilla, Cuthbert bent his knees and thrust his barrel chest forward, taking Kirkstone's weight on his shoulder so that the lighter man lost his footing and slid sideways.

As he fell on his own carpet, in his own narrow hallway, Kirkstone curled his arms around Cuthbert's knees and yanked. Violet's hefty husband lost his balance and hit the wall, leaving a mark on the wallpaper. The younger man scrambled to his feet and launched all his weight, but Cuthbert pushed back just as hard, and in the narrow space he held his ground. Panting and grunting, they locked together like wrestlers.

Maddened, Kirkstone slapped the heel of his hand against his opponent's chin, sinking strong fingers into Cuthbert's rubbery lips, stretching his hand across his bulbous nose. Violet heard her husband's neck crack as Kirkstone shoved Cuthbert's face backwards. The caveman-coalman swung a punch at Matthew's ribs – but he couldn't reach.

Then the peace-loving Arthur Linden grabbed Cuthbert by the trouser belt, attempting to yank him off, and all three fell out on to the landing.

Fists were flying now and poor Arthur was trapped in the middle of frantic, clumsy punches. He kept trying to push the opponents apart, but both men were stronger than him and the more they hurt him, the rougher his own shoves became. Instinctively protective, Arthur shouted for his wife to get herself safely out of the way. Obediently, Mary started to flee down the stairs but, reluctant to miss the action, she ran back up again.

It disgusted Violet to see Mary join in, punching at them all with her small gloved fists, grunting with the effort. As the fracas moved towards the top of the stairs, her turquoise hat, with its dead feathers, flew over the banister and dropped down the stairwell.

Douglas Hythe was inching backwards along the wall, with his piano-playing fingers tucked safely behind him. Janice Kirkstone was tugging at her husband's shirt.

And Violet saw a tiny dark-haired girl cowering in the flat doorway. Her own body as still as the core of a tornado, she stared at the child called Jan.

❖

How did it happen?

Cuthbert had found a new balance. His face contorted as

277

he jumped and rammed his forehead at Kirkstone's. There was a crack of skulls. All three women yelped and everything stopped. In the background the child was crying. Matthew was holding his bleeding nose. Cuthbert was panting. Arthur put his hands on his hips and bent to catch his breath.

If only it had stopped there. But, as Arthur wearily walked between the two opponents, they both took a final swipe. One blow hit Arthur Linden on the temple, the other in the chest. The momentum sent him spinning towards Mary. Unbalanced, his elbow dug into her chest. Furious, Arthur's wife shoved him off her with all her strength.

He did not tumble down the stairs.

There is a place at the top of most staircases where the rising banister meets the landing banister. Just on that top stair the junction has an inadequate geometry, a deceptive design flaw where protection is not as high as one might presume. The vulnerable spot usually goes unnoticed, unless, like Arthur, you happen to be pushed backwards towards it.

He didn't scream. In a smooth movement, like a clown in the circus, he spread his arms and fell straight down the centre of the three-storey stairwell.

His body broke several tiles on the floor. Mary's hat, with its unlucky peacock feathers, lay next to him.

❖

At first no one dared look. Then Janice, the nurse, flew down the stairs. Cuthbert and his opponent galloped down behind her. Violet leaned over the balcony. The nurse looked up into her eyes and shook her head.

All Hell was let loose.

Kirkstone fell to his knees. He grasped the corpse's lapels, trying to shake some life back into him. Janice tried to restrain him. Behind the tableau, poor Cuthbert was whining like a baby, grasping his scalp and tugging at his red hair.

Next to Violet, Mary had covered her face with her gloves and was running on the spot, stamping her feet down hard – bang, bang, bang – as if she could trample away the horror. Just as suddenly she stopped, and fainted. Douglas Hythe, plastered against the wall, watched her fall. Terrified, traumatized, the musician made no attempt to catch her, so she landed with a thump and a head thud, knocking herself out. Mary Linden lay at Hythe's feet, a widow.

Only Violet remained calm. Her shock was full of stillness.

'Mammy! Mammy!' The toddler sat nimbly on the top step, then began to shuffle her bottom down one step at a time. Instinctively Violet bent to pick up the little girl who was exactly the same age as Alice.

'Mammy'll be back in a minute, pet. Is that your dolly's pram? Where's dolly?' She lifted little Jan and took her through the flat door, down the narrow passage and into a front room. Babies must be protected. Someone had to look after this child. Someone must work out what to do.

A long windowsill was lined with potted geraniums. Violet said a silent prayer to the sky – but great black thunderclouds hung over Newcastle city, blocking her view of Heaven.

We're all damned, she thought.

Toys littered the floor. In the corner was a rocking chair. Violet sat down and hoisted Jan on to her lap. The child's rosebud mouth quivered, but Violet still had her package and, as soon as she started opening it, the little girl's fingers grabbed at the book. Violet kissed the top of Jan's head and began to read.

There was muttering outside, footsteps running up the stairs. Violet sat still, nursing the child. I'll have this minute, she told herself. I'll have it despite everything. She stroked the little girl's hair. Baby Jan was smaller than Alice. Her fingers were slim and agile as she traced the pictures. Dark hair, wavy rather than curly, finer than Alice's, framed a heart-shaped face with such delicate features that babyhood seemed to have fled too quickly. There was a seriousness, an intelligent knowing in those blue eyes.

I won't let them hurt this child. They won't hurt any more children, Violet vowed. A decent man lies dead, maybe this little girl's grandad, and for what? For the love of a child, they killed a man. My own husband has taken a life. Mary Linden, Hythe, even this young Kirkstone lad, all grabbing, manipulating. Hurting children. Hurting one another. Killing. Over babies. It must stop. I'll make it stop.

Janice charged into the room. 'Put her down!' She dragged her baby from Violet's lap, crying, 'Don't touch her! You're all insane. You've killed a man and you'll hang. I'll make sure you all hang.'

'An accident,' stammered poor Cuthbert, who had followed her into the room. Tears were dropping down his fat nose and his mouth was slack. 'Accident. Holy Jesus!'

Douglas Hythe was dragging the prostrate Mary on to the settee.

'Get out of my home!' Janice Kirkstone cried. 'What are you doing in my home? Go away. Please go away.'

Violet rose heavily from the rocking chair. 'Where's your lad?' she asked, impressed by the calmness of her own voice. 'He's in serious trouble, you know that?'

'It wasn't Matt's fault.'

'No? Depends how you look at it. Mebees the Lord above knows it *was* an accident, but the police'll twist things. Blame somebody.'

'It was them!' Janice pointed to Cuthbert and Douglas.

'I never touched him.' Douglas's hands were twitching at the air. 'They were all fighting – not me. Your husband had a motive.'

Cuthbert had his eyes closed, as if trying to see his memory. 'It was Mary what pushed him!'

'WE'RE ALL RESPONSIBLE!' Violet's shout startled the child. 'This must end! D'you hear?' She had already scanned the next few hours, days and years, and she thought she was thinking straight. 'We need to agree what to tell the police!'

Suddenly Mary sat up, her eyes wide with horror. 'My Arthur! Who's looking after him?' She started to stagger off the settee. 'He's dead, isn't he? I've killed him. My Arthur!'

'Oh, Mary!' Violet felt heady with control. 'The accident wasn't your fault.'

'They were punching him. And I didn't mean to . . .'

'Mary, listen! These stupid bastards know right well what they've done. But no one planned to harm Arthur.'

Matthew Kirkstone appeared at the door, white as a sheet, vomit stains down his shirt. 'I've sent Jess to call the ambulance.'

'Listen, lad,' ordered Violet, 'we must think straight! Did that Jess see what happened? Any other witnesses?'

'You can't lie about this!' Janice Kirkstone had backed into a corner and was holding her baby tight.

'If we don't, your man might hang. Aye and mebees mine anall.' Violet was thinking fast. 'Was anyone watching up the stairs?'

'No. No.'

'Right.' Violet looked compassionately towards the young couple. 'I'm sorry for what we've done here today. You want to keep yer bairn. And you, Mr Kirkstone, don't want to go down for murder. So what we'll say is this – Arthur was TAKEN ILL – CLUTCHED HIS CHEST – HAD SOME SORT OF SEIZURE – AND FELL. That's what we've got to say.'

'It's a lie,' whispered the nurse.

'Aye, and a very black one. But the truth's even worse. Protect my man and we'll protect you.' She grabbed her husband's shirt sleeve. 'Tell them, Cuthbert. And you, mister,' she glared at Hythe, 'promise you'll leave this family in peace.' They both nodded. Violet felt the pressure of tears in her chest as she vowed to Janice, 'Keep this tragedy between wuselves and you'll not see these greedy, possessive men again. My word on that.'

'I'll go now,' gabbled Douglas desperately. He made for the door, but Cuthbert grabbed his shoulder.

'Now hod on, mister . . . !'

'He complicates things,' reasoned Violet. 'Best if the whole baby-switching thing is kept quiet.'

'Absolutely right.' Douglas was opening his wallet.

'Put your money away.' In a small, astonished part of her mind Violet was thinking – it's me that the girls get their brains from! I never realized. 'Now, everybody! Concentrate! We were just . . . visiting. We've all known Janice since Sylvia was in hospital. We came for tea. Poor Arthur was feeling poorly. Said it was indigestion. Held his chest, leaned over the banister, and before we knew it – he fell.' She pointed at Hythe, 'As for him, if anyone noticed him, we'll say he was that Jehovah's Witness – just happened to be calling. So, Mr Hythe, bugger off. No one ever wants to set eyes on you again.'

Douglas bolted.

Janice Kirkstone was trembling visibly. Clutching little Jan, she edged into her bedroom. Violet waited for a second, then followed her.

On the settee Mary rubbed her head. Cuthbert helped her up, while Matthew Kirkstone wrapped his arms around his waist, looked out of the window and started making deals with God.

Consciences

wept in silent torrents. Guilt was as heavy as the overburdened sky. And fear was very dark indeed. Yet, for a brief, nervous pause in history, they thought that they had got away with it.

❖

DI Howard, contented bachelor, who never ate Sunday lunch because he couldn't be bothered to cook it, was supping a bottle of Newcastle Brown and crunching pickled onions, when his telephone rang. With a deep belch, he turned off the wireless and listened carefully. A nasty accident in Kenton was looking suspicious. Man dead. Body, blocking access to flats, needed removing urgently.

He went to his sideboard and pulled out a blank exercise book, which he rolled up and slid into his jacket pocket. With a straight back and a supercilious chin, he marched down his garden path.

Howard was renowned for his panoply of dubious

crime-solving techniques, including the slippery smile, the sympathetic 'Tut tut', the empathetic blown nose and the inappropriate joke, all designed to disarm suspects by encouraging a false sense of trust. 'Better get this off your chest, pet. Oh, I understand completely. Dear-oh-deary-me. A saint would have been tempted.' His frustrated superiors squirmed and colleagues chortled as Howard befriended his suspects with a stretched grin as dangerous as a tiger's.

Oddly, however, this smart, upright man, this great ferreter after truth, possessed a shrouded emotional instinct which could compromise simple facts. Howard believed in things 'both seen and unseen', and was privately smug when he experienced acute sensory reactions which bypassed logic.

On that Sunday, as his colleague, DC Eric Butterwell, drove him to Kenton, Howard had no idea how deeply his closet sensitivities were about to be tested.

Staring at the corpse, imprinting the broken image in his diagrammatic mind, he wrote 'ARTHUR LINDEN' on the front of his book. As his colleagues prodded, poked, marked and noted, Howard began penning information on feint ruled lines, in algebraic shorthand.

Where to start? There were witnesses upstairs, a family called Kirkstone, but Linden's wife, it seemed, had already been taken home. Raw, fresh widows were as tender as rare steak, and they had to be tackled immediately, before complicated emotions toughened up their fibrous fibs.

❖

Ten minutes later, in the dead man's kitchen, Howard flattered Mary Linden with some solicitous hand-patting, while

Butterwell made tea. The fluffy widow, delirious with panic and horror, waded through her story with trembling, wringing, pacing conviction. Fascinated, Howard watched her lips as the peachy words slipped around.

'Nine out of ten for shock, Butterwell,' he remarked, as they hovered over the kettle. 'Eleven for dramatics. Sharps still here? Let's see what they have to say.'

Cuthbert and Violet had brought Mary home. They waited, both shock-white, at her dining table.

DI Howard smiled broadly, as if a death was no more than a crossword clue. He remembered the couple from the teenage runaway incident, three years ago. Now they were holding hands awkwardly, Howard noted, as if trying to remember love. They answered his questions with tightly twinned words.

The Inspector sighed over their loss of Sylvia. 'And you've never heard from her again? Dear, dear. I understand Janice Kirkstone was the last person to see her before she left the hospital that night.'

'We've kept in touch since the babies were born. Especially when Janice got the gypsy's baby.'

'Has she ever shed any light on Sylvia's disappearance?'

'Not really. No.'

'Expecting you, was she?'

Nodding in tandem.

'You didn't bring Alice to play with Jan?'

'She's away with her great-gran, Ethel Linden.'

'Ah, yes. Poor lady has lost her son. Has anyone told her yet? Mm. You say the Lindens went with you, to the Kirkstone flat?'

'Invited. As well. For tea. We all used to visit Alice in the Maternity Hospital. And we got to know Janice.' Violet put her hanky over her face. 'Next week, it's the bairns' birthdays.'

'Marks, sir,' asked Butterwell, later.

'Nine for sorrow. Ten for fear.'

'And truth?'

'Four.'

Arthur's death was already pitiless news. Only minutes after Howard and Butterwell left, Mary had to slam her front door in young Roger's face.

❖

Back at the flat in Kenton, Howard climbed the concrete stairs. He paused on the top landing and allowed his stomach to follow Arthur Linden's descent down the stairwell. 'Poor sod,' he murmured, holding his chest, as he imagined the final thud which drove the soul out of Linden's body.

The Kirkstones invited him into their pristine flat. Howard began his questions, but he found himself momentarily distracted by a small child with serious eyes, who clung to Janice Kirkstone's skirts. Startled by an irrational wave of emotion, the policeman experienced a queer sense of déjà vu triggered by that wary little face. His pen hovered. Gypsy blood, he thought, I can smell the spice of it, alien, yet uncomfortably erotic.

What? He asked Matthew Kirkstone to repeat himself. Nice! Very nice. The Kirkstones were emphatically denying any acquaintance with either the Sharps or the Lindens! They claimed to be astounded by the accident which had happened outside their flat before the doorbell even rang.

Howard simply smiled, listened and wrote.

Naivety – ten.

At the bottom of the stairs things took an even more delightful turn. A woman with massive hair was telling Butterwell about a smart man wearing a dark suit who had fled from the building as if his bum was on fire.

❖

Monday morning, Cuthbert Sharp was shovelling coal in his yard.

'Who was this pretty bloke in a suit?' asked Howard.

Cuthbert leaned on his shovel. 'Oh aye, there was a feller. Forgot about him. One of them Jehovah's Witnesses.'

'Did he witness Linden's fall?'

'Aye, but he didn't stop.'

'Did you take his name?'

'Never thowt.'

❖

In the security of Halstone House Douglas opened the lid of the grand. Martin heard his emotional crashings and drew his own conclusions. Behind his locked bedroom door the devoted dancer felt the music in his belly and began to prance fiercely, responding to the tantrum in the musician's fingers, resenting the private passion which inspired it, for this was surely the sound of a broken heart. Martin's hands clenched and stretched. The muscles in his abdomen contracted. He twisted his torso, pivoted, then leapt.

'I can't even arrange my own dad's funeral,' David bleated, trapped in his broken body. The lad was in a bad way. DI Howard watched the nurse inject and then sat waiting for David's forehead to relax.

'The funeral won't be for a while yet. Forensics.'

'Oh, God. They'll chop him up.' Words were slowing, slurring. 'Mother won't explain properly. What happened. I have a right to know.' The detective nodded, unable to draw his eyes away from the ridge of flesh knotted together at the corner of the boy's mouth. David's Adam's apple began heaving up and down. Howard pulled the curtains around the bed.

'Treating you like a child won't take this pain away, son.'

Howard did not ask questions. Not yet. Instead he did the compassionate thing and answered some. He told David the mystifying truth, as he understood it – about the Lindens and Sharps visiting the Kirkstones, about baby Jan being the child who was abandoned at the same time as Alice. Mercy today would surely reap rewards tomorrow. As David began to drift into a drugged doze Howard found he was talking to himself, weighing aloud those inconsistent stories.

❖

As the train dashed across the Scottish border, a spirited Geordie girl scowled at the hills. At this stage of the unfolding saga Katherine was barely noticed. Certainly DI Howard never thought to question her, which was his loss, since the girl was so furious that she would have told him everything. Because –

Sylvia was back.

The people around her were making a terrible mistake in underestimating Katherine's devotion to Alice. Because she was still a child herself, they were dismissing the premature motherly instincts which had flourished as she bathed Sylvia's baby, held her bottle and paced the floor through teething and gripe. Yet why? Why should her possessive adoration be any less potent than that of Violet, Cuthbert or Ethel? Why should her love be cheaper than Janice Kirkstone's?

Through nurturing Alice she had learned the disciplines of patience, tolerance, persistence. Perhaps that was why she had skipped naive teenage crushes and rushed into a full-blown sexual passion for David. For months she had been plaiting together triple strands of happiness, one for David, one for herself, and one for Alice.

But Sylvia was back – and Katherine had learned a new facet of love. Its ferocity.

With astonishing insensitivity, Katherine's parents had sent her scampering up to Ayr on a rescue mission. Ethel had lost her son, she needed to get home. Alice must be kept out of harm's way till they were sure she was safe. For Katherine, this enforced holiday meant taking time off school. With exams in a couple of weeks she knew she would once again pay dearly for Sylvia's mistakes. 'I wish the bitch had run to the edge of the world and fallen off,' she said aloud as she humped her suitcase along Ayr platform.

By the time she found the hotel she was exhausted with vexation. Ethel was waiting in the lounge. The old lady was bent over an ebony stick, as if her backbone had collapsed, but she stared unusually hard at Katherine.

Unsure of herself, the teenager bent to kiss Ethel's cheek. The thin flesh quivered and Katherine thought – this old lady has lost her son. If Alice died . . . even as her imagination fluttered over the notion, a physical pang of dread clenched her. In years to come she would remember that moment of attempted empathy, and realize that her imagination was completely inadequate.

'I'm ever so sorry about Mr Linden.'

Ethel nodded. 'I want to talk to you, lass.'

'Where's Alice?'

'Upstairs, with Nanny. Don't scowl. I know how protective you are, but this woman has already proved indispensable.'

'But I'm here to look after Alice now. I'll just pop up and check her.'

Ethel grabbed Katherine's arm. 'Sit down.'

Resentful and nervous, the young girl obeyed. Ethel lifted her several chins and confessed, 'Kath, my heart is weary and my lungs feel as if they've shrunk, but my brain won't let me rest. One minute I feel spiteful as a blunt knife, the next I want to die, so badly that I try to stop breathing. But no, I can't go before I know the truth about Arthur.'

'The truth?'

'I don't believe he was ill. I suspect foul play. And I suspect Bloody Mary! Now, tell me what you know.'

Shortly afterwards a woman in a grey uniform carried a tousled, sleepy Alice across the hotel lounge. Katherine stood up. She looked Clara Blake straight in the eye and, with assertion beyond her years, held out her arms. Little Alice reached out too. 'Tatwim!'

Nanny Blake smiled as she handed over her charge and said, 'You don't mind a spot of babysitting while I take Mrs Linden home?'

'It's not babysitting. It's Alice.'

❖

With a mouth set in wrinkled concrete, Ethel refused Clara Blake's arm and boarded the train to Newcastle.

Left alone in Ayr, Katherine carried Alice down to the beach. Over the blae-blue Firth of Clyde, a band of high pressure whisked swirls of silver through a cobalt sky, and the sea breeze lifted goose pimples up their arms. Katherine found Alice's cardigan, and wrapped a towel around her own bare shoulders. The trusted teenager kept her charge close, playing safely with bucket and spade, building a sand-castle.

A gentle peace stilled the troubled girl's mood. Why not enjoy these few days? She had a swanky hotel room, money for ice creams, and Alice all to herself. Away from Newcastle, she could try to control the wretched bitterness which curled inside her.

Sylvia was back. Ugly, half dead, and loopy. But back.

She gazed across the Firth towards the lavender contours of Arran. Beyond that, a long grey smudge – Kintyre – and then the Atlantic.

'America,' she sighed aloud, looking into Alice's puzzled face, 'But how could I leave you, my little flower?'

The child had eloquent eyebrows which lifted right up under her fringe. Such an actress! Pointing her small finger, she said, 'You not did dis right, Tatwim. Falling down now!' She took her spade and smashed the castle back into an amorphous pile of sand, giggling, then breaking into a dreadful screech when glassy particles blew into her eyes. But infant tears washed out the debris and for a long while Katherine sat holding Alice close, her lips straying along the delicate skin at the child's nape. How she could possibly be separated from this dear little soul? She should have become Alice's mother, if only . . .

Suddenly Katherine looked down at her charge. Good God! Only in that moment did she face up to the fact that she could be holding the mad gypsy's baby.

❖

When Cuthbert Sharp drove his lorry to Fontbury, it was followed. Outside the veterinary surgery, although Violet Sharp tried to avoid showing her stocking tops as she climbed down from the cab, Butterwell glimpsed her pale thigh flesh.

Howard was blessing his own cotton socks. 'Knew it,' he boasted. 'Sharp was bound to contact our fleeing, besuited man.'

'Ten out of ten, sir.'

'Go down the village. See what you can find out about this vet.'

❖

Sylvia sat with her ankles pressed together and her back straight. She was alert today; all her senses seemed sharpened, and her head felt clearer than it had for months.

Her mother was as pale as flour. 'Dad's here, pet. Wait'n outside. He'll not come in unless you say so.'

'Will he shout? I can't remember him doing much else.'

Sylvia was fascinated at the sound of her own voice. It was low, mature. She wondered what her mam was staring at, and realized that it was Sam's hand, squeezing her shoulder.

There was a menopausal sheen to Violet's skin. 'Bluster, love, that's all it ever was . . . because Dad cares too much, not too little. When he's worried, he gets in a fettle. I've learned that. He's sorrier than words can say, pet. And now that young David's lost his father – from a heart attack – life's just too short. Arthur doted on owa Alice. Oh, heavens . . . !'

Sam interceded, 'Sylvia, shall I ask your Dad to come in?'

She nodded, rewarded by her gentle vet with a stroke of her newly cut, newly dyed, dark auburn curls.

Cuthbert shuffled through the door. He looked sick. His ginger hair, overwhelmed by wiry grey, was fading to dirty yellow. His face had a jaundiced tinge and there was a purple plumpness in his lips.

Silence stood like a soldier between them. Eventually Sam walked forward and took the other man's hand.

Violet covered the awkwardness. 'Cuth! Tell Sylvia why we kept Alice. Go on.'

Cuthbert's bloodshot eyes blinked as he stammered, 'For your sake, lass. I'd made a turrible mistake. Owa Alice is a smasher. Wouldn't be without her for the world.'

'How's your friend the baker, Dad?'

'Listen pet, a'm trying to say that a'm very sorry.' Suddenly Cuthbert lost control and sobbed, 'Lass, I thought you were dead.'

And Sylvia, with no compassion at all, thought – I was, fuggerit.

❖

Tactfully, Sam took Mustard for a walk. When he returned the coal lorry was gone and Sylvia was alone, fast asleep on the sofa. For a full minute Sam stood watching her pale face in repose. Had he finally got her back on the right track? Would that milky skin regain its youthful bloom? Would her hair grow long and lustrous?

The surgery bell jangled. A man stood nonchalantly tracing Sam's brass name plate with a graceful finger.

'Afternoon, Mr Phillips. DI Howard. A word?'

Sam's heart was banging because he knew it was time to lie and he couldn't remember what he was supposed to say. Damn Alexandra, he thought. Damn her!

In the vet's surgery, the detective sniffed loudly, as though savouring the smell of frightened animal. 'That lorry. The one that just drove away. Belongs to Cuthbert Sharp.'

While Sylvia slumbered peacefully in the aftermath of her painful reunion, Sam fumbled for words to protect her, dodging questions like a cornered fox, catching himself out time and time again. After a while Howard simply folded his arms and looked Sam straight in the eye, the sort of challenging gaze which says with absolute confidence – this is utter bollocks.

With a deep sense of betrayal, Sam finally thrust off the

suffocating blanket of deception. 'You had a telephone call, Inspector. A man claiming to know where Sylvia Sharp was.'

❖

Thus the cat leapt out of its bag and into Howard's arms.

'I brought her home, to the Sharps, but it all went wrong. There was a dreadful accident.'

'Motorbike smash.' Within the Inspector's gathering euphoria something deeper stirred. Second sense. Foreboding. 'Let me guess. Nicoletta What's-her-name.'

'We found her at the coast.'

'Sylvia Sharp is here? Bless me!' Like a terrier, Howard was back in the corridor, flinging open the doors of Samuel's private rooms.

'Where?'

'Please . . . she's asleep. Fragile . . .'

'And your relationship with her is?' He found the kitchen.

'Friend, just friend. She's ill, hovering on the edge of a breakdown, too vulnerable to be questioned. Please don't push her.'

'A man's dead.'

'I know. But it has nothing do with Sylvia.'

'It has everything to do with Sylvia.'

The vet had his back against the sitting-room door. Howard brought his face close. 'The other woman, the one driving the car – she your wife?'

'Alexandra? No. Just a . . .'

'Another friend? Lucky man. Now, let's go and see this slumbering queen of tragedy, shall we?'

Reluctantly, the vet opened the door. On a sofa, Howard

saw a girl curled up like a five-year-old. He tilted his head to study her sleeping face.

'Sylvia Sharp. By God.'

'You can see, Inspector, she isn't very well.'

'Skin and bone! Never seen such a rake.'

'She just needs proper care.'

'Daft kid. Wrecked her own life and maybe a few more.'

'Please keep your voice down. None of it is her fault. She was only a child.'

'She knows about Arthur Linden?'

'Yes.'

'Wake her up.'

The vet bent to stroke the girl's pale cheek. Howard shivered as the tenderness of the gesture blew a whiff of sexuality into the room. Sylvia Sharp, darker-haired and long as a pole, opened her eyes and caught the vet's fingers with a sudden, beautiful smile.

How old is she now, Howard wondered. Not eighteen yet. He watched the vet smooth her hair, like a woman with a doll. Except that the doll stretched very sensually.

'There's a gentleman here wants to talk to you, Sylvia. A policeman.'

Howard beamed, all teeth. But a mottled flush was spreading under Sylvia Sharp's skin; her eyelids dropped, her mouth slackened as she retreated into herself.

Seven out of ten.

'Nothing upsetting, pet,' Howard reassured. 'By lass, I'm delighted you've come home! Your folks must be over the moon.'

No response.

'Especially young Alice.'

Still the girl seemed struck dumb.

'Three years.' Howard sighed, very, very sincerely. 'She'll be a toddler now. Probably chattering away. Have you seen her yet? Oh, I do like a happy ending!'

Affability was getting him nowhere. Sylvia's eyes strayed to the hallway. Howard turned, but all he could see was a grandmother clock with cardboard taped over its face.

'Mr Phillips. Could you manage us a cuppa?' The vet was about to argue, but Howard whispered authoritatively, 'Better here than at the station. I can see the problem – I'll be careful.'

Once they were alone, Howard sat beside the girl.

'Wherever have you been, lass?'

Interestingly, she wasn't afraid to meet his eyes. This was no eloquent silence, this was a combative void. But the Inspector was not a man to be outpowered, nor was he too proud to fill the wordless gaps. Tactics were just tactics.

'I can imagine how you felt,' he empathized, 'when you ran away. Lonely. Miserable. Sylvia, did anyone ever explain to you about "baby blues"?'

She was caressing her own fifteen-deniered knees, perhaps subconsciously, or perhaps not.

'Sometimes, after ladies have babies, they feel sad for no reason at all. It's chemistry or biology or something.'

Her hands clenched the hem of her skirt, knuckles bone-white. Little twitches, or tics, fluttered over her features. Madness, or mischievous restraint, or was she simply a child with a manipulative pet lip?

He scratched his head like a friendly old uncle. 'Anyway,

you're home, safe and sound. New chapter. No need to be depressed now. If you want to be happy, take a tip from me, lass. Whenever you can, try to find the funny side of things.'

Sylvia looked back towards the hallway and muttered something, although Howard couldn't make out what, because her voice was as low as a man's.

'Shall I tell you how I brighten my darkest moments?' he carried on, blustering over his frustration. 'Composing limericks. The blacker and dafter the better.'

To give himself time to think, he walked to the window and began trying to compose some lines which rhymed with Sylvia – which was impossible. So he tried Sharp, and said aloud, 'Harp. Carp . . .'

He did not see the girl's brow smooth, nor her lips lift. 'But when the melancholy fit shall fall
Sudden from heaven like a weeping cloud
That fosters the droop-headed flowers all,
And hides the green hill in an April shroud;
Then glut thy sorrow on a morning rose
Or on the rainbow of the salt sand-weave . . .'
The policeman turned and raised an eyebrow, then slowly clapped his hands.

'Keats,' she said, in her provocative, Garbo voice.

Like a resentful waitress, Samuel Phillips thrust his tray through the door and began clattering teacups.

The policeman took a biscuit and asked, 'How did you meet your veterinary benefactor, Sylvia?'

She shrugged. 'Through Greta.'

Scorched by an inexplicable heat in his hands, Howard snapped his digestive, dropping crumbs on the floor.

'Greta Korda, the gypsy? Is she still your friend?'

The teenager looked at the vet, who looked at the crumbs. Howard's head snapped backwards and forwards between them.

Phillips pre-empted him. 'If you've finished with Sylvia, Inspector, perhaps you'd come into the surgery?'

❖

'Greta?' Howard was tapping his thumbnail against his teeth.

'Alexandra Hythe. One and the same.' The poor vet looked sick.

A bubble of giggle humphed down Howard's nose. 'My, my. Gypsy mother of one abandoned baby. Three years later turns up with plums in her pretty mouth.'

'She wasn't always . . .'

'And a gob full of lies.'

'You don't understand.'

'No.' (I bloody soon will.) 'Her baby is fostered by Janice Kirkstone. Arthur Linden dies very mysteriously at the Kirkstones' flat. The Sharps are there. You, sir, are harbouring their daughter and are also romantically involved with same posh gypsy who seems to be at the core of the whole grisly catastrophe.'

'Alexandra had absolutely nothing to do with that man's death. I can vouch for her.'

'It's not a woman I'm looking for. An unidentified man bolted from the scene. Mr Phillips, perhaps you would be good enough to furnish me with a recent photograph of yourself?'

'Watch out,' Alan whispered into his mate's ear. 'Here comes the powlice.'

Hendo had only been conscious for eleven hours. He kept drifting in and out of sleep, but refused to sink back into coma. Although his speech was slow and his vision blurred, with the exception of his pot leg and wrist, his body functioned normally. Signs were good for a full recovery and prayers of thanks were due to be offered on Sunday by Gosforth's entire Methodist congregation. Alan, however, felt a keen need to protect his friend.

DI Howard's presence dominated the ward. 'Now then,' he grinned, 'I won't ask you if you're feeling better, for fear of being cussed. But I heard you were back from fairyland and I need a chat.'

Howard turned to Alan. 'How's things with you, Watson?' As he fished in his pocket for notepad and pencil, he noticed a shadow of alarm flicker across Alan's reddening cheeks. The small, charismatic lad twitched his floppy blond fringe, and rolled his eyes towards the door. The Inspector was quick to understand. He deliberately laid his pencil on Hendo's bed, and put his arm across Alan's shoulder. 'A word with you first, Watson? Before you get off?'

In the corridor Alan shuffled. 'No one's told him about Arthur Linden yet.'

'Breaking bad news is my trade, son.' Howard sniffed, scenting anxiety. 'What's bothering you, Watson? You know, I've had several different accounts of Arthur's death, and I'm not sold on this seizure bit. What do you think?'

'He was a good bloke, David's dad.'

The detective watched the boy's conscience squirming, and he sensed that Alan's hesitation was loaded with intelligence. 'My job to stick up for good blokes. Especially when they're dead. Arthur Linden's got no voice now, poor sod. Someone should speak for him.'

'I wasn't there.'

'Right.'

'But I was at the accident. When Hendo and David got smashed up.'

'Something you didn't tell us at the time?'

'A lot. Sorry.'

❖

Through torrential rain they came again, from north and south, those gypsies and travellers with their red traction engines and shiny chrome caravans, to struggle in the Newcastle mud and pierce the drizzle with a million determined light bulbs.

History would show that the decision to bring the Hoppings forward a week was a bad one. On Saturday, 18 June, rain gushed down the spiralling troughs of the three helter-skelters. Two Big Wheels stood soaked, empty. Mud lay thick and squelchy between the rides. Vehicles were bogged down, caravans sucked into liquid earth. Money would be lost, so moods were as filthy as the conditions.

Nothing, however, could muddy Howard's excitement as he stomped along in his boots, his trousers splattered and soggy. DC Butterwell, a man well rounded by buttered lardy cake, plodded miserably behind. Howard bought them both toffee apples, which they chomped in the shelter of an awning, while watching the Zipper spin through the spray. The ride was now manned by a young lad with a yellowish ponytail. After washing his sticky hands in the rain, Howard went to talk to the dirty youth, after which he moved from ride to ride, stall to stall, question to question, until he came to Binnie.

The old Romany woman stood bent beneath dripping tarpaulin, her movements slow, her back painfully curved, as she pocketed her sixpences. She seemed to look right through Howard, cloudy with either wisdom or cataracts, and although she nodded at Greta's name, beyond that she pretended deafness.

'Greta was married to Dick Korda. Had his child.'

Binnie shrugged.

'Your friend's done rather well for herself. Got a new name. Alexandra Hythe. Money too. She forgot all this.' He threw a careless arm across the scene.

The arthritic gypsy tried to straighten her back. 'Where is the child?' she demanded.

Howard was taken aback. 'I can't divulge that. Tell me about Greta.'

'Where is the child?'

'Why?' He was puzzled by the old gypsy's intensity.

She paused dramatically. 'I have the sight.'

'How nice.'

'The child is in danger.'

Howard's spiritual eye saw the Kenton flat, the stairwell

and the broken tiles, and he suddenly felt anxious. 'Who from?'

Again, Binnie shrugged. She held out her hand. Howard put sixpence in it and she handed him seven marbles.

'She is close. I can feel her.'

'I believe you can.' Howard looked believing.

'A thread of trust ties me to her. Life and death. Tell me where she is.'

'What danger?'

'Who protects her?'

'Who threatens her?'

'Bah.' Again Binnie walked away.

She returned a minute later and said, 'Life and death, I say. Tell me.'

'Butterwell, would you mind guarding this lot? Binnie and I are going to have a chat somewhere private. Your place, Binnie?'

In the gloomy but spotlessly clean caravan, he said, 'Look. About the child. Perhaps, without compromising anyone, I could give you some – reassurances.'

'She's well looked after?'

'Yes. But something bad has happened to someone tied up in this old story. Tell me, Binnie, did you actually see Greta's baby?'

'I delivered her.' Binnie lifted empty trembling arms. 'Marked her. Where is she?'

'Marked?' Howard grinned. 'You're playing games with me, Binnie.'

'Give me your hand.' Her stained finger pressed the fleshy muscle at the base of his thumb. Fascinated, he watched her eyeballs move beneath wrinkled eyelids, wondering what pictures her 'second sight' could see. His own spiritual eye must have been closed, because he had absolutely no idea that in the throbbing pulse of his wrist Binnie could feel – Greta.

Howard stumbled away from the Town Moor, trying to shake off the spell which seemed to have wagged his tongue. Why else would he have given the tricky old gypsy such information?

Minutes later, Binnie was surprised when a young man helped her down from her caravan. She touched Roger's hand, and felt the power of truth. So she stopped and listened.

❖

Guilt felt like a collar of woven brambles around Mary's throat. The house itself was shivering. Ethel's presence was demonic. Even although the wretched old woman was upstairs Mary could feel those hooded eyes on her back.

Her fingers dialled. 'Douglas!' she whispered. 'Whatever shall I do? He keeps asking such difficult questions. This Inspector – Howard, he's called – implies things. I have a dreadful feeling! Oh, Douglas, I think they might arrest me. It's so unfair, it was an accident! No, of course I won't say anything. I'd never let you down, dear.'

The hooded eyes above blinked. There was nothing wrong with Ethel's hearing.

❖

'It *was* Sylvia then.'

'Aye. She's written to uz. And to Davy boy.' Hendo

handed Alan the letter and wriggled his bum against the starched sheet.

The note was humble, sincere with apology.

'She's never bothered to write to me,' complained Alan.

'You're not all blood and bandages. Remember playing catchy kissy in the yard? You always chased Sylvia, and you couldn't catch her on account of her long legs.'

'Oh, she did let me catch her a couple of times. Smooth lips.'

'Aye. I remember. Me memories keep coming back – and every one is like – precious.'

'They're calling you Hardskull Hendo now.'

'Take more than a crack on the head to knacker my brain. Mind, I'd rather forget flying through the bloody air. I keep gett'n mixed up between what I've dreamed and what really happened. The body's amazing, how it heals. Molecules regenerating themselves. Little electrical impulses.'

'So, your willy's working then?'

❖

Dear Sylvia,

I really appreciated your letter. Losing my dad, and under such mysterious circumstances, has made me look hard at my life.

You ask my forgiveness. I ask for yours. You must have been wretched when you ran away and it was all my fault. Actually, much of it was my mother's fault. She said you didn't want to see me, that your father was threatening to kill me, that you'd been sent away to Torquay or somewhere. I should have tried harder to find out the truth.

*We are parents, you and I. Alice is a wonderful little girl.
I love her dearly and have refused to go away to university,
because I can't leave her. Will you come to see me? We should
make plans for the future, when they let me out of this bloody
hospital.*

*Katherine is angry. She and I have become close, but never
in the same way that you and I were. We were too young,
that's all. Do you remember the daft poems I used to write?*

*We are grown up now and have a chance to put every-
thing right, both for ourselves and for Alice. Although I
wouldn't blame you for hating me, I hope you don't. Come
and see me, please, and be prepared! That road made a mess
of my face, but if you sit on my good side, I look just the
same.*

*Sorry this letter isn't very romantic. When you went away
I wrote lots of love letters to you, but had nowhere to send
them. Perhaps one day you'll read them!*

Love from David. X

❖

Katherine wished she'd stayed in Scotland. She wished she'd
grabbed her opportunity, taken Alice and run as fast as her
legs could carry her. To Edinburgh, Glasgow, London, America, anywhere other than mucky Newcastle with its filthy,
traitorous population.

So! She slammed the iron down on the board and wriggled it up into a gather. So! Sylvia had written to David, and
David thought he should write back. So! She hadn't been
allowed to read 'said letter', because it was PRIVATE! So!
(SLAM) Sylvia was coming here this afternoon. So! (SLAM)

307

And Alice would now be told that Sylvia was her mother. So! She was left ironing Alice's dress, like bloody Cinderella! So! (SLAM SLAM) SOD them all! Ouch!

Home?

No.

The same china dog sat on the new mantelpiece, alongside Aunt Maud's candlesticks and a familiar plastic cyclamen. Old olive-green curtains hung against the new window, not quite fitting, the hem just dusting the sill.

Sylvia soaked in all the remembered paraphernalia of 'home'. Oddly, much of it was positioned in exactly the same way, yet dislocated in a room with a higher ceiling and wrongly positioned door.

Her mam, as ever, was flapping a tea towel, but her dad was acting completely out of character. His upper lip was pulled high over his gappy, tombstone teeth, in an attempt at a smile.

'The nanny's bring'n Alice,' explained Violet. 'Ethel always takes the bairn to Sunday School. Have a seat, Sam. That's right. Better keep the doggie on its lead. Here, Sylvia, have a spam sandwich.' She called into the kitchen, 'Kath! Fetch the tea.'

Katherine entered, carrying the brown pot, with her

shoulders back and her chin high. Her breasts were each as big and round as the teapot! Sylvia had to place a discrete hand on her lips to discipline the furious voice inside screaming – she's all swish and sex! Her lips are shiny with it. There's sex in the snaky look she threw me. She's seen David's penis and I can't remember what it looked like.

❖

At the door, Clara Blake handed Alice into Violet's arms.

'Is Ethel bearing up?'

'She's coping. I'm taking her back to Corbridge tonight. Yesterday she spent a long time talking to that policeman – shouting at him, to be frank. But I suspect it was him that persuaded her not to stay in Gosforth.'

'How's Mary?'

'A bit doolally.'

'When's the funeral?'

'It's delayed because of the autopsy.'

Violet buried her horror in Alice's innocent curls.

Clara left with her usual dignity. She never kissed Alice in public.

❖

The beautiful little girl chose Sam's knee. She sucked the hem of her dress and flirted with him, with large blue eyes. Was it his imagination, or were they the same colour as Alexandra's? Sylvia had pale eyes, greyish with a hint of a green which could almost be turquoise. Sad sea eyes.

This little blossom liked an audience. If Alice remembered anything about the attempt to snatch her, it was locked into her subconscious. She was as bright and mischievous as a child should be. Delightful. Sam's paternal instinct stirred: a pure, forbidden lust.

I could have been her stepfather, he realized, if I'd accepted Alexandra's proposal. She could have lived in my home, been my eldest child, sister to those who would follow.

He looked across at Sylvia. Her slender fingers were fiddling with the little gold watch he had bought her, to mark this special day, and her pale eyes were greedily following Alice's every move.

What sweet torment this must be for her, thought the vet. How can I tell her that Alice might not be hers? Have I done the right thing, letting her enjoy this long-awaited reunion, untarnished by doubts?

As Violet adjusted Alice's bow, the child stood with her hands on her hips in front of Mustard. For once, the fluffy dog was behaving beautifully. His tail began to wag, leaving yellow hairs on the carpet.

'Does he bite?' asked Violet anxiously.

'He's ever so gentle,' replied Sylvia in her uncomfortably deep, measured tone. 'Do you want to stroke him, Alice?'

Sam felt an embarrassing urge to cry as the little girl put her hand into her mother's. How can I tell her the truth, he thought again. Yet how can I not?

Alice's eager fingers laced through Mustard's golden fur. Very slowly, Sylvia laid her own trembling hand on the child's shoulder. But Sam noticed that the caress was not soft. Sylvia's fingers were rigid with tension, almost clawed. He looked at her gaunt face and noticed the clench of her shoulder muscles. With renewed shock he registered the chasm of her bitterness.

It's grief, he realized. Her daughter has been taught to walk and talk by other people. It must be crucifying.

Mustard, meanwhile, unable to restrain himself, licked the little girl's cheek. When Alice giggled, the dog barked, a great deafening shout of enthusiasm right in the tot's face.

In one quick movement, Cuthbert Sharp swept his granddaughter up into his strong, protective arms.

The vet watched as Sylvia's frown slowly meet her father's, like for like.

❖

Afterwards, driving away in the Hillman, Sam said, 'That went well.'

'They've possessed her.'

'They adore her. But she's still your daughter. Be patient.'

'Is she like me at all?'

'She's beautiful, just like her mother.' God forgive me, thought Sam. Greta seemed to be staring at him through the windscreen.

'I can't seem to match her to the baby I remember holding.'

The weight of Greta's guilty secret ached across Sam's shoulders. 'You've missed some important years.'

Sylvia did her thoughtful clucking, then quoted, 'I will restore unto thee the years that the locust hath eaten.'

'Pardon?'

'Sorry. Bible text. Just popped into my head. I learned loads at Sunday School – Plymouth Brethren, in the hall over the Co-op. But, Sam, how can God restore my years? Even he can't make tempus fugit backwards.'

'I know you can't have Alice's babyhood back, but maybe there'll be blessings in the future, to make up for the past.' He patted her knee, then realized he shouldn't. 'You've a very retentive memory for texts and quotes,' he probed. 'Did you spend your time in Scarborough learning poetry?'

'Only favourite bits. But I used to read everything aloud. And when Tony made me study *Othello*, I spoke the parts in funny voices. Now, I hear those voices in my head saying lines I can't even remember learning. If I'd stayed at school, I think I'd have been clever.'

'You are clever. School or not.'

He thought – she is very intelligent. If I can get her through this, she could become a remarkable woman. She's fragile, but she's also an adult. I have to tell her the truth. The longer I protect her, the closer she'll get to Alice and the harder it will be. It's now or never. If I can't live with never, it has to be now.

'Look,' he suggested, 'we've got some time before hospital visiting. Let's take a walk around Exhibition Park.'

A thickening summer haze was rising towards the sun. With Mustard tugging on his lead, they meandered along laurel-lined pathways and, while Sam kept putting off what he needed to say, they chattered about things he thought didn't matter: dreams and eagles, guillemots and ghosts, the lipstick beaks of black swans. He watched Sylvia's animated face, laughing at the ducks, seeing a girl who was blossoming beautifully with hope. Her optimism was terrifyingly sad. He found himself wanting to touch the vulnerable smile on her lips, the fluffy curls, newly styled at the nape of her neck, the pearls clipped on her lobes.

❖

Euphoria was novel and shocking. Sylvia felt her skirt flowing sensually around her legs and such joyful energy swirling around her that she could have danced to the brass band's clumsy um-pah-pah waltz, which was blasting from the bandstand. She was back in Newcastle, strolling with a handsome, mature man, who had reunited her with Alice, and who would make the most wonderful stepfather in the world.

She caught Sam's hand and swung it, reading things in the innocent vet's careful smile which would have shocked him. He looked embarrassed, like a boy in the playground.

'Sylvia, I'm going to put Mustard back in the car. Wait here for me? I'd like to talk to you, before you visit David.'

And in that buoyant, naive instant, Sylvia convinced herself that Sam, jealous of her old love for David, was about to declare himself. Why else would he want her alone, without even Mustard to distract him? In this gentle place of fragrances and willow curtains she sat watching other couples cuddling, sharing ice creams, laughing, kissing, and her expectant heart beat so hard that she was sure people could see her ribs jumping.

When Sam returned, she slid her fingers through his, trying to relax her hands.

'Let's take a boat out on the lake!'

Laughter jarred the sultry air as they wobbled into their seats. Sam rowed strongly across the man-made lake, face coming close to hers on the forward lean, back arching into the pull. In the shelter of some greenery he stowed his oars and Sylvia stretched out her skinny legs, folding her arms behind her head.

'My soul is an enchanted boat,

Which, like a sleeping swan, doth float . . .'

'What's that poem about?' he asked.

'A Voice in the Air, Singing. Sam, do you ever hear voices in the air, coming from no one?'

'No. Although – and I'm only admitting this to you – I do sometimes imagine animals are trying to speak to me. Wishful thinking.'

'Do parrots and budgies understand what they're saying?'

'Probably not. Can I change the subject?' Sam had stopped smiling again. He leaned forwards and grabbed her hands. 'There's something serious we must talk about.'

Sylvia sat up, and moved her face close to his.

'It's about Alexandra – Greta.'

A voice in the air swore, *Fugger Greta!*

'She did something very bad.'

'Left me on a train.'

'Worse. It's about Alice.'

'I don't believe a thing Greta says. Neither should you.'

Sam began massaging Sylvia's rigid fingers, stretching them out one by one.

'The night you ran away from the hospital – she says she went back for a moment . . .'

'I remember.'

'. . . and she sort of muddled the babies up. Put them in the same cot. So we can't be sure . . .'

A spiteful tickle, like broom bristles, swept down Sylvia's spine.

Cunning whore of Venice!

This time the Shakespearean voice had bellowed from right across the lake. Or had it bubbled up through the water? Or was it in the rumble of thunder?

Above the trees, hot moisture was gathering, changing the light, dimming the picture. Sylvia stared at her new watch. Held it to her ear. Listened to the ticking, to try to deafen the other shouts ringing all around her.

She hardly heard Sam say, 'I can't believe that the hospital didn't know which baby was which. Your family is convinced Alice resembles both you and Katherine. Unfortunately, when Alexandra saw Alice, her emotions got the better of her . . .'

'Where is MY baby?' Something sharp was digging into her spine, gouging between her shoulder blades. She felt her heart being tugged, dragged out of her, and hoisted up into funneling currents, towards the storm.

'Alice is your baby. Almost certainly. The nurses, doctors, they must have noticed things, birth marks, skull size . . . Sit down, love. You're rocking the boat!'

Sam took the oars and rowed hard across the lake. Drops of condensed moisture were now falling, pinpricks on bare arms. As he helped her on to dry land she dropped the watch and it disappeared into the muddy water.

'I'll get you another.'

'NO MORE WATCHES!'

High above, lightning leapt.

Under a leafy chestnut Sylvia pressed her head into Sam's

shoulder, clutching at his waist until her fingers bruised him. She tried to silence her ranting mind by alerting all her sensory nerve endings to the warmth of his body. But Sam had even more to get off his chest.

'Sylvia, there's something else. About Arthur Linden's death. Your parents, I'm afraid, witnessed it. You see, they had located the – other baby.'

MY BABY?

'Apparently they all went to this flat in Kenton, where Linden fell. Except that Howard doesn't think he fell by accident. He thinks David's dad was pushed.'

Out of Sylvia's stifled mind exploded a voice crying, *O, falsely, falsely murder'd!* But part of her knew these were learned words. A much louder voice was ranting somewhere behind her, mad, furious sentences, punctuated by clacking, deafening TOCKs, warning her that her father was a murderer, that he had Alice and would do anything to keep her, that he had even gone looking for another little girl.

'The police are saying that an unidentified man ran away from the crime. Unfortunately, for complicated reasons, Howard thinks this mystery man is me.'

A powerful back-tug yanked Sylvia out of Sam's arms.

'I'd already lied, to protect you; only I'm not good at lying. By the time I told Howard the truth he didn't believe a word.'

Was Sam crying?

His tears, blinking painfully from bloodshot eyes, sucked Sylvia back into her own body. Everything stilled.

Summer rain began to rustle in the branches and drip

down their backs. She leaned again towards his chest, not from compassion, but with a sense of power. Sam needed her.

'We'll sort it out, pet,' he was saying. 'Trust me.'

Oh, the quarrelsome, contradictory mind, and the contrary, disobedient human body, which will giggle at bad news, and tingle at the sight of blood. Sylvia's personality had its own alchemy. With her bony frame so hard against Sam's muscles, she felt a deep, familiar throb. Feathery fluttering tickled her backside, making her buttocks clench. She closed her eyes, and felt a gentle weight pushing against her spine.

Pitter-patters on the leaves overhead. Their backs were cold and wet, their fronts, pressed together, began to warm with intimacy. Sam's breath panted on Sylvia's forehead and his arms tightened around her waist.

Throb.

Her fingers moved up his chest to his neck, stretched out across his jaw. Slowly, eyes locked with his, she pulled his face down to hers until their mouths were just touching. At first his lips were soft over hers, then she felt tiny muscles around his mouth move as his grip on her slender body tightened. Suddenly he was kissing her back so hard that her neck was bent backwards, her breastless chest thrust into his.

Throb. Throb.

Her hands tugged his wiry hair, strength surging into her fingers, into every part of her body, as the sensation on her lips gathered momentum, the throb pulsing up from her vagina and through her belly.

At last Sam pushed her away.

'Well!' he breathed.

'Well!' she replied, touching her bruised mouth.

A chemistry of joy bubbled up from her trembling insides. Unable to stop herself, Sylvia giggled.

❖

Sam was shocked. One minute this woman-child seemed to be on the brink of total breakdown, the next she was seducing him. What was so bloody funny?

He longed to touch her again, but he denied them both by marching smartly back towards the car, while she skipped behind him.

Sylvia walked into the hospital with a new air of confidence. Sam's lips still burned. His heart pounded with astonished novelty. How had it happened? Why? While his instincts were screaming RIGHT, his conscience screamed WRONG! She was too young. He had taken advantage of her vulnerability. It was just hero worship. Gratitude. But alongside rational thought, simplistic plans began to stream through his mind. He could heal Sylvia, discover her, love her, make love to her. The skinny arms which had held him could be fattened up. He could personally supervise exercises to strengthen her young body so that when he finally had the right to possess her, she would come to him with pride. Oh, sod it, no! No! That wasn't what he wanted. He knew the very bones of Sylvia Sharp, and given half a chance he would kiss each protruding rib, knee bone, hip bone right now, tonight . . .

Yet David Linden, the father of her child, lay waiting, injured, deserving pity, craving forgiveness. How would Sylvia feel, with her female senses already stirred, her fragile ego lying open as a sun-thirsty buttercup? How much would it take for David to pull her back to him? Would their young romance blaze again or would that impudent, kissing Sylvia emerge from the jumble of hospital buildings, ready to leave first love behind?

❖

A complex wash of endorphins shielded Sylvia's emotions as she stood before David's bed, uncomfortably aware of his scrutiny. Her perception of her own appearance was that she was fat, yet shapeless. Was that disappointment in David's lopsided smile? Couldn't he see the real Sylvia beneath her short fringe? Had time and sadness and deprivation made her totally unattractive?

David looked terrible. One side of his face was a map of yellowing, swollen tissue. His mouth was distorted. But it was more than that. His eyes, once so honest, now shifted uncomfortably.

'Thanks for your letter.' Twice they began to speak at the same time, and twice the conversation fizzled out. Sorrys hung defenceless in the air. Nervous smiles expanded then shrank. 'That gypo you ran off with. Madwoman. You've heard what she said, about swapping babies?'

'Sam just told me. But he's sure the hospital wouldn't have let the babies get muddled.'

'I agree. I love Alice, quite instinctively. I know she's mine.'

'Yours?'

'What shall we do, Sylvia?'

Then Katherine bounced in. She kissed David soundly on his sore side and smiled triumphantly.

❖

Sylvia found poor Hendo, still prostrate, with his leg slung in the air. Part of his head was shaved, yet, miraculously, Hendo's rueful smile touched the girl who used to be Sylvia Sharp, reawakening, momentarily, her true self. Laying her hand on his arm, she tried to find words of apology.

'Belt up, bonny lass!' He hoisted his leg and shifted his bum. 'Howay, hinny, tell uz a good story. Distraction's the best medicine and a'm bored out of me bloody mind. Tell uz about the gypos. Life in a caravan. Can you tell fortuncs yet?' He stretched his good palm towards her. 'Ger a look at this. What d'you see?' Sylvia smiled and took his hand, tracing his mount of Venus with a slender finger.

'Long lifeline. Significant career. More money than you can spend. Two wives – no three – and just let me count these creases – seven kids.'

'Bloody Nora! Now then, Syl, your turn. Where've you been while wus lads have been pick'n wer nebs?'

'Oh, Hendo, I'm supposed to keep it secret.'

'Howay kiddo, give a body summut to think about other than bedpans. Just start at the beginning . . .'

Why not? Why not tell him about Greta the gypsy who dumped her on a train, after secretly trying to swap babies? Craving Hendo's sympathy, courting it, Sylvia drifted into her own words, as she described living alone in a cold, damp cottage, talking to a photograph, counting every tock of the fuggering clock. Lost in her own gloom, she hardly heard

Hendo's account of difficult exams, school trips, foota on a Saturday, until . . .

'I was court'n your Katherine for ages. Aye, that surprised you!'

Hisper Cottage melted away.

'My sister?'

'Aye. But she was always flirting with Davy. Mebees it was inevitable – them two end'n up together. Have you seen him? He's not as handsome as me now. Poor sod's bruises are as yella as diarrhoea.'

'Kath was with him.'

'She chased him.'

'How fast did he run?'

'He waited for ages, but you never showed.' Hendo scratched his bandage. 'Alan realized it was you, when we seen you knock the door. Even with that black mop. Much better now, by the way. Reddish-brown.'

'Auburn. Hairdresser says.'

'Alan's always fancied you.'

'I know. Is he still going to be Prime Minister?'

'Oh aye. Probably start his own Party.'

'What about you?'

'University. Wanna be an architect. This broken leg might get uz out of serv'n Queen and Country. You should hear Alan gan on aboot conscription – he'd bore the knackers off you! Anyhow, Syl, I don't suppose you fancy being one of me three wives?'

❖

During the ride home to Fontbury Sam's sentences were clipped. 'Good visit?'

'Katherine was there.'

So, thought Sam, young Katherine wrecked the poignant reunion! Bully for her! Why shouldn't the younger sister put up a fight? He pressed hard on the accelerator.

As the purple humps of the Pennines came into view, Sylvia started her old tutting, clicking habit.

'What's up, pet?'

'All this talk about University – even Katherine. They're just school kids, playing at being intellectuals.'

'Is that fair? You're not the only one who's suffered. David has just lost his father. He's had to cope with the stigma of having a daughter. He's helped bring her up. And so has Katherine.'

'To serve her own purpose! To catch David, with his good prospects and family money. Oh, I can see right through her. "OWA ALICE", she called my baby. They both did. As if I never gave birth to her! Kath's always been a conniving little cat. But I'll fight her, Sam. I'll see her rot before . . .'

'Before she marries your David?'

'She can have David on a plate with butter on. But she'll not get my baby!'

Sam's right foot pressed down hard again.

Alice should have a birthday cake. Violet dripped red cochineal into the icing sugar, seeing the blood collecting around Arthur's head. Her daughter had been returned to her, but the cost was unbearable. Happiness was unthinkable; joy lost for ever down a tragic well of secrets.

Violet had another tiny secret. Tucked away in the bottom of her underwear drawer was a set of doll's clothes, a lilac dress smocked with dark lavender threads, knitted shoes with tiny silver buttons, white frilly pants. A pretty birthday present for a little girl. For baby Jan.

She'd promised for the men, not for herself.

❖

Katherine stormed away from David's bed. While Sylvia had been there she'd managed to keep up the act, enveloping her boyfriend in possessive charm, but as soon as her weird sister had left, David had become extremely snotty.

'I've a lot on my mind, Kath,' he had complained. 'Need to sort my feelings out.'

'You said you loved *me*,' she reminded him bitterly.

She was furious with herself for being so blatant. It never paid. Her love for David Linden was so deep and so strong that it was terrifying. This shocking, compromising jealousy was anguish.

Outside, she dragged on a Woodbine for a few minutes, then took her mortification to Hendo's bedside, where she moaned on, berating Sylvia, her parents, David, swearing with a viciousness which made the lad's sore head ache.

'Bugger off, Kath. You're getting on me wick, bleeding spite owa me sickbed, when just a few weeks ago you dumped uz. If neebody likes you, you've only got what you deserve. Do a body a favour – get lost!'

All the way home Katherine fought tears. Outside the house she found Alan leaning on the wall.

'What are you here for?' she snapped.

'Charming! Just wanted to find out how the visit went, with Sylvia.'

'She brought a stupid dog that made Alice bubble. Then she went to hospital and made David huffy. Ever since she came home everybody's been miserable.'

'Aye. Especially you. Cacked on your schemes, hasn't she?'

She pushed past him.

'Aren't you glad to have your prodigal sister back?' Alan sneered.

'She's a selfish bitch, and no one can see it.'

'Tut tut. You know what they say – takes a bitch to call a bitch.'

'Back on yourself, Alan. Caller called. Bitch calls bitch. She's a bitch, I'm a bitch and you are the biggest, or should I say smallest, bitch of all!'

'Tell me, Kath, did you chase Davy because he was Alice's dad, or because he was Sylvia's lad?'

'Both. OK?'

'You hurt my mate.'

'So?'

'Played Hendo along, while you bent down in front of David, letting him see your stocking tops.'

'Bastard!' Katherine hissed. 'You could swallow yourself with your own gob. Lasses aren't exactly stampeding your gate are they, TITCH?'

'Raving nympho!' the small lion roared.

'Back on yourself again. Takes one to call one. You're just jealous because I took Hendo, then David, away from you! You were left, a lonely little boy, playing with yourself behind the Scout hut!'

For one split second Alan was nonplussed but, when it came, his retort cut Katherine deep and bloody.

'Some women are just born bad. Poison seeps out of their fingernails. In the olden days they were called witches and villagers ducked them.' The tirade went on and on, until Katherine slapped Alan's face, very hard, and fled into the house.

Poor Katherine. There was little welcome for her in her own home. Alice had been scolded and sat wailing on the floor, Violet was clanking around the kitchen, and her father, uncharacteristically, stood with his arms outstretched against the mantelpiece, staring down at the empty grate. He turned on his second daughter the minute she entered the room.

'Where've you been, Katherine Sharp?'

'Why?'

'Hospital?'

'What if?'

'When you knew Sylvia was to see David, for the first time? By, you're a crafty madam. Bitch on heat. Can't think of any bugger but yourself! Totally SELFISH!'

Katherine felt drowned in injustice. Out it spurted – truth mingled with gall. 'Hypocrite! If I'm selfish,' she yelled, 'I've got a flam'n good teacher. You want to posses owa Alice till you're sick with it, but I never saw you change a shitty nappy. While me and Mam paced the floor, you just snored, and you still had to have your bloody bait ready.'

'Hold your gob, girl!'

'Why? Why don't I matter, Dad? Sylvia left Alice and David to rot. She left Mam to grieve, think'n she was dead.' Katherine was blinded by fury. 'Well, I'm not glad she's back. David asked me to marry him months ago. Alice will live with us, the parents she knows. Maybe I didn't give birth to her. But maybe Sylvia didn't either. Maybe the gypsy did. I don't care a flying fanny. I love that bairn.'

'Wus all do!'

'Aye. And you fondle her a bit too much!'

'Are you suggest'n . . . ?' Cuthbert's spittle flew across the room.

'I'm suggesting that Alice needs a healthy family life. Not mauled over by a . . . pervert.'

Katherine bent to pick up the screaming Alice, but Cuthbert grabbed at the back of his daughter's dress and yanked her around. The flat of his hand landed hard on her jaw, jarring her neck. She sprawled across the settee.

Back on yourself, Katherine.

Little Alice was beating her tiny fist against Cuthbert's leg as he grabbed Katherine by the throat. He would have strangled the life out of her if Violet hadn't hit him over the shoulders with a saucepan.

Katherine flew out of the house. Violet picked up Alice and chased after her daughter, but couldn't catch her.

❖

Two hours later, once she was sure her dad's lorry had gone, Katherine sneaked back into the house to find it deserted. Her bed was unmade. A pot of face powder had tipped on the dressing table scattering pale dust into an open drawer. Every-thing was messed up. Everything!

She hugged herself tightly. Why was it wrong to love someone so much that you were prepared to fight for them? Why did everyone hate her?

'It's not fair!' she cried aloud.

Katherine lit a cigarette. One by one, she assessed the people in her life, examining how she felt about her nearest and dearest, before cancelling each of them out. All except Alice. Sweet, trusting Alice.

In the kitchen she found a note from her mother.

CUTHBERT AND KATHERINE.
YOU'RE BOTH BEHAVING DREADFUL! IT'S
NOT FAIR ON ALICE. SHE'S BEEN CRYING FOR
AGES. SO I'VE TAKEN HER TO ETHEL'S. SHE
CAN STOP THERE TILL YOU TWO CALM
DOWN. YOUNG ALAN IS DRIVING US IN HIS
DAD'S CAR SO I'LL BE HOME BY BEDTIME.
BEFORE I GET BACK, MAKE SURE YOU SAY
SORRY TO EACH OTHER.

'Bugger that for a game of soldiers!'

Katherine stubbed her cigarette in the sink. The soggy butt was her sign of final rejection. Then she reached into the larder for the biscuit tin which contained grocery money – two pounds, twelve shillings and fourpence. That would do for a while.

Ten minutes later Katherine had packed clothes,

toothbrush, face cloth and photo of Alice. Fighting bitter tears, she marched down the street.

❖

Of course Ethel was pleased to have Alice for a few days. The old lady felt contrarily energized by grief and anger. Growing certainty of Mary's betrayal with her unknown lover, of her guilt in Arthur's death, kept Ethel from stumbling under the massive millstone of mourning.

When Violet and Alan arrived, she cautioned herself to mind her tongue, just as DI Howard had directed. Alan took Alice upstairs to find some toys. Daphne had already left, so Clara volunteered to make supper.

Violet was edgy. Ethel wondered about that, as they walked slowly down the lawn. The grass, drenched by the sudden shower, gistened in the low sun, and the air smelled of lilies.

'Where is Sylvia now?' inquired the older woman.

'Fontbury. Staying with that vet friend of hers, Sam.'

Ethel raised her furrowed brow. 'Is this an appropriate arrangement?'

'God knows. She's eighteen soon.'

'And Alice is three on Friday.' Both women sighed. 'Could we hold the party here, Violet? It would mean so much to me. David is coming out of hospital. Clara is going to nurse him. We could make it a good day, in the middle of all the madness and sadness. Sylvia can come here, with her vet friend, of course. But there are private corners in this house where the young people could talk.'

Alan walked towards them, holding Alice's hand. Ethel

bent down to her. 'Would you like a picnic for your birthday party, pet? Here on the lawn? Uncle Alan can come too.'

What could Violet say? Her husband had helped kill Ethel's son.

'Owa Kath could help. She loves coming here. Poor lass is hurting bad.'

Alan, privately ashamed, agreed. 'David should decide which girl he really loves, then tell them both straight.'

Ethel snorted. 'You teenagers are idealistic. Love is either pure as snow or black as pit dust. Sadly, Alan dear, there's a lot of muck in between.' Turning to Violet, she changed the subject suddenly. 'Do you think Alice is our baby, Violet? What about this other child, Jan?'

Alan interrupted again. 'You can't have both bairns. What would you do? Swap them back? Give Alice away?'

'Sh!' Violet hissed. 'Little ears! Of course we keep Alice. We've loved her, all of us, every minute of her little life. My days have been full of her, wiping her sticky hands, tucking her into bed at night.'

They all watched Alice crushing lavender seeds. Violet sighed. 'Yet something strange – when I held that little Jan . . .'

'What?' breathed Ethel.

'I felt . . . oh, Lord!' Violet turned to look at the older woman. 'A think there's been a turrible mistake. I think Jan could be owa Sylvia's daughter.'

'Why?'

'A mam sees things in her own bairn, little gestures, expressions. Even as a tot owa Sylvia had a way of making uz feel guilty. She didn't scream and paddy – well, not until she was thirteen. But when she was little, we'd get the turned-down lip and big sad eyes, enough to turn a body inside out. It was there, Ethel. A saw it again . . .'

'Dear Lord!'

Clara was shouting over the lawn, summonsing Alan to fetch Alice indoors. After goodnight kisses, Gran and Great-gran slowly wandered the garden, each hiding private terrors.

A profound silence hovered over the evening, worried by the whisper of a million midges. Ethel finally drew a long breath of scented air.

'Tell me about this mystery man. Don't shake your head. I've heard Mary speaking to him on the telephone in very desperate – affectionate tones. You can't protect me from the sordid truth. The baggage has been having an affair. Her lover killed my son.' Ethel watched the other woman's ashen face. 'Violet, I'd stake my life on your own innocence, but you were there, and I beg you, in utter humility, to tell me what you saw.'

To Ethel's surprise, Violet let out a great racking sob. Trembling hands flew to cover her face. When the dreadful gulping subsided Violet lifted her wet face to the other woman's pale, suspicious eyes. 'Sorry. Haven't got over the shock. Arthur just fell, honestly. Clutched his chest and fell.'

Ethel's shrivelled mouth pinched.

❖

The river widened through Fontbury, badious water running so shallow that when Sylvia and Sam stood on the small foot-bridge, they could see fishy shapes wriggling over the pebbly bottom. It was a fierce sunset. Ruby clouds, empty of rain and streaked with lemon beams, reflected in the burnished river.

Molten gold seemed to be flowing beneath their feet, streaming across the shadowy land. A magical evening, an idyllic spot.

'You're too young, Sylvia. I took advantage of your trust. When you kissed me . . . I'm only human and you're a beautiful young woman. Now listen, love,' Sam insisted, taking her by the shoulders, 'you mustn't think of me in a romantic way. Perhaps you'll fall in love with David all over again, or maybe you haven't yet met the man you'll eventually marry, but what you feel for me has grown out of dependency. I've almost manufactured it and I feel hideously guilty.' He pushed her gently away. 'As long as you are under my roof, that mustn't happen again.'

He walked away, leaving Sylvia staring down at a pair of swans gliding towards the reddening twilight.

She willed the great dreambird to enter her body and peck away the pain, imagining how it would feel to grow wings between her shoulders, to dive down into the water and murder a trout.

And then, as she felt its fluttering presence behind the mask of her face, she realized that it wasn't a bird at all.

A gross mutilation of a man

sat on Douglas Hythe's chesterfield. The musician despised ugliness. His stomach was too sensitive for the grotesque, and the stench emanating from this monster's body was foul with stale alcohol and shit.

Lord! What a face. One glinting eye. An eye cheated of its partner, bitter, resentful. Folds of skin sewn across an empty socket. A nose with such a kink that one hairy nostril was stretched wide and the other compressed to a black slit. One perfectly formed, ringed ear. The other joined to a roughly shaven face by a mass of tangled scar tissue. Black teeth.

Douglas smoothed his own silver hair and looked towards the piano for comfort.

'This is insane. You expect me to believe that my daughter is married to you? And that this child . . . is yours?'

'Just tell Greta – sorry, Alexandra – that you've seen me. That I'm alive, and kicking like a fucking pony.'

The dreadful man suddenly lunged and grabbed Douglas by the collar, pulling his face towards the horror of his own.

Nose to nose, he spat, 'Pretty, isn't it, sweet Alexandra's hand-iwork? No, don't you bloody turn away!'

'Why not speak to her yourself?'

'I will. Eventually. Meanwhile she'll be looking over her shoulder every minute of every day – waiting.'

'I've no idea where she is. Alexandra has a wonderful habit of disappearing.'

The working half of Dick's face leered. 'Takes a nice pho-tograph, Greta. Even looked good on newsprint. You know, when we got married, I vaguely remember noticing the name on her birth certificate wasn't Greta, but then, neither was mine Dick!' He flashed a mischievous gold tooth. 'A fair bonus, after all these years, to find myself married to MONEY.'

'You'll get nothing out of me.'

'How's your career, Hythe? Would publicity help? Daugh-ter attempts to kill gypsy husband?'

'Pity she didn't succeed.'

'Reckon she'd agree. But I hung on . . .' his strong, filthy hands splayed, '. . . promising to feel Greta's neck one more time.'

Douglas locked fear behind his lips.

The evil man sneered, 'Just for now, I'll let Greta run free. She'll know I'm behind her. She'll shake when she hears foot-steps, blubber with fright at every noise in the night. She'll never stop running. Tell her this, Hythe. She owes me, and she'll pay. In cash. In pain.'

'Pain?'

'Tell me, Hythe, where is my kid?'

'No idea.'

'Liar.'

Douglas looked up into the towering, distorted face. A shaft of light glinted off something metallic in the ugly man's hand.

'I'm not a rich man . . .'

'Oh, Hythe. If I took your money, Greta would just laugh.' Dick scowled. 'It's blood money I want. Money for blood.'

❖

Sam was surprised when Douglas Hythe announced himself on the telephone.

'Alexandra isn't here. Where? Er . . . I'm not sure,' he lied, 'but she promised to ring me tonight. Yes, I'll give her a message. Urgent. I understand.'

For a few more seconds Sam listened, his expression changing to absolute horror. 'JESUS!' he swore. This information merited the absolute. As Sam replaced the receiver he was already dialling Scarborough.

'Alexandra, call your father urgently. He's leaving the country – a tour or something, but he must talk to you. He wants to warn you – that – Oh Hell . . .'

'What is it, Sam? Is it about Alice? Tell me for God's sake.'

'Alexandra. YOUR HUSBAND! Dick has been at Halstone House. He's looking for you. And your baby. Alexandra. ALEXANDRA . . .'

The phone went dead.

❖

DC Butterwell was positively crowing.

'Juice be aflowin, sir! Had a bloke in – Provy man – sells

335

insurance to Mary Linden. Saw same lady having lunch with suave geezer, just a couple of days before her man took the tumble.'

Smiling serenely, Howard ordered, 'Bring her in.'

Butterwell rubbed cake crumbs off his trousers. 'Sir.'

'And, Butterwell, you start the interview. I'll watch.'

❖

Howard folded his arms while Big Boy Butterwell tenaciously wore Mary down. Deference to her bereavement was abandoned as the interview dragged on through the day. Time and again the inquisitor demanded the name of her lover. Time and again she denied all knowledge. At about four in the afternoon Mary feigned a faint.

DI Howard plied her with sips of water, attentive as an apologetic lover.

'Sorry if Butterwell's upset you, Mary. Would I be right in guessing that this man you're protecting is married?'

'No! But I am. Married. Was.'

'Men don't like sharing. Did your lover kill your husband?'

'No! I keep telling you, he's not my lover! He's totally innocent in all this. Just a friend. Barely a friend really.'

'So why protect him?'

Her eyes glazed slightly. 'He's – famous. The newspapers would make something of nothing. We had lunch, that's all. A chat. Entirely innocent, I swear. I hold – held – my wedding vows sacred.'

'Politician? Royalty? Archbishop of Canterbury?'

'Musician.'

Howard opened his notebook. 'Name him, Mary.'

'You can't make me.'

'Don't be daft. Of course I can.'

She bowed her head. Howard let silence tick slowly, before sniggering,

'There was a fair lady intent on . . .

romance, and she found herself lent on

by a dashing musician,

with a vain disposition

and a passion for women from Kenton.'

'Fool.'

'No, Mary. You're the fool.'

'Why don't you ask the others?'

'The Sharps? Do they know him?'

'Yes.'

'So I'm going to find out anyway.'

'I don't want it to be me – that betrays him.'

'Oh, Mary. Misguided loyalty. Your husband was murdered and, well, any minute now I'll have to say it.'

'What?'

'Mary Linden, I'm arresting you for the murder of your husband, Arthur Linden, etcetera, etcetera.'

Her face blanched under the powder.

'Someone pushed your man over that rail.'

'No one pushed him. I swear. Arthur just held his chest and fell.'

'His name, Mary,' Howard ordered sternly.

Her personal concerto was played out. 'Douglas Hythe.'

Tea in a trembling cup.

The muddled babies story. Mary rather enjoyed Howard's

surprise. But she still firmly maintained that Arthur had taken a seizure. The stress. Too much.

Eventually Howard stood up, warning her not to leave Newcastle. But Mary's mind was already dashing down several different escape routes.

'Can I make funeral arrangements yet?' she sniffed.

'Your husband's body should be released next week.'

'My mother-in-law wants him buried in Corbridge.'

'Ah.'

'And we've arranged for David to convalesce there.'

'Shouldn't he come home?'

'Doesn't want to.'

Howard sighed with something which might have been sympathy. A measured thought crossed his face. 'A car will take you to Corbridge, tomorrow.'

❖

'Late, sir. We both need some kip.'

Howard carried on doodling.

Butterwell asked, 'Do you believe all this bollocks about muddled bairns?'

'Oddly, I do. The lover and husband scenario was always a tad trite.'

'Weird sort of crime, swapping babies.'

'No evidence unless blood tests show something. It's hearsay – unless the horse's mouth confesses.'

'Alexandra Hythe?'

'I've asked Wiltshire to pick up Douglas Hythe and track down his wandering gypsy daughter. But, Butterwell, I don't care which kid is which. I want to know who killed Linden.

Six liars on that landing when he toppled, one of them, maybe two, pushed.'

'You don't think he fell?'

'You can't fall over a banister. It takes momentum.'

'So who's your money on, sir?'

'You say first, Butterwell.'

'Sharp. There's a dirtiness about the man. More than coal dust.'

❖

Another man, with a different dirt in his heart, was helping Douglas Hythe to load the car. Suitcase, blazer, brogues and a case of manuscript.

Martin was in torment, but he wanted to stay beautiful for these last minutes. He hummed romantic melodies from *Kismet*, *Showboat* and *Carousel*, while they did the checklist together. Wallet, passport, reading glasses. Fresh bandages. TCP.

Blood was still seeping under the dressing where Martin had fastened the bits of his master's skin together with elastoplast. And for his pains, his tenderness? Douglas was leaving him – for a woman.

Oh yes, the great musician had, with rare humility, explained it all. That he had become involved in a fatal accident. That it wasn't his fault, yet he had to keep the wife quiet because she could blame him.

It didn't help. The car pulled away. Not even a kiss goodbye.

'And this is my beloved,' sang the butler sweetly, leaning against the grand piano. 'Dawn's promising skies, petals on a pool, drifting . . .' The melody hurt too much. He tried to dance and couldn't. So he thumped his fingers down on the keys, bashing and bashing. An ear-shattering dementation rang through the empty house.

In the garden, Dick Korda sat listening, rubbing a dirty handkerchief along the blade of his knife.

❖

Mary checked out of the window to see if anyone was watching. Loosening the heavy curtain cord, she wound it through her fingers and thought about hanging.

The telephone jangled. It was Douglas himself, ringing from a box, his seductive voice dripping with tenderness. Mary's hand shook. She'd Judased him.

He sounded very keyed up. In her own despair it took a while for her to comprehend what he was saying. An entirely shocking notion! His proposal winded her. Heart and eyelashes began to flutter. Madness. Delicious, rebellious, defiant madness.

As she laid the handset back in its cradle, she was racking her brain to remember something Arthur had once said. To do with tax. A box in the attic.

She hauled the heavy wooden ladder up to the landing. Climbed it. Flicking on David's Scout torch, she pressed the wooden lid into the dark abyss. Then she glanced down. The stairwell curved away beneath her feet, down, down . . . she could feel the ghost of Arthur, pushing . . .

Fighting off a sweaty hot flush, she hauled herself upwards and crawled along splintery beams to be rewarded with a find which surpassed her own greedy expectations. Clutching a wad of notes, she whispered to herself, 'Arthur Linden, you crafty old sod.'

❖

The door opened just enough for one eyeball.

'Hello, dearie. Buy some pegs?'

Janice Kirkstone slammed the door in the gypsy's face.

Old Binnie took her painful bones down the stairs again. She leaned on a brick wall at the end of the road, and worried. The evil was closing in; she could feel it in every prickling, silver hair. How could she protect Greta's baby?

❖

With every gin slug Dick Korda pushed his foot harder on the accelerator, rueing his losses: money, pride, face, years, and the Zipper! He ached for Zipper power, Zipper speed, Zipper screams, Zipper cash bag, Zipper swagger.

But Greta had hurt him so badly that he hadn't been able to work for months. And she had taken all his money. Now, all he could do was to work for pennies, for the Zipper's new owner.

Another slug.

The Zipper. Gone for ever. Yet – maybe not. Round and round. Purples and reds and flashing lights. Round and round.

❖

On Howard's desk lay an old hospital report of Dick Korda's horrific injuries. His inner vision was swimming with bloody

341

pictures of a burst eyeball. Could this monstrous attack have been perpetrated by the beautiful Alexandra Hythe?

Her face and body were imprinted on Howard's memory. She was physically magnificent, strong enough, certainly; but was her capacity for violence this grim? He imagined her above him, wielding a knife, eyes flashing. Oh yes, he could picture that. All his instincts screamed that the raven-haired vixen was highly dangerous. And yet, how could he deny the intelligence which had immediately intrigued him?

These were not loose ends, these knotty, twisting threads of muddled babies, accidents, madness and violence; these were all part of weave. He needed to question Alexandra Hythe. Badly.

❖

The same woman was driving across the county in a second-hand Land Rover (bought from a farmer, in Tony's name), trying to convince herself that release from the horrendous guilt over being a husband-murderer felt good. But as Greta focused on the road, the wretched ghost who had haunted her for three years became more and more solid. Dick. Not a ghost at all. Damnedly alive!

Her father's panicky orders, disguised as paternal protection, had sounded ugly and sad. How naive to expect her to obey his precise, calculated instructions. Greta knew what she had to do – get to Dick before he found the two little girls in Newcastle.

There were several things Greta did not know.

Firstly, that her father had already found both Alice and

her legal daughter, Jan. Secondly, what Douglas had endured at Dick's hand, to protect his grandchild.

Thirdly, the dangerous depths of a certain dancer's jealousy.

❖

The rain stopped on Wednesday night. In Newcastle the sky cleared and the North Star shone down on a lonely girl, huddled on a park bench.

By six in the morning Katherine was hitching a lift to Corbridge. In the last two days she had already been to London and come back again. Loneliness in scruffy hotel beds had even made her spare a thought for Sylvia's solitary, missing years.

Missing.

Missing was a funny word. Absent. Also – longing.

Did longing describe what she felt for Alice, and for David? Was love missing? Was missing love?

Alice's birthday, tomorrow. Katherine had sent a card from London. It was going to be horrible, not being there, helping her open her presents. But she couldn't go home. She could not!

In Corbridge she jumped out of a lorry and headed for Twin Elms, the house she had hoped her little family would one day inherit. Not that she wished premature death on Ethel. David's grandmother was the one adult she wholeheartedly admired.

With relief she walked the last half mile, tired, but hopeful that Ethel would take pity on her.

Unfortunately, as she approached the house, she saw

Mary Linden being helped out of a police car. The last person she wanted to bump into! Frustrated and hungry, Katherine went down to the river bank and found a large stone to sit on.

Where could she go now? She was so hungry she began to suck her thumb. Exhausted, she laid her head on her arms. The rush of the river and its peated smell soothed her and blessed sleep began to hover behind her eyelids.

But a substantial shadow roused her.

'Eee, hinny. You'll get piles!'

Daft Daphne was blocking the sun. Her limited vocabulary was thick with Northumbrian dialect.

'Mary's at the house, Daphne. I don't want to see her.'

'Cud freeze a pan o'chips, that'un.'

'Can you let me in the scullery door and tell Ethel I'm upstairs? She'll understand.'

'Howay round the back. And watch oot fer that nanny. She's in a right bossy fettle.'

❖

Ethel was puffing by the time she reached the upstairs nursery, where she found Alice playing with her doll's house and Katherine Sharp prone on the little girl's bed.

'What's up, pet?'

'Oh, Mrs Linden, I'm so glad Alice is still here!'

To Ethel's surprise, and Katherine's, the teenager began to cry. Ethel put an awkward arm around her shoulders. Suddenly, tears also swam across the old lady's cataracts, as a wave of grief swamped her. Ethel and the girl who would never be her grandson's wife sobbed heavily together. Alice, puzzled, came and put her little arms on both of them and very quietly joined in the weeping, the mystery of adult sadness too uncomfortable to bear.

But Ethel and Katherine were strong, obstinate women, and after some determined hanky blowing they began to talk. Afterwards, seeing that the lass was shaking with exhaustion, Ethel took her up a second flight of stairs to a quiet attic bedroom. Unable to resist sleep any longer, Katherine lay down under the eiderdown.

In the kitchen the atmosphere simmered with resentment. Nanny Clara Blake was boiling Alice's egg. Unfortunately she had noticed Daphne's inadequate washing of some raspberries and had instructed her to check for maggots. Since Daphne's arthritic husband, Tom, had grown the rasps himself, this caution threw her into a massive huff, and she laid the table in silence.

So, because no one told her, Clara never knew that Katherine was upstairs, sleeping off her sad exhaustion.

❖

Ethel and Mary sat on opposite sides of the lawn. Each had a book, and a glass, and both were sighing as if they had entered a sighing competition.

The air was still. No breeze ruffled the trees. Birds were too lethargic to sing. Flowers sat motionless in their beds. In an atmosphere more fragile than old crystal, the endless afternoon limped into a curious evening.

Supper brought a surprise guest to Twin Elms, a neighbouring farmer called Ernest Wood, who held his sherry glass in his huge hand and sipped from lips which seemed too big for the glass. While Ethel fussed her old friend, Mary watched Alice charm him. Fleetingly, she recalled her own childhood and the men who had brought her up. In a swift, sharp lance of wisdom, she comprehended why she had become – herself.

The little girl was dancing with excitement, telling Ernest that tomorrow was her birthday. Would he come to her party? Her daddy was coming, in an ambulance, 'specially'. Also 'Tatwim, Dwandad, Gommom and pwetty lady Sylvia wif dat man who mended doggies'.

The nanny hurried Alice off to bed and returned, freshly bloused and blushing, to take her seat next to Ernest Wood at the dining table. Mary sat opposite the clumsy man, automatically adopting a supercilious manner to underline his lack of sophistication.

Nanny and farmer discussed dogs. Mary hummed. Daphne ladled soup. Dripped it down her skirt. The farmer smiled kindly at the dim woman and Mary wanted to smack them both.

Conversation became threadbare. Candles quivered. Ernest ran out of pleasantries. Ethel's bitter mourning, however contained, salted the raspberry crumble and her deep suspicion poisoned the wine. Around the shadowy table, they ate to avoid speaking. No eyes met. No laughter relieved the suffering.

Finally Ethel herself spoke. 'By the way, Mary,' her chins trembled triumphantly, 'I've bought David a present. I don't want him getting another confounded motorbike so I invested in a new Ford Anglia. It's behind the old stable. Clara says it goes well. Do you think Arthur would have approved?'

Mary shrugged. If Ethel wanted to pay for David's

luxuries – fine. Nevertheless, she felt uncomfortably sorrowful, thinking about her son.

'I'm very grateful to Violet Sharp,' Ethel continued, 'for explaining about Arthur's death. Upsetting, yes, but better to know. And I understand, Mary, why you found it difficult to tell me the truth. I suppose you've heard about the arrest.'

Mary was jolted. 'Arrest?'

'Mary has been so brave,' Ethel informed Ernest sweetly. 'Coped very well – under the circumstances. She could have been bitter.'

'Who's been arrested, Mother?' Mary was flushing up from her genitals.

'Why, that man who pushed him!'

'No one pushed him! He had a seizure. For God's sake! You're embarrassing your friend.'

'Oh, I assure you . . .' Ernest remonstrated.

'Friend of yours, wasn't he Mary? Special friend?'

Mary stood up. Ernest automatically stood too, out of politeness.

'What are you accusing me of, Mother?' Mary knew this was exactly the wrong time to lose her temper, but she was so tense she wanted to scream.

Ernest laid down his napkin. 'Late. Best be off. Thank you . . .'

Stiffly Ethel escorted him into the hall and returned with her slack face quivering. Clara stood up and sat down twice.

'Stay, Clara,' Ethel ordered. 'I'm so angry I might have a heart attack.'

In a fury of fear, Mary hissed, 'How embarrassing! How dare you?'

The old woman's face had changed, all feigned gentility gone, her frown cool and goading in the candlelight.

'I've heard you telephoning him. Your dirty friend.' She punched her arthritic finger in her daughter-in-law's chest. 'Arthur was worth a hundred of you, you black-hearted whore!'

That did it. Mary blew. 'Your son was a jelly-livered, pathetic excuse for a man who didn't have the balls . . .'

'Unlike lover boy.' Ethel sneered, as if the reference to sexual parts proved Mary's immorality.

'He is not my lover!'

'No sex? What a disappointment.'

Clara's eyes were wide. 'Mrs Linden! Dear! Perhaps you should . . .'

'This woman and her lecher MURDERED MY SON.'

Coherent words failing her, Mary banged the table with her fist.

Ethel moved in for the kill. 'Listen well, Mary. You'll never get a penny of Arthur's money. I told the police everything. Telephone calls. Dates. The way you and Arthur fought, divorce threats. Asking him for money in return for his freedom. They've got your motive, Mary dear. You'll go to jail. Or hang.'

'No I bloody won't!'

DI Ernest Wood, concealed in the hall, was scribbling in his notebook. Any minute now he would have a confession! But, no! A different truth was about to be revealed.

'It was Cuthbert Sharp. That's who killed my husband. Cuthbert bloody Sharp!'

❖

Between the elm trees a shadow moved.

❖

Violet Sharp sat in darkness, beyond tiredness after another round of police questioning. She had stuck faithfully to the story until Butterwell accused her of having an affair with Arthur! How had she answered the madness? She couldn't remember. Her head was still buzzing.

Eventually they'd allowed her to go home. Here, the worst misery of all. Katherine had still not returned. Four whole days. In the middle of the nightmare, their youngest had flown, just like Sylvia. Tomorrow things would have to be done. People informed. Comments accepted. Again.

Past midnight. The front room wallowed in gloom. Cuthbert came and sat in his chair.

'A've done the till,' he said. 'Money's ready for the bank. Housekeeping's on the bench. Ten bob for Alice's savings.'

Violet nodded. A death sentence hovered between husband and wife. A noose of doubt, distrust and mutual recrimination was tightening around their marriage. Perhaps, by sitting it out, this long warm night would never end. The sun would never rise to shine on the horror.

Violet looked at her husband. Slayer of Arthur. Alien. Old. Nose too big. Face too florid. Eyes shifting craftily.

He scratched his crotch. Violet stared at his black fingernails. In her head, she heard the word Katherine had used. Pervert.

'Doomed! A'm doomed!' moaned Cuthbert suddenly. 'They'll hang uz like a bloody chicken.'

'It was an accident.'

'A should of telt them that in the first place. Your lies, woman, have made it twice as bloody worse.'

'I was just protect'n you. Now it's just as bad for me, and I'm innocent. They said it took more than one pair of hands to hoy Arthur over the banister.' She went to the ironing pile and handed him a clean handkerchief. 'If it comes to it, Cuth, if the truth outs, will you tell them it wasn't me?'

'Oh, aye. And while they'll drag uz to the bloody gallows, you can knit.' He blew his nose.

'Oh, Cuth.' Violet felt a deep, remembered emotion. A long-forgotten urge made her sit on his lap. He was hot, his thighs rigid, and, as she laid her head on his chest, he made no attempt to cuddle her.

'Made me mind up,' he said, 'to turn meself in. First thing the morra.'

'It's the bairn's birthday.'

'Aye, and we should be doin the party, not Ethel. But mebees now – it's fer the best. Happy birthday, pet lamb. Yer grandad's not here. He's gone to jail. And he won't be around to see yer fourth.'

Violet felt his chest heaving, and suffered a sudden wash of jealousy. She took his red face in her hands.

'What about me, Cuth? What about my next birthday?'

He grunted, his eyes screwed up. His silence was as hard and cold as a cell door. Perhaps, behind his eyes, his mortality was glaring too harshly.

Violet rose clumsily from her man's lap. 'You don't give a

fly'n fanny about me, do you?' Her worst fears slipped off her tongue. 'Cuth. The cops, they'll ask – why you got so ferocious with Kirkstone.' She waited for a moment, hating his bleak weakness. 'The way you are with Alice – it's hurt all of us. What owa Kath said. Is there any truth? Do little girls make you feel . . . ?'

Cuthbert's bloodshot eyes bulged.

But it was too late for Violet to stop. 'You see, there are three empty beds in my home. Why, Cuth? Why have I lost me lasses?'

Cuthbert rose from his chair, and walked slowly to the door. His body seemed leaden, as if injustice was weakening his bones. 'That's it then. Aye, that's it.'

Violet listened to the roar of the lorry and a tear rolled into her mouth.

❖

Katherine woke abruptly. From her room in the attic of Twin Elms, she could hear someone moving around in the bedroom below. Clara? Was there a problem with Alice? She went to the top of the narrow stairs to listen. No, she couldn't hear the bairn crying.

There was a draught, as if a window or door was open. Prickles flurried over her skin. She tiptoed down into darkness. Feeling her way along, she opened the nursery door.

And Katherine's kismet lurched.

A yelp

in the darkness. Alice? Was she sick?

Eyes stinging, Clara pushed her feet into pompomed slippers and pulled on a cardigan.

The bed in the nursery was empty! She tossed aside cold cotton sheets. Wide awake now and worried, Clara opened the bedroom door just in time to hear a scuffle, a mewing sound, and someone shuffling clumsily down the stairs.

'Who's that?'

No reply.

'Ethel?'

Surely Ethel would have switched on the light.

'That you, Mary? What's the matter with Alice? Why didn't you call me?'

Sixth sense suddenly urged caution. Why would the most unloving grandmother in Christendom be taking Alice downstairs, secretly? Indignation turned to panic as Clara heard the back door click, then footsteps crunching on gravel.

NO!

There was a slam of a car door and the burp of an engine.

MARY'S STEALING ALICE!

Clara flung open the back door, just as a van turned out into the road. In a futile gesture she ran to the end of the drive and waved, shouting loud enough to waken the whole household. But there was no answering flare of lights in windows.

EMERGENCY! EMERGENCY!

Once upon a war, Nanny Clara had driven ambulances around London. Now, instinctively, she dashed back to the hall table and grabbed the key to David's car. Still in nightie and cardigan, she spurred the little vehicle out into the road.

She caught sight of the van on the far side of the bridge, where the driver had pulled up and was checking the back doors, slamming them again. It certainly wasn't Mary. It was a man. And as Clara drew level, he climbed back in and zoomed off into the night.

I can't let this happen, she thought desperately. Who is this dreadful man? Why has he taken poor little Alice? She'll be terrified!

Over the hills, through the inky night, Clara chased the van, until, in a moorland gully, it stopped. Turning a sharp bend, Clara came upon it too quickly, so she flared her headlights and overtook him. The beam coloured the van blood-red.

Terrified, she drove around a bend and pulled the Anglia behind a stony outcrop. Tucking nightie into knicker legs, she threw herself into high fern and hauled herself up to the top of the ridge, to look back down the road. She could just make out the man moving around the van again.

Night blackened. Ferns swept against her face. A thorn bush grabbed her cardigan. Clara wrenched herself free, angry at her own hesitation. Dare she tackle the man in the van? Could there be two of them? Kidnappers or murderers? Her life suddenly felt very fragile. But horrific thoughts of what might be happening to Alice drove Clara past her own fear. She hurried back to the car and hunted in the boot for a weapon, grubbing desperately in the darkness for something with which to slash tyres,

– or slash a man's balls.

Just as her hand fell on the spider wrench, the van flashed past again. Clara swore and scrambled back to the car.

Hurry! She drove like a demon, until eventually a pair of pink lights appeared ahead. In the darkness Clara started praying. God answered by trimming the night clouds with silver as she trailed the van back towards Newcastle, crossing the High Level Bridge, then through the city to the Town Moor, where the van bumped across the field, towards the sleeping jumble of caravans.

Clara parked as near as she dared and followed on foot, her slippers soaking in the dew, the spider wrench clutched under her cardigan. Like a spy, she slid from ride to ride, tripping over trailing cables, half-eaten toffee apples and broken bottles. In the first blush of dawn the Ghost Train's garish colours hung dirty as death. Overhead a carriage on the Big Wheel squeaked.

I'm a brave woman, she told herself. My Fred always said I was brave.

About to risk her own life, the memory of her husband flared, her own agonizing, unhealed war wound.

Oh, Fred, without you I'm like an ambulance bell without a clapper. I thought a nanny's life would be peaceful. I thought I could fill my empty photo albums with other people's children. I thought I could settle down with Ethel Linden in a tranquil house; time to stroll leafy lanes, take long baths and read adult books. Oh, Fred, there's more to me than Peter Pan. Here I am, only half-way through the first chapter of *Lady Chatterley*, and look, I'm wandering around Newcastle Town Moor in my slippers, ready to . . .

She raised her hand to knock on a caravan door. Behind her back was the spider wrench.

❖

Friday, 24 June.

While Geordies slumbered, the sun rose across the saga, glistening on dewy strawberries and milk-bottle tops.

Violet roused herself from the armchair. 'Cuthbert!'

The house rang hollow.

Just before eight, the postman delivered an envelope addressed to Miss Alice Sharp, with a second-class stamp and a London postmark.

❖

In Fontbury, Sam was picking sweet peas at the bottom of the garden.

Schizophrenic heart, he self-diagnosed. That's my problem. And starved libido. One minute I'm lusting after Alexandra, the next I'm maddened with confusion over Sylvia, a skinny, neurotic teenager with so many problems that she would test a skilled psychiatrist.

She's ill. Her mind is too full. Her body too empty. The

skin under her arms is as papery as an old woman's. But her vulnerability titillates me. This is not love, it is power.

Sam argued against himself until, inevitably, his earthy instincts won. He took sweet peas to her bedside.

'Forgive me?'

Her eyes opened. The clock ticked. Mustard turned over in his basket and went back to sleep. Through the open window they heard the clink of the gate as the postman pushed letters through the box. The church bell chimed eight times.

Sylvia sat up and sniffed the sweet peas. She whispered softly,

'Love, who bewailest

The frailty of all things here,

Why chose you the frailest

For your cradle, your home, and your bier?'

Very slowly Sam lifted his fingers to stroke her brow. This time the teenager did not giggle. She took his hand, opened it, and kissed his palm. Sam felt the heat from her lips surge down to his testicles. As he lay down beside her on the soft eiderdown, a sweet sadness flowed through him. Her needy bones reached out, her lips became soft and sensual.

The preparatory movements of the fabulous dance began. Joy, sated and salty, washed over them. Sam's troubled conscience fled out into the morning and only holy love-lust remained.

Sylvia's wasted muscles felt petal-soft. Enveloped in pale blue nylon, her bones were as long and hard as a bunch of knobbled sticks. Her breastless nipples were locked into privacy by pink ribbon bows. Sam's gentle fingers loosened the ribbons, but as the fabric slipped, Sylvia's hands flew up to stop him, and she sat up as if startled out of a dream.

Sam groaned and rolled away. As his thudding heart slowed, common sense returned with a vengeance. 'God, I'm sorry, love.'

But Sylvia's fragility was the vet's weakness. The more she craved reassurance and love, the more empowered he felt to heal her. This bodily shyness was a new challenge. Irresistible.

❖

From a telephone box, Violet dialled Fontbury.

'Sam, can you take Sylvia to Corbridge for Alice's party this afternoon? Ta. And thank you, lad, for look'n after my lass. Me and Cuth owe you a lot. Bless you.'

It took two buses to get to the Kirkstones' flat. In the echoing entrance, she skirted around the spot where Arthur died, and climbed the stairs. She left the parcel containing the dolly's clothes next to the Kirkstones' door, then, with shaking hands, pushed a letter through the box.

Back at the bus stop, she prayed, 'Dear God, let me get to Corbridge, before Ethel finds out.'

❖

Janice gasped. 'Hell's teeth! Gypsies and murderers. I knew they'd keep coming back.' She hurled the doll's clothes into the bin. 'What does the letter say?'

Matthew's hand was trembling. 'SHITE! That old bugger Sharp has only decided to go and confess! OH, MY GOD! The coppers will come – TO WORK! I'll be arrested in front of EVERYBODY!' He turned on his wife savagely, 'It's all your bloody fault!'

'Mine?'

'I should have fathered my own bairn! Not borrowed one!'

Janice turned his poisonous words over in her stomach before saying, very quietly, 'God gave us Jan.'

'But I'm trapped. With you. Loving a bairn I can never call my own.' Matthew pushed a clean hanky into his pocket. 'Sharp can say what he likes, I'll deny everything.' He shook his finger in her face. 'And you'd better do the same!'

'I can't lie any longer.' She bit her fist with worry. 'It's a sin.'

'Saint Janice!'

Matthew strode into little Jan's bedroom, his face twitching with emotion; yet with infinite tenderness, he picked up his sleepy child. 'Kiss for Daddy, bonny lass?'

As little Jan snaked her pale, slender arms around his neck he swayed and sang softly, 'Bye baby bunting, Daddy's going hunting . . .'

Janice watched them from the hallway. In this triangle, she was always a voyeur; the most loving, the least loved. She accepted, in that moment, that her marriage was an empty kettle, boiled dry, burnt. Matthew did not love her. He was a coward who had killed a man and would lie to hide his guilt. This callousness threw the whole Christian sum completely off the heavenly balance sheet, because his sin was just too big, even for Jesus to forgive.

He left.

Janice crossed the toddler's kilt straps and brushed her dark hair.

'Swing park, Mammy?'

'No, we're going to see a man down the town.'

An hour later, alighting from the trolley bus, Janice carried little Jan up narrow stairs, praying that the solicitor could help her to keep Jan and divorce her husband.

❖

Sylvia was studying her body in the mirror. She talked to the feathery spirit who could slide in and out of her body, loving her when she could not love herself, feeling things she dared not feel. Today he was moving around the room, no more than a judder in the dusty air. Being naked in front of him was intensely erotic.

'Why did God give me such huge nipples? Fuggering freckles everywhere. Ginger hair on my triangle. Dad's mark. Alice grew in this belly. Born between these thighs, three years ago today.'

❖

Ethel had slept in. She woke feeling tired and lethargic. Pushing herself out of bed, she dressed with as much haste as her weakening limbs could manage, then made her way downstairs.

'Clara!' she shouted. 'Katherine!'

No reply. Her head felt strange, muzzy.

'Clara!' she shouted again.

Eyes wouldn't focus properly.

'Mary! Where is everyone?'

The pain hit like a series of hammer blows. It emanated from her shoulder, but quickly enveloped her whole body. Knees collapsing, she slid on to the Chinese rug and rolled over, struggling to push her mind out of her feeble frame and upwards towards a place somewhere above the crushing pain in her chest. 'I will not give in. Not now. I cannot give in. I will not . . .'

❖

'Sorry to be leaving you, mate.' They had wheeled David along to see Hendo. An ambulance was due to take him to Corbridge.

All right for some, thought Hendo resentfully, watching his friend hitch his pot leg around. 'Your face is a bloody mess!'

'That's rich, from a gorilla with his head shaved. Listen, I'm sorry about Katherine.'

Hendo hesitated for a moment, too proud to admit pain. 'D'you love her? Or d'you still love Sylvia?'

'I think I'm terrified of both of them.'

'So! Happy families, this afternoon?'

'Daggers out and me in the middle.'

'Old Sharpy'll be watch'n like a hawk.'

'Miserable bugger. He's never bothered to visit.'

'Nor me.'

'Bastard. Obviously doesn't reckon he owes us anything.'

'Well. It wasn't for his sake, was it?'

'No.' David looked out of the window. 'I'm dying to see Alice.'

'Davy, are you absolutely sure that Alice is . . . you know . . . the right one?'

'POSITIVE! Do me a favour – don't ever ask again.'

'Sorry, mate. Here, luk. A've gorra birthday card for 'er. Mam bought it.'

A pink envelope passed between them.

It would never be delivered.

'When you get out of here, Hendo,' said David, 'we'll have one hell of a booze-up.'

'A've got just one ambition, kiddo. To rock-and-roll!'

❖

A telegram, penned late yesterday afternoon.

DI HOWARD STOP KIRKSTONE SHARP AND LINDEN HAD FIGHT STOP LINDEN FELL STOP ACCIDENT STOP I WAS INNOCENT WITNESS STOP DAUGHTER ALEXANDRA HAD NOTHING TO DO WITH IT STOP WE ARE BOTH INNOCENT STOP DOUGLAS HYTHE STOP

Butterwell knocked. 'Sir? Cuth Sharp's not at his house or the yard.'

'Find the bastard. Where's Kirkstone?'

'Cell number one.'

Howard rubbed the side of his nose. 'Truthie toothy time.'

❖

Alan arrived at Twin Elms just before one o'clock. As far as he could tell, no one was in, which was a bit puzzling. He was

361

further surprised when Violet walked up the drive, looking exhausted.

'Where's Mr Sharp? I'd have given you a lift, if I knew he couldn't fetch you. I've knocked. No answer. They must have gone down the village. Are you all right, Mrs Sharp?' She was clutching her stomach.

'Alice!' she shouted. Then she began dashing around the house, looking in windows. Alan instinctively joined her. From one of the low sitting-room casements, he could see through to the hallway.

'Flaming Hell, look!' he roared. 'It's old Mrs L. On the floor. She's dead!'

'Jesus Mother of Mary! Break the glass!'

So Alan hurled a stone at the glass, removed the shards and climbed in. As he approached the old lady, he was terrified of touching her, because her face was like candlewax. Thank God, just then, he heard a car crunch into the drive. He rushed to unbolt the front door, and was relieved to see that it was the vet, with Sylvia.

'Quick!' He shouted. 'It's Ethel . . . !'

Alan stood back, while the vet knelt and put his hand to Ethel's neck.

'She's alive. Get an ambulance.'

There was a telephone on the hall table. History repeats itself, Alan thought, dialling 999. While he was giving information to the operator, he watched Violet Sharp trying vainly to talk to the unconscious old lady. 'Where's Alice?' she was hissing. 'Who's looking after Alice?'

Sylvia was still standing outside, looking dazed and oddly

unmoved. Violet shouted out of the door, 'Find Alice, Sylvia!'
Then to him, 'Alan, find owa Alice!'

They both ran then, through the house, searching every
room, every cupboard, under beds. Eventually they met at the
top of the stairs and just stood looking at each other.

'Have you got her?' shouted Violet.

'The nanny must have taken her out for a walk,' called
Alan, still holding Sylvia's gaze.

At that moment the ambulance arrived, followed by a
second, carrying David to his daughter's birthday party. As
David was wheeled in, his gran was carried out.

'Heart, I think,' said Sam. 'I'll go with her.'

Violet shook her head. 'No. She doesn't know you. I'll
have to go.' Her face was grey. 'David, you stay and help find
owa Alice. Dear God! What's happened to the bairn?'

Once the ambulance had left, they searched. Waited.
Searched again. After an hour they knew for certain that there
would be no birthday party. Neither the adored three-year-
old nor her nanny returned.

DI Ernest Wood arrived. Slow and meticulous, he
inspected beds, noting that Mary Linden's had not been slept
in. He examined tyre tracks, but with two ambulances up and
down the drive, there was nothing to be gleaned. Wood tried
to reassure them that, any minute now, the missing persons
would walk back through the door.

The vet seemed desperate to leave. He led Sylvia to the car.
She was clucking and muttering to herself, like a mad old
lady, obviously traumatized.

Alan was left with David, to sit through a long, long afternoon, looking at a birthday cake with three candles.

As soon as Sam was back in his surgery, he dialled Scarborough. Liz sounded flustered and Tony was singing opera like a strangled horse with bad vibrato.

The singing stopped.

'Greta's gone away. Said she had something to do.'

❖

'Where the Hell is Cuthbert Sharp?'

'Lorry found in Penrith station car park.' Howard studied the clock on the wall behind the Superintendent's head. His boss was furious.

'So he could be anywhere? North or South. Where's Mary Linden? Is Alexandra Hythe with her father?'

'Don't know. The lads in Wiltshire got there too late. He'd already scarpered. She may have gone to her family in Italy. The Marlettis.'

'Please God! Not the bleeding Mafia!' groaned the Super. 'So, where is Janice Kirkstone? What about this nanny and the kid, Alice? I can't make out who's been kidnapped, who's been murdered and who's done a runner. What in tarnation have you been doing, Howard? You find Sylvia Sharp and lose the whole of bloody Tyneside. Eight people missing! EIGHT!'

❖

No, actually. NINE.

A ninth person was missing.

Missing was Katherine Sharp's word.

Now bits of her were missing. She had no sight. No vision.

364

She couldn't feel her feet, or her hands. But she could still hear her heart, even though she willed it to stop. And still feel a sensation of wetness under her thighs. The flow of her blood as it slid away from the pain in her core.

She prayed for death.

Then for life.

Then for death again.

❖

Janice Kirkstone was found at her mother's. She announced her intention to divorce her husband and, at last, confirmed the facts about Arthur Linden's death, including Mary's last push. Butterwell described it as a remarkably boring truth, all things considered.

But the pressing new crime was KIDNAP. DI Howard consoled himself with the theory that Alice had been taken out of love. A child so jealously coveted could have been snatched by any one of the missing people, especially Alexandra Hythe, who had already tried it once.

Yet again, Howard hauled in Violet Sharp, who wept and pleaded ignorance.

'You're lying. Protecting your man. Where is he?'

'I don't know! Just find my family. Please!'

The tragic Mrs Sharp let out an involuntary wail, and handed him an envelope.

'What's this?'

'She's ran away to London! Owa Kath.'

Howard groaned aloud as he read the birthday message and checked the postmark. London, 2 June. Dear God! The lass had scurried away, just like her sister, to disappear, along with too many runaways, into the smoke of the flagitious capital.

They would never find her.

The frustrated policeman stared at the card, struck by the thought that a vulnerable teenager in London had selected this naive picture of a petal-clad fairy. She was hovering on translucent wings between cornflower stalks, and had dark ringlets, like Alice. But there was something impure about this fey. Her eyes were tipped seductively. Sheer coincidence, that's all it could be, that the slanted gaze reminded him of Alexandra Hythe.

Binnie would never leave Newcastle again. She had rented a flat in Jesmond, and sold the stall and lorry to a young traveller, for cash. She left her ancient caravan where it was, on the edge of the Town Moor, for the Council to discover and dispose of when the Hoppings cleared.

There were enough sixpences in her Post Office book to keep her for a few years. The old Romany woman walked sadly up Osborne Road. Roger carried her case.

Screams

dragged Clara Blake back to consciousness.

She found herself in a dark space with two small porthole windows, on a heap of stinking sacks. She recognized the smell. Blood.

Her perception of time was distorted and she panicked, like an old lady with dementia, open-mouthed, silent, trembling.

Then she screamed.

Then she stopped, because her yells were drowned in other fairground shrieks, and the thunderous organ music of the Hoppings.

Her memories began to tidy. Red van. I'm in the red van! She bashed at the doors with bare fists. After a while she calmed down enough to breathe.

It was dusk. Dawn to dusk! Almost a whole day since she had woken suddenly in her nice bedroom in Twin Elms, thinking she had heard Alice cry out.

Clara slumped against the metal walls and checked her body parts, limb by limb.

Perhaps attacking a monster with a spider wrench had not been her very best idea.

❖

Time to remove the sack. He'd had her many times now, while she couldn't see him. The thrill of doing it with a completely helpless young girl was exquisite, especially when she bled and he reckoned he was breaking her. This was not the first unsuspecting woman Dick had raped since Greta wrecked his face. Whores were expensive and the bitch had taken his money, so when the urge had come upon him – well, needs must.

This 'opportunity' was a fair bonus, a distraction to make up for the disappointment of finding himself on a wild goose chase.

Not that his information had been wrong. The nancy boy who lived with Hythe had told it true. Oh, how willingly the wimp had bleated, especially when his legs were threatened.

The kid, Alice, his own daughter, had certainly been in the big Corbridge house that afternoon. Fascinated, Dick had watched her play in the garden. She reminded him of his long-forgotten sister, with her black ringlets and plump cheeks.

When the two old biddies took her indoors he had felt oddly disappointed. Then he spotted the girl with the big, bouncing titties, sneaking in the back door. Taking his chance, Dick slipped in behind her, easing from corner to corner until he could get upstairs and hide behind a bedroom door.

When the old lady took the titty dolly up another flight of stairs, Dick silently opened the nursery door. The kid, his kid, was playing on the floor. Dick looked at the little body and felt strange. He wanted to speak to her, to touch her, and yet he couldn't.

Slipping back out of the house, he spent the evening hovering in the shadows, thinking and drinking. Later he dozed in the van, his dreams full of leprechauns; until his internal alarm woke him. Burglaring hour.

Dick slipped back into the darkened house. In the nursery he opened his sack.

But where was the child? She should have been there, slumbering innocently, waiting for her daddy to take her away. Frustrated, he tucked the sack in his belt and flicked his torch over shiny lino, a rocking horse, a pile of bricks. On the empty bed was a glass-eyed dolly.

Now he had his own dolly.

The young filly shouldn't have been tiptoeing around the house in such a flimsy nightie. She had wriggled in his arms, her large breasts soft beneath his right hand as he clamped her mouth with his left. One swift punch on the temple and the fleshy girl slumped in his arms. She smelled delicious – and he needed information. Good enough reasons. He pulled the sack over her head and torso, then bundled her down the stairs, across the yard, and out into the road, where he threw her into the van.

He drove a mile or so, then, just over the bridge, pulled up. Looking over his shoulder at the sleeping town, he dug in his pockets for his knife, flicked it, opened the back doors. She was still unconscious, so he climbed in, lifted the sack to her neck, and roped her arms to the upper part of her body. He worked by touch. Because the night was dark and exciting, he eased the lashings across her breasts so that he could feel her nipples protruding between the cords. Knowing that her body was entirely in his control, he couldn't help himself. With the knife between his teeth, he ran callused hands over her bare knees and up under her nightie.

A car passed him. For what Dick wanted to do, he needed privacy, so he locked the girl in the back and drove off into the hills, his lust fizzing and spiralling. Urgent with greedy need, Dick stopped in a quiet gully, and opened the van doors. She was awake, whining. Dick was not gentle. Viciously aroused, he threw his weight on top of her and used the knife to rip at her underwear. She was hard to enter, but once he'd mastered her thrashing body and pressed through the invisible barrier, he ejaculated almost immediately.

Now the fun was wearing off. The girl was almost a corpse. The last time he had set about her, she'd lain listlessly, her head thrown to one side. A rag doll.

And what the hell was he to do with the second dolly? The old china locked in the van?

❖

Clara dozed again, then woke on a fresh wave of panic. Terrified, claustrophobic, she shouted and shouted, bashing her knuckles raw on the metal panels, but the van was parked in the middle of heavily thrumming engines, so no one heard her.

❖

Katherine opened her eyes to feel a knife at her neck.

A wretched, one-eyed mask swam before her. Leathery breath hit her in the face. Trembling like a dying dog, Katherine tried to beg for pity or merciful murder, but she couldn't move her swollen tongue. Tied spread-eagled to a bed frame, she moved her hips across a slick of her own bodily fluids, anticipating rape or death, or both.

The man lifted her head and poured scorching gin into her gullet. Thirsty beyond madness, she swallowed. He slugged some himself, then began to question her.

Her fuddled brain tried to give clever answers, but logic was a distant, irrelevant relic of mortality. Only this moment was real, a terrifying ballooning trice.

He slapped her face. Lusting for the suck of death, she murmured, 'Alice is not the gypsy's baby. Jan is the gypsy's baby. Alice is mine. Alice is mine . . .'

❖

The sound of Dick's body slamming drunkenly against the side of the van shook Clara awake. She heard his muttered curses and waited in dread. But the engine revved beneath her. They were pulling away from the site. With nothing to hold on to, she bounced around, knees and knuckles bruising as she struggled to keep her balance.

❖

Greta had seen his face, the man who was her husband, seen the hideous scars she had inflicted, seen his drunken swagger. She had watched him stumble on the platform of the Zipper, heard him quarrel loudly with a younger man whose yellow hair was tied back in a ponytail. Sickened, yet perversely entertained, Greta had followed Dick to the caravan they used to share, warning herself to wait, to stick to her plan.

371

When he drove off in his van, she went to find Binnie, but a younger woman was working the stall.

'She's gone.'

'Where?'

'Her business. Hey, I know you – Korda's bitch.'

Greta turned away. She spotted Binnie's caravan, and, without conscience, took a screwdriver to the lock.

❖

Smoother road. Stop and hand brake. The driver's door opened and slammed.

Clara waited.

Through the porthole windows, she saw that they were in Gosforth High Street. Would he open the doors? She drew herself into a frog crouch, feet firmly braced against the floor, ready to leap. Seconds ticked by. Her knees cramped and she fought down the urge to cry.

But the villain had different plans. The vehicle pulled off again. Minutes later, and it stopped in a gloom of black trees and navy sky.

This was far worse. Pinned hard against the wall of the van, face tucked to the side of the window, again Clara crouched. She heard the lock turn carefully.

Click.

She hurled herself against the doors. They crashed open. Fists clenched before her like train buffers, the nanny leapt out, throwing her full weight at his chest. Dick fell backwards, still clutching a dribbling steak pie. Pushing and pummelling at his sluggish body, Clara scrambled to her feet and kicked him in the testicles.

Then she sprinted. Loose hair flying, cardigan held tightly to her chest, she ran through the trees in her slippers, faster than decency, her heart bursting.

❖

Hello, Joe.

In Binnie's caravan, Greta tucked her peasant skirt into baggy trousers, tied a shawl twice around her midriff, then fastened Tony's old baggy jacket over the ensemble. Her breasts were disguised in what appeared to be rolls of beer gut. She pulled a large cap over the bun on the back of her head and checked the tools in her pockets.

Anticipation quivered in her stomach. She turned up her collar, dropped out of the door, strode across to Dick's caravan and leaned against it, waiting for her prey, her undead husband.

What was that noise? A groan – muffled, weak. Female.

The door was open. She edged into the dark interior and flicked the torch over naked, pale skin. On the bed, splayed out like a human offering, blood over her thighs and breasts, lay a young girl.

What kind of monster had her husband turned into?

There must be time. She couldn't leave this poor girl. Fumbling at the knots, she released the binds. Two dilated eyes opened and closed again.

How to cover her? Greta grabbed Dick's stinking old coat and drew it over the bare, bruised, abused body. Without speaking, she hauled the trembling young woman out of the van.

At first the girl could not stand. Her knees repeatedly gave way as Greta manhandled her twitching body. But the young woman began pushing and kicking, her feet slipping on the grass, as if she wanted to run out of a nightmare, but couldn't.

Jesus! She thinks I'm a man!

'Hush. I'm a woman. I won't let a bloke near you.' She threw her strong arm around the girl's waist and took her weight on her hip. As they staggered together towards Binnie's caravan, Greta could never have suspected that this was Sylvia's sister.

❖

On the edge of the Moor, a police lamp hung outside the 'Blue House'. Clara fell through the door in her nightie and slippers. It took many repeats of the name DI Howard to convince the constable that she was not a madwoman escaped from the asylum.

By ten o'clock, fifty policemen took their positions, to watch and wait behind Howard for the opportunity to corner Dick Korda. But they were ordered to tread cautiously; Alice's life might be at stake.

❖

At least, thought Greta, she'll sleep for a while.

She had done her best. The nameless girl was under a sheet, with Greta's own face cloth stuffed between her legs.

By the smell of her breath, she was dead drunk. Clearly, Dick had abused her beyond most women's wildest fears. If that were me, she persuaded herself, would I want doctors prodding my sore, private places? Police asking every sordid

374

detail? No! I'll look after the girl until she can talk. Perhaps she's one of the gypsy kids I knew years ago.

Justification was now absolute. Time to go hunting. Greta checked the tools in her pockets. Each heavy spanner and hammer was a potential weapon, but she hoped she would need none of them. The Zipper was dangerous. Usefully dangerous.

Joe's costume was cumbersome, as he/she hitched Binnie's old caravan to the back of the Land Rover. Then, wearing thick gloves, and boots with metal toecaps, Greta waited in the shadows.

The red van returned. Dick was limping awkwardly, as he entered his caravan.

Greta felt a surge of power. It's me behind YOU.

❖

The rag doll had escaped! Dick crashed back out of the caravan and stood on his step, puce with rage, rolling his single eye around the fairground. Suddenly a face moved into the light and there in front of him – grinning like a Cheshire cat – was a fat man. A man who looked like . . .

GRETA!

Greta dressed as a bloke! Blowing him a kiss, arms outstretched as if she longed to hold him. Weird! That gin must have been off.

The Greta man moved away. Fascinated, he stumbled after her, towards the Zipper.

Surrounded by people – unsuspecting witnesses – Greta felt secure, as Dick lumbered behind her.

The Zipper was spinning. Greta leapt on to the platform,

dodged between two lurching carriages and sprang on to a lethally whipping metal arm. She was used to the crazy motion, having spent many a night balancing precariously, taking money, hopping from carriage to carriage.

The lad with the ponytail yelled at her from the centre control platform.

Dick seemed mesmerized. As the undulating ride took Greta up and down, above him and then below him, she smiled tauntingly.

Riders and spectators, deafened by organ music, took little notice as Dick clawed his own face and bellowed, 'Like your handiwork, your ladyship?'

Come and get me, bastard, Greta willed him. Come on.

Dick snarled and leapt forward, instinctively hurdling the metal arms until he was on the one next to hers. Then he made a grab for her. But Greta was nimble. Rising and falling, she ran along the arm and dropped into an empty carriage.

A lone drunken eye disadvantaged Dick's balance. He stood for a while with each foot planted on a jerking arm. Then he lunged. Falling on top of her in the carriage, he grabbed her by the throat, but she booted him with a toe cap. Vaulting from the carriage seat, Greta jumped up and grabbed one of the umbrella spokes which supported the canopy. Swinging her legs, she kicked him in the chin and sent him sprawling back on to peeling leather.

The crowd ahhhed.

Ponytail had pulled back the drive lever, but Greta was there next to him. As the ride slowed and Dick struggled to his feet, Greta hit the young man's fingers with a giant spanner and pressed the lever forwards, till the carriages began to pick up speed again.

Riders yelled as the ride went too fast, out of control. Dick's arms grabbed at air. He lost his balance and was about to fall between the dreadful metal arms, when someone leapt into the carriage and hauled him back to spinning safety. DI Howard had Dick Korda in an arm lock.

Police pulled the ride to a halt.

Greta was running, chased by Butterwell's posse.

❖

Howard bellowed in Korda's face, 'Where's the little girl, you bastard?' He had hold of the bastard's collar and was shaking him. 'Blood all over your caravan.' The shaking became increasingly violent. He couldn't stop himself. Korda's head was banging against the metal carriage. 'Where've you dumped her little body? Touch her, did you? Play with her? You twisted git . . . you . . .'

Another officer attempted to intervene; the carriage swayed on its tilted casters and they all fell. Dick took his opportunity. He pushed them off and, more surefooted now, nipped across the metal arms to the back of the ride, slipping between sections of green tarpaulin and out into the milling crowds, upturning stalls and pushing over slow pensioners, leaving a trail of devastation to delay his pursuers.

Only a showman would have risked running between the alternately plummeting sky rockets as they plunged and reared. The crowd screeched with thrilled fear when Dick missed being sliced in two by a whisker. He bolted towards the main road, dodging through the traffic, and by the time the police arrived at the kerb, Dick Korda had vanished.

Greta, meanwhile, was dancing between dodgem cars and under guy-ropes, through trick mirror passages, finally finding refuge in the tented chambers of the Ghost Train. It was enough. Joe metamorphosed.

It took several minutes for Butterwell to halt the ghoulish ride, switch on torches and brave the horrors, but Greta had long since emerged from under some muddy canvas with a completely different identity. As graceful as a cat, she sauntered through hysterical crowds, her long black hair swinging over her bared shoulders and her sea-green skirt folding and flowing around her shapely brown legs.

Searching

began on the moors, around the gully where Clara saw Dick's van stop. The hills were ringing with whistles and dog yelps as a farmer moved his sheep away, and a line of policemen, pulled by alsatians, began poking and slashing. Sam joined their ranks, his garden hoe grasped in his fists.

Sylvia sat in the Hillman, watching. DI Howard said she shouldn't be here; she should be with her mother, who was now all alone in Gosforth, frantic with worry about her missing family. But Sylvia didn't care about her mother. She needed too much parenting herself.

She took fascinated solace from the spirit which seemed to flow in shivers around her. Sometimes his wings embraced her, or supported her from behind, or else he walked before her, as a shield. But, with each savage turn of events, he kept cheating his way under her skin, his mellisonant voice echoing around her skull with increasing insistence. Usually he just recited learned lines, but when he was upset he muttered a foul, private language, a stream of evil thoughts scurrying like mercury, neat, glistening droplets of poison.

In calmer moments, especially when wrapped in Sam's embrace, Sylvia begged him to go away, to give her peace. But the voice was beautiful in its seduction.

In the wide-awake world of disciplined reality, Sylvia kept hopping between two oppositional paths of trauma. Alice might truly be her daughter – but she had been kidnapped, and might even be dead. Or the other child, Jan, might be hers – given away to some woman in Kenton.

Jan or Alice? This pain or that pain?

The agonizing binaries were unstable. So was Sylvia.

On the horizon, a policeman stooped suddenly. He was pulling at something . . .

Alice's body?

Don't look! said Dothy, who was kneeling on the passenger seat, biting her nails.

Ah . . . ! Sylvia breathed out again. Just rags on the end of a stick, put into a sack.

'I can't bear this. Don't cry, Dothy.' She patted the little girl's shoulder, wondering how to comfort her. 'Do you ever see him? My angel? Does he talk to you?'

I like the other one better.

'There's another one?'

But the little girl didn't answer. She was snivelling, nose pressed wetly to the window. So Sylvia sat stroking her imaginary friend, while she watched the police line make its way across the hilltop.

'Don't worry, Dothy. God punishes bad people.'

With that consoling thought, Sylvia closed her eyes.

❖

A loud tocking started to thud around the car. It hammered, like a monster woodpecker, on the walnut dashboard, clattered across the windscreen, thwacked the leather upholstery. The whole car rocked with pulsing bangs. Every strike was more violent, the noise booming, echoing, louder and louder until the metal car was clanging like a massive church bell.

A man's voice bellowed in their ears. *Her lies will be stifled by Desdemona's pillow. She will fall for eternity through the bottomless, burning pit!*

Dothy screamed, opened the car door, and pelted across the moorland. Sylvia charged after her, until the two of them stopped at a pile of rocks, staring up at the sky.

Pray! ordered Dothy. The dimples around her mouth were pinched in fear and her eyes were frantically roaming the heavens. But the vault was huge and empty.

Where are you, God?

TOCK.

Please, God! Was it Sylvia shouting, or Dothy?

TOCK! TOCK? The voice of the angel was TOCK!

He soared across the sky, screeching, *The Lord searcheth all hearts, and understandeth all the imaginations of the thoughts. Atishoo. They all fall down.*

Sylvia fell into the heather, curling up, closing her eyes against Heaven, seeing only godless Hell. And in that devilish freedom, violence, lustful as sex, balled her fists and kicked maniacally through her legs, as she wrestled, punching, ripping, biting, with an unseen enemy.

It was Dothy who shouted, *Stop it!*

Sylvia shot across the hilltop. She reached Sam and fell against him.

'Stay with me. Keep me awake. Keep talking. Please.'

Sam dropped his hoe. Tenderly, he led her back to the inert car.

❖

Later, as they lay together on Sam's sofa, Sylvia felt amazingly calm again. Perhaps she had only slipped, by some queer trick, into Dothy's nightmare. She studied the knobs on the radio, wondering if she had something similar in her head which turned down angel volume.

'It's possible,' Sam was musing, 'that your dad's quite innocent. Maybe he just went down to London to find Katherine.'

Sylvia was surprised when her own voice sounded quite normal. 'You don't know his temper. He killed Mr Linden in a rage, then got scared. He's a murderer. He'll be hung, won't he?'

'Actually, they've just voted on the death penalty. New convictions should only carry a life sentence.'

'Prison for ever.'

'It's a terrible thing for a man to face. If I thought Howard could really pin something on me, maybe I'd vanish too.' He frowned. 'This whole saga, it's all about running away.'

'Like I did.'

'Flight is a basic survival instinct.'

'Does that make it right?'

'I don't know. I'm only a vet. Animals don't understand bravery. It's just humans who call each other cowards when it's entirely rational to duck or run.'

'Ironic, isn't it, that they all dote on a baby that may not even be mine. Sam, explain the blood thing to me.'

'Unfortunately you have a very common blood group – "O" Positive. Howard has had little Jan tested and she does share your blood group, but so does a third of the world. If they could test either Alice or Greta, then something might be proved.'

Sam closed his eyes, drawn into private regrets.

Sylvia watched his eyeballs shifting under his lids. He was thinking about her again! Fuggering Greta!

Tock came hurtling through the window.

The angel crash-landed, and stood for a moment looking down at Sylvia. He smiled softly, nodded. Slowly, he pulled his silver gun out of his diamond-studded holster and twirled the chamber.

❖

Already, all the national broadsheets were running headlines about Alice. The young journalist Roger was getting ambitious. He was spitting frustration because he knew every facet of the story and his boss at the *Chronicle* wouldn't listen well enough to write the facts with proper cohesion. Worse, the text contained outrageous innuendo about witchcraft and covens. So many adults had disappeared, implying 'multiple guilts surrounding an innocent child' that the 'OCCULT?' slant on Alice's disappearance read with unholy plausibility.

On Tuesday, the headline 'ALICE, The Italian Connection', purpled an already garish story. Once again, the police were appealing for Cuthbert Sharp to come home.

'Hardly likely to turn himself in now,' grumbled Roger to Binnie.

They were sitting in her tiny upstairs room. The landlord's lampshade rocked unsteadily on its base and the table wobbled as Roger put down his teacup. There was no saucer.

'You're a bright lad. Found Greta's baby for me. Thank goodness your paper hasn't mentioned her.'

'You're sure that Jan is Greta's baby, not Alice?'

'Am I sure?' Binnie poked her ear with a long, bent fingernail. 'Bring me something,' she said suddenly, 'that belongs to this child, Alice.'

'Why?'

'To test destiny.'

❖

Roger was good with women, especially older ones. He found Violet Sharp in her husband's yard, standing looking at a pyramid of coal.

'Need some help?' he asked. 'Bagging up or something?'

'Me husband's a wanted man. Who'll buy coal from us now? What am I to do with this lot?'

'Sell it cheap?'

'Where've you sprung from, lad?'

'Mate of David and Hendo. (A lie.) And I know your Katherine. (One shared cigarette.) I could do with earning a few bob.'

She looked at his young, kind face and clean hands. 'Howay into the office – I'll make a brew.'

In the wooden hut Violet fetched two tin mugs. On the

384

coal-black floor Roger noticed a little toy trolleybus, with a jelly baby pushed into the cab.

❖

Howard threw the *Chronicle* into the bin. 'Bollocks!'

Again he broke his pencil. He was now working in two separate notebooks – blue for Arthur Linden and green for Alice Sharp. The back page of the blue one bore the underlined word, CONCLUSION. He was fairly content, now, that Linden had died as a result of a violent tussle and a final shove from his wife.

Beneath the heading was a list:

> *Kirkstone* – MANSLAUGHTER.
>   Case scheduled Quarterly Assizes.
> *Sharp* – MANSLAUGHTER
>   (catch fucking bastard!)
> *Janice Kirkstone* – PERVERSION (silly cow)
> *Violet Sharp* – ditto (crafty cow)
> *Hythe* – ditto, possibly AIDING (clown)
> *Mary Linden* . . .

DI Howard jabbed his pencil point in her name. It broke. He resharpened, then wrote:

> – MURDER?

Was that last push deliberate?

Howard drew a hangman's noose on the bottom of the page. He let his mind stray again over moorland and sea. So many bastards missing! Each had vanished so perfectly that there were barely any tracks to sniff. But, reflected the policeman, the Law is a hungry dog.

The green book, Alice's, looked like a teenager's geometry homework, all triangles and parallelograms. Cuthbert Sharp was connected to Alice with a heavy red arrow which continued over several pages. Had the besotted grandfather spirited his granddaughter away? He turned to his page headed 'FAIRGROUND FIASCO', and drew another series of rings around the name GRETA KORDA.

Howard chewed the end of his pencil. He had his own guilty secret. He knew it had been her face under the cap, her slender waistline glimpsed as the 'fat man' swung across the Zipper, but he hadn't actually mentioned this in his report. Already reprimanded for lack of control when he almost throttled Dick Korda, reprimanded again for losing the bastard, he simply didn't trust his own memory enough to risk further ridicule.

Was there another reason? Was it because, in that split second when the 'fat man' almost caused Dick Korda to be sliced up by the Zipper, he remembered willing her to succeed?

Had the gypsy with two faces taken Alice? Is that why his intuition kept worrying at her name? If so, the poor child could now be anywhere in the whole damn world.

Interpol were treading cautiously in Italy. Yorks Constabulary had interviewed Torricelli and Liz Baxter in Scarborough, but Alexandra Hythe, latterly known as Greta Korda, was as free as a vixen.

The vixen did not feel free. She crushed the newspaper angrily, then threw it into a ditch, determined to keep its contents from the girl until she was stronger. Injustice choked her with impotent fury, all her rage focused on Dick.

Where was the bastard? Lurking behind her? Or dirtying another innocent, like the pathetic creature lying pale and feverish in her caravan?

The sorcerous gypsy grapevine whispered nothing of Alice. Why had Dick gone to Corbridge? What happened that night? Had the teenager been unconscious long enough for Dick to have taken Alice and passed her into another pair of hands?

Dear God! What if the bastard now went for the other baby, the child who was legally his – Jan? This final worry made Greta crawl with guilt. She herself had caused the moral scales to tip. If, as a result, Dick was sliding further and further into evil, it was her responsibility to shift the weights.

❖

'Push more harder!' Little Jan flew backwards and forwards on the swing. Janice Kirkstone pushed, staring into space. A chiffon scarf was knotted tightly under her chin.

The park was adjacent to the block of flats in Kenton. Janice had returned to the home which was now hers and hers alone, because Matthew was going to be in jail for a long time. It had taken just one afternoon to pack his case and clear him out of her life.

Janice's parents, mortified and cowardly, had already fled

to Brighton. At a time when Janice most needed help and support, the young mother found herself isolated, even from her nursing friends.

Old Binnie was wearing the smartest clothes she'd ever owned, a black coat with three buttons at the waist. Beneath it was a dove-grey dress which was much too hot, but these clothes would have to last summer and winter. A silver hairnet gathered unruly grey tufts to her scalp and a new purple hat sat on the top of her head like a pansy seeking the sun.

For several afternoons she had waited on the park bench, rolling thumb over thumb. One day Roger had sat with her, discussing everything from Elvis to Hitler. When he gave her Alice's toy trolley Binnie had let its cold metallic message pass through her, but the sensation was so dreadful that she could only shake her head.

Binnie smiled and nodded at the woman in the scarf.

Janice Kirkstone was vulnerable. Life had become a parched desert, thirsty for normality. So when the old woman said, 'What a pretty child,' Janice was ready for empty conversation with a stranger.

Double dare. Take off your nightie.

Tock, huge and commanding, suddenly appeared at her bedside. He slid a hand under the sheets. Only half awake, and highly aroused, Sylvia wriggled.

It's dark. Go on. Slip into his bed and his body will do the rest.

Sylvia whispered, 'Why do my hands grip so tight, and my thighs clench till I hurt him?

Because it feels good.

'Bad feels good? I thought you were an angel.'

The hosts who had left Heaven and had not reached Hell flew into the holes of the earth, like the stormy petrels.

'I never read that.'

No. You didn't. Now be a bad girl. Take off your nightie.

❖

'NO!' Sam shot out of bed. 'NO!'

He dashed for the bathroom and stayed there until his erection shrivelled. Splashing water on his face, he berated himself until he could exert some control over his body. When at last he emerged, Sylvia was huddled on the bed with the eiderdown over her head.

'I'm sorry, love.'

'You had sex with her.'

'Don't bring Alexandra into it.'

'It's because I'm ugly, isn't it?'

'No, Sylvia. It's because I love you.'

'As a woman?'

'As the child I never knew, the teenager in trouble, the bride in a veil and the woman who will sleep in my bed, until we are both, I hope, very old.'

Sylvia's sad sea eyes emerged from the covers.

Sam had no idea that a dark angel called Tock was frowning, and that a little girl called Dothy was whispering, *Please may I have a sapphire?*

On the following Sunday, Tock spread his wings over Sam and began a countdown of ticks. Ten, nine, eight. A single second before noon, the vet, helplessly, hopelessly animal, slipped inside Sylvia, and could not slip out again.

The romantic sprite child, Dothy, dismayed by his grunts, hid at the bottom of the garden. Needing to stay in her own world of fairytales, she peered into an old book which she had taken from the shelf beside the grandmother clock. But she was only a little girl, and she couldn't read it.

What is the use of a book, thought Dothy, *without pictures . . . ?*

On a bank,

nowhere near Oxford, a little girl is sitting with her blue dress spread in a circle around her. Her apron is crumpled, the soles of her feet are grass-stained, and her hair is fastened away from her brow by an Alice band. She is playing with a peapod, picking out the juicy peas, one by one, popping them into her mouth.

Such a lovely, hot day! Fat fluffy bees are dancing through clumps of purple clover. A crafty blackbird is happily pecking strawberries. There are probably fairies dozing under the rhubarb leaves.

Our Alice is in her own Wonderland.

Smell those carnations! Take off your jumper and feel the sun on your arms. Isn't this Heaven? While Alice toddles behind a wall of weeping runner beans, let's sit here for a while, and rest. Settle down on the lawn, which is long and lush, emerald as Ireland, studded with daisies and leggy dandelions. Listen quietly to all the twitters and small buzzings, the scuffling of a rabbit . . .

Of course there's a Rabbit. But this one is humble grey and

he is locked in a hutch behind the vegetable plot. Stormy by name and by nature, they can't let him out because he bites ankles.

Bunny and Alice are twitching noses at each other. Do you think she can hear him talking, as he scissors through carrot tops? Perhaps Stormy stares so hard at the little girl because he is trying to warn her that there are dangers in Wonderland: floods of tears, a cruel Queen, and someone as mad as a Hatter who talks to Time.

Part Two

And on a different bank,

an older girl slipped off her dress and stumbled down to a river. She stepped into the flow, letting the rushing, crystal-clear water tug around her ankles. Smoothest white rock, moonlike, felt silken against her soles. She shivered, despite the hot sun on her back. Bending slowly, hands distorted in the glassy rush, she eased her body under, until the sore places juddered, then numbed.

In a wooded cleave, high in the Yorkshire Dales, where the River Wharfe ran shallow and fast, polishing its solid stone bed until it shone like dimpled enamel, Katherine submerged her whole body in pure, ice-cold water. Across breasts and buttocks it gushed, through armpits, between legs, eddying around her head, tangling and untangling matted hair. She filled her mouth and spat. Filled again, pushing water against teeth and under her tongue.

When the cold became painful, she dragged herself across the white rocks and pulled a towel around her shoulders. Gradually the caress of warm air smoothed away goose pimples, but as soon as the sun evaporated the water on her face, the feeling came back. Filth.

She flung off the towel and pushed her body back down into the rippling surge, rubbing vigorously at her skin as if the bruises would wash away.

❖

Tock loathed being dirty. Coal dust crept into every bodily fold and orifice.

Sylvia finished writing up her father's order book, locked up the yard and walked back to the house in South Gosforth. In the kitchen she scrubbed her hands, slid on her new sapphire engagement ring, then fried some Craster kippers. The house reeked of smoked fish.

A cumbersome month had passed, lumpy with jumpy emotions and flawed logic. Sylvia had stopped trying to reconcile hatred with joy, finding she could accommodate both, simultaneously, if she allowed Tock free reign. When Sylvia thought about Alice, the majestic angel came swiftly to her shoulder, pointing his gun at everyone. Unfortunately, his ferocious intensity was the cause of the present problem. It was Tock's fault that Sylvia had to live with her mother. He enjoyed sex too much.

When Sylvia lay in Sam's arms, her mouth watering, sweat oozing from mysterious glands until she was slippery as a siren, Tock shook the air with his great wings. He tocked in time with thrusts, and his feathers fell on the bed. Only after orgasm could he tuck his head down and sleep.

The vet, struggling with his lack of control, had begun worrying about his reputation, so he had taken Sylvia to the jeweller's in Newcastle, kissed his temptress openly in Northumberland Street – and deposited her on Violet in Gosforth.

Fuggerit!

Ironically, the vet's bid for cleanliness sent Sylvia into her father's dirt. Tock clawed walls with frustration, while Dothy, whose job it was to guard the ring, sat contentedly on the dressing table, staring into the dark blue depths of the sapphire, waiting for a happier angel.

❖

Violet was dozing in Cuthbert's armchair, her mouth slack with bitter exhaustion. Sylvia laid the kipper tray on her mother's lap. Tock looked down into the mother's curly perm, despising the coal dust between her hair follicles. He couldn't resist it. He tipped the tray slightly . . .

❖

Violet wasn't sleeping. She caught the movement before it became one accident too many.

Had she understood about Tock, Sylvia's mother would simply have spat in his eye. Lost in her own troubles, she sensed her daughter's gathering madness but could not deal with it. Sylvia's apparent clumsiness – the broken clock on the mantelpiece, the burn on the tea towel, Cuthbert's smashed mug – was vexing enough, but the mysterious thread of threat which tied her broken heart in knots was too complex to unravel, so, to begin with, Violet ignored it.

One human heart, they say, is capable of love for an infinite number of people. Our potential for joy is therefore immense, but it is matched by an equal, cataclysmic vulnerability. Violet's heart, overwhelmed by multiple griefs, was now paralysed, and that angst was locking up her body. Her elbows and shoulders had stiffened, because her arms ached for Alice's warm, wriggling little body. Staring at the soot dust on her windowsill, Violet allowed herself another insane moment of imagination, picturing her granddaughter's body. Her throat wanted to scream for ever.

And Katherine! Where was her own little girl? Barely sixteen and wandering around London by herself. The worry was an itching sore in the middle of Violet's chest which made her bra feel like a tourniquet.

She tried to stand up, but her legs shook under the weight of Cuthbert's betrayal. Whether he stayed away or came back to face prison, he would never again be her husband. The lonely path ahead looked steep and dark.

Still in her forties, yet an old woman, she fell back in the armchair. The hearth was empty. Soon it would be autumn and she would need Cuthbert's coal. The only thing left was coal. A mountain of the filthy stuff.

The tray lay on the floor. She picked it up. The kippers would be eaten, neither wasted nor tasted.

❖

Each night Howard took his exercise books to bed. His private equations made unsettling bedtime reading and his question marks were doodling works of art.

Kirkstone had a figure eight wrapped around his name, the number of years he would get for 'Manslaughter'. Sharp would do ten, once he was caught. The Inspector longed to see that red face flaming in the dock. He longed for it so badly that he was tempted to put down his pencil and pray.

Inside a near-perfect parabola were the names Mary Linden and Douglas Hythe. He changed the shape to a heart and put Alice's name between them. Then he rubbed Alice's name out. Sharp, Katherine and that bastard Korda all had better reason to take the child.

But Howard's primary suspect (he drew five Olympic circles beneath it) was the woman who thought Alice was hers by right of birth, Alexandra Hythe.

❖

One wearily warm afternoon Howard visited Ethel Linden, who was staying in the Gosforth house, helping David to sort out his father's affairs. They, along with Clara Blake, now coexisted as a cell of 'left-behinds', tacitly avoiding rubbing one another's emotional scabs. If Ethel (doubly depressed after her heart attack) wept, she was not fussed over. If David locked himself in his bedroom to blow his sax, no-one grumbled. And if Clara Blake repeatedly needed to soak in the bath because the smell of blood on the sacks would never quite leave her nostrils, then she was welcome.

Howard spoke gently. 'Ethel, pet, we must find Mary. Any chance she's contacted David?'

'I watch the post like a hawk and I've had the telephone moved beside my chair. Nothing. Any leads on Alice?'

'As the weeks go on . . .' Howard frowned. Time to prepare the old lady for the worst. 'The blood samples we took from Dick Korda's caravan were "O", the same group as Sylvia's, so there is a possibility that it was Alice's.'

'But "O" is common.'

'You're right, it proves nothing.'

'What else?' Ethel snapped, 'Don't insult my intelligence. What else did you find?'

'Semen. Pubic hair . . .'

'Dear God! Clothing?'

'A woman's undergarments. Brassiere and such. By all accounts Korda is a bit of a . . .'

'Sex maniac? Men like that steal little children.'

'Not necessarily. Paedophilia is a very specific sort of . . . em . . .'

'Abomination?'

'Ethel dear, there was no sign of a child having been there at all. Don't forget, Korda thinks Alice is his daughter.'

'Mad is mad.'

She was ranting, yet again, about the whore-bitch Mary.

'Now Ethel, here's a juicy surprise for you. It's doubtful that Mary is, or ever was, having an affair with that particular gentleman.'

'Rubbish!'

'Rumour has it that Hythe is – em – he . . .'

'Spit it out!'

'. . . prefers men to women.'

'Ye gods and little fishes!' For the first time in many weeks, Ethel's lips twitched. 'How do you know?'

'An informant. Ethel dear, you'll give yourself another heart attack.'

The old lady was wheezing. 'Give me this informant's address. I'll send the bugger fifty quid. Cheered me up no end!'

Romantic Paris. The 'lovers' sat in a Gauloise haze sipping liqueurs, sharing mutual hatred. Sauntering over to a battered piano, Douglas leaned elegantly on an elbow and fingered a note or two. Mary crossed her legs and folded her arms as the performer eased himself on to the stool and spread his hands over the keys. Slowly, softly, he slid his music into the café, as gently as cream over a spoon. Poignant notes filtered through the smoke. One by one the customers nudged each other and began to listen. A silver lock fell over his brow. His jaw dropped slightly, and he closed his eyes as he played, seemingly oblivious to his audience.

Of course Mary knew he wasn't. The man was as vain as a flaming peacock!

Oh, it had been so exciting at first. A rendezvous in the middle of the night. Hasty embraces. Hovering fearfully around Newcastle's Oslo Quay until they could board the ship to Norway. When Douglas's delicate stomach had rebelled against the vessel's motion, he had clung to her like a baby chimpanzee. Once on dry land she had accepted his polite preliminaries with affected shyness, always craving more passion than he volunteered. The wanting had driven Mary daft.

Daft indeed. Passion had never flared, not even smouldered. The man had no conversation, no manners and no – SEXUAL DESIRE! As cold as a dead haddock. The whole exhausting episode had left her feeling stupid, fat, middle-aged and ANGRY.

She fished in her handbag, calling, '*Garçon*!' The fresh-faced waiter did not respond. He was leaning on the bar with his chin propped on his hand, staring at Douglas.

'*Garçon*!' bellowed Mary again.

The boy roused himself and sauntered across with a bottle.

'*Non*!' Her hands flapped the bottle away. '*L'ADDITION*, FOR GOD'S SAKE! No good looking at him! The monkey on the organ can't pay. Hasn't got a bloody bean. I'll pay for my own. He can sing for his supper.'

Douglas missed the harsh scraping of her chair as she left. His music was reaching its climax and his shoulders hunched as he pounded the surprised instrument, vibrations echoing through polished floorboards, sending waves of emotion into each corner of the room and a shiver of excitement into the *garçon*'s tight trousers.

Stunned to discover that the broken teenager she'd rescued was Sylvia's younger sister, Greta basked in Katherine's gratitude while, in turn, the young girl took refuge in the gypsy's audacity. They swiftly established an intimacy which neither had achieved with Sylvia. As she watched the girl's fight to recovery, Greta began to understand her own pain and self-loathing. Equally damaged and defensive, set ruthlessly against the world, they toured in Greta's Land Rover, pulling Binnie's old caravan behind them, continually painting new names on the door. Gypsy Marie, Dora-belle, Roseanna; paint over paint, place after place, they concealed themselves within gypsy communities.

When Greta felt Katherine was strong enough to hear

about Alice's disappearance, she was unprepared for the girl's anguish. At first they quarrelled and accused. Then they talked the mystery into a theoretical pulp. All Katherine's anger was directed at her father.

'He's obsessed. Capable of anything. I must go home. Tell them it wasn't me. As soon as I'm better . . .' Yet how could she face them with the unspeakable, intimate horrors of Dick's violation?

The teenager quickly became accustomed to this earthy life as she grubbed in hedgerows and washed in streams. She grew like the Earth itself, divided into strata, soft layers eroding beneath a stony crust and, at her core, the burning fire of humiliation.

Greta knew the old travelling routes, places where a caravan could park overnight leaving only a pile of litter for a frustrated farmer to find. Gypsy havens: moorland lanes next to cool burns, railway embankments rich with blackberries, bunny banks alive with rabbit, stonewalled fields popping with white mushrooms. While Katherine hung half-washed clothes on makeshift lines, Greta did the manual work, hitching and unhitching the caravan, cranking the lorry, building fires. Sorties into shops were swift and nerve-racking. Both faces had graced national newspapers, so they bound their heads tightly with scarves, obscuring features with sunglasses.

July seemed endless. On some afternoons, Greta tried her hand at telling fortunes. During these 'séances' Katherine would wander through crackling wheat and cool woodlands. Where rivers ran sluggish beneath bridges, she fought nettles to get into the water. The need to be clean became a compulsion which drew her to towpaths and gushing streams.

Greta was good company. Her stories about Venice and her Italian relatives were riddled with humour and her circus adventures sparkled with bittersweet nostalgia.

One enormous lie stood between these two females. Katherine was deceived. This was no aimless wander. What she perceived as escape and freedom was, to Greta, a man-hunt. The huntress was stealthily pursuing the very monster Katherine thought she was fleeing.

And Greta couldn't find him. Was Dick in front of her or behind? When she found the bastard, would she also find her daughter? The gypsy grapevine told her that the Zipper had been sold abroad. Occasionally, she heard, Dick would turn up amongst his cronies to help set up rides, but often he lay for days, sprawled on urine-soaked sheets, dead drunk.

At a site near Dumfries Greta recognized Binnie's stall. She tackled the new owner again, and was eventually given an address in Newcastle. Why there? Unless . . . was it conceivable that Binnie had taken Alice?

Ironic, thought Greta, how every path seems to lead me back to the North East. To Sam.

As she drove the Land Rover, she found herself aching for those gentle, scrubbed hands and his soothing, yet passionate embrace. With naked frankness she talked to Katherine about sex, reassuring her that Dick's abuse could be healed through the kind of love Sam had once given her.

Meanwhile Greta's new-found talent for fortune-telling empowered her psyche. During the short summer nights she lay awake trying to link with her mother.

'Mamma. Can you lead me to Alice? Or is she with you?'

❖

The Eiffel Tower straddled Mary's head like a giant toy. After two days of her own company, enveloped in clamorous, incomprehensible French gabble, her nerves were shattered. She felt lost and homesick. But if she returned to England where English people spoke English, what would happen? A prison sentence seemed marginally preferable to facing folk on Gosforth High Street.

She gazed upwards into the criss-cross of girders. With one final burst of courage she willed her footsteps towards the lift. She would probably never see Paris again, so she'd go up the bloody Tower or bust. Then she would go home to Newcastle and face humiliation. Money had become a serious problem. What a gullible fool she had been. And to think she had been ready to go the whole way! (In the dark of course, Douglas was never to see her varicose veins.) But he hadn't wanted her at all – just Arthur's money.

Yesterday, standing in Notre Dame, the old church smell had queered her head. GOD (or a miserable devil) seemed to place a terrible image in her mind, and a really uncomfortable feeling to go with it. She was transported to Arthur's funeral, the one she had caused, and missed. There, gliding down the aisle, were the pallbearers shouldering Arthur's lily-laden coffin. Limping manfully behind it, his proud nose in the air, his Adam's apple gulping, she could see her son, David. Mary was overwhelmed by a curious longing to comfort him. Miraculously, in Notre Dame, Mary Linden had actually knelt and prayed, for a full five minutes!

The Tower lift shot up. She got out on the top platform

where gusts of wind were making the mighty girders tremble. Clinging to a rail, she looked down on the cream and gold city and let tears trickle freely through her powder. There was no practical way to jump, but anyway – death would mean Hell, and she didn't fancy that much either.

OH, bugger! A man was watching her! A bloody Frog! With a bald head and enormous, bristly sideburns.

Hastily scrubbing her cheeks, Mary glowered back at his impertinent stare. The man raised a white eyebrow of apology and turned away. His gaunt face was sallow as he looked down, and he visibly shivered, as if Mary's coldness had penetrated his immaculately tailored black coat.

Oh, Lord, thought Mary. If I go back, everyone one will stare like that.

Suddenly feeling as if she was standing in front of the whole of Tyneside in her French knickers and knobbly blue veins, Mary pulled her lapels tightly together. Checking first for bird shit, she sat on a bench.

Slowly, the man turned, his grey eyes confident and direct. 'Life, it is short, *oui*? You are English, Madame?'

OH! Thank God! A comprehensible English conversation! Mary tilted her head so that her little nose stuck up in the air. 'Have we been introduced?'

'*Enchanté*, Madame. I apologize for my . . . what you call it?'

'Rudeness. What made you think I was English?'

'*Les chaussures*, Madame. The shoes.'

Without moving her head, stiff-necked, Mary dropped her gaze to her feet. 'Well!'

'*Désolé*, Madame! I make bad joke. Today I am *triste* –

how you say? Sad. So my joke falls like stone from La Tour d'Eiffel.' His white eyebrows drew into a frown as he looked out across the city. 'Ah, Madame! You and I, we are both sad, and Paris – she is not so beautiful today.'

Lip quivering, Mary bowed her head. He came to her side immediately, attempting to hold her hand, which she snatched away. Damned sauce! The Frenchman returned quickly to the rail, clutching it, inhaling deeply through extended nostrils.

Arms wrapped around herself, Mary stared at her English shoes, but as her eyes misted, she saw the pink slippers she had left at the front door, next to Arthur's tartan ones.

Poor Arthur. Poor David. Poor Me.

The Frenchman was humming a sad tune. Yes, in this unlikely place and time, they were *triste* together. She lifted her head, rose gracefully from the seat and moved to his side.

'I wish my son was three again,' she said. 'Do you have children, Monsieur?'

❖

A week of thunderstorms bogged down Greta and Katherine in mud and depression. Desperate for home comforts, they drove across the width of England to Scarborough. Dumping the caravan in the field next to Hisper Cottage, they took turns to luxuriate in a bath, Katherine changing the water twice before she would get out. Then, under a roof which didn't rattle, they slumbered like innocents.

Katherine slept in Sylvia's bed. She tried to imagine the cottage before Greta had improved it. She tried to understand Sylvia's loneliness, but found that rather than fearing it, she craved it.

After this brief relaxation, Greta announced her intention to go to Newcastle. 'I want to talk to Sam, face to face. We need his help.'

'Do we? Are you clear about what you want from him?'

'Yes. Respect. And I'm going to ask Sam to mediate between me and the Lindens.'

'I'm not coming.'

'I know.'

So Katherine remained behind in Hisper Cottage and, like Sylvia, trusted that Greta would return.

The miracle of cell regeneration which had healed the teenager's physical injuries hadn't begun to cure the pain inside. She didn't want to get better. 'Not minding' seemed the worst possible self-betrayal, so she clung to the nightmare, replaying it time and again.

On the day after Greta left, the sky finally cleared, rain clouds scurrying away on a sharp breeze which whistled across the moors and out to sea. Katherine walked the beach beneath Hisper Cottage feeling comfortable in her cloak of solitude. Sodden sand beneath her bare feet, heavy denim trousers stained to the knees, she let Dick the Devil drift from her mind for a few precious minutes. Stretching her arms wide, Katherine savoured freedom. Who needed people? Who needed love, ties and rejection?

Oh, this watery emptiness was bliss!

Unfortunately, the fat Italian was calling again tonight. She could not abide his brooding, suspicious eyes, nor the way his trousers hung beneath his belly, nor the smell of garlic. He didn't like her much either. Afraid that he would report her, Katherine had persuaded Greta not to disclose that she was Sylvia's sister. Partly in jest, Greta had told him she had rescued Katherine from teenage prostitution. Poor Tony's compassion was sorely stretched.

So, thought Katherine, Sylvia existed here alone, when Hisper Cottage was little more than a hovel. She laughed at herself. Was this a charitable thought? Was she really wondering if her sister had been terribly cold, bored, scared? Had Sylvia missed home, maybe even her sister?

Salty spray dampened her face. What would Greta find out in Newcastle? Where was Dad? How was Mam managing?

'No!' she shouted, running into the noisy sea. 'I can't afford to care. How could I go back and face them now? I'm filthy. FILTHY.'

❖

On the island of Islay, off the west coast of Scotland, a man knelt on a pew, in a chapel. Cherubic chants echoed around him as the choir practised a psalm. The man was drunk, having consumed half a bottle of single malt, directly after his square sausage breakfast.

He wasn't exactly praying. But he was letting something spiritual flow into him, as he gazed at the crucifix. It felt like – courage.

❖

There was no surprise in Binnie's features as she opened the door. Greta hugged her briefly, neither woman comfortable with such gestures. While the old lady moved around her shabby kitchenette, Greta asked questions, receiving oddly evasive answers. Finally, in the dim light of the drab sitting room, Binnie found her tongue.

'Your daughter, Greta. I've seen her.'

Greta stared, incredulous. 'You DID take Alice!'

'JAN, Greta. That's the name your daughter was given.'

'Oh. You've seen the other little girl?'

'We must watch over her.'

'You stayed in Newcastle, Binnie, to look for my baby?'

'I held your baby as she was born, and I felt the singe of Hell. She must be protected.'

'It's too late!' Greta felt a deep flush of foreboding. 'Someone's already taken my baby. Oh, God!'

'You talk of Alice Sharp? Oh, lass, I heard that you muddled the babies. All you did was to confuse destiny and throw both children into the cauldron.'

'Binnie, your sight is legendary. Please, tell me what you see. Do you know which child is which?'

'Only God knows now. But I am drawn to Jan. I feel my destiny wound in hers.'

'Your destiny?'

'Yours too.'

'But Binnie, when I saw Alice, I felt instinctively that she was mine. I don't have your sight, but I have my own intuition.'

Binnie went to a drawer, took out the toy trolleybus and laid it on Greta's palm.

'Whose is this?'

Greta tried to open her mind. 'It's cold. I . . .'

'Yes?'

'I can't breathe.' Startled, Greta dropped the toy to the floor. Binnie picked it up and held it to her own chest.

'What do you feel, Binnie?'

'You, Greta. I feel you. And sudden darkness.'

'Death?'

Binnie shuddered and put the toy down with distaste. 'I was told it belonged to Alice, and yet the first time I held it, another name came. Dorothy.'

'Dorothy? Perhaps it belonged to another kid. Or . . . maybe a woman called Dorothy took Alice?'

Binnie shrugged. Her cataracts glazed. 'But I have held Jan and the trill of death was a scream in my chest.'

'It's all my fault.'

'No, lass. Old Nick picks his own victims, and very carefully.' Binnie grabbed Greta's hand. 'Take your child away from this place. Change her destiny.'

'But I might be leading her straight into it!' Greta shook her head. 'Somewhere out there Dick is threatening to kill me.'

Binnie's voice rose on a wheeze. 'Dick Korda haunts my dreams.' She began to tremble and her mouth slackened. 'His spirit stinks like rats' piss in a sewer.' Her breath began coming in short, sharp gasps and she seemed focused on something beyond Greta's head. Her hunched body became languid, but her eyes were so wide that white showed around each iris.

'What else do you see, Binnie? Tell me!'

The old lady's arms began flailing. Greta grasped her hand. But as their fingers touched, Binnie's chest began to heave, her breath coming faster and faster. 'Behind me. I can't run fast enough.'

'Who?'

Binnie whimpered. 'No, Dorothy! NO!'

❖

In the bathroom of his B&B, Cuthbert Sharp tried not to spill dye on the lino. He was touching up his roots. Taking an ironic leaf from his daughter's book, he had first dyed his hair in a ladies' toilet near Glasgow.

Using his coaly takings (which he never did bank) to buy train and steamer tickets, he had arrived in Islay, where he now spent his days tramping through sheep droppings and his evenings propping up a bar, telling fairytales about being a lonely widower in search of peace.

Peace? Could a wanted man ever know peace? Widower? He might as well be. His wife thought he was a pervert.

He'd read what the papers said about Alice's abduction. Seen his own picture. He knew he should do something about it, but what? If he showed his face in England he would be arrested.

So he had wallowed in whisky, depressed, mentally inert, trapped in a paralysis of pointlessness.

Until today. Today something was changing.

He walked out into the storm. Rain was lashing the island, blowing horizontally across the rocky hills. Everything was mud and thunder. The narrow, turbulent channel between Islay and Jura was a mountain range of surging waves, terrifying to watch, vicious and unforgiving, as ruthless as God.

But, perhaps the Lord was answering his prayers. Perhaps

he was bellowing – Cuthbert Sharp – get your cowardly arse home. Tell your wife you love her. Tell her that you haven't got a perverted bone in your body. Tell the police the truth about Arthur. Take your punishment like a man. Jail can't be any worse than Scottish freezation. The Lord helps them what helps themselves.

'Go forth . . .' Cuthbert shouted at the howling gale. 'I will go forth. Mebees even fifth.'

Black dye dribbled into his eyes.

❖

The Town Moor was bleak and empty as Greta strode over it. Was this where it had all begun? In the mud, where her child was born? In the caravan, on the afternoon Dick impregnated her? Or was it years before, on the night of her mother's funeral?

She kept turning Binnie's words. Think, she told herself, think. Piece the puzzle together. Who the hell is Dorothy?

❖

The surgery phone rang. Greta's breathless, female voice swooped across the wires and plummeted straight into the vet's conscience. He flushed. His hand trembled.

Sam had never told Sylvia about the other empty calls, of those maddening seconds as he'd held the handset, saying, 'Who's that?' and knowing it was Alexandra. Sought now by press and police, she was once again a creature of secrecy.

'I must talk to you,' she said.

'Where are you?'

'Newcastle. Could we meet?'

'Are you bringing Alice home?'

'Sam, I don't have Alice.'

'Why should I believe you?'

'Because I promised. Jesus, you hate me!'

'I don't hate you. But if you're lying . . .'

'I'm not! Oh, what's the use?' A pause, but she didn't slam the phone down. 'Whether she's my daughter or not, Sam, I'm very afraid for Alice. I'll never rest until she's safe. And . . . I have reason to be equally worried about the other little girl, Jan. I suggest we all get together; perhaps we can solve this between us.'

'Get together? Who with?'

'Sylvia. Her mother. David Linden and his grandmother. Please, Sam, meet me somewhere. The coast?' she suggested.

Sam rubbed his chin. Could he justify this? Alexandra the beauty. Greta the liar. Despite her denials, she could have taken Alice. Perhaps he should meet her, for Sylvia's sake.

❖

Two hours later, he was the first to arrive at the rendezvous. He sat playing with a plate of fish and chips, looking out over Whitley Bay's windy promenade. The day was miserably dull for this, his final scene with Alexandra. The wind was enough to give a man earache.

Sam pressed his eyelids. Would she even turn up? Did he want her to? Why had he hidden his assignation from Sylvia? For Alice! Just that. Nothing else. With grudging respect he acknowledged that Alexandra's tenacity might well lead them to the child. Finding Alice would heal his young fiancée and give them all a future.

He began to ferret for flakes of fish in a mess of greasy batter. Head down, he would have failed to recognize Alexandra if she hadn't sat opposite him.

Familiar perfume floated through the oily atmosphere, but everything else had changed. Gone the silken, glamorous Alexandra he once loved. Before him a woman who resembled the one he had met three years ago in Kings Cross. Hair wild, tangled about her face in an obscuring black mass. Clothes dark, hanging listlessly about her frame, nondescript. Shoulders hunched beneath a utility gabardine. Glasses!

His shocked expression seemed to amuse her. She began to smile and the smile widened into a grin. Sam felt his gloom lift as she looked at him bewitchingly over thick brown rims. Those mischievous, catlike eyes! God, she was sexy, even in the rough!

It was as though nothing had changed. A brief, warm kiss. Sharing chips. Pulling coats around themselves as they braved the wind and strode up the promenade towards Spanish City. When she took his hand, he held it.

'Keep moving,' she said. 'Don't stop anywhere long enough for anyone to register your face. That's how I live.'

'If you've done nothing criminal, why not turn yourself in? This whole mess needs sorting out, especially which baby is which. Do you know your blood group?'

'No.'

'Take a test. YOU could hold the key. I'll come with you, stand by you, plead for you . . .'

'They'll lock me up. We both know that.'

'Not if you explain about Dick. Convince them that you're a victim.'

'Dear Sam. You haven't changed.'

'Actually, I have.'

Greta placed a penny in a one-armed bandit and pulled the handle. The wheels rolled and three fruits jarred to a halt. No payout.

'I WILL find Alice. Perhaps when I've earned a modicum of self-respect, then I'll come forward. In the meantime, you've got to help me.'

'Here we go! What now?'

'Arrange for me to talk to Ethel Linden.'

'Poor soul's not well. You can't go upsetting her.'

'I must speak to David Linden too.'

'The lad's life is a tragedy. He's lost everyone. Father, mother, daughter . . .'

'He has his old girlfriend back.'

'No. There's nothing between David and Sylvia.'

'After all that? No romance?'

'Actually, there's something I want to talk to you about. It's difficult.'

'Need some help playing Cupid?'

'No. That's not what I need.'

'Whatever you need from me, Sam, you can have it.'

Her flirtatious smile pierced him. He touched a strand of her hair. 'Understanding?'

She held her breath for a second, then said, 'As I need yours.'

'Oh, Alexandra, I should have told you sooner . . .'

'What?' Her arm snaked into the warmth of his jacket.

'I'm so sorry. I've fallen in love – with Sylvia. We're getting married.'

Greta held his gaze for a split second, then slowly withdrew her arm. Turning sharply, she pulled the metal lever again and watched the machine roll. Sam began to mutter apologies, but she wasn't listening. More money in the machine. Pull. Roll. Click. Pull. Roll. Click. The machine shook on its housing.

Sam rested his hand on her shoulder and she stopped abruptly, sniffing long and hard, her proud head high. She turned to him and he was astounded to see tears in her eyes, not glittering with anger, but huge and baleful.

He wrapped a strong arm around her and drew her back out into the wind, crossing the road to the cold metal railing above the bay. For a few tender minutes they stood together looking out on the thrashing sea, coats flying, Greta's black hair whipping Sam's face. She asked nothing. He offered nothing, except to gently pull her into his arms and kiss her lips with a melancholy, salted tenderness. Before he had time to utter words he had been rehearsing, like respect, friendship, loyalty, she turned her back and walked stiffly away. When he followed, she quickened her pace. When he shouted, she ran.

Let her go, Sam.

❖

It was Alan's first Saturday home since starting at Durham University. He and Sylvia were going to visit Hendo in the Rehabilitation Centre. They were standing in a queue at the trolley stop and Alan was waffling nervously about his lectures, his halls, his new mates.

Sylvia seemed unimpressed. Understandable, Alan allowed,

under the circumstances. He couldn't stop looking at her, though. Looking up at her, actually, because she was wearing high heels and was taller than him anyway. Despite all the heartache, Sylvia was regaining her prettiness; Alan was seriously infatuated. Lank black locks gone, her red hair was cut so short that it bubbled in natural waves which clustered in kiss curls around her forehead. An attractive layer of flesh now softened her bones. She even had a small bust. There was a maturity in her face which Alan respected. Flighty young females bored him. Sylvia had lived. Endured. Sylvia had more to think about than lipstick, Cliff Richard and hula-hoops. She had an air of knowledge, a consciousness above and beyond his. It's sex, he thought. With a man who is too old for her. A bloody vet!

She was quiet today. In fact Sylvia had hardly spoken. Always either enthusiastic or bombastic, Alan could blether for both of them. Running his finger around his collar, he was mid-flow about the Students' Union, when Sylvia turned abruptly to the man standing at her other shoulder and asked, rather sharply, 'I beg your pardon?'

The chap, surprised, shrugged and looked away.

On the trolley Alan gave her the window seat and paid her fare. They sat shoulder to shoulder and he savoured the tingle where Sylvia's bicep touched his. Suddenly it was as if a warm wind blew over Sylvia's features and she began to chat quite normally about the way Newcastle was changing. In turn he told her about the car his parents had promised him.

'Just a jalopy. But I'll be able to drive back from Durham for weekends.'

'Unless you get a clever university girlfriend. Then you

won't want to come home.' Sylvia was smiling conspirationally. Was she asking him something?

'I've necked a few. At parties. But nothing serious.'

'And how do clever girls taste?'

'Probably better than vets.'

She laughed. And said to the window, 'Shut up!'

❖

Hendo was ecstatic. 'Why, ya bugger. Luk what the tide's washed up! Humans! Watch out for the Gestapo. They beat your arse if you're caught sitt'n doon.'

'So how's the physio, kiddo?'

'Take uz home – take uz home . . .'

'It's for your own good.'

'Your bloody backside isn't black and blue. By, Sylvia, you luk a picture. How's things, pet? Any news?'

'Still no sign of any of them. Let's not talk about all that today.'

Alan said, 'How's this for a crack? You know that bloke David's mam ran off with? Turns out he's a queer!'

'Bugger me! And bugger him.' Hendo laughed, great golden guffaws, lightening the day, making them all feel young again.

'It's not funny,' rebuked Sylvia, grinning. 'Imagine how David must feel.'

'How is the lad?' Hendo asked her pointedly.

'Sylvia's courting Sam now,' Alan explained tactfully. 'The vet.' He caught Sylvia's slender left hand and pulled it towards Hendo, so that he could see the sapphire.

Hendo absorbed the irony of the two hands with the wrong ring between them.

'Gonna get married?'

'Uhu.'

'But he's ancient!'

Alan defended her. 'Sylvia's a lot more grown up than most lasses.'

'Is this the real thing, pet?'

She nodded.

'Alan, son, looks like ye and me's gonna be bridesmaids!'

❖

On the way home Sylvia felt very restless. They got off the trolley in Newcastle city centre and, while Alan went to City Library, she did some window-shopping for wedding presents. Ironically they agreed to meet under the Goldsmiths' Clock, with its naked, inviting Venus, reaching towards Heaven.

Sylvia arrived first. Looking up at the Goddess of Love's guilded buttocks, she noticed, perched on the top corners of the hanging clock, four winged cherub heads.

One minute passed. Four hands on four massive clock faces ticked simultaneously.

Yoohoo! Dothy was sitting right on the top, next to one of the cherubs.

Sylvia waved. Her neck was hurting from looking up. She felt a shudder, then a wonderful surge of security, as she turned to see a smiling face.

Hello, Fuggerit, called Dothy, *we've been waiting for you.*

An Angel of Seconds took Sylvia's right hand.

Immediately Tock appeared, and took her left.

Alan came towards her, grinning sheepishly. She grinned back.

❖

Greta knocked on Ethel's door. Introducing herself as Alexandra Hythe, she was relieved that the old woman did not suffer another heart attack. In fact Ethel leaned on her stick and received her caller with dignity.

'David,' she called, 'you'd better come down.'

Another woman stood in the hallway. Greta felt herself examined by a pair of very sharp eyes. The famous Clara Blake, as featured in national newspapers? With exaggerated formality, the woman retired to the kitchen.

David approached Greta with an ugly scowl, worsened by the mess of his face. 'Ransom time?' he sneered. 'How much?'

Greta shook her head and studied the stitching at the corner of his mouth.

'I'm so sorry – about the accident . . .'

'Where's Alice?'

'I swear I had nothing to do with Alice's disappearance. That's why I'm here. The police have so many suspects that they're tying themselves in knots. The field must be narrowed otherwise Alice will never be found. Perhaps together we can work out who did it.'

'Where's your father – and my mother?'

'Don't know. But my father is no lover of small children.'

'Nor is his mother,' echoed Ethel. She was watching Greta, weighing her intelligence.

'I know you despise me. But please, put that aside . . .'

'Easier said than done.'

'Mrs Linden, we have an advantage over the police. Between us, we know each of the suspects. How they tick. I've risked everything to come to you with some information about Dick, which might help. I want to ask you about Sylvia's mother. Could she and her husband have conspired, and hidden Alice somewhere?'

'Violet is as angry and lost as the rest of us.' Ethel was intrigued despite herself. 'The police have put her through Hell. I don't suspect her at all.'

'Could Cuthbert Sharp have run away with another woman? Someone perhaps called Dorothy?'

'A laughable scenario. I imagine you could dream up many more, just to detract attention from *yourself*. Now, what is this information you have, Miss Hythe?'

Greta hesitated. 'How do I know you won't ring the police as soon as I turn my back?'

'I expect you know I will.'

'Ah. I think I'd better leave.'

'No.' David grabbed hold of Greta's wrist. 'Tell us what you know.'

Greta glared down at his curled fingers. 'Let go.'

His grandmother was more shrewd. 'Speak, woman, then you can run to the ends of the earth for all I care.'

Greta wrenched her arm free. Taking a moment to compose herself, she walked to the window.

'The blood in Dick's caravan. I know whose it was. It wasn't Alice's.'

David felt pricking behind his eyes. 'Thank God . . .'

'Dick hurts women. Sexually.' Greta looked into Ethel's eyes, woman to woman, communicating the horror of rape.

The older woman met her gaze solidly. 'Whose blood was it?'

'A teenage girl. She was badly . . . damaged. I found her. She told me that, as far as she knows, Alice was never in Dick's caravan. On the other hand,' Greta continued, 'Dick *was* in Corbridge when Alice disappeared. And he has reason to believe he is her father. He was . . . is . . . my husband.'

'A man who hurts women?'

'Yes.' Greta let her black hair fall over her face.

Ethel spoke quietly. 'Would he also hurt a child?'

'Yes. Because she's my child.'

David suddenly raised his hand to his forehead, as if the pain of fear had hit him between his eyebrows. Ethel sat down heavily, silenced for a moment.

'A wicked world you live in, woman.'

'I'm sure your world is just as wicked as mine.'

'Alice!' shouted David. 'Tell us anything else you know. Please!'

Greta looked at his scarred, scared face and saw in this man/boy a love for Alice which humbled her. 'I do know a little more, David. But I'm not sure you'll understand . . .'

'Spit it out, woman!' snapped Ethel.

'It's possible that Dick had an accomplice. I have reason to believe that someone called Dorothy was involved.'

'Reason to believe?'

'You may find this difficult to accept.'

'Try.'

'I have a friend. An old gypsy woman. She – sees things.'

'In a crystal ball? Give me strength!' Ethel scorned.

Greta's fingers traced the latticework on the window. 'My friend is a true Romany; she has sight.' She lowered her voice, deliberately chilling the room. 'This woman delivered my baby. But when she held my child she felt a thread of evil which would wind in and out of her little life. I remember she whispered an incantation. Call it a spell, or a charm. In the same way that godparents make vows, my friend bonded herself to my baby. This bond is as real and indestructible as . . .'

'How much more of this rubbish must we listen to?' Ethel banged her stick on the floor, as if she could stab all gypsies with it.

Greta smiled slowly, the kind of bleak, knowing smile Dick himself used. 'Swallow your ignorance, Mrs Linden. You said my world was wicked. Yet my friend has done a very remarkable, brave and unselfish thing. She's very old, and she has chosen to spend the remainder of her days here, close to the child. To try to protect her.'

'In Newcastle? Has she got Alice?' David's brain was searching for another logic.

'No.' Greta's feet clicked across the parquet flooring. 'But she feels her somewhere close. She speaks of danger, and of Dorothy.'

'Tosh! Lies! Fairy stories.'

'Of course, there is a problem. We don't know which child my friend speaks of. She thinks that Jan Kirkstone is my baby, but I believe that Alice is my child. It may be that both children are in danger.'

'YOUR FAULT!' Ethel's stick became a pointing sword of accusation. 'If you hadn't told that dreadful lie about swapping babies, then my son would still be alive today. BY YOUR HAND HE DIED!!'

Greta faltered, suddenly Alexandra Hythe again, vulnerable, misunderstood, yet proud. 'Dick is brutal. That's why I left my baby in the first place. We must find Alice! And watch over little Jan, who could be your real great-granddaughter. You seem quite callously unconcerned about her.'

Ethel was incensed. 'How dare you? Enough of this codswallop.' She reached for the telephone.

'Don't.' Greta laid her hand on Ethel's. 'I can't find Alice if some zealous policeman puts me in prison. Turn me in and you risk both girls' lives. Help me and we could prevent another tragedy.'

'Blackmail!' Ethel turned to her grandson. 'Show her out. Push her out if you have to. Gypsy charms, indeed! What about curses? There's blood on your hands and you'll stink of it for the rest of your days.'

Greta absorbed the anathema with more humility than Ethel would ever comprehend. As she passed David she stopped, rather dramatically, and asked, 'Your nanny. Clara Blake. Are you sure that's her real name?'

Having planted her seed of suspicion, she swept out. David followed.

❖

Clara glided into the room. 'What's going on?'

Prune-like, Ethel's mouth twisted this way and that, the silver hairs on her chin bristling. 'You had no need to hide in the kitchen.' She looked hard at the nanny, trying to recall the letter of reference she brought with her. Her stick fell from

425

her grasp. Clara picked it up and held it defensively against her own chest.

'Our caller was the famous Alexandra Hythe,' offered Ethel slowly.

'Glory! What did she have to say for herself?'

'Lies and fairytales. She's a complete lunatic.'

'But did she take Alice?'

Ethel's worn face sagged. 'It seems – unlikely.' The old woman struggled to her feet. Any exertion still left her breathless.

'This is all too much strain, Mrs Linden.' Clara handed over the stick and Ethel leaned heavily on it. 'You're still not well.'

'I've lost my son. I'll never be well again. This house, it echoes of him. But the echoes are dulled, because it's Mary's house too and I can't mourn my son because I'm so busy hating her.' Rare tears were gathering in the folds of skin around Ethel's nose.

'Let's go home. Away from the mucky Newcastle air.'

'Oh, I long for my own bed in Twin Elms, but what about David?' Ethel tipped her head thoughtfully. 'Would you mind, Clara dear, staying here to look after him? Just for a while?'

'But how will you manage?'

'I expect Daft Daphne will do her best to poison me.'

'She's a good woman.'

'Drippy as suet. But her heart's in the right place. I'm getting better; I'll be fine. David can't boil an egg. He's hopeless.'

'He's been orphaned.'

'Eventually, we are all orphaned.' Ethel coughed chestily. 'Clara, I fussed Arthur too much. His life ended wretchedly because he couldn't face up to his wife. David won't develop any strength of character unless we encourage him to stand on his own two feet. I'm going to withdraw now. He knows where I am if he needs me. Meanwhile, if you could just stay with for him for a week or two, teach him how to cook a bit, and wash his own underpants.'

'If he'll let me.'

Ethel leaned on Clara's arm. 'My dear, David and I owe you more than we could repay in two lifetimes.'

'I love the baby too, you know.' Clara rarely said words like that. Both women sighed heavily.

'Yours is a strange profession. Constantly caring for little souls, then handing them back. You are a wonderful nanny. You should be looking after babies, not a crotchety old woman and a moody young man. We are repaying you with selfishness.'

'But when Alice comes back . . .'

'If Alice comes back, things will change, my dear. And I'm wondering . . . is it time to let you . . . move on?'

'You're dismissing me?'

'Of course, I'll write you a glowing reference.'

Ethel picked up the telephone handset. 'Inspector Howard, please.'

Clara Dorothy Blake's face went blank.

Cuthbert

needed a vehicle. With only coppers in his pocket, barely enough for a pint, he considered going into his own coal yard. No. He'd be picked up immediately.

Having hitched lifts as far as Gosforth Park, he was now hiding behind massed rhododendron bushes, dead scared. Scared of capture. Scared of prison. Scared of the end of his mission, of discovering some unimaginable truth.

Cuthbert stepped on to the road.

'Right! Onward, Christian soldiers.'

Tuneless humming helped propel his feet. It was a long walk. Trudge. Rest. Trudge. Rest. Tired and thirsty. Push on. Even when he was finally within sight of Prestwich Colliery he wasn't sure he could go through with it.

David limped after the posh gypsy as fast as his bad leg would allow. How could he dismiss any lead which might bring Alice home? The madwoman got into her scruffy Land Rover and opened the passenger door.

'Come with me, David.'

'I'm too old to be abducted.'

'I'm going to see the other baby – Jan.'

Like a speeding train clicking over a series of points, a rush of decisions flashed through his bright brain. He tipped his arched nose in the air and sat his backside on the seat, pulling his stiff leg in behind him. Greta drove off.

Resting his elbow on the open window, he spat, 'My daughter or yours?'

'One day we'll know. I'm so sorry, David.'

'I expect you are.' He stared out of the windscreen, his headache tightening like wires across his skull. 'I'm not interested in this Jan. ALICE is my daughter. Did you take her? DID YOU?'

'No. I swear! Your dad wanted to get to the bottom of this. You should respect what he was trying to do. I've never seen Jan either. I happen to know that today a babysitter is taking her to a swing park. Perhaps we'll see a likeness, something obvious.'

'Stop! I'm getting out. Last time you did this, you tried to swipe Alice. And look what happened.'

'You had no part in this disaster? I remember what Sylvia went through giving birth. So damned hurt and lonely.'

'I didn't know. They told me lies.'

'Excuses! Would you settle down with Sylvia now, David?'

'Nope. That vet bloke is welcome to her.' Greta flinched. 'And Katherine?'

'What about her?'

'I expect she took it badly, Sylvia coming home.'

'You're asking if Kath could have taken Alice? Yes, she could. I keep having nightmares about sleazy rooms in Soho.'

'Was she that kind of girl?'

David found himself remembering Katherine's giggles and the way she had always stopped his hands. Eyes locked on the road he acknowledged, 'No. She was – a virgin. Determined to stay that way.'

'Were you in love?'

'Sort of. We were Alice's family. She loved the bairn too much. She was just using me.'

'How was she using you? She already had Alice, every day, every bedtime story. Her love for you was separate, naive and innocent.'

David's eyes rolled slowly sideways. The pain over his brow may be dulling his ire, but his brain was working over-time.

'How would you know?'

❖

Cuthbert seriously considered eating some rosehips. His stomach kept cramping. Hunger and fear were a bad combination for bladder and bowel.

Nostalgia bruised him. It seemed a lifetime since he'd worked down the pit with the lads. The shift was changing. Clean faces in, black faces out. Sets of white teeth grinned at each other as the miners walked off together, flasks swinging.

He crouched in the lane opposite the entrance and counted. One. Two. Three. GO . . .

Keeping his face down, he sidled through the gates and dodged away from the main throng. He knew where to hide until the moment was right. In an empty shed Cuthbert rolled across the floor like a puppy, blacking his clothes, rubbing filthy hands over his face.

It would be easy enough to grab a spare helmet. The hard bit would be getting the keys.

The lorries were lined up, waiting.

❖

In a world reverberating with tragedy, Sylvia was inappropriately happy. She got off the bus in Fontbury feeling glamorous in one of Katherine's blouses (her younger sister's breasts having burst the buttons) and her mam's full dance skirt.

Sam, however, looked silly. He was wearing a tweed flat cap. He was also somewhat overladen, with chocolates under his elbow, flowers in one hand and Mustard's leash in the other. The dog was a whirl of golden fluff and pink tongue. Hugging was clumsy, full of laughter and, mercifully, the cap fell off.

Once behind closed doors, Sam drew Sylvia towards the sofa. He opened the chocolates, popped an orange cream into her mouth, then ran his hands through her auburn curls, grasping her head like a football. Sylvia was still trying to swallow the sweet when he kissed her.

The nausea which had plagued her for years vanished in a combination of sweet taste sensation and lust. In an instant she throbbed. The throb became a tidal wave of throbs and all through her spare frame muscles began to contract.

'Go and play chess or something, Fuggerit,' she muttered.

Sam frowned, frustrated. He thought she was talking to him. 'Well, if you'd prefer to . . .'

'Not you.' Bold and potent with sexual power, Sylvia pushed her fiancé back on the sofa and straddled him. Her bony fingers gripped his shoulders. It was an odd way to have a conversation, with their groins twitching together.

'Lord, I've missed you.' Sam was already undoing her buttons. 'I should be down the garden, cropping my beans. Don't laugh, Madam!'

'They say we should get married, really soon. Next month.'

She shrugged off the blouse and arranged her skirt so that her bare thighs were rubbing against his corduroy trousers. Sam began fingering the smattering of childish freckles across her breastbone.

The shimmering air in front of the clock twitched, as Tock shivered.

'Who says?'

'My friends.'

The fumbling lovers rolled off the sofa and rearranged their limbs on the carpet. Sylvia stroked Sam's chest, hands stretched wide to discover the arch of his armpits as he held himself over her.

Fuggerit stopped picking his nose, and knelt down to watch.

Afterwards, lutescent sunlight filtered through the leaded windows, making chequered patterns on naked bodies. For a while they savoured the quieter sensations of intimacy. Sylvia glanced through the door at the newly repaired grandmother clock. Tock was leaning against it, arms folded moodily. Fuggerit was studying the face, trying to move the clock hands.

Sam began to stroke her limbs again.

'What a lovely bride you'll be.'

Dothy peeped around the door.

Sylvia sat up, pulling her jumper back over her head.

'What's the matter?' His hands were following her.

'I fancy a chocolate caramel.'

❖

Cuthbert Sharp was not built for deceit. A bulldozer by nature, he was a difficult chap to overlook. An electrician called Ernie did a double take at the sight of a large man attempting to tiptoe across the yard. Ernie instantly recognized the frame of his old friend. Innocently he shouted a greeting, automatically raising his hand. But the electrician's hand remained suspended in mid-air as he remembered that Cuthbert Sharp was wanted by the police. For MURDER!

Ernie shouted and gave chase. Poor, exhausted Cuthbert ran.

❖

Two phone calls came within seconds of each other.

'Moles creep out of their holes! Quick, Butterwell!' Howard was out of the door like a whippet, his sidekick stumbling behind. 'Alexandra Hythe's just visited Ethel. And Sharp's been spotted at Prestwich Colliery.'

At the pit they were met by an army of shamed black faces. Apparently Cuthbert Sharp had disappeared. Every inch of every building had been searched. There was only one conclusion. Somehow he had got into the cage and down the shaft. He could be anywhere in an endless maze of tunnels.

Howard switched on his helmet lamp and held his breath. He hated lifts. He hated heights. Worst of all, he hated depths.

❖

David felt a fresh wave of heartbreak. The little girl's dark hair reminded him too much of Alice, although Jan had a finer build. There was arrogance in the way the child ordered her strange, elderly companion to push her higher and higher on the swing.

He and Greta sat on opposite ends of the park bench like quarrelling lovers.

'David, for God's sake, tell me she looks like your granny or your Aunt Fanny or even Great-uncle Cecil.'

'Why should I put you out of your misery?'

'I – MADE – A – MISTAKE! Sorry. A thousand rotten sorrys. But let's be objective. My family is Italian. She doesn't resemble any of my cousins. She's pale . . .'

'Her skin is fairer than Alice's.'

'My father is fair.'

'Your father's a poof.'

'So what does that make your mother? Desperate?'

For a moment David thought he might cry. He started rubbing his leg. 'My dad is dead. We're all in Hell and you put us there. For the last time, Alice is my daughter. And at this moment my guts have a hole in them. No other kid could fill that gap.'

'Yet this child could be yours . . .'

'No, lady. Life is not that convenient.' He rounded on her.

'You did take Alice, didn't you? Tucked her away somewhere, telling her lies, buying sweets and toys. Go on, deny it again. Tell me that this isn't some elaborate ruse, palming this other kid off on me.'

'I do think that Alice is my daughter. But I did not take her, and I can prove it.'

They watched little Jan climb the steps of the slide. She was wobbly at the top and David had to fight the urge to run over and help her. She slid down on her back, with legs and arms flailing. In an instant she was running towards the spinning 'teapot lid'.

Those damn things were so dangerous! David never allowed Alice . . .

The old woman in the purple hat who was supposed to be minding the child couldn't move quickly enough. Little Jan grabbed the metal bar and, placing one foot on the running board, scooted the other along the ground, mimicking the older children. Old Binnie reached out with curled arthritic fingers in a feeble attempt to grab the handles of the ride and halt it, but big kids were pushing it faster and faster.

David was on his feet and limping painfully across the park, but Greta overtook him and swiftly mounted the dizzying ride, catching her arm around Jan's middle. Using her strong legs, she stopped the ride, prised Jan's fingers loose and deposited a stunned child into David's arms.

The proud lad looked down his nose at Jan. The child against his shirt scowled at him suspiciously. Gently David placed her on the floor, took her hand and led her over to Binnie. The old woman stared, with shocking intensity, into David's face. He met her grey eyes for a split second, then walked past her, limping angrily past the big swinging cone of the iron teapot.

He winced as Greta grabbed his arm.

'Can I trust you?'

'You're joking.'

'We must help each other. End it.'

'Why me? Why not Sylvia, or the police . . .'

'Because we have a mutual problem. God forbid, our mad parents might even marry.'

'Jesus spare me! Your father's a bloody poofter.' David stood tall to face her.

'He married my mother. And fathered me.'

'Hallefuckingluia.'

'Oh, drop the schoolboy sarcasm! Will you help me find Alice or not?'

David folded his arms. 'You know where Katherine is, don't you?'

'Can I trust you?'

'Trust a bitch with gypsy under her posh skirt?'

Greta turned on her heel so quickly that her long dark hair flicked across his cheek. Tucking herself neatly into the Land Rover, she slammed the door and fired the engine.

❖

Young romance echoes around the globe, patterns folding and unfolding, rituals timelessly obeyed. Magic words are confessed with such boring lack of originality that it's a wonder the whole world isn't deafened with the universal clang of 'that phrase' (I-L-Y).

This particular ritual was taking place on a railway

embankment, not far from where Sylvia once experienced her own first sexual awakening. Here the track to the colliery ran high above the harvest-shorn fields, and in the distance the giant pit heap pierced the skyline. It was late, her mother would be worried, but the teenage girl lay spread-eagled on the slope, trying not to slither down flattened grass. Her skirt was bunched around her waist.

She was waiting to hear it. Willing those three precious words to tumble from her boyfriend's mouth. Lying on her back, she tried to stop her mind from wandering while he fumbled with zips and elastic. She was unprepared for the sharp pain of penetration. Biting her lip, willing her body to expand and accommodate, she felt an hysterical need to simultaneously giggle and scream. Her handsome prince looked like a seven-year-old boy riding a rocking horse. Up and down. Up and down. Shouldn't she be feeling something other than pain and disappointment?

And he hadn't said it! A perfect moment soiled. Up and down. Up and down. The sun melted into the horizon and as she gazed over his shoulder she studied the sky's luminous twilight, a blanket of satiny turquoise, flocked with gliding patches of purple velvet.

But the perfect firmament was slashed by two overhead lines of coal buckets; great black troughs swinging on wires above her lover's head, screeching as they wound their lonely way from pit to depot and back again.

The girl panted appropriately, but all sensuality had dissolved in regret. Why was she allowing her body to be violated in this ridiculous pantomime? Up and down. Up and down. Taking for ever. His grunting became obscene, and then it was all over. She felt sticky and ashamed. His collapsed weight was uncomfortable, but the girl endured it, still looking upwards, asking herself which lad she would try next week.

Silhouetted against a glowing sky, the buckets came to a sudden halt in their overland trek. Full buckets to the right, empties to the left.

There was something different about the shape of the trough overhead; long bits sticking out, hanging down like droopy tulips.

Violently, the girl pushed her boyfriend off. Her hand went over her mouth. The tulip heads were shoes, the stems bent legs! Her scream shrieked into the night, stilling every wild animal in the rustling fields.

Stinging

sand flurries, whipped by an offshore wind, snaked along the beach in fabulous, shifting designs. Katherine was sitting high on a rock. She could have been a mermaid with her legs wrapped tightly in Greta's green taffeta skirt and damp curls tossing around her head. Bare white arms clutched a thin shawl to her shoulders and her face was upturned towards the rushing sky.

David was mesmerized by her aura of stormy solitude.

Greta gave him a hearty push and retreated back along the beach.

'Katherine. Can I talk to you?' he called, raising a hand.

Her head moved slowly in his direction, then turned back towards the sea.

David's brow wrinkled in the face of the wind, and a familiar, bullying ache began in his temple. He limped forward, his shoes squelching. Even as he reached up awkwardly and touched her waxy arm, she would not respond.

'Aren't you cold?'

He wondered fleetingly if the drops of water clinging to

her long brown eyelashes would taste salty. In true gentle-manly fashion he removed his jacket and offered it, but she pushed it away and rounded on him.

'Why have you come here? Why did that bitch tell you?'

'I begged her. There are things you should know. Kather-ine pet, I've come to take you home.'

'By God, you have not!'

David tried clumsily to hoist himself on to the rock beside her, but the surface was slippery and pain shot through his bad leg. He cursed with frustration and hopped down towards the sea where great rollers were crashing. Icy spray stung his scarred face. He was at a loss. How could he make her listen?

'It's bloody freezing,' he shouted. 'Why don't you come up to the cottage and make me a cocoa?'

'David, do me a favour. Say what you have to say, then piss off.'

'If that's what you want, but I'm damned if I'll talk here. Let's get into the warm.'

'No.'

'Why?'

'I stay near the water.' She stood up suddenly, leapt down from the rock and, on white toes, ran down the beach. Pass-ing him, she splashed into the glacial North Sea, arms outstretched as she balanced herself against the push and drag of the pounding waves. A wet stain crawled up the green skirt as it danced in the eddies.

'You don't want me anywhere near you, David. I'm soiled. Even a bloody great ocean can't wash me clean.'

'Very dramatic! For God's sake, get out of there. That

water is enough to turn you purple. We can't talk in a howling gale. Katherine, this is terribly important.'

She stepped even deeper into the brine, allowing a cauldron of water to pour over her shoulders. The shawl was washed away, leaving only a tight white cotton blouse to cling to her breasts. Another wave smashed into her small frame and she stumbled, falling forwards into the arms of the greedy sea, her dark curls floating.

David dashed into the waves and yanked the hair, pulling Katherine's spluttering face out of the water. Throwing his arm around her waist, he struggled to keep his balance on his weak leg.

'Silly bitch,' he shouted in her streaming face, as he limped and stumbled back to safety, pulling her along with him.

He badly wanted to comfort and calm her, but instead he found himself holding her by the shoulders, shouting, 'So some pervert forced you to have sex. What difference do you think that makes to me? It wasn't your fault! You're right that the sea won't clean you. This is a waste of time. A waste of your life, Katherine. Clean comes from inside, not outside.'

She wrenched herself from his grip. To his utter amazement, she began to peel off her sodden garments, dropping the skirt to the ground and standing in it, a puddle of jade. The blouse caught in the wind and was whisked away. She stood trembling in only a pair of thick, rose-pink pants. David tried to look away, but his eyes were drawn involuntarily to the forbidden vision of milky breasts, heavy and quivering as the wind puckered her nipples and sand gathered in her collarbone. Her eyes were as cold as the North Sea itself.

'Go on, have a good look. Enjoy it,' she laughed. 'Oh,

441

what a big man you are, David! So grown up! What do you know about clean? Did Mammy teach you to wash your hands when you had a wee-wee?' She held her arms above her head, revealing soft brown fuzz in her armpits. 'This body has been washed in rivers, washed in the sea, washed a hundred times and then again. Do you think it's clean enough for you to touch? You think water can reach the parts that stink? My insides are poisoned, David Linden. If I could pour disinfectant into my guts I might be happy again, but I can't.'

'Katherine, don't do this to yourself. You're a good person; a warm, loving, funny girl. And you *are* clean inside.'

'And you're a dirty shit!'

Deaf to what Katherine was really trying to tell him, he shouted tender words into the wind. 'I know, Katherine, and I'm so sorry. Sylvia and I – we're not . . . it's you I care about.'

The naked apparition threw back her head and laughed hysterically, breasts heaving. 'You saying you love me, David Linden?'

'We're friends . . .'

She grabbed his jacket, flung it around her shoulders, then stumbled off along the beach. Limping after her, David called, 'What the Hell is wrong with you Kath . . . ?'

She stopped. Her toes gripped the sand. 'I'm pregnant – by the bloody Devil.'

❖

DI Howard ate his chips, then screwed up the newspaper and chucked it over a hedge. It was late. The pubs had shut. He felt like doing something really bad, but a bit of litter dropping was as strong as a policeman dared get.

What a job! What a tedious waste of time. Chase, chase, and keep bloody missing. Damned, damned frustrating! One suspect down, but no nearer the truth. Cuthbert Sharp was swearing on everyone's life that he hadn't taken Alice, that he only came home to try to help find her and his second daughter, Katherine.

Howard believed the miserable coalman. He also hated him. Oh yes, the crafty old bugger would now go down, but he had taken Howard's pride down with him. With profound shame, the Inspector remembered his panic attack as the pit cage had sunk deeper and deeper into the black earth. Howard's nerve had shot like a bullet from a gun. He had actually screamed, like a silly bloody woman, 'Take me back up! Fresh air – help! HELP!'

All the while, Old Sharpy had been having a doze in a bloody bucket! Made a canny little nest for himself, shuffling the slack until he could lie easy on it. Crafty sod, he almost got away with it until the poor kid in the field got caught with her knickers down.

Meanwhile Howard himself had been sent home, like a sick kid from school.

And as for that flaming elusive Alexandra Hythe! Always one step ahead, leaving devastation behind her. What mischief, upsetting Ethel Linden with that garbage about gypsy charms and visions! What an amazing talent for evasion! Like a laughing ghost, she seemed to haunt him, holding invisible strings, while he danced.

Howard was drunk and maudlin. He looked over his

shoulder and peed against someone's backyard wall, mumbling, 'Next time you show your hand, Alexandra Hythe, I'll catch it, and break your sodding fingers.'

❖

In the tiny front room of Hisper Cottage, four voluble people sweated before a roaring fire. The argument which crisscrossed the hearth was approaching boiling point. Tony Torricelli had resorted to loud, bombastic use of his native tongue, which only Greta understood. He was heartily sick of being used to harbour her waifs and strays! What right had she to install a pregnant gypsy prostitute in his cottage?

Poor Tony's temper was not improved by Liz repeatedly telling him to 'Shurrup!'

David Linden was pointing his finger at Greta. For no logical reason at all, his anger at this enigmatic woman had somehow melded with his anger towards his mother.

Liz tried to calm things. 'Paper says they've caught Sylvia's dad. No sign of the bairn, though.'

'But,' argued Greta, 'he could have an accomplice. Maybe he was having an affair.'

'Old Sharpy?' David sneered. 'Bollocks.'

'Bollocks back,' snapped Greta. 'There's a woman in this somewhere. I keep telling you – Binnie sensed a woman called Dorothy.'

'Your bloody father made a crusade out of finding your kid. So he's as likely to have taken Alice as anyone. And if he has, I'll kill him. Yes, I'll kill him. He seduced my mother. And my dad died because of him! Died! He's dead . . . my dad . . .'

'Come on, lad.' Liz put her arm around David's shoulder

444

and hissed at Tony, 'Shurrup, you garlicky old fart!' But the Italian continued swearing and gesticulating.

Greta took a breath. 'Look, David, I have my own reasons for hating my father, but from what I'm told, your mother was Arch Bitch of Newcastle.'

Despite everything, David felt a perverse desire to defend Mary. 'She was seduced by a pervert! He used her! To get his evil hands on MY DAUGHTER!'

'Why did your mother want to run off with anyone, when she'd just lost her husband? What's wrong with the woman?'

'What's right with her?' This from Katherine, who stood, dry-clothed, in the doorway. Liz rushed to draw the young girl towards the fire. Katherine, true to form, resisted and curled up on a cushion in the window.

Tony, who had no idea that Katherine was Sylvia's sister, assumed that David was staring at her because she was a prostitute. He couldn't have been more wrong. The only lust in the young lad's heart was for comfort. David looked at Katherine's white face and full figure and suddenly wanted to sink his head into her bosom, to let his locked-up tears flow over her blouse. And in that moment, David Linden realized that Katherine, despite her young years, had always mothered him.

Greta was in full flow. 'The point is, how do we find them? And can we lure them back here?'

'NO MORE HERE!' Tony exploded. 'You promise me you keepa dis place secret. SHUT UPA YOU ALL! For what reason we not know, but your papa, he make friends with his mamma and they make plan about *nipote*. Isa nothing we can do. Now I sick, sick, sick of dis all.'

'Miserable old bugger.' Katherine actually winked at David. It was not a friendly gesture. He watched, open-mouthed, as she sashayed towards the ruddy-faced Italian, theatrically assuming her wanton role.

'I know when I'm not wanted.' She pursed her lips in a mocking kiss.

'*Prostituta!*' Incensed, Tony hitched up his trousers and hooked a finger at David. 'You sleep on Ristorante floor.'

'Wait for me . . .' Liz struggled into her coat.

David stretched his stiff leg. He kept his head down as he passed Katherine's warm body and cold gaze. This new woman of frightening extremes was so changed. With great sadness he looked down at her socks; he knew the toes inside of them, remembered touching them with his own during stolen nights in Corbridge, as they huddled under the covers, wrapped in a comforting, fleshy embrace. Yes, he had abused the security of Katherine's adoration. Awed by her rebelliousness, he had failed to respect her qualities – her unfailing devotion to Alice and the strength of her personal resolve.

She had been determined to remain a virgin. Oh, how mischievously she had teased and touched him, always leaving him wanting more; but her full body used to be her most guarded treasure. Why? David asked himself in that split second, looking at her feet. Was it because she feared pregnancy, or was it because he had done it with Sylvia and she couldn't bear his comparison?

Now Katherine's dreams, her pride and courage, were mangled. With shocking frankness Greta had described how the greasy gypsy had ripped her insides – with his thing! The older woman's words had painted debauched pictures in his mind. They made him feel odd, revolted and yet titillated. Shamefully suppressing the horror of his own lust, he pitied the girl whose spirit was defeated and whose body, defiled for ever, would now have to swell with a child she must surely loathe.

At the door of Hisper Cottage Katherine's voice, sharp with sarcasm, pinged through his headache. 'School on Monday?'

'I have my own problems, Kath, but I came to help you.'

She shrugged and turned away.

Tony growled like a bulldog all the way back to town. In the flat above the Ristorante he hurled a blanket and pillow at David, then retired into his own bedroom.

David's headache peaked during the night. Suspicion pricked behind his throbbing eyes. Why had Greta brought him to Scarborough? To prove that both she and Katherine were innocent? Or to try to rekindle a dead romance? Was he supposed to marry Katherine; to cover up the pregnancy and give the little bastard a name? His brow cramped in agony and he fled to vomit in the kitchen sink.

Katherine and Greta also stayed awake late.

'He'll tell everyone!'

'He won't. I made him promise.'

'David's promises! Ha! Cheating toad. His face is hideous and I hate him.'

'He is bloody sanctimonious. I'll put him on the train first thing tomorrow.'

'No! I haven't finished with him yet.'

Katherine poked the fire. Greta read her expression, understood the bizarre nature of human attraction and laughed out loud. 'What a little madam you are!'

It was a good feeling, being close to another female. In one of life's ironic twists, Dick Korda had unwittingly bequeathed them each other.

'Greta, what happened when you saw Sam? I know you were hoping . . .'

'Hoping? Was I? In a way I think I already suspected what he eventually confessed. I just didn't want to open my eyes to it. My dear, soft-hearted vet has fallen in love with his own bloody lame duck.' She laughed wryly. 'Your sister.'

'Sylvia the Tragic? Never!'

'Daft bugger's going to marry her.'

'I'll be bridesmaid. You can be matron of honour.' She saw Greta's fingers clench. 'God, I'm sorry.'

'I'll be sorry for the rest of my life. But what about you? Will you go home with David?'

'I'll never go home now.'

'He's got some other bits of news for you, Kath. You've got some harsh realities to face up to.'

'What are these harsh realities?'

'Talk to him in the morning, after a good night's sleep.'

'I've been asleep for months. Tell me!'

'Your father,' Greta delivered her bombshells in the kindest way she could – blunt as the wrong end of a hammer, 'is being tried for manslaughter. His business has collapsed. Your mam is broke. As for you and me, there's now a price on both our heads. Courtesy of Ethel Linden.'

Katherine stared into the flames. 'I wish I *had* taken the bairn. I honestly do.'

'Come with me, then. Help me find her.'

'How?'

'Eliminate suspects. Kath, you must understand this. I'll do anything to find Alice. We may never know if she's my baby, but I can't bear to think that HE might have her.'

Katherine shuddered. 'How could he have taken her? He was too busy with me that night.'

'You were unconscious. What if he went back into the house for her? He could have handed her on to an accomplice. Or . . .'

'Killed her and dumped her body.'

'I'm going to find him. For Alice's sake, are you brave enough to come with me?'

'Have you got a gun?'

Greta saw her own sin in Katherine's young face. What was this? Could they both be contemplating murder so calmly?

'Katherine, I'm not a good person. Don't let Dick rot your soul too.'

'My insides are rotten already. I can't afford a conscience. I already have to kill this bastard in my belly.'

Greta felt unaccountable revulsion.

'No!'

'Why not?'

'Your baby could be Alice's brother, or sister.'

'Or her cousin. A mess, isn't it?'

'Kath, my baby was conceived in violence, just like yours. Perhaps that's why I could walk away from her three years ago. Now I'd give anything to have her back. If you destroy your baby, you'll never have that choice.'

Despair crumpled Katherine's pretty face. 'I don't want this to be happening,' she wailed. 'It's growing, punishing me for something I never did!' She pounded her fists against her stomach. 'I just want it out of me.'

'Strange. I once remember your sister saying exactly the same.'

❖

Mario Marletti stood by his father's carved mahogany chair. At fifty-six, Mario was an educated man who had lived, since the cradle, with the promise of great wealth and status. Although callously overbearing towards the younger members of the family, in this palatial room he was always calculatedly subservient to his father. Some day soon, he would finally inherit the Marletti fortune, and sit on the comfortless chair himself. Then, his turn at last, he would guide the family wisely, invest appropriately, divest even more appropriately! He had no time for parasites, and the man who stood before them was a contemptible worm. Mario's linguistic skills would cope with the interview, but his emotions couldn't. He felt as if his dear dead sister, Sophia, was watching him.

Mario's father's body was bent and frail, but the Marletti power still saturated the immense room like pungent frankincense, oppressing all comers, ensuring that only desperation brought supplicants to humble themselves before him.

The senior member of the Marletti dynasty, the man whom Greta called Nonno, listened to Mario's translation of Douglas Hythe's plea with repugnance. He did not look at his son-in-law, but stared instead at his own hands. Transparent skin stretched across his fingers and he could clearly see his own vein system like the roots of a tree, still pulsing with lifeblood.

'No.'

'*Suocero*,' (father-in-law) 'please . . .' Douglas grovelled.

Mario translated his father's spiked answer. 'Age has not dimmed my intelligence. You embarrass yourself by begging.'

'Alexandra is your granddaughter. She needs help.'

'She knows where I am.'

'Have you heard from her?'

The old man tapped a long fingernail against wood. Mario folded his arms.

'*Suocero*, she is in great trouble. There are things she may not have told you.'

Italian words flew on spittle and Mario translated instantly. 'I dislike ambiguity. State facts.'

'Her life is threatened. By a dreadful gypsy.'

'Give this man a name.'

'Dick Korda.'

'An Italian family? I will investigate.'

'I doubt he is Italian. He is her husband.'

'WHAT?'

'A filthy horror of a man. I do not understand it myself, *Suocero*.'

'When did she marry?'

'Many years ago. Before her time with you here in Italy. I fear she never told you.' Douglas felt a degree of satisfaction as he witnessed the shadow of disappointment in the old man's eyes.

'This gypsy husband tries to kill her?'

'He is mad. Very, very dangerous. There is more. She is in trouble with the police.'

'What trouble?'

'Suspected – theft.' Douglas was thinking quickly. 'Sir, I must go to her. Please help me.'

'Why?

'To protect . . .'

'HA!'

'I swear.'

'Do not insult me. Fatherhood was never your priority. No! You want money for yourself – and your lover!'

Douglas flinched, but he made a last attempt to salvage his pride, delivering a speech so honest that he almost made himself weep.

'Sophia was a most wonderful, amazing woman. I hurt her, as men often do the purest of women. The pain of my guilt is hard to live with. God made me, sir. With my . . . confusions. And I hope He loves me still. I tell myself that I am not a bad man, and yet sometimes I believe perhaps I may be, for I am not instinctively kind. But I love my daughter. I admire her strength and her will, and the more she rejects me, the more I crave her forgiveness. Let me try, sir, I beg you, to help her.'

Mario began translating the reply, speaking very quietly

like a slick ventriloquist, so Douglas had to strain his sensitive ears to hear. 'You killed my daughter. The disease took her life because you had destroyed her soul. Sophia was a great woman. She died wretched. Now you crawl to me like a dog. There is no forgiveness. I spit on your head. I curse your curse, for the devil inhabits your soul.'

Sick with humility, Douglas stuck to his point.

'I've addressed several letters to Alexandra in Halstone House and more recently via her friend Samuel Phillips. Each note has included a cryptic message with instructions to meet me in Monte Carlo on her mother's birthday.'

'October eighth.' Mario spat this on his own account. 'Two weeks ago. We put flowers on the memorial.'

'Alexandra did not come. If she has not contacted you either, then I'm very afraid for her safety. But if you do know where Alexandra is, for pity's sake, tell me she is safe.'

'Return here in three days.'

'*Suocero* . . .'

'No money!'

'There is a child. Your great-granddaughter. She is three years old.'

The old man's body twitched. He spread his hands across the arms of the chair.

Mario spoke for himself. 'I telephone Antonio Torricelli.' His call would be two days too late.

❖

Neither Fuggerit nor Tock expected Sylvia to get drunk.

Alan called for her in his ageing Austin A40. The boot was loaded with Newcastle Brown, and Hendo, mercifully

453

released from 'rehabilitation', was sitting with his leg extended across the back seat, one great hairy hand waving out of the open window.

Sylvia jumped into the front, subconsciously loosening the taut restraints of her mother's accusatory depression and Sam's virtuousness. It was bliss to be youthfully gay as they zoomed down Gosforth High Street, proud as muck. Sylvia put her mouth to a bottleneck. The bitter taste suited her palate. By the time they reached open countryside, they were all singing and burping and shouting obscenities at mesmerized cattle.

Something drew them, that day, towards Hadrian's Wall. They drove along the old Roman Road, which marches east to west, from hill to windswept hill, undulating madly. Sylvia laughed hysterically as Alan drove too fast over the rises and her bottom repeatedly left the seat.

They stopped at Housesteads, and admired the snaking Roman Wall. Far from sober, they settled down to personal conversation.

'When's the big day then, hinny?'

'Hinny? How common, Hendo,' Sylvia giggled.

'Prefer Mrs Poshy Pants? Or Mrs Very Veterinerararary?' Hendo smiled drunkenly.

Fuggerit smiled too, standing there in his purple toga and helmet. How brave and fearless he looked, as he studied the grooves carved in stones by Roman chariots.

'Nowt wrong with common.'

'Don't let yourself down, Hendo,' Alan lectured. 'Let's not perpetuate the world's opinion that Geordies are thick!'

'Why not? That way the bastards never see us com'n.'

'You and me and Davy boy, we're all going to be famous. You'll redesign city centres. Davy'll discover a cure for cancer, and I'm going to blow the whole face of politics to smithereens.'

Hendo winked at Sylvia. ''E will anall.'

'Watch out, world! The brainy Geordie boys are a-coming.'

Standing high on the Wall, Alan opened his arms to the wind. His blond hair blew all over his face.

What about the Geordie lass who used to help you with your Latin homework? Tock, dressed in armour from head to toe, stood at Alan's shoulder, with his leather gauntlets folded. The protective angel started spouting a blether of resentful Latin, with a final spit of, *alis volant propiis* – she flies with her own wings.

Sylvia took a swig from her bottle and climbed up the stones. Her head was swimming, but she needed to tell Tock to stop, so she put her hand over her mouth and started mumbling at him.

Hendo, well inebriated himself, thought she was drunk. Alan, however, watched her hisses with hazy puzzlement.

'First sign of madness.'

She looked blankly at him. With exaggerated courtesy he helped her down from the wall and began asking about her own plans.

'Will you be Sam's receptionist? Or will you get a proper job?'

Fuggerit started picking through Alan's hair, as if looking for nits.

'Sexy secretary,' hiccoughed Hendo. 'Or sexy nurse or sexy summut.'

Alan, earnestly wanting to help, said, 'You could try the Ministry. You'd have to go in at the bottom. Clerical Assistant. But you'll sharp work up to CO. You used to be quite clever, didn't you?'

Tock, walking behind Sylvia, dug his gauntlets between her shoulder blades, and slipped under her skin, armour, feathers and all. He pointed his gun out of her mouth.

Used to be?

Alan was in full flow. 'But anyway, in a year or so you'll be pottering around a nice little house, making jam, knitting, ironing Sam's hankies.'

Our minds have been to places you could never imagine. Shall we show you?

Alan tossed his bottle at a cowpat. 'Of course, you'll need to earn a few bob just now. Save up for your bottom drawer and such. You used to work in a shoe shop in Scarborough, didn't you? You could try Timpsons on the High Street.'

Hendo was limping along the Wall, singing,

'When I was just a little girl,

I asked my momma, what will I be?

Will I be pretty, will I be rich?

Here's what she said to me . . .'

Fuggerit, who still had a sense of humour, put his arm around Hendo, and like a debauched Roman joined in the chorus,

Que sera, sera, whatever will be, will be,

The future's not ours to see . . .

456

Tock took Sylvia's angry, drunken mouth and fastened it on Alan's.

Que sera.

❖

Missing hearth and home more than she'd care to admit, Katherine found life on the road tedious. Back in the caravan, weather ruled their lives. Cold brought one kind of misery, rain another – damp sheets, damp blankets, damp clothes and a chill which clung to that dampness till there was no comfort anywhere. The caravan did have a small fireplace, but during afternoons and evenings Greta told fortunes, so for long hours Katherine found herself killing time alone.

She had taken to working with some of the other showmen, pegging tents, stacking shelves with prizes, loading air rifles, taking money. Befriending these itinerants meant that Katherine could ask questions about Dick Korda which his wife couldn't. But the trail had gone completely cold. The bastard seemed to have disappeared. Part of Katherine was very glad – but her own fear of the rapist was less important than the search for her sweet, innocent, missing Alice.

This life was very strange. Swamped by vibrant colours, music and milling crowds, she felt invisible. People didn't look gypsies in the eye. Richer by a few bob, she would return to the caravan perished and exhausted, welcomed by the smell of superstitious bodies who had sat on the divan which doubled as her bed. The harder she tried not to mind, the more she did.

Whenever they were near a big city, Katherine still insisted on finding the local swimming baths. Despite her embarrassment over her gently swelling belly, she and Greta, equally competitive, would race each other up and down the pool.

Between fairground stops Kath's eyes seemed perpetually focused on tarmac. The ROAD became a dirty word. Life was a constant fight for cleanliness – MUD the arch-enemy. As she went into her fourth month of pregnancy the nausea lessened, but she developed a highly sensitive bladder. Purgatory was trying to pee behind a hedge in the dark, with rain on a bare bum and a gale howling between her legs.

❖

A single letter lay on the mat. Postmark Italy.

Sam's hands trembled as he slipped the pages into another envelope, which he addressed to Scarborough. What else could he do? Huddled into his duffel coat, he sat on the bench at the bottom of the garden trying to convince himself that he should tell Howard.

❖

Katherine's back ached. This journey was taking hours. They had sung every Doris Day song, played I-SPY and debated Elvis Presley's mascara. Now, as the miles slunk wearily by, Katherine was quietly wondering how bouncing around on the Land Rover's hard bench hadn't already aborted the thing in her belly. Daily she shocked her body with ice-cold water. She had jumped from high rocks. Banged herself in the stomach. Greta had even helped her with the gin remedy, which would have been funny if she hadn't been so sick.

Too late, now, for the needle.

Perhaps it was just as well she hadn't killed it. Katherine

believed in the earthly balance: goodness earns blessings, badness begets more badness. So, as she fretted about her darling little Alice, she hoped that her own bad luck and endurance were earning the little lass some happiness, wherever she was.

And if Alice was dead? How could abortion balance the books?

Once the kid was born, she would have to have it adopted. 'It' was not a baby. 'It' was Dick's sperm. 'It' was morning vomit and bladder accidents.

But what if Alice's soul was trying to be reincarnated inside Katherine's own belly?

Oh, God!

They were heading towards Halstone House. As Greta drove along in her own daydream, Katherine also fantasized. Maybe some day, when Alice was found, when Dick the Devil was out of their lives for good, Greta would invite her to make a new life here in the South. What sort of life would that be? A lilac bedroom? Caviar (whatever that was)? Sunny mornings wandering around manicured lawns, armed with a great woven basket and an even greater woven hat? New clothes? Rich men?

'You look shattered,' commented Greta.

'Past myself.'

'Nearly there.'

When they finally glimpsed Greta's home, Katherine was disappointed. She'd expected something bigger, posher. It had started to rain and the poplars along the pitted, puddled driveway were whipping. Beneath the dark windows of the boxy building, fallen leaves from a Virginia creeper lay in sodden heaps, and only the old plant's clinging tendrils seemed to prevent Halstone House from disintegrating under its own melancholy.

At the bottom of the drive, Greta drew to a halt.

'We'll tuck ourselves behind the kitchen garden, hidden from the road. As long as it keeps raining we'll have enough water for some tea and a good wash. Then you, young lady, can have a doze, because tonight we are playing pussy cats.'

She drove them to one side of the house, past a thick copse, through a quagmire and alongside a high brick wall.

'If anyone comes nosing around, you know what to do.'

'Cough a lot. Wipe nose on back of hand. Ask where to buy fresh eggs.'

'I'll have to stay hidden.'

'Weird, burgling your own home.'

By midnight deep layers of black cloud blotted out the moon, promising yet more rain. Katherine clung to the older woman's macintosh as they trudged blindly along the length of the high wall. In the dripping copse Greta's torch guided their wellingtons under branches, through prickling brambles and over running gullies. Emerging from the cover of the trees, Halstone House loomed large before them, black against black.

Greta slid her key into the lock but the door refused to budge.

'Bolted from inside!' she hissed.

They crept like shadows around the house. Greta had her tool bag. She jemmied the back door and almost fell into the scullery.

Katherine's heart was pounding. The walk through the dark had been exciting, but now exhilaration shifted into full-blown fear. Stepping tentatively across the threshold, they were welcomed by a stench of sulphurous cabbage water. Scurrying mice nattered and stopped. Greta flicked the torch between stained pots, picking up a fantastic cobweb strung from a pan handle to a grey-green loaf of bread. On the slate floor were muddy footprints.

Swiftly they passed through the kitchen and up into the main hall. Anther long cobweb, hanging from a chandelier, tickled Katherine's face. She turned, so that she was walking back to back with Greta. They entered a room at the front of the house. Suddenly Greta stiffened and screamed, slamming her hand over her own mouth to silence herself. Katherine's whole being, inside and out, began to quake.

'What?' she hissed, fully expecting to see a dead body on the library floor.

'BASTARD!' Greta's fists clenched in fury. In the centre of the room torchlight fell on Douglas's grand piano. The shapely top had been wrenched from its hinges and thrown across the floor. From the beautiful instrument's guts, spewed tortured strings, hanging like broken spider legs.

'Twisted ferret! I'll murder him.' Greta laid her arms across the mutilated instrument.

She suddenly snapped off the torch. 'What was that?'

They both froze, but there were no sounds at all.

'It feels so dead. Come on, Kath. Job to do.'

Back in the hallway Greta bent to pick up a pile of letters. Every envelope had been ripped open, the contents torn or crumpled. 'Damn, damn!'

Katherine whispered, 'Burglars?'

She held the torch while Greta tried to piece together bits of letter.

'Someone much closer to home. Hell and damnation!' she cursed again. 'What's this? Keep that light still!' She was joining four parts of a handwritten page.

Katherine focused the beam on a few lines of writing:

Your Mother's birthday.
The place you first tasted champagne.
The hour Sheba was born.

'What is it?'

'A message from my father. Crafty sod. What date is it today? Bloody Hell, I've missed him!'

'I don't understand. Who's Sheba?'

'My pony. She was born near midnight. I drank my first champagne in Monte Carlo. He's given me the date, time and place, but that was two weeks ago!'

Suddenly the windows lit up, as a bolt of lightning shot its incredible, heavenly energy to the earth. Automatically Katherine counted. One. Two. Three. Four. Five. The storm was five miles away. 'Can we go now, please?'

'I must look in my father's room. And his study, although I bet the safe is already empty. Let's hope he left some clue about where he was going.'

Another great flash.

One. Two. Three.

The sky groaned. Spatters tickled the windows.

'Greta, this house feels like something I saw at the

pictures. Daggers came out of the walls and the ceiling started coming down, and they were trapped . . .'

'Don't be daft. This is my home.'

Just as she said it, the torch blinked off. Plunged into total darkness, Katherine whined, but Greta was alert with frustration.

'The damned gods are definitely not on our side tonight. Stay here, Kath, I'll find some candles. Try singing.'

Katherine fumbled her way to the windowsill and gripped it.

Greta was groping through the house, singing, 'Once I had a secret love . . .' Her harsh contralto voice echoed around the high ceilings. Katherine joined in, her shaky soprano holding contact with her friend.

'. . . that lived within the heart of me.'

'All too soon my secret love, became impatient . . .'

Flash.

One.

Thunderous rumble. Rain lashed against the glass.

'. . . to be free. NOW I SHOUT IT . . .' The top notes quivered and fell into giggles as, ghost-like, Greta's illuminated face appeared in the doorway, grinning from ear to ear, candlelight flickering under her chin, from a branched candelabra. She handed it to Katherine and beckoned her upstairs.

After that Katherine's sole priority was protecting the precious flames from guttering, as she followed Greta from room to room, listening to her swear.

'No bloody good! We need daylight. I'm going to wait here until dawn. Do you want to go back to the caravan?'

'On my own?'

'You're tired, but I need to keep searching.'

'Someone might see you.'

'Got to risk it. I'll grab a couple of hours in my bedroom. Hey, it might be the last time I ever sleep in my own bed.'

'I'm staying with you.'

The four-poster bed was almost as big as the caravan. It was strange to see Greta's belongings picked out in candlelight, standing lifeless, waiting. They huddled under her feather eiderdown, lying close together, yet separately cocooned. Despite fears of ghosts, ghouls and bogeymen, Katherine's exhausted, pregnant body relaxed into fitful naps, but in the early hours she awoke bathed in sweat.

Every sinew in her body was tense. She fought to stay awake. Time dawdled to a standstill. Hunger pangs gnawed at her belly. Slowly, so slowly, the strangeness of the night began to melt as the sky outside softened from black to grey.

Birds began to twitter.

Greta snored on. Katherine studied the faded room and wondered how a woman from such a background had ever married Dick the Devil. How had she endured his filthy squalor; stayed with him when she found herself impregnated?

Why did Greta want her baby back now, child of a brutal man?

And yet, Greta's baby could be – Alice.

With the first tiny red crescent of sunlight she made her decision. It fitted as tidily as the last piece in a jigsaw. What to do when 'It' was born.

She would give it to Greta.

'Oh, what a beautiful morning,' sang Howard, as ecstatic as a lonely, middle-aged policeman could be. 'Oh, what a beautiful day. I've got a beautiful feeling . . .'

While an exhausted Katherine fought her way back to the caravan through wet branches, and Greta continued her search of Halstone House, the inspector was running for the train.

❖

Ducking under windows, Greta savoured each room: threadbare carpets, peeling wall coverings, dripping taps – nonetheless, home. At last a wellspring of childhood nostalgia could flow, because her father was not there to soil it.

'Mamma.' She sat on her mother's bed and remembered the blanket of love which had wrapped them together. Peace settled on her troubled mind as she touched the mattress where Sophia had died, and instead of seeing her agony, she saw her mother's beautiful healthy smile. She sniffed, searching for the smell of cologne, remembering the touch of a lace handkerchief on her cheeks.

Rising, she crossed to the dressing table, lifted an ivory hairbrush and pulled long threads from it. Like a handle turning in a door to the past, the brush opened a part of her heart which had long been closed, and her mother's ghost reached out to touch the hurt little girl who was once Alexandra, forgiving, understanding, comforting the woman who had grown into Greta.

'*Grazie*, Mamma,' Greta whispered into the mirror, seeing

Sophia's face instead of her own. 'I've lost my child, Mamma. I gave her away and I'm so sorry. Help me find her, please.'

A noise downstairs! Greta jumped to her feet. Tap tap tapping. Rhythmical beating like a hammer, or a war drum. She tiptoed towards the door and listened. A familiar tune. Humming. Tap tap tapping.

❖

The morning was fresh, washed clean by the storm, blown gusty and bright. Katherine leaned against the high wall, watching the copse. As she willed the sun to defeat the lethargy of pregnancy, she felt increasingly anxious. It was now nine o'clock and Greta had still not returned.

Only a vague silhouette of Halstone House was visible between leafless branches, but she could see part of the drive. Something smooth and shining flashed, and then it was gone. A car?

Katherine turned back to where the caravan stood embedded in mud. Someone was moving around the front of the Land Rover. Someone in a uniform. She pressed herself against the wall, slid along it, and slipped into the kitchen garden.

❖

'I'm singing in the rain.' Tap tap tapping.

Greta could hardly breathe. She followed the high-pitched refrain to the dining-room door, then, standing well back, pushed it open with her foot. The clattertap continued. She poked her head round the door. Glowing in morning sunlight, the long french-polished dining table extended the entire length of the room. As if this were a scene in an American musical, a man danced along the table's lustrous surface, twirling an open umbrella on his shoulder, tap tap tapping.

'Neat footwork, Martin. I'd forgotten you were so talented.'

'Ah! Such sacrifices I made for your father, my dear.'

Greta was shocked. As a servile young man, Martin had always been effeminate, but now his voice was even higher than a woman's! His theatrical grin was the comical mask of a debauched clown. Mannerisms exaggerated, language overly contrived, he was using his homosexuality like a weapon.

'He adored me, darling, from the first moment he saw my face in the follow spot. "Star quality," he said! But once I heard him tinkle those ivories, sweetie, I was lost. Simply knew that I must for ever play second fiddle. What were a few piddling pirouettes compared with his mastery? I worshipped him.'

'So you took a pickaxe to his piano.'

'He left me. For a woman.'

'Tell me, Martin, do you bathe in your own tears?'

'I swear I do, darling.' With a flourish Martin leapt into the air in toe-touching splits, landing with a shuffle-hop-step at Greta's feet, smugness creamed all over his puffy face.

'Now don't be spiteful.' He spun the open umbrella between them, the point close to Greta's face. 'I've come to bring you a message, my sweetie.'

'Stick it up your accommodating backside!' She turned from his madness and walked towards the door.

'Nasty, nasty!'

Suddenly the umbrella became a weapon. Martin used it like a sword, digging her in the back, pinning her to the door, the tip pressed hard into her spine. A shock of pain winded her. She arched her body and tried to grab backwards at the taut fabric, but even when her fingers caught an edge, she couldn't shift it. So she kicked like a horse. But the torture only increased.

'Can't have you running out on my little welcome party, dear. I do so love police uniforms.'

'Get off . . .'

'Be a good girl and listen to your message.'

'My father? Ah!'

'No. A Scarface. Permanent wink. Not my type at all. Oh dear, Alexandra, you've been a naughty little girly-wirly. He's vewy cross!'

Greta was coughing now. The point of the umbrella had slipped lower, into the soft tissue under her ribs, threatening to break the flesh and impale her.

'Pretty Dicky left you some very important instructions. And I'm rather excited, because I've had the wickedest notion.'

'This has nothing to do with you.'

'No? Any minute now you'll be arrested. But how can you possibly fulfill nasty Dick's instructions if you're in jail? You need a servant. A very well paid one, who keeps his mouth shut.'

'I've no intention of going to jail. Or listening to Dick's perverted messages.'

She fought again, twisting against the pain, until Martin said, 'Don't you want to find your itty-bitty baby?'

'Just spit it out, bastard!'

'He wants four thousand quid – for old times' sake. New-castle Town Moor, Bonfire Night, seven o'clock. I think his words were, "Payment ensures her safety; secrecy secures her life." My fee is half of his. Hope you've got the dosh, darling.'

Footsteps crunched on the gravel outside the house.

Martin (suddenly playing the butch hero) shouted, in bass-baritone, 'Here she is, officer.'

Then he whispered, 'I'll visit you in jail, darling.'

Bluff?

A cruel, money-grabbing hoax? Or did Dick have Alice after all? How could she get that much cash by November the fifth? What if she was in prison, and couldn't make the rendezvous?

Please God, Greta prayed, make this message the twisted ranting of a pervert. Let Alice be safe in Europe with my foolish father and Mary Linden.

Policemen were invading Halstone House, fussy bluebottles buzzing. Every door was opened, every cupboard explored. Floors and walls were banged to check for secret hiding places. They were looking for Alice.

The local DI sat Greta down at the dining table. He lacked Howard's finesse; his interrogation was fast and furious. Why did she take Alice? Where had she hidden her? Where was her father? On and on he rattled. Greta became surly and obtuse.

'We've found your caravan.'

'That must have been difficult. Such a tiny thing.'

'Cut the sarcasm.'

In Douglas Hythe's study a telephone jangled. Bluebottle

activity froze. A constable moved to pick up the receiver, but the Inspector hauled Greta to her feet.

'Answer it.' He stood by her side, his breath on her face.

'Nonno! Oh, Nonno!'

Sweet Sophia's hand had indeed stretched from Halstone House, right across Europe.

'My grandfather,' Greta explained curtly to the policeman. 'A very frail old man. Please let me talk to him for a moment. Pick up the phone in the hall if you wish.'

The Inspector motioned an officer to guard her, while he stomped away to pick up the other handset.

'Are you well, Nonno?'

The reply was in fast, vexed Italian. 'You are in trouble, Alexandra.'

'I am, Nonno . . .' She tuned into her grandfather's Italian gabble, praying the Inspector could not translate.

'We could not find you. Mario sent messages to Antonio Torricelli and Samuel Phillips. Also, we telephoned the house every day. The servant promised to get our message to you.'

'Where is the pain exactly? Have you seen a doctor?'

'What is happening?'

'Excuse me, Nonno . . .' Over the handset, to the Inspector, she said, 'My grandfather doesn't understand much English. He's been ill.'

Switching swiftly to her mother's tongue, Greta rushed on in fluent Italian, 'The police are here.'

'Why?'

'I am accused of stealing a child.'

'Guilty?'

'NO!'

471

'I have been told of this child, by your weak, homosexual pa . . .'

Swiftly staunching the word papa, she asked, 'Is my parent there with you?' The language became familiar again across Greta's tongue, words tumbling casually. 'Nonno, did he bring the child to you?'

'No. Such disgrace, Alexandra! Your child is a member of my family!'

Her outward demeanour suggesting only polite conversation, Greta gave no hint of the desperation in her words. 'Don't trust my parent, Nonno. He fled from England because a man died and he was involved. Nonno, I must find out if he took my child. If it wasn't him, then it may have been another man.' Idly, for the sake of the young constable guarding her, she picked her fingernails.

'Your husband? Of whom you told me nothing?'

'I was ashamed. He is evil. He has asked me for money and threatens to hurt her. It could be bluff. Please, Nonno, can you make quite sure the infant is not with . . . my parent.'

'Mario will investigate.'

'If you find her, keep her with you, Nonno. In England she is in great danger.'

While the voice on the other end rippled on, Greta simply listened, looking bored, smiling apologetically at the policeman. She hoped to God that none of them understood when she mumbled, 'Four thousand pounds for November the fifth.'

'I will send it.'

'I will repay you.'

'You will.'

'Via a friend who lives by the sea?'

'One week from today.'

She placed the receiver back in its cradle. As the Inspector's fingers bit into her arm, Greta did not flinch.

❖

By the time they took her down to the station, Katherine was over two miles away, tramping up a busy road with her thumb held high in the air. Greta had taught her well. If in doubt – run.

❖

It was late in the evening when DI Howard entered the locked cubicle. The woman he had sought for so many months lay dozing on a narrow bunk, her forehead pressed against cold green tiles. Howard studied her long, muscular legs.

'At the risk of sounding corny, we meet again, Miss Hythe.'

He extended his hand. She didn't even sit up, but rolled over and stared at his sausage fingers.

'You've refused to speak to my colleagues.' Howard's fingers, still hovering in the air, reached down to her face.

'Understand, Alexandra, that I am not a bully.' He traced her jawline. 'Not like your husband. Not at all. I simply want your version of the truth.'

With a violent crack, Greta slapped his hand away.

Howard let his arm remain in the air for a second, then he deliberately brought his hands together and rubbed them slowly.

'Sit up!' She did not. 'Sit up!'

Howard felt power push through him as the woman

gracefully raised her torso. Her black hair was wild; he noticed grey threads at her temple.

'Dick Korda. Your husband. You attempted to murder him. Twice.'

Howard found himself riveted by her empty gaze. Something dual about the woman, her hot/cold, alluring/repulsing sexuality made him brusque.

'Was it self-defence? There were plenty of witnesses to his brutality when you were in labour.' Her eyes flickered slightly. 'No doubt you thought you'd done away with him then. But no! Back he comes to haunt you, and you make a second attempt, this time dressed as a man.' If this was a duel, Howard momentarily lost his advantage because a flicker of laughter twitched the corner of her eyes. 'I was inches away from you. And that spanner you were wielding.'

The spanner hung between them again, poised to break Greta's silence or Howard's patience. This spanner moment began to stretch as Greta refused to answer.

The extraordinary policeman rarely lost a battle of wills. But, as he watched the woman who was both Alexandra Hythe and Greta Korda, his spiritual antennae twanged. He was looking at the hollow in the base of her neck, watching a small tick of life. In her pulse he felt a wave of something excruciatingly uncomfortable – female vulnerability, loaded with pride and shame.

In that instant Howard's tangled web of theories began to weaken. Threads snapped. Doubt crept in. He pictured Dick Korda and let a wash of empathetic, perhaps telepathic, fear rush through him. He imagined trying to escape from the man's brutal grasp. Running. Fleeing. Not looking back because the picture was too terrifying. And suddenly Howard was running inside his own head, on a black night with some unthinkable pain both behind him and in front of him.

Through these time-distorted seconds the policeman's face remained impassive. His glance flicked to her temple, then round her hairline to her forehead. He looked at the pale skin and thought – her brow is smooth, without creases. As if she has never been puzzled, never cried, never even been truly angry.

And as he pondered this, a lightning flash of cognition crossed from Greta's intelligent eyes to his. It was loaded with integrity.

Abruptly Howard stood up. He looked down on her black, tangled crown and said, 'I'm afraid Alice is dead.'

Then he walked out.

❖

Two hours later he returned. Her head flew up. The flush on her high cheekbones, the sickly white of her chin and nose, chest rising and falling too fast, these changes were too subtle to be feigned. She was really upset.

Howard was unprofessionally glad.

'Your insides were mashed up. The day after you attempted to kill your husband, your injuries were treated in London. You returned to your father and became Alexandra Hythe again. Then you went to Italy.'

'Alice? Please . . .' Her brow was still smooth. But her mouth had slackened wetly, like rotting raspberries.

'Talking to me now?'

'Alice? Tell me.'

'Did you attempt to murder your husband?'

'No!' Her stare skewered him. 'How cruel you are, Inspector. As cruel as him. Is my daughter dead? Have you found her body?'

'This is where we exchange information.'

Greta threw her head back and began to laugh. The guttural sound echoed around the cold tiles. As her hair fell back, her long neck arched towards him, almost as if she was offering it for strangulation. Howard knew this wasn't helpless hysteria; her false mirth was bitterly self-conscious. It stopped as abruptly as it started.

'Inspector. Have you ever been so terrified that you would run anywhere, just so a man's eyes don't fall on you? Do you know what it's like to cower like a dog in a corner, waiting for the next beating? No? Try to imagine what it's like to give birth, then find that your lifeblood seems to have drained out of your legs, so even although you desperately want to run, you just can't!'

'The point being?'

'I delivered on Newcastle Town Moor. That was the last time I ever saw Dick. From the moment I was taken to hospital, all I wanted to do was run. But I couldn't, so I staggered. And just kept staggering.'

'With Sylvia Sharp?'

'Not my choice. She begged to come. We were both as weak as kittens. Spent a night in a hotel . . . I'm sure you know all that. Now will you tell me about Alice?'

'You told Sylvia you were taking her to Scarborough.'

'The girl was a pain in the backside. I told her to go back to her parents, but she just clung to me, and I didn't want it.'

'So you dumped her?'

'Sent her to friends.'

'Noble. And, that afternoon, in Durham, what did you do?'

'For pity's sake. Tell me about my baby . . . has a body . . . ?'

'No body. Keep talking.'

'I remember hobbling up to the Cathedral, sitting for a long time, trying to think where to go.'

'Pray, did you?'

'I don't pray.'

'Witnesses?'

'Possibly. I left a bloodstain on one of the pews. Women bleed after childbirth. There's no strength for murder.' She took a deep breath. 'I can't bear this any longer. Tell me, for Christ's sake.'

Howard sniffed, long and hard.

'I lied.' He smiled. 'So did you.'

❖

A nurse took a blood sample. The interval gave Greta time to compose herself. She needed a different technique for handling the manipulative Inspector. Calculatedly, she shifted her perspective. Beginning to understand her adversary, Greta was unsurprised and unimpressed by his apology.

'I had to see your reaction. My absolute priority is Alice, and weeks are slipping by. I said I was "afraid" she was dead. Meaning afraid of the possibility. A play on words. I'm good at that. But you are right, I was cruel and I'm sorry, Alexandra. Or do you prefer Greta?'

'Alexandra. Greta was Dick's wife.' She deliberately pitched her voice to be low, intimate. 'I've told you the truth, Inspector. I confess, I did once try to snatch Alice from the Sharps. A kind of mad desperation gripped me. But that is my only crime in this horror story.' She swept the tangles away and lifted her head. 'I have terrible regrets about what I did that day. One look at David Linden's face is enough to remind me of the havoc I caused.'

'You've left a few other scars behind you.'

'I wear my own privately.'

'I dare say.' He leaned forward. 'Your father – and David's mother. Did they take Alice?'

'No.'

'So certain?'

(She wasn't, but if the Italians found Alice she was safest with Nonno.) 'If Father had taken Alice, I would have found her by now. Ask Ethel Linden and David. They know I've been searching for Alice myself, in my own way.'

Howard nodded slowly, his eyes soft as melting candle-wax.

'Hilloe! I wonder if you can help me. I am proud to say that I was instrumental in assisting with the arrest of Alexandra Hythe yesterday. Look – scratches to prove it. Has the lady been charged? May I speak to her?'

'Sorry, mate. She's been taken out of the area.'

'Oh, baggar! Where to?'

'Can't divulge that.'

Martin bowed slightly and left the police station.

❖

At Durham Jail, Violet told herself not to bubble. She didn't feel sorry for her husband, she felt sorry for herself. Cuthbert, sitting opposite her, with his ridiculous, blotchy brown hair, had little to say. Their marriage would never again be free of blame and bitterness.

'Case'll be heard January,' he muttered. 'If you're interested.'

'What did the lawyer say?'

'Ten fuck'n years of me life. For a fuck'n accident.'

'Kirkstone only got eight. That Janice was on the bus, so he must still be in here.' She sniffed. 'She looks at me as if a'm summut on her shoe. And yet she's got a bairn that could be owa granddaughter.'

To Violet, baby Jan was like a tiny flame of hope, a small soul she had briefly touched, but who seemed destined to remain just beyond her loving grasp.

'No sign?' Cuthbert was asking, his face humble with powerlessness.

'No sign.'

Neither could bear to speak their names. Katherine. Alice.

Violet watched the keen open in Cuthbert's heart. She resented his pain, because it left no room for hers. And no room for her.

Cuthbert looked up. 'We cocked it up. Lost the lot. My temper and your lies.'

'Try'n to protect you!'

'Well, divent tell no more porkies on my part! A'm not ashamed of the truth.'

'I am, Cuth. I am.'

'Go to bloody church.'

'What for?'

'Te pray. Helps.'

'Well, start pray'n for owa Sylvia.'

'Why her? She's in fuck'n clover. It's the rest what's bug-gered.'

Violet rolled up her left sleeve and showed Cuthbert some livid red skin where the kettle had scaled her forearm.

'She's crackers, Cuth. Owa Sylvia's gone bloody crackers.'

❖

Alan drove home from university looking forward to going to the Three Mile for a beer. It was the favourite Friday meet-ing place of last year's sixth form, and it was great to catch up with his old mates. He hated drinking alone; he liked talk-ing too much.

As usual, he called on Hendo first, but the big lad was taking a nurse to the Odeon. David didn't even answer the door, so Alan decided to call on Sylvia.

'Come on,' he encouraged her. 'You'll meet some of your old friends. Moira's often there. Joyce sometimes comes with her lad. She's engaged, like you.'

'Is David going?'

'Na. He's all morose, blowing his horn.'

Sylvia smiled, quite bewitchingly, and nodded.

'I'll pick you up.' Alan normally felt swanky when he said that to a lass, but he couldn't impress Sylvia because her fiancé had a smart new car.

Alan called for her later, feeling very flash with his black pencil tie and his blond hair washed and fluffy. Sylvia had made an effort too, wearing a tight turquoise jumper and vivid jade eye shadow. Her lips were losing their creases again, smoothing out, glossy and pink. If he expected her to be nervous, she wasn't. She was as warm as a girl who was engaged to a vet could be, which was bloody frustrating because Alan was so deeply attracted to her.

The Three Mile was busy. Most of the throng were lads, although Joyce was there, wearing her new fiancé on her arm like an umbrella. Sylvia seemed completely unable to make conversation. She settled against Alan's arm, watching the giant young men, deaf to their banter, unimpressed by their boasting. They, in turn, were shy around the tall young woman whom they hadn't seen for so many years. Tragedy, Alan realized, flummoxes people.

Sylvia sipped her lager and lime, leaving lipstick on her glass. Alan smiled at her, their faces close enough for him to notice her mascara. He felt a surge of emotion and thought it was forbidden, denied love.

'I want to go,' Sylvia said, abruptly. 'Feel a bit strange.'

Unfortunately Alan read his own meaning into 'strange'. He laid his hand in the small of her back as he helped her into the car

'Can we park up for a bit?' she asked.

Wishful thinking washed Alan in testosterone.

At the end of Broadway East was a little footbridge which crossed over the mucky burn, to the allotments. For decades, this spot had been used as a dark place of secret courtships.

They got out of the car and clanked on to the metal bridge. Alan, very unusually, couldn't speak. He didn't even dare take her hand. What the poor lad could not see was Tock and

Fuggerit standing either side of him. They both wore leather jackets with upturned collars.

'Did you know Hendo's got his place at uni?' Alan asked finally.

Sylvia was leaning on the handrail, and she began muttering to herself, '. . . A is for Architect. B is for Baker, Banker, Bookie. C is for Copper. D is for Doctor. E is for . . .'

'Engineer?' laughed Alan, puzzled.

'M is for Mother. V is for Vet.'

'You'll be W of V. Wife of Vet. And I'm going to be PM – Prime Minister.' Then he added, with nervous overconfidence, 'Or G for God.'

Sylvia stopped mid-flow. 'No, Alan. GOD is God.'

Two angels nodded in unison.

Then, very slowly, Sylvia came and pressed herself to him. Her pelvis made contact with his.

'Sylvia,' Alan stammered, his hands automatically sliding around her back, 'do you really, really love Sam?'

'Yes,' she said. Then she kissed him. She grabbed the back of his head, fingers grasping his fluffy hair. Alan found himself swamped by her mouth, by her teeth and tongue.

The kiss stopped, wetly. Fuggerit, mischievous as ever, lifted Alan's hand and placed it on the turquoise jumper. Tock, the tactician, helped Sylvia unzip her victim's flies.

The bridge itself shuddered.

❖

Alan was on Hendo's doorstep the next morning.

The big lad was studying. 'Test uz on this,' he demanded, throwing over a Physics book.

Alan threw it straight back. 'You've left me way behind.'

'A've left meself behind. Oh, why didn't a do English? At heart a'm just a romantic.'

'Actually, I've got a bit of romantic news. Me and Sylvia.'

'What?'

'We did it.'

'Bugger me!' Hendo was jealous.

'But there's something else . . .' The blond lad looked perplexed. 'Afterwards, in the car, she kept muttering. And none of it made sense. I thought she was singing some daft song at first, but . . .'

'Was it guilty muttering? About the vet?'

'No. Something about thieves.'

'Well, she has had her bairn nicked.'

'Thieves of Joy. That's why I thought it was a song. Oh yes, and "the dirty coal slave".'

'How much had she drunk?'

'Couple of lagers. Oh, Christ, I've just realized. She's probably on tablets. The booze must have gone to her head.'

'And you took advantage?'

'Fuck!'

'Aye. Fuck.' Hendo picked up his science book. 'Life's perfection lies in its imperfections,' he asserted. 'Which is why Physics is total bollocks.' He made a paper dart and threw it across the room. 'Gonna end in tears.'

❖

Howard had never enjoyed a train journey so much. Travelling at his side, occasionally even touching him, was a rare beauty. Although he didn't trust her a jot, he enjoyed the proximity of Alexandra Hythe immensely. In fact, he could be hypnotized by her mobile upper lip, as he coaxed conversation out of her, privately marking her every phrase for truthfulness. Very stimulating!

Such a proud woman. Chip off two old blocks. Head high, jaw tight, shoulders square, the very smell of the woman exuded animal femininity. Her companionship was as exquisite as that of a tame panther.

Perhaps he should have handcuffed her, but they were accompanied by three other officers, all bored and flicking newspapers. She couldn't do a runner. Nor would she try. Not yet, despite her habit of evasion, bluff and identity switching.

Apparently eager to set all records straight, Alexandra Hythe had made long statements, about her father, her initial flight with Sylvia, muddling the babies, and her first attempted abduction of Alice. Howard was convinced she did not have the baby now. However, despite her denials, he certainly was convinced she had twice tried to kill her husband. Until he had some hard evidence, or a confession, he had no grounds on which to charge her.

How had he persuaded her to come back to Gosforth with him? By doing a deal.

In the green-tiled cell, she had explained that she had been chasing Dick, to see if he had taken Alice. Also, she claimed that Dick called on her father, threatening her life. Sooner or later, husband and wife would come together, and Howard wanted to be there when it happened.

So, why not? Why not use a pretty sprat to catch a one-eyed mackerel?

On the condition that she report to him every morning,

Alexandra Hythe was to remain free. The Superintendent wouldn't like it, but Howard did. It gave them – a relationship. He was drawn to her, even if her tactics were as transparent and cold as an ice cube. The more he opened his sensitivities to this fascinating woman, the more he wondered if, beneath her charisma and her recklessness, there was only emptiness. No happiness to risk, no love to defend, no dignity to surrender.

'Inspector,' she was asking, 'since we have no way of knowing whether or not Alice is Sylvia's natural baby, can I actually be accused of a crime?'

'Various parties could make a civil case against you. What will you do about baby Jan?'

'Whatever I decide, I'll do it officially. Janice Kirkstone has always known that she could never be her legal mother. The husband is in prison. Hardly an ideal family unit now.'

'And yours is? Mrs Kirkstone adores her. Another heart broken? What could you offer Jan that Janice can't?'

'Some good bedtime stories. Lots of Italian cousins.'

'You'll need more than that.'

'I suppose wealth counts for something.'

'Not necessarily, in Geordieland.'

It was when the train halted in York station that everything began to fall into place.

'I have another confession,' she said. 'I kept the baby charts. At least, I lodged them with Tony Torricelli, in Scarborough.'

'Wonderful! I'll have them collected.'

'I'd prefer to go myself. Tony is my trustee, on behalf of my grandfather. If I'm to stay in Newcastle, I'll have to pay for a hotel. I could do with arranging some funds.'

'Your grandfather is a powerful man in Venice, I understand. Shipping?'

'Nonno has many interests.' The Marletti empire was built on unusual commodities. Howard knew more than Greta realized.

'Perhaps you could come with me?' she flirted. 'What if we met him here, in York? We could have a day out.'

Howard's mouth twisted. He was sorely disappointed at her predictability. But why York?

'Today is the twenty-fourth,' he said. 'Live like a saint for a week. Next Wednesday – thirty-first – we'll discuss it. You must realize that if you break our agreement you'll never live comfortably again. You might enjoy life on the hop, but one day you'll want to settle down. Stick to my rules and that may be possible. Deceive me, my dear, and all our good work will go down the proverbial lavvy.'

❖

Mario drove out of Venice and up through France. Conversation was minimal. In his ignorance, the Italian was exhausted, having been unable to sleep while sharing a hotel room with a homosexual. At Calais the Italian folded his arms and watched the ferry plunge out into open sea. He refused to wave, but silently wished his brother-in-law good luck. Douglas was travelling on a false passport and carrying the equivalent of four thousand pounds in various currencies. A ransom for Sophia's grandchild was a ransom that must be paid. If Douglas was picked up by Customs – God help them all!

The once-glamorous musician now looked like a refugee. Unshaven for several days, his chin had the charm of a cactus.

His practised stoop was convincing. With an overlarge, threadbare overcoat hanging from a humped back and those suave, silver-blond locks cut close to his head, he had sacrificed a great deal of vanity to perform this service for his daughter.

❖

Howard summonsed his team. 'Alice is still out there somewhere. Cuthbert Sharp and his missus are ruled out. No sign of Katherine Sharp, Mary Linden or Douglas Hythe. That bastard Dick Korda could be anywhere from here to Kingdom Come. Remember that the latter did his best to murder his kid the day she was born. Not exactly father of the year.'

'Sir.' This from a spotty young man with ambition. 'Could he have sold her abroad?'

'He could have nicked any kid to do that. Why his own? I agree though – if Korda took her, money's the motivation.'

'Or revenge.' The Superintendent had entered the room. 'Where have you lodged Alexandra Hythe?'

'The Chester. Harry and John watching.'

'You're mad.'

'Am I? She can't lead us to Alice if she's locked up.'

'You think she's planning to try something on this trip down to York?'

'Maybe.'

'Too obvious. You're underestimating her.'

'Perhaps I'm overestimating her. But wherever she goes – my lads will follow.'

'Is Torricelli being tailed?'

'Sir, Torricelli doesn't piss without the Yorkshire boys knowing about it.'

❖

'Tony, darling!' Greta was ringing from a telephone box in Newcastle.

'Not give me this "darling" shit. What you want?' He puffed strong coffee fumes into the phone. 'Damn blasted women – gypsies – *prostitua*! How many more you gonna dump on Tony? I send her away . . .'

'Who?'

'Big-mouthed bitch witha waggy tail. I no want bad women in my place. I no PIMP!'

'You mean Kath? She came to you? OH, thank God. But you sent her away?'

'Sure.'

'Tony, she's Sylvia's sister!'

Silence.

'Tony, where has she gone?'

'Why you never tell me this?'

'I'm sorry . . .'

'Ha!'

'Tony, we'll find Kath later. Right now there's something even more important. Nonno is sending a messenger with a parcel for me. A ransom for Alice.'

Fighting his surly reluctance, she laid out her instructions. Aware that he was listening but not agreeing, she was ruffled when he said, 'If Nonno send messenger here – messenger can also bring parcel to you. I busy.'

Humbled, Greta pleaded, until Tony grumpily conceded.

❖

Did she have a friend left in the world? Teatime darkness shrouded the telephone box. It stank, but offered some shelter from the biting wind. Greta had walked and walked, followed, unsubtly, on bicycles, by her two 'escorts'. One had a huge Elvis quiff; the other had noticeably large feet, plod-like, in his balloon-toed boots.

Impulsively she picked up the phone again and dialled Sam's number. When Sylvia's youthful voice answered, Greta couldn't speak.

Alone in that tight cubicle, lost in a suburb of Newcastle, she wrapped her arms around herself to hold in the pain. After a while she blew her nose and walked down a shadowy road, shivering. Her coat was too thin to keep out the northeast wind, and her followers' eyes felt like chains.

Where was she? In the middle of some council estate of boxy prefabs with oversized windows and privet hedges. A group of kids was dragging around a pram chassis, with a floppy doll made out of a stuffed jacket and battered trilby. 'Penny for the Guy! Penny for the Guy!'

When Alice is found, thought Greta, this is where she'll grow up: in this strange, cold corner of the world. Where people work hard, play hard and spend even harder. A city where the working man despises riches, yet where ambition is almost a disease. Where beauty is on the doorstep, if you look past the pit heaps. Where the wind is sharp, and the clouds are laden with coal dust. Where the sky, so often grey, can be bluer and higher than anywhere else I remember.

When Alice comes home, this will be her life.

The money

arrived in a battered violin case. It sat on the Ristorante floor, along with several old shopping bags, next to an ashen, ragged, unshaven old man. One of his shoes was tied with string; a pocket was hanging off his coat.

Liz approached him with her pad, and sniffed. The 'gentleman tramp' smelled of alcohol, but nothing more foul than that.

His tone was laughably pompous. 'Red wine. French. Preferably Burgundy.'

'Tea do?'

Perhaps, thought Liz, he's an old soldier, traumatized by the war. Or an unloved, homeless widower. Or a fugitive from justice. Or a Russian, taught English at spy school!

'Bring me a plate of anything that IS NOT PASTA.'

(They taught posh English at them spy schools.)

'Sausages?'

'Wiltshire?'

'Cumberland. Mash and onion gravy.'

'Delightful. Thank you.'

While the part-time kitchen help, Florrie, refried some of the breakfast sausages, Liz took tea and buttered bread to the man's table. The tramp grabbed her hand.

'Antonio Torricelli?' he whispered.

'Ow! 'E's out. Let go!'

'Where?'

'Mind your own.'

'I've come from Italy.'

Liz's eyes grew very round. She looked down at the violin case and whispered, 'The MESSENGER!' It was her turn to grasp his wrist. With the shapely case in one hand and man in the other, she dragged him away from the table and behind the counter. Pushing open the door, she shoved him by the backside upstairs, hissing, 'We was told to keep you hid.'

Douglas Hythe groaned. What a flaming charade! Sighing with weariness and indignity, he threw himself down on Tony's sofa.

Liz brought his bags and the sausages upstairs. Half an hour later the gravy was drying on the stained plate and Douglas was snoring.

❖

Temper as filthy as the weather, Tony was in a pub, quarrelling with some mates about the escalating political situation over Egypt's determination to nationalize the Suez Canal. Europe stood perilously on the brink of a Third World War, and Tony could only recall his internment with anguish. What should he do? Pack up and return to his fatherland?

Beneath his fury was miserable guilt over Katherine. Why hadn't they told him Katherine was Sylvia's sister? Why was he now expected to aid Greta in more cloak and dagger schemes? Why was Liz shouting at him all the time? Oh, for some peace!

Peace?

Would going back to Italy salve his soul, console his gathering self-pity? Swiftly fleeing middle age was depressing him, exaggerating his enforced isolation and the prospect of a lonely old age. Perhaps, in Italy, his family would reabsorb him; surround him with nephews and nieces to fill the gap of frustrated parenthood. Or – perhaps they wouldn't.

It was late when he stomped back into the Ristorante. Ignoring his customers, he scowled murderously at Liz. 'Old bat! Why you no tell me she Sylvie's *sorella*! I no even likea kid, all sexy hips and big titties . . .'

'Hush!'

'You women, you makea war inside my head. I am like nuclear bomb. I will implode. I will be a mushroom of deadly fury-cloud. My fallout, it will . . . will . . . fall out!'

He flung himself up the stairs. Swinging open the door of his flat, he discovered a prostrate TRAMP on his sofa! His ferocious Italian curses were enough to curdle the carbonara.

Douglas, startled out of his snooze, rolled off the couch, landing in a heap on the floor, instinctively raising his hands to protect his face, as Tony's bellowing bulk towered above him.

During the ensuing cacophony of insults (on both sides), Douglas crawled to his haunches and pulled himself on to the sofa, gathering a cushion protectively across his chest. Finally he screamed the name 'Hythe'. Tony's Italian blasphemies stopped mid-spit.

❖

In a pub on Gosforth High Street, Greta drank gin until she
fell off her stool. The landlord pushed her out of the door and
one of Howard's lads took her to her hotel. At about two in
the morning she wandered along an unfamiliar landing to
vomit in a musty lavatory. At eight, waiving her fried breakfast, she went out in search of clean air. She felt like a dog on
a leash; a dog with a very bad headache. And it was raining.

Gosforth High Street was awash, and prickling with
umbrella spines. As Greta hunched in a shop doorway, people
around her shook themselves, bemoaning spattered nylons
and shoes which had 'taken in'. The hangover left Greta's
blood feeling thin as cherryade. Dressed only in a lightweight
coat, she was chilled to the bone. Reluctant to part with what
little money she was carrying, she purchased a plastic mac
with a ridiculous pixie hood, to keep out the rain and wind.
Minutes were dragging. Over two cups of black coffee in the
Toddle Inn she moaned to herself, 'Trapped in this bloody
place for a whole week! While Dick's out there, maybe with
Alice. I should be doing something. DAMN!'

When the pubs opened at lunchtime Greta dripped
through a door into smoky gloom, but the stench of stale beer
and smoke turned her queasy stomach, so she carried on
walking.

By four o'clock the rain had eased to a fine drizzle and
Greta stood at the school gates. It wasn't hard to pick out
David, a giant among midgets. At his side was an even taller
friend – on crutches.

Greta closed her eyes in dismay. Just as she turned to flee, David spotted her. His scars were livid in the drizzle.

'Wait, Greta! I can't run.'

She stopped, suddenly feeling old-ladyish in her plastic mac.

David's mate hopped up behind him. He had large, blue eyes and his chin was dark with stubble. Greta faced him squarely.

'You must be Hendo. What do I say? "Sorry" seems – pathetic. But I am. Deeply. One day I'll try to make it up to you.'

Very slowly the big boned, big hearted lad stretched out his hand. Humbled, she matched his grip.

'At least me and Davy'll never have to do square bash'n. Mebees we gor off lucky.'

She felt bathed in shame.

From across the road, a group of lads hailed them with what sounded like a Red Indian salute, 'How!'

'How!' Hendo replied. Turning on his crutches, he hopped back over to them.

'Kath?' asked David gravely. His concern made him look older and Greta realized how much she liked him.

'The police collared me. She made a run for it. I was wondering if she'd come to you.'

'No! Jesus. She's pregnant. Where would she go?'

'She's been back to Scarborough, but Tony threw her out. Still thought she was a pro.'

David uttered worried expletives. 'I'll go down and look for her!'

'No point. She could be anywhere. All we can do is wait.

If she's likely to contact anyone it'll be you, David. I know she gave you a chilly welcome in Scarborough, but she really does care about you.'

'Cold as a fish.'

'She's hurting and scared. You haven't told anyone?'

He shook his head. 'No. I promised. Anyway, Kath's a bit of a sore subject between Hendo and me.'

'David, there's more bad news. Or it may even be good, if we handle it right. Dick's sent me a ransom request for Alice.'

David's questions choked around his contracting Adam's apple.

'I need help,' she whispered urgently, 'I don't know if I believe him. But if he has got her, and I tell the police, he might do something terrible.'

Still David did not speak.

She pressed on. 'Help me. Please. I'm getting the money, but . . .'

On the other side of the road Hendo was watching, obviously puzzled by the closeness between them.

'Tell me!' David hissed between clenched teeth.

'Can we go somewhere dry?'

'My house.' He was already limping away.

'NO!'

'Gran's gone back to Corbridge. Come on.'

As they walked, it began to pour down. Heads bent against the spatters, Greta told David about Martin, the message, and her arrest. Approaching the elegant house which legally belonged to the absent Mary Linden, Greta asked, 'What about that other woman, Clara?'

'She's really livid at Gran. Thinks she's been sacked for losing Alice.'

'What sort of woman is this nanny? Could she have taken Alice? Could she be in league with Dick, or someone else? Could she have passed her on that night? People do sell babies.'

'In a way, the "selling" theory comforts me. It's better than my nightmares. But Clara would never harm Alice, or anyone. She's gentle and brave. Kinder to me than my own mother, which isn't exactly hard. Nursed Gran with the patience of a saint.'

'Is she so kind that she might help a sad woman who needs a baby?'

'Good question. But then why still hang around with me? And why did she chase your husband that night?'

'Katherine says she vaguely remembers a woman knocking on the caravan door and having some sort of tussle with Dick.'

'She told me she belted him with a monkey wrench.'

'It's time I met Clara.'

In the tiled hallway they shook themselves dry.

Clara Blake came and stood solidly before them.

'Your gran would NOT like this.' She turned to Greta. 'But I want to talk to you.'

'And I want to talk to you, Mrs Blake.'

'David! Kettle on.'

They ate fruitcake and hunks of cheese. When the teapot was empty they drank Mary Linden's gin.

Greta eventually managed to stagger back to her hotel. The following morning, Saturday, while David lay prostrate with a hangover, Clara and Greta walked the width of the Town Moor together.

❖

Howard looked up at the beautiful Alexandra Hythe.

'Blood test,' he said, 'unfortunately proves nothing. You all share the same blood group, Sylvia, baby Jan, you. "O" Positive. Common stuff.'

'Damn!'

'You can say that again.'

'DAMN!'

'I hear you've befriended David Linden.'

'News travels suspiciously fast.'

'Ethel will be furious.'

'And you have to tell her?'

'At some stage . . . possibly . . .'

'I'm getting to know Clara Blake. Call it – investigation.'

'Ouch. You're standing on my toes.'

As far as Greta could make out, Clara Blake was a saint. Heroic Blitz ambulance driver, patient nanny and nurse, she now claimed to prefer minding healthy children to sick ones.

'Don't like suffering,' she admitted. 'Too much of it about.'

She was full of her own questions too.

'So, you were a trapeze artist? What made you stop? Have another sandwich. Go on. You've kept your figure. Did you ever fall off? Did you not fancy being an actress, like your mam? She was so lovely in that film . . . what d'you call it? You're very like her. So, you've been to Italy? I'd love to travel. What's your hotel like? I'm doing chops for tea. You will stay? Lord, listen to him blowing that thing!'

Upstairs David was blasting his terrified soul into his saxophone.

'He's a good lad,' said Greta.

Clara nodded. 'My lad was a good lad too. Only seven when we were bombed.'

'You lost your baby?'

'There was nothing left to find.'

Greta shuddered. 'I can't imagine your agony.'

'And you just left your bairn in a hospital. I can't imagine that.'

Both women gulped gin.

'Can't you, Clara? You met my husband.'

'Why on earth did you marry that evil bastard in the first place?' asked Clara. 'Here, put your feet up. I'll fetch some coffee.'

Later that evening Clara asked, 'What on earth are we going to do about this ransom?'

Call it – investigation!

❖

So, unknown to either Ethel or Mary, Greta's enforced sojourn in Gosforth was much softened by Linden hospitality.

Clara was giving David driving lessons in the Anglia. Each morning he drove it to school and she drove back, dropping Greta at the police station. For the rest of the day the two women sat together in Mary's front room, talking. The talk, of course, became a plot. Or plots.

As Dick's 5 November deadline approached, a cautious

elation began to infiltrate Greta's defensive shell. Resolution and a normal life seemed only a whisper away.

And yet the whole thing was a lie.

❖

'Sir? Clara Blake's on the blower.'

'So many spiders in this web! Put her through.'

'Inspector?'

'How's my friend Alexandra Hythe?'

'You've agreed for her to go to York. I'd like to go with her.'

'Why?'

'In case she's collecting Alice.'

❖

It was on the train, on Friday, 2 November, that Greta really began to understand just how tightly Howard was binding her. He had permitted this meeting with Tony, as she knew he would, but she was now sandwiched between him and Butterwell, their masculine bodies rubbing against hers, rocking with the train's motion. Doubtless there were other discreet officers around, watching corridors and doors.

Clara was unpacking a picnic bag. 'I've always wanted to walk the York City Wall,' she enthused. Butterwell refused her sandwich as if it might be poisoned. Howard, however, munched happily.

'Windy day for it,' he warned. 'Mind you don't get blown right off.'

'Take more than a little puff to shift me, lad. Sausage roll?'

Greta found even this mild banter irritating. Altogether too sociable. She needed to keep alert.

In York station, she scanned the busy concourse. Where was the Yorkshire Constabulary? Her eye fell on an attractive male in a pinstriped suit, rummaging in a briefcase. Another man, casually sitting doing a crossword, momentarily glanced at her face. An older chap, hands in pockets, trailed them through the portico, slightly too slowly.

Ah yes. There was the Newcastle lad with the Elvis quiff.

Howard gave instructions. 'Not far to the Castle Museum. We'll walk.'

Taking his arm, Greta smiled sweetly. 'You'll let me meet Tony alone? You did promise.'

'For a few minutes. Just stay in my sightline.'

Clara gave her a swift, efficient hug. 'Good luck, lass. See you back for the train.'

The grey stone rampart was directly opposite them. As Clara strode across the road towards it, Howard nodded at Butterwell, who hesitated only for a second before following the most innocent nanny in the world.

Twenty minutes later, outside the Castle Museum, Greta was relieved when Howard moved away from her. His dominance was becoming as oppressive as Dick's.

The wind was whistling across the broad pavement, chilling her ankles, lifting the swing coat which Clara had loaned her. Feeling clean and smart, more like Alexandra Hythe, Greta adjusted a scarlet wool beret over her black hair.

How long would Tony make her wait? Bless him, he might be angry, but he would never let her down.

After ten minutes she was shivering, striding up and down with her hands buried deep in the coat pockets, feeling some sympathy for the pinstriped man with the briefcase, who was sitting on a bench. Poor bugger looked perished.

'Greta?'

Tony's voice rumbled behind her. She swung around to meet her friend's limpid gaze. Ready to confront his ire, she found herself enfolded in a bear hug. While he clung, he spoke.

'You are not alone?'

'The Inspector is over there. A few more beady eyes around.'

'But they not know about ransom?'

'Best not. Alice could get hurt. You do understand, Tony?'

He relaxed his grip and picked up the holdall at his feet. 'It matters not if I understand. Mario ask favour. I simply oblige. Here. Take.'

'Oh, Tony. Don't be angry.'

'Of course I angry. But now we visit dis splendid museum. Come. It is very important you come.'

Puzzled, Greta looked at her watch. 'I must catch the three-thirty.'

'Come! Now!'

Tony had hooked her arm and was dragging her towards the museum. Greta felt nervous, almost giggly, knowing that Howard would be striding angrily behind them. She could feel the Inspector's fury fastened to the back of her head, like a spiteful hair pull.

Through the moody museum halls Tony steered her. He kept up some pretence of interest in the exhibits, pausing momentarily to look at staged rooms from other centuries, with his arm tight, too tight, around her shoulders. All the time Greta could feel Howard's eyes watching. Defensive senses heightened, she was aware of everything around her – the eyes of a stuffed cat on an Edwardian hearth, empty shoes under a bodiless dress.

'Come see this place!'

Greta yanked Tony to a halt. They had entered the famous Victorian cobbled street, a storybook world of bow-fronted shop windows, where ladies in muddied petticoats once gazed through pebble-glass panes at bonnets and ribbons.

Standing motionless on the cobbles, frozen in morbid decay, was a black horse, harnessed to a carriage. Something about the cold bit in its mouth, the disintegrating mane and leather shackles horrified Greta. The stuffed beast looked trapped between life and death.

As Tony pulled her towards some gallows, a chorus of turning keys clanked in Greta's head. She was being walled in, by Tony, by Howard, a pin-striped suit, even Clara. Cornered by a stampede of wills.

The street's atmosphere was too real. She looked down at a worn stone doorstep. She wanted to be a child again, in bare feet, under a gas lamp, on a snowy night. She wanted to be the Tinder Box Girl, with her last light, looking at the face of an angel. Cold and alone, but free.

Someone touched her arm.

Alexandra Hythe turned and saw a sallow old man, bent

almost double. He moved away to look in a sweet-shop window which was luscious with sugar mice and aniseed balls.

❖

Above Greta's head, where a cantilevered upper window gave an excellent view over the dramatic stage set, a young man with a huge quiff watched the top of Greta's head. He couldn't see her surprised tears.

❖

Despite her bravado, Clara found it perishing cold up on the high City Wall. She climbed down some stone steps and made her way to Brown's Department Store where she was very relieved to find the Ladies toilet.

Butterwell, hovering in Haberdashery, was bursting, but he didn't dare go.

❖

Tony's van was followed all the way back to the coast. He knew it, so he drove recklessly.

Douglas, travelling separately, dozed on the bus. Back in Scarborough, the ragged musician entered the Ristorante like any other diner, and prayed that no one would realize he hadn't come out again.

How skilful Alexandra had been in concealing her surprise, as she stood next to him, peering at barley sugar twists. A meeting of eyes, a single 'Pardon me' of forgiveness, and then Howard had appeared at her shoulder. Softly, Douglas had moved on.

❖

The holdall, with the Maternity Hospital charts and Greta's clothing, was now in the police station.

However, the packet which Clara had collected from Liz's daughter, Sally, in Brown's toilet had travelled home in her picnic box. There were also two envelopes, which Greta would read privately.

She opened the brown paper parcel on the Linden dining-room table. As the wads of notes spilled out, she stifled a scream of horror. There were no pounds! No fivers! Francs, pesetas, lira . . . currency from countries all over Europe.

'Nonno, you crafty bugger!' she murmured. 'If the bastard wants to spend his four thousand pounds, he'll have to get out of the country to do it.'

Clara asked, worried, 'But will Dick accept this foreign stuff?'

'If it's a real ransom, an exchange for Alice, then no, I don't think so. But, if he's bluffing, he may take what's on offer and run. It'll be dark. He'll be in a hurry. I'll put some pounds on the top and hope he doesn't check too hard.'

'But what about Alice?'

'If he doesn't bring her, someone needs to follow him.'

'Oh, Hell. That'll be me then.'

❖

Alone in her hotel room, Greta opened the first envelope. It was from Tony, and contained what remained of the money which she took from the caravan all those years ago, along with a single line:

Thank God to be rid of this.

She took her time, reading the second letter.

My Dear Alexandra,
Nonno charged me with the task of carrying his gift to
you. I wish I could help more, but sadly I must quit the
country again.
Please know that I am innocent of all charges
against me. Linden's death was a terrible accident.
True, I must take responsibility for orchestrating the
overture, for I was guilty of ruthlessness in probing into
your past – with very dreadful consequences. The
knowledge that you had a child, my grandchild, filled
me with a terrible desire to discover the truth. The
thought that I may lose that grandchild made me rash
and irrational.
It must be desperately hard for you, not knowing
which child is yours, also with Alice missing and Jan
so possessed by her foster mother. It troubles me that
I do not know how you feel. You have always been
such an enigma, Alexandra. Your chilly privacy punishes
me.
For over twenty years I have been haunted by your
disapproval, yet don't believe myself a sinner, rather a
victim of Mother Nature. Age and loneliness, however,

*have helped me realize that passion is not love. I want
you to understand that I cared for your mother deeply,
and that I have always loved you. Perhaps my mission
to find your child was a subconscious search for
someone who might, one day, love ME.*

*But, Alexandra, I did NOT take Alice. Mary Linden
did offer to bring her to me, but I rejected the idea, and
Mary arrived alone, at our agreed meeting place, at 3
a.m. I last saw that lady many weeks ago, in Paris.*

*I can prove nothing, so, until Alice is found, I must
live this dreadful existence of exiled vagrant. My career
is over. I daresay I will end my days plonking on some
appalling instrument in the corner of a bar in
Casablanca.*

*When you find your baby, love her for me and for
your mamma, and try to make those personal sacrifices
which I never achieved, because, as God is my witness,
my secrets have cost me dearly.*

Good luck my darling.
Papa

Greta's limp fingers dropped the pages on her abdomen.
The sensation in her chest was beyond logical thought.

❖

This life of subterfuge was hard on Douglas. The humility of
his shabby disguise had crawled under his skin, entering
where loneliness had opened a painful fissure. His nerves felt
tethered and taut as, day after day, he remained in the company of Antonio Torricelli. Friction crackled between them,
and the nastier they were to each other the more miserable

they both became. Liz, threatening to knock their heads together, put it down to middle-aged jealousy. Perhaps she was right. Alexandra stood between the two men like a humourless goddess.

'They're changing the Guard at Buckingham Palace,' Douglas sang sarcastically as he peered through lace curtains. Regular as clockwork, the police surveillance on the Ristorante was changing shift. 'They can't know I'm here, so must be watching you.'

He began again, 'Christopher Robin went down with Alice . . .'

'For a musician, you no can sing,' grumbled Tony.

'But where, oh where is Alice? Torricelli, I do believe they think you're Christopher Robin.' He turned to meet the other man's eye. Not for the first time, a flicker of homosexual recognition slid between them. 'Are you, Tony?'

The Latin man's eyes bulged and his chin stiffened.

Douglas smirked. 'Fear not, old chap. I'll be gone tonight.' He lifted a tiny corner of the curtain. 'Oh look, we've got Bill and Ben with matching macs. Poor sods must be freezing. At least the night shift gets a car.'

'*Bastardos!*' Tony joined Douglas at the window, keeping a safe distance from the pianist's shoulder. 'High tide – four o'clock. See boat with yellow stripe? You getta this boat half past three exact. My friend take you down coast to Hull. Then big ship tomorrow.' He pointed out of the window. 'How we getta ridda them?'

'A decoy?'

'*Si*. I suppose.'

'Dear God, I wish it was anything other than a fishing boat. I'm sick on a duck pond.'

Tony laughed. 'Choppy, choppy.'

❖

In the early hours of Sunday, 4 November, Tony left the Ristorante and sneaked past the night surveillance's Humber Super Snipe. Carrying a spade which served no purpose other than to intrigue the watchers, he headed for the great point which led around to North Bay. Sure enough, the car door clunked and Tony heard footfalls behind him.

Under the massive cliff, night swallowed Marine Drive. Against the sea wall deep water was writhing and crashing with monstrous power. This road beneath the Castle had been notorious since the Viking invasion for the giant waves which, during storms, could spit silver plumes higher than three houses, and suck silly souls right off the road.

Tonight the sea was grumpy but not furious. Waves were running along the wall, occasionally spouting up over the railings, cascading down with hefty splats, then sweeping over the road and back again. Tony was walking in a salted void, because the cliffs were lost in blackness, the cobbled road smudged out. Only the metal railing was real and although it robbed Tony's fingers of any vestige of warmth, he daren't let go.

When he considered that sufficient time had elapsed, the mischievous Italian brought his march to a sudden halt, and pivoted around to face his pursuers. The silhouettes of two men were barely visible. Very slowly Tony began to walk back towards the detectives who had stopped in their tracks. As

Tony approached them he slung the spade from one shoulder to the other. Passing heavily through the air, it must have looked like a formidable weapon. He grinned maliciously as the policemen hesitated and looked at each other. One of them moved to the other side of the road while his colleague held on to the cold, wet railing. Tony readied himself to pass between them.

Just at that moment, the tide chose to surge. A great wave hit the sea wall and backwashed, to slap against the next incoming wave, hurling a giant plume of salt water twenty feet into the air, which landed with a great crash – on the policeman. He clung to the railing and kept his footing, but the poor man's neck was jarred and he was utterly drenched.

Tony, compassionate if not sympathetic, dropped the spade and rushed to the staggering man's aid. Between him and the other bobby, they drew the chap to safety. The next great wave licked the road and took the spade into the greedy sea.

❖

The greedy sea was Douglas's arch-enemy. Terrified, he slid along the back alley and out towards the harbour where the boats were bobbing like toys. The musician thrashed through his memory for some comforting refrain, but all he could hear in his head was 'For Those in Peril on the Sea'.

The vessel which Tony had pointed out was half-way along the harbour wall. Already sick to the pit of his stomach, Douglas pulled his coat tight and lurched towards his doom.

❖

Above the Ristorante, Tony's little flat was as warm as a womb. The Italian felt euphorically heroic, having helped the shivering policeman back into the Snipe. They'd driven off now, so for the first time in several days the Ristorante was without watchers, also without the uncomfortable presence of Douglas Hythe. Tony climbed into his voluminous pyjamas and farted, sighing contentedly at the luxury of privacy. While the kettle boiled for his hot water bottle, he put the light out and stared out of the window at the harbour lights, which were swinging in the rising wind.

It's got too rough, he suddenly realized. The skipper won't take her out on a night like this. Tony made his hot water bottle and, clutching it, went back to the window. Ten minutes later his worst fears were confirmed as he saw the sizeable bulk of his fisherman friend walking back across the road. Behind him, a hunched shadow was vomiting beside the fish shed.

As the fisherman began to bang on the Ristorante door, the Snipe slid back along the road.

'FUCK,' swore Tony, with a Yorkshire accent.

❖

Douglas puffed up the hill towards the train station. At least it would offer him some shelter. He had absolutely no intention of going back to the dreadful Italian.

Suddenly there was a loud 'vrrum' behind him. A motorbike wobbled to a stop.

'Get on, stoopid *bastardo*.' Tony's moustache flared beneath a red crash helmet.

'Certainly not!'

Tony reached out and grabbed Douglas by the collar. 'Miserable coward. Get on fuckin *motocicletta*.'

Trembling, Douglas lifted his leg over the machine, behind the wobbly Italian. He hesitated, but as Tony kicked the bike into gear, Douglas wrapped his arms around the broad torso in front of him. The Italian's generous waistline was as solid and comfortable as an old sofa and they were soon speeding along at a fair lick. Bracing his chest against the Italian's back, Douglas hid his face from the icy draught. Endurance became elation as they sped up Staxton Hill, and southwards towards freedom.

❖

Meanwhile, Tony's van was lurching across the misty moors, over twisting, plummeting bends and curves. Each dip held a treacherous layer of falling cloud, but the fisherman knew these roads well. He also knew the two men in the Snipe which was following him. Played darts with them in the Packet. Nice lads, both. So he slowed down a bit and turned up the van's heater, chuckling about how cold his mate Torricelli must be on his motorbike.

❖

On Sunday afternoon Hendo and David limped to a local recreation field. Clenching fists into waists, they both tried to run.

'We can't do this,' cried David as he watched his friend fall to the ground in pain.

'Aye we can, man. Howay, give uz a hand up. Let's start on a bit of a trot . . .'

'This is ridiculous. We're bloody cripples. How can we chase a gypsy over the Town Moor?'

Hendo was struggling to get up. 'Wish Alan was home.'

'I shouldn't even be involving you.'

'That's what mates is for. So tell uz, Davy boy, is there summut gannin on between you and the "older lady"? Is she learn'n you a few tricks?'

'You're joking! No!'

'She's a bossy cow. Personally, a wouldn't mind a bit domination.'

'Hendo! This is about Alice!'

'Sorry. But what a useless team! Two knackered lads, plus Nanny Goat and Jane Russell.'

'Clara's as brave as a butcher.'

'Doesn't mean she can run a three-minute mile. Her knickers'll probably fall doon!' Hendo guffawed, but very quickly became serious. 'It's not gonna work, son.'

'I can't risk Alice's safety by telling the police.'

'Wharaboot Sylvia's veterinary?'

❖

Sam answered the phone and returned to Sylvia looking as if he had lockjaw.

Sylvia was miffed. 'Something wrong?'

'Nothing a cuddle won't cure.'

As lovemaking began with mechanical caresses, distraction frayed at the bonds between them – and Sam shrivelled.

Awed by her failure to arouse him, Sylvia felt agitated all the way back to Gosforth. But there, on the doorstep, Dothy sat waiting, in pink satin ballet slippers and a Sugar Plum Fairy tutu.

❖

Dawn. Hull docks. Two middle-aged men sat huddled beneath a tarpaulin. One of them was shaking.

'Thank you, Torricelli.'

'Probably waste my time. You gonna die on ship of bloody sickness.'

Tony fished in his pocket and pulled out a hip flask.

Douglas grabbed it and desperately sucked down the brandy. Wiping his mouth, he asked, 'You love my Alexandra?'

Tony's liquid eyes saddened. 'As uncle . . . maybe.'

'Or aunt?' Douglas shook his head wearily. 'D'you sing bass or tenor, Torricelli?'

Tony's moustache twitched. 'I singa better than you.' Very quietly he started to croon, 'De fishermen of England, sail out on de stormy sea . . .'

Hythe's belly suddenly contracted. 'Jesus! I'm going to perish in a rusty hull on the bottom of the ocean and no one will give a damn.'

'You very sorry for yourself.'

'And for you.' A siren sounded. Douglas took another swig. 'Here's to Hell. Let's go.'

They crawled from their shelter and faced each other.

Douglas held out his fine hand and, very cautiously, the bigger man took it.

Abruptly Douglas let go and walked away, pulling his collar around his face, hunching his shoulders as he had grown accustomed.

Guy Fawkes

was perched, cross-legged, on a battered harmonium. His pyre of dry branches, railway sleepers, orange boxes, toilet seats and several hundred copies of the *Evening Chronicle* was ready to burn.

❖

Clara left the Linden house and walked several streets until she found a telephone box.

When she returned, she shut her bedroom door and packed her most treasured belongings into a carpet bag. While Greta and David were otherwise engaged, she tucked it in the boot of the Anglia, covered it with blankets, then stuffed around it the other provisions Greta had laid out: torches, sandwiches, flasks, tools. Lastly Clara pushed in her own lumpy shopping bag.

If they had to follow Dick Korda to find Alice, they were prepared.

And if the worst came to the worst, if they found out what she had done, she would take her carpet bag and disappear.

Violet placed her hands on her hips.

'Stuck in that place, your dad's just faded away. You don't care tuppence. Are you even listening? You've never understood, have you? Nor never tried to. It's easier wallow'n in self-pity!'

Sylvia tapped her shoulder. 'Got to watch my back.'

'Wash your back?'

'He killed one man for Alice. I might be next. You might help him.'

'What stupid notions are these?' Violet was shaking. How could her daughter's attractive face conceal such insane, bitter thoughts? 'I'm your mam. Why would I hurt you? And you know full well Arthur's death was an accident.'

Sylvia's coldness was so mystifying that Violet felt exhausted with incomprehension. 'All Dad did was love your bairn too much. Aye, remember Alice? Your daughter? The little lass who's been stole, who you abandoned before she was two days old?'

The bomb of blame fell between them, too bright to look at, too destructive to bear.

Sylvia shrugged. 'Well, of course, I'm not allowed to be happy.'

'Happy? Alice might be dead! How, in God's name, can you be HAPPY?'

Violet watched Sylvia turn to her right and extend her hand downwards, towards – nothing.

'Sh, Dothy!'

This was neither the first time, nor the last, when Violet

thought she saw the fleeting ghost of a child on the floor. She remembered Sylvia with pigtails, playing with a doll's tea set, her freckled face serious as she arranged two yellow plates, two spam sandwiches and two pink wafers; slopping orange juice into two tiny cups.

❖

Nearly four o'clock. Sylvia thought she should take Dothy home. Real home. By the time they arrived in the street where she grew up, she felt more awake again.

Dothy ran up the garden path. Shoulders hunched, Sylvia stood for a long time looking at her old home. Fuggerit and Tock, however, weren't interested. They kept walking up the road, passing Hendo, who was loping towards her, school scarf flying in the wind.

'Hiya, Syl. Visit'n council alley?'

'Just felt nostalgic. A bit sad.' She did feel sad. And lonely. Yet clear-headed, as if, for a moment, she had climbed out of one world and into another.

'What's up, flower?'

'Nothing.' Sylvia shrugged carelessly, then shivered. 'God, it's freezing.'

'Well, hinny, it *is* November.' His face split into a grin. 'Bonfire night. Got your sparklers?'

Sylvia brightened. Hendo made her feel so normal. 'Will there be a big bonnie on the Town Moor?' Her mood leapt suddenly. 'Shall we go?'

'What? You and me? Sorry, pet. Gorra stack of homework.' Hendo looked at his watch. 'Ee! Luka the time!'

Sylvia didn't listen to Hendo's excuses. She was looking up at her old bedroom window. Dothy was waving.

❖

At five-thirty precisely, Clara and David drove off in the Anglia. Greta watched them go, then scanned the road for Hendo. He was late. Was the plan already going wrong?

❖

'What's young Henderson doing here?'

The big lad was hopping down the avenue on one crutch, his school scarf muffled around his face.

Butterwell frowned. 'Good lad, that. Shouldn't be involved with this lot.'

In the home of an obliging dentist, Howard stood at a darkened window, watching the little tableau. His fascinating sprat looked sexily mannish tonight, her lovely long legs hidden in black trousers, her square shoulders wide under a sheepskin flying jacket. He felt a voyeuristic twang when, in the most unexpected of gestures, the beautiful woman suddenly kissed Hendo's cheek. And, as she swung a haversack over her shoulder and began to walk, Howard was caught by a wave of anticipatory eroticism.

'Lads in place, Butterwell?'

'Aye. I've told them to follow, not to apprehend.'

'We get Alice first.'

'Let's hope, Sir.'

'Jacks are jumping. Let's go fire some rockets.'

❖

518

Violet sat alone at the kitchen table, looking at the wallpaper. A long brown gravy stain dribbled down the roses. On the carpet was a pile of cold liver.

'What's to be done?' she muttered to herself. Then she repeated the same question over and over again. 'What's to be done?'

Her eldest daughter was crazy. In a way, Violet could understand the girl's coldness, because sometimes she too felt tempted to withdraw from the responsibility of love. With life so full of betrayal, even the girl's sudden violent outbursts held an uncomfortable logic. But this latest development, Sylvia's new way of looking at the floor and chattering in a fast stream of unconnected sentences, was terrifying.

It was weird. For patches in any day Sylvia was lucid and normal, even plausibly caring. And then suddenly, it was as if the soul of Sylvia fled, to be replaced by a demon.

'Possessed,' Violet muttered. 'Me lass is possessed. What's to be done?' Violet's bowels groaned sulphurously. 'How can I fight the bloody Devil? Jesus!'

She cleared up the liver, then grabbed a wet dishcloth and slapped it at the wallpaper. Tears fell down her sallow cheeks as she rubbed at the brown stain. Harder and harder she rubbed, until the paper's surface broke and the roses crumbled.

Mad people were put in the local sanatorium. Rumour had it that it was like a prison. Violet looked at the ruined wallpaper. Her nose was running.

'Put ME in the bloody padded cell, God!' she whimpered. 'Put me in it.' She leaned against the wet wall and slid slowly down it.

Dothy wouldn't sit still on the bus; she was so excited about the fireworks. Fuggerit was cheerful too. He was wearing red gloves and a black and white Newcastle United scarf. But Tock . . . Tock was dressed in a flowing black cape, his head cowled in a hood.

'Why are you dressed like that?'

I wear what I'm told to . . .

❖

'Trust Hendo to be late,' David grumbled nervously as they drove.

'He wouldn't chicken out, would he?'

'Never.'

Sticking to Greta's plan, Clara parked the car in St George's Terrace, then she and David marched across to the Moor, where a crowd had already gathered, waiting for the bonfire to be lit. Guy Fawkes's pyre had been built fairly near the road. David took his position, slightly away from the crowd, on the Gosforth side. Being the better walker, Clara strode past the throng, in a westerly direction, where the rolling moorland stretched and disappeared into a wide darkness.

She looked lonely and vulnerable, clutching her old shopping bag.

❖

Although Clara did not know it, Sam had been following them. He parked close to the Anglia, then followed some woolly-clad kids over the road, anxious not to be spotted.

David's information had been given confidentially, but he could hardly have let Greta face Dick Korda with only the protection of a nanny and two half-crippled lads.

Again the vet asked himself if he should have alerted Howard, but surely Korda would be on his guard; any sign of a detective's raincoat and he would bolt; the tentative trail to Alice would be lost. Tonight Sam, unseen, must somehow protect Greta, and find Sylvia's daughter.

❖

It was bitingly cold. Greta and Hendo left the same trolley, but walked independently. He hobbled to his assigned post nearest the Great North Road, where he could watch Greta moving around the bonfire. Over her head, poor Guy Fawkes sat cross-legged, ludicrously smiling down at a man with matches.

'Stand back! Stand back!'

A crackle. Smoke. A tiny flare, then an orange, licking flame. 'Aaah,' breathed the crowd as flames lit up the night, glowing on upturned faces.

❖

Rockets hissed, soared and exploded. Tiny silver stars cascaded around Dothy's glowing face. Sylvia pulled the little girl's pompom hat down over her ears and, removing her own red gloves, took out a hanky to wipe Dothy's sweet little nose.

Suddenly Tock touched her arm. He pointed. Sylvia's eyes were drawn to a tall man who seemed to be scanning the crowd for someone. Was it?

Oh, Sam! He'd come after all! He was looking for her!

Fuggerit laughed. Tock didn't. Sylvia took Dothy's hand and began pushing past people to get to her fiancé. But Sam's eyes were riveted on something, someone else. Greta.

The scales shall fall from her eyes, intoned Tock.

His birdlike claws sank into Sylvia's shoulders, stopping her, forcing her to stand back and watch Greta's head turn slowly to meet Sam's gaze.

❖

Howard strode across the moor, passing David without noticing him. Urgent, almost panicky instincts were dragging him towards the ball of fire.

Butterwell, who could never keep up, winked at several plain-clothed officers as he passed them.

❖

Around the raging flames, sparks danced in clouds of billowing smoke.

Greta could feel Dick everywhere. Her eyes darted left and right. Her body twisted. For some reason, in this absurd setting, her mamma's ghost felt very close, and Greta began to pray, not to God, but to Sophia.

Walk with me tonight.

She snatched her head around to look behind, but the only face she recognized was Hendo's. Her gaze swivelled back more slowly. Across her left shoulder her eyes connected with a piercing stare. A tall man. His attention entirely locked on her. Knowing eyes. Dear face. Sam.

In the same instant another man appeared out of the smoke. His silhouette, outlined against the fire, was instantly recognizable. For a split second, Greta stood between the two men who dominated her life, one loved, one despised. And in the triangle, she felt powerful.

Sam remained absolutely still, but Dick approached. Behind Greta, Hendo tensed. Behind Hendo, Howard stopped breathing.

❖

Sylvia witnessed the invisible cord which bound Sam to Greta, a living, twanging thing, tightened by rejection. She wanted to grab a flaming ember from the fire and burn that cord to cinders.

In this dreadful moment, her perfidious angels seemed unmoved, careless about her pain. Their matching noses were pointing skywards to where stars were bursting in the heavens. Tock and Fuggerit. Opposites and equals.

They're twins!

'Help me!' she yelled.

But they simply faded away.

A skyrocket whistled up and disappeared in space. Sylvia jumped, startled by some young lads, who were setting off bangers.

Fists clenched, she pushed past a granddad who was carrying a little boy on his shoulders. As Sylvia circled through the crowd towards Sam, she saw another man moving in on Greta. He was hideous, darkly glowering. He put his hand on Greta's shoulder, placed his wet, twisted lips on her ear, and yanked at her haversack. But Greta held it tight and shouted in his face.

Sam was watching them, his face muscles locked. Sylvia

approached her fiancé on his left side. Even standing next to him, he failed to notice her. Was this love? When he couldn't even sense her presence, two inches away? When he cheated and lied to meet bloody Greta!

Monstrous jealousy expanded inside Sylvia until it exploded with a scorching blast. She clenched her bony fist and, with every ounce of strength, punched Sam in the side.

Astounded, Sam's taut nerves only registered pain and alien attack. Automatically, his forearm lashed backwards, smacking Sylvia in the chest, a hefty blow which lifted her off her feet and sent her sprawling.

Sylvia lay prone on the muddy grass, winded and wincing with pain. Sam dropped to his knees at her side, but for all his tumbling words of apology and mechanically groping hands, his eyes were still being dragged through the smoke towards the scene being enacted by Greta and Dick. Sylvia saw, and, through her haze, desperately summonsed Tock.

But it was Hendo who came to her side. Hendo who was supposed to be too busy doing homework. His stiff leg prevented him from kneeling, but he held out his hands. As Sylvia found her feet, she saw the ugly man drag Greta into the shadows.

And she saw Sam follow.

In that moment, Sylvia knew she would never marry Sam Phillips. Breath flooded back into her lungs and fury into every sinew of her body.

❖

Greta saw none of this. Dick pulled her away from the golden, leaping fire, and out over the common land, into the shadows, where Clara was waiting in the darkness, with her hand in her bag, gripping her monkey wrench.

Greta barely resisted. This was a game. Hissing spiteful words and threats, like children fighting over a toy, she and Dick each had a grip on one the haversack's straps, and they were tugging backwards and forwards.

'No child, no money.'

'Listen, bitch. This money is mine. You nicked it from me.'

'I earned everything I took. Whores get paid.'

'Not if they like it enough.'

'Bastard! Have you got Alice or not?'

A slow smile creased his twisted face. He let go of the bag and Greta staggered backwards. Taking advantage of her imbalance, he flung his arms around her, holding her close, squeezing tighter and tighter. She could feel his erection against her belly. Teeth roaming over her cheek, he bit into the tender flesh where ear met jaw, pulling skin away from bone. When she yelped, he licked the wound he had inflicted. His foul breath was on her face as he whispered, 'They say revenge tastes sweet. You know my appetite, Greta. So I brought my little knife. I could slip it in without anyone noticing. Just about here.'

He slid a hand beneath her jacket and pushed his fingers between her breasts. Then he placed his stitched mouth over hers. Bile rose in Greta's throat. She spat it out.

'Poor old Greta.' He pinched her nose and twisted it cruelly. 'All dried up and wrinkly now. Inside and out?'

'Where is Alice?'

'She's where you left her, Greta.'

He let her go and nodded mischievously towards the

Great North Road and the windows of the Maternity Hospital beyond.

'You've left her there?'

'Seemed appropriate.'

Greta dropped the haversack. Desperate to believe what would turn out to be a pitiless lie, she started striding urgently towards the Great North Road and the distant lights of Princess Mary's. As she walked, she pulled out her torch, turned the switch to green, and signalled backwards to Clara, forwards to Hendo.

❖

The scene Sam had just witnessed nauseated him. Standing fifty yards away, he had misread their embrace, seeing only the foul man kissing Greta's neck, touching her breasts. Deeply shocked, he let Greta walk away, and stayed to watch Dick loosen the straps on the bag, dig his hands in, and surreptitiously examine its contents. The kidnapper had his ransom, his greedy hands rummaging urgently in the haversack, pulling out and checking notes.

And then Sam felt a presence behind his shoulder.

'Leave this to us, Mr Phillips. Move along now.'

The irritating DI Howard elbowed him to one side.

But in the same instant, Dick bellowed like an enraged demon. He threw a handful of paper lira in the air, then, clutching the bag, began to pelt after Greta.

Instinctively Sam chased. So did Howard. The two men pounded and panted alongside each other. When they saw that the villain was going to catch Greta near the bonfire, they both bent lower into the sprint.

❖

Greta heard Dick shouting ferocious abuse behind her. She too began to run, veering to the left of the fire. But, like a crafty sheepdog, Dick curved around, coming up on her side, so that she was forced to dash right. Sprinting hard, she pushed over a spectator. The crowd parted and swore. Children were snatched out of her way.

Her eyes flicked everywhere. Where was Sam? Where was Hendo? David? On the far side of the bonfire, she caught sight of two men in uniforms, their silver buttons gleaming, and she ran towards them.

❖

Butterwell, knowing his limitations, blew his whistle. He threw his arm in a bowler's circle, and a couple of raincoats followed Howard in pursuit.

But Dick heard that whistle and realized that he was being chased. With the slipperiness of a startled fish, he changed direction, towards a dark spot where a nanny happened to be waiting for him with a monkey wrench.

Looking over his shoulder, Dick saw that Howard had slowed, overtaken by two younger men, presumably coppers. But a faster man was right on his heels. Suddenly Dick felt a metal weight hurled against the back of his legs. The haversack shot through the air and he was down, falling hard on Clara's monkey wrench. It hurt like hell, but it was a useful weapon. He grabbed it. His nearest assailant was over him. Dick lobbed the wrench at the bloke's chest.

It broke two of Sam's ribs. The brave vet sank.

Korda pelted away across the moor, chased by two plain-clothed policemen, and Clara. Although he sprinted well, he was tiring. Eventually he stopped, slipped his knife out of his belt, and feigned surrender. There, with only Clara as his witness, Dick Korda stabbed two good men.

Even as he ran on towards Fenham, where he had left a motorbike and sidecar, he knew he would have to get to Holyhead by dawn. He'd be safe in Ireland.

❖

Greta, meanwhile, was only aware that she was being chased. She had no idea that Dick was already gone and that one of the breathless sprinters was her friend DI Howard.

The crowd was hampering her. Around the fire, where it was too hot to stand, was a clear circle of about ten feet. Convinced she was fleeing for her life, Greta rushed straight into the roasting space. Too near the flames, she felt the bonfire's heat blasting one side of her face. Her hand, outstretched to balance, was licked by fiery breath. Frightened, she curved back out of the heat. At last she spotted Hendo,

with Sylvia standing next to him.

❖

But Tock was also waiting, his black cape crackling with sparks, his mouth pursed around clucks, *Tock Tock Tock Tock*. He slammed into Sylvia, pushing her forwards, propelling her towards the thieving, cheating gyspy woman who wasn't even worth loathing.

Fuggerit floated above the crowd, shouting, *Damned thou art!*

And out of the fire roared a chorus of voices, chanting sinful psalms, a ranting crescendo of scripture with a countermelody of curses.

Sylvia heard Dothy screaming. The fairy child was standing in the blaze, her pretty hair flying in the flames.

Tock shoved Sylvia one last time. He was beating his wings, fanning the inferno. As Greta came through the smoke, the two women collided. Without thought, without conscience, Sylvia pushed.

❖

Greta stumbled and fell backwards. She heard charcoaled sticks crack under her back. One leg of her trousers took light. The flying jacket protected her shoulders, but not the tender skin of her neck. Her hair frizzled and stank and was gone.

Someone was hitting her in the face with suffocating fabric. Rolling her over and over. Hitting her again and again. A child was wailing.

❖

As Butterwell helped Sam to his feet, the crowds round the bonfire began shrieking like demented witches. The vet shouted, 'No!' and limped towards the hellish clamour. Puffing, exhausted, Butterwell had to catch his breath before following. Dutifully, he paused to pick up the haversack.

As he bent down, he was nicely popped over the head with something small and heavy, concealed in the hand of a new figure who had tripped stealthily out of the shadows. Panting hot breath into his balaclava, Martin picked up the haversack and was gone.

❖

David heard the cacophony of screams and fought to suppress his own. The crowd was scattering like disturbed ants. Out of the swarm came a fleeing nanny with an empty shopping bag.

He was young

the doctor, and mad.

Sylvia answered him with a politely posh accent, feeling utterly disdainful. Whilst her intelligence was billowing around her head in a cloud of superiority, he, poor man, could only frown and twitch.

For weeks she'd been warning him about her mother, the thin woman sitting next to her, with shiny eye sockets and cheekbones; the crafty woman with dishcloths and knives in her handbag; the woman who helped her father kill Arthur Linden.

The doctor was using a word – 'schizophrenia'.

'Rubbish,' Sylvia said haughtily.

Peering over his spectacles, the doctor, whose eyes were unlined, and whose cheeks were positively chubby, ignored Sylvia and addressed Violet.

'In young women it usually surfaces during early twenties, but in Sylvia's case it has been triggered early, by trauma. We've tried various medications. But Sylvia fights us.'

Violet, weeping pathetically, patted Sylvia's knee. 'Can these electrical thingy convulsions actually cure her?'

'Cure? A quantitative and qualitative perception; we can only keep, em, situations under control. You must understand, Mrs Sharp, that Sylvia's voices are as real to her as I am to you. And her suspicions are truly terrifying.'

What's truly terrifying, thought Sylvia, is the poison you shoot into my veins, that hurls me into a dark tunnel. I wake up and my senses feel broken; eyes and ears, burst and split. Dothy's not well, and I can't reach her.

The doctor was passing a paper over his desk. Her mother signed it.

❖

As the door closed behind Violet, the doctor demanded Sylvia's attention. 'Now, let's talk about Angels.'

'This infernal pit shall never hold Celestial Spirits in bondage!'

'Yes, I understand you've been reading Milton.'

'Until you confiscated it.'

'Why would an Angel tell you to push your friend into the bonfire?'

'Because,' said Sylvia, as if he was the stupidest man on earth, 'she was burning Dothy.'

'If the woman had died, you would have been a murderer.'

'Like father, like daughter.'

'Not all angels are good, Sylvia. Quite a few fell out of Heaven, remember.'

'Into Chaos.' Sylvia giggled suddenly. The twins were

draped in white, and Fuggerit was holding a glowing halo, lopsided, over the young doctor's head.

'Sylvia, you must let go of your Angels. There's a way I might be able to help. Tomorrow you're going to a special room. We're going to try a therapy called ECT.'

❖

Her mother's visits were always excruciating. Violet kept looking over her shoulder as if expecting to be attacked. Or worse – witness a patient doing something embarrassingly sexual.

Months ago, Sam came, but only the once. Sylvia had begged him to take her away, begged him to forgive her, begged him to kiss her; then, in desperation, she had begged him to fuck her. When he wouldn't oblige, Sylvia lifted a chair and hit him over the shoulders. After that incident the doctor injected her with a syringe full of nightmares.

But Alan came every Saturday without fail, looking puzzled and inquisitive, as if her imprisonment and illness fascinated him. Always overconfident, he seemed convinced he could make her better, keeping her mind awake, with crosswords, chess and Lexicon. He even took the trouble to research 'schizophrenia' in the university library. It was Alan who comforted her with the theory that Saint Joan of Arc may have been schizophrenic.

On the night before her first Electrically Stimulated Convulsion, Sylvia lay drugged on her mattress, her limbs as rubbery as her undersheet. Inside her head she floated helplessly in an emotional void, where passions weren't even memories. But she clung to the certainty that the doctor's shadowy world, his pathetic half-life, was false. Her world, where truth was as bright as the sun, was the real one.

That night Fuggerit came and dressed her in a suit of armour, while Tock placed a flaming sword in her hand.

❖

Greta, by comparison, had many visitors. This woman, who had always lived on the edge, suddenly found she had FRIENDS. Daughter of the legendary Sophia, she would never be physically beautiful again, but pain and patience were blessing her with a more attractive personality.

The fire up the back of her neck and across her head would not surrender, but proud Greta lay on her stomach saying she felt fine, that she didn't give a toss about the permanent loss of her black locks or the purple puckered skin across scalp and brow. She said she was just glad that the heavy flying jacket saved her life.

With a craving which surpassed gluttony, she awaited Sam's visits, twisting and turning crossly between the starchy sheets when he was late, lying dejected and humourless when he left, because he never kissed her goodbye.

Thank God for David and Hendo who made her laugh, and especially for Clara Blake who gave Greta the essential gift of PURPOSE. Just when Greta's pain seemed almost too much to bear, Clara would come up with another incredible PLAN.

Conversations about Dick Korda and Alice were still acid with worry and determination. Of course, the kidnapped child had not been left at the hospital – she was still nowhere to be found. As soon as Greta was sufficiently recovered, both women were equally resolved to take over where the police were failing.

Clara, of course, had her own secret reason for fussing Greta. Guilt. She prayed that DI Howard would never betray her duplicity.

He too was one of Greta's frequent visitors. At first Howard's visits were official but even after every question had been answered, he kept coming. His frustration at his inability to untangle the web which had swallowed Alice infuriated him. Crime, however, would not stand conveniently still and other urgencies kept crowding Alice out, so he used his free time to sit by Greta's bedside, finding her absurdly bewitching, despite being robbed of her looks. Perhaps, just perhaps, in the midst of her idle chatter there it would be – the missing fact, the pointer, the lead.

On Christmas Day, he came close. He was feeling smug, having brought Greta a present which he knew she would enjoy, an illustrated atlas. But when she opened it, a photograph of a child fell out. Jan.

She stared at the picture for a while before asking, 'Will her mother spoil her today?'

'Janice has no money. But she's a good woman, so she'll do her best.'

'Is she a good woman? I wonder. Has this Janice ever mentioned a teddy bear to you? You see, I left one, in the cot, under my baby's blanket.'

'You did?' A tingle.

'It was tiny. My mother helped me knit it.'

Howard took Greta's hand and surprised himself by kissing it. 'Couldn't you have mentioned this earlier?'

Janice Kirkstone denied all knowledge of any knitted teddy. Howard interviewed Ada Parks and her colleagues, but their work was full of knitted teddies and no one could remember anything.

❖

Douglas Hythe never reported back to the Marlettis, otherwise he might have heard about his daughter's 'accident'. While she was enduring her agony bravely, her father was suffering in his own way, as he wandered across the South of France with only his fingers to earn him a crust. He was paid a reasonable fee for playing in Cannes on New Year's Eve, but January 1957 was a pitifully hungry month. February was starvation.

And too easily, Douglas Hythe became a beggar.

❖

In a 'Christian' home which helped girls 'In Trouble', Katherine's baby was lifted bloody from her thighs and swiftly removed. Those excellent women had done their very best to 'Save her Soul' and persuade the teenager that giving her baby to a childless couple was an 'Act of Charity' which would earn her 'Heavenly Forgiveness'. Katherine did not fight them. She was even afraid of seeing the baby's face, in case it looked like Dick. If a decent couple could love an infant born in sin, good luck to them.

However, the baby was born orange. That is to say, she had tangerine hair and very jaundiced skin. This unbeautiful little mortal was immediately taken to a nursery and hidden from Katherine. At this stage some mothers became crazed, even violent, and it was practice to give them sleeping tablets. While Katherine swooned in a drugged haze, the baby's prospective parents came to inspect her.

It was hardly love at first sight. The orange child was bellowing. Her mouth was huge, her toothless gums yellow. Greenish pee was leaking out of her nappy. They hesitated.

Perhaps they should come back when the jaundice was better.

Katherine knew none of this. All she knew was that she had given birth to a girl. Although she was supposed to stay in bed for a week, she desperately wanted to get away. So, three days after giving birth, she padded herself up and packed her modest bag. As her elder sister had done before her, she left hospital too early, by a door behind the sluice.

It was necessary to cross a small courtyard to get to the outer gate. Against the rear wall was a long bench. On it were five carrycots. These were the jaundiced babies who needed the sun's rays to correct their chemistry. Something drew Katherine to the nearest one. She looked into the carrycot and saw – her father. Sure enough, the label tied to the baby's ankle read, 'Sharp'. It might as well have said 'Cuthbert'.

The baby opened her eyes. They were dark blue, lashed with lemony fluff. Katherine felt something weird happen in her breasts, a prickle, as if every blood vessel was popping. She looked down to see two large wet patches spreading across her blouse.

Still Katherine found the strength to walk away. But just outside the gate a young couple were arguing.

'I couldn't call that one Carol, after Mum,' the woman whined. 'She'd always get called "Carrots".'

'Do you want it or not?'

'I'm not sure I can love that one.'

'I thought you said you'd checked. That the mother was the same colouring as you.'

'It must be a throwback.'

'You've pushed me into this adoption stuff. I'm not sure I want to be saddled with a ginger kid that's clearly not ours. I want a family that looks like a real family. Or none at all.'

'So you don't want any kids, unless they look like you?'

On and on they went. A conversation rattling with 'it', 'I', 'want' and 'ginger'.

Katherine went back to the carrycot. The child was dozing – lashes on cheeks, palms open to the sun. A tiny bubble in the corner of a tiny mouth. A tiny chest, rising and falling. Vulnerable as a butterfly.

Katherine found she was holding her breath, trying to stem a sensation under her ribs. As she finally breathed out, she said, 'Doesn't look like you'll ever be called Carol.'

Then she grabbed the two canvas handles, picked up the carrycot and strode out of the gate, straight past the unworthy couple.

At first Katherine walked quite quickly, but soon she was exhausted from heaving the awkward canvas box from one side of her body to the other. In a public park she found a quiet corner and set it down on the grass. Tenderly, she unwrapped the baby, who stared quietly at her mother.

'You need sunshine, treasure.'

Katherine explored lemony legs, fingers, the shape of her

daughter's skull. Her breasts prickled again. She turned her back on the world and unbuttoned her blouse.

An hour later the baby's nappy was oozing. Katherine found a telephone box, gritted her teeth and rang the Ristorante.

'Liz? OH, LIZ! Please can you get a message to Greta for me?'

Scarborough was nearly eighty miles away. It took Tony Torricelli less than two hours to drive those miles.

And so, for the first time in his life, Tony held a newborn baby. Her ugliness made him love her immediately. This man, whose emotional generosity was even larger than his waistline, this man who would never have a child of his own, laid her on his chest and felt her little heart touch his.

Hisper Cottage became Katherine's home. Liz scrounged a cot, and soon Katherine was proudly walking through Scarborough pushing her month-old baby all dressed in white (she would never wear pink), in a coach-built pram which Tony had bought second-hand and polished until it shone like a Rolls Royce.

Hazel Sharp had entered the saga, with a will and a story of her own.

❖

When Liz brought the news to Greta, she lay on her stomach, waiting for jealousy, but finding she only felt warm and hopeful. She wished upon every star that one day the two children fathered by Dick Korda would truly become sisters.

Katherine still insisted on remaining in obscurity. Difficult though it was to keep the news from David and Sam, it was rather delicious to hide the luscious titbit from DI Howard.

At the end of May they moved Greta to a convalescent home and, as the month of new blossom languished towards perfumed June, she walked the shaded veranda pushing others in wheelchairs, chatting cheerfully and hiding the pain.

One day, when the sun's fire was safely hidden behind some sullen clouds, Greta was sitting near a neglected flower-bed, nose deep in rose scent and Agatha Christie. A man sat down next to her. She was so absorbed in the plot that she failed to acknowledge him.

'You owe me four thousand pounds.'

The words danced on the page. She could feel the knives of fire in her hair again. The book thudded on the grass, as she jumped up. But when she looked down she saw an old man who was squinting up at her from crinkly eyes which were loving and familiar and full of compassion.

'Nonno!' she breathed.

'You think I not come?'

His body felt so small as she embraced him. 'You've been ill. Zio Mario wrote and explained.'

Nonno touched one of her scars with a knobbly finger. In his tenderness, she felt his grief for her lost beauty.

Mario walked into Greta's clouded vision. Taking her hand gently, he said, 'We've come to take you home, Princess.'

❖

Polishing his knife had become an obsessive habit. Dick sharpened it, then trimmed a little off his beard. His hair was now long and filthy, but it wasn't enough to hide his face, so he rarely removed his crash helmet and scarf.

At night he tucked the bike into quiet lanes, where he slept in the sidecar, usually drunk, lusting, not for women, but for money. And every morning, he moved on.

Ireland was difficult. His accent drew attention. It was also harder to nick things in small communites, so, after months of successfully evading capture, he felt complacent enough to cross back to England on his motorbike, with his face behind army surplus goggles.

❖

Sam nodded with meek acceptance when Greta announced she was going to Italy. 'Howard doesn't mind?'

'No. Such a strange man.'

'He fancies you.'

'Delicious, isn't it?'

'How do you feel about him?'

'Not the same as I feel about you.'

Damn! Sam had some news to tell her, and didn't know how. It was all the more cruel because she was trapped in a bed, and couldn't fling her head, storm off and disappear.

Wasn't her pride more important than his guilt? How could he let her humble herself to him again? Or was he simply excusing his cowardice?

Greta covered his silence with brittle brilliance. 'Come and visit me in Italy! Free holiday!'

For the first time in almost a year, Sam kissed her cheek, seeking out a place where the skin was still whole and smooth. He mumbled promises he wouldn't keep, because he couldn't bear to say the words he had rehearsed.

Greta lay with her damaged head twisted sideways on the pillow, blinking her lashless eyes. 'You know what date it is, Sam? June the twenty-third. My baby's birthday.'

'Come on . . .'

'Is it my fault Sylvia went mad?'

'She has an illness. It just happens, like cancer.'

'Do you visit her?'

'They advise me not to.'

'I want to go.'

'It wouldn't help either of you.' He touched her shaking shoulder.

'Got to go.' Sam bent his head again, this time to press his lips to the puckered flesh on her brow.

'*Ciao*.'

❖

Violet's posh home had been sold. The Council rehoused her in a flat in Fawdon. She visited Cuthbert and Sylvia when she could and, for the rest of the time, sat listening to the radio. Sometimes, because there was no one to hear her, she even sang along with Tommy Steele, 'Singing the Blues' –

'Oh, I never felt more like crying all night,

Everything's wrong and nothing ain't right . . .'

How she longed for a television set – but it was a struggle to afford a pound of mince.

Hating long days alone in the flat, she took to riding her old bicycle through the countryside. On Alice's birthday she cycled up towards Woolsington, where the verges of the lanes were speckled with wild flowers.

At the little airport, a plane stood waiting to whisk passengers to Jersey. She stopped and leaned against a gate with a cigarette between her fingers.

Could I ever go up in a plane? Is there a life beyond this misery? Katherine used to talk about America . . .

And, looking at the aircraft, Violet wondered again if that was the answer. Had Katherine laid her hands on some money and taken Alice abroad? Were they both living out some kind of happy ending in Cowboy Land?

❖

For little Jan's fourth birthday Binnie made jelly mice with liquorice tails. It was a Monday afternoon; Janice Kirkstone's flat was bouncing with balloons which ten noisy children were trying to burst.

Through the mess and hubbub, Janice smiled. Life had calmed. No communication from either police or solicitors for ages. Thanks to her eccentric friend Binnie, she was managing well. The old woman was always available to babysit, morning, noon or night. Janice had even started going out with some of the other nurses.

Yesterday had been quite thrilling. What better way to spend a summer Sunday than driving into the hills with a handsome, serious doctor?

❖

Traditionally, at the end of June, the Marletti family removed themselves to a delightful nineteenth-century villa at the head of Lake Garda, where sheer-faced mountains reflected the heat and light breezes skimmed the water.

For poor Greta even the slightest glimpse of the sun set her raw nerve ends on fire, so she was forced to remain behind closed shutters. Clara, on the other hand, was having a glorious time. When she had befriended the woman accused of stealing Alice, she couldn't have expected such a bonus – a sojourn in Italy. These bright days found her riding the cable car, gazing down at the shimmering lake, wandering narrow streets between creamy villas, or hiking manfully along mountain paths.

Clara's obvious delight frustrated Greta, who was as ill-humoured and restless as a wasp.

There came an amber evening when the air was damp and unbearably hot, as moisture bubbled up into great puffy clouds to wreath the blue mountain-tops. After supper Mario pulled out the photograph albums. Greta had seen them all before. By far the most photographed member of the Marletti family was beautiful Sophia. Her healthy gaze, reduced to sepia monochrome, was too much for Greta to bear.

She left Clara to Mario's inebriated reminiscing and, drawing a scarf around her bald head, trod swiftly down wide steps to the poplar-lined road.

At the water's edge lazy waves lapped beneath flower-decked balconies. As the sun sank towards the craggy skyline, the deep, dark lake twinkled with squares of reflected light from the village's elegant windows. Rose, vanilla and lemon scented the evening air, heady as Turkish delight.

She had a special place, where a pine and a palm stood side by side and where, on a finger of land which protruded into the water, some thoughtful person had placed a small bench. Here, so many years ago, she used to sit curled against her mother, watching sunsets.

'Am I right, Mamma, thinking Alice reminds me of you? Or is there something of me in serious little Jan? The old pictures are sad, and they tell me nothing. Oh, Mamma, you were so perfect. Would my daughter find me repulsive?'

Huge raindrops began plopping in the lake. Greta threw off the scarf and allowed the sudden deluge to spatter against her skull, streaming down her face and into her cleavage. Denied tears mingled with the rain, and she found herself praying that Jesus would reach down, touch her and make her whole again.

Gently, the cascade eased to a shower, and a sharp breeze whipped the water. Shivering, slipping in squelching sandals, she made her way back through the village with her dress clinging to her body.

Passing a small café, a young man shouted, 'You're soaking. Come in!'

His face was familiar. He was the son of the cook, up at the villa. As a small boy, Lorenzo used to play in the garden.

The lad was handsome now, with an air of impertinent confidence. He was dragging tables and chairs into the shelter of an overhanging balcony which was dripping from sodden geraniums. Light from the doorway spilled across the pavement, catching red and orange petals as they lay like wet confetti on white tabletops.

Greta followed the youth into the warm, coffee-flavoured room, accepting a stained towel gracefully. A draught of local liqueur burned its way down her gullet and the young man's smile warmed her. Lorenzo did not turn away from the scars. With sympathy but no drama, he asked her all about it.

The café was empty, the chef replete, dozing in the kitchen. Young Lorenzo placed the bottle between them and poured another two glasses. By midnight Greta convinced herself that God had sent her a salve, in the form of sweet Italian firewater. Lorenzo's hand slipped on a fresh bottle and they both giggled as the sickly, sticky liquid sloshed over the table.

Greta lifted her glass. 'Wet the head of my wery wet friend's baby. To Hazel!' She burped. 'To Katherine the Soggy! You'd like her . . . what's your name again?'

'To you! Cheers!' said Lorenzo, showing off his English.

Greta's eyes slid up into her lids and her head sank slowly to the table.

❖

At about three o'clock the following afternoon she awoke with a thick head and total amnesia about the night before.

'You're up then.'

'Clara. What time is it?'

'Time you stopped drowning your sorrows. Some bloke brought you home in a bloody cart. A lad half your age.'

'Oh, God.'

'Mario's furious.'

Greta tottered to the sink to splash her face. 'I remember him as a kid, running around with a bit of rosemary hanging out of his mouth. Ye gods! He must be nearly twenty now.'

'Eighteen. Talk about cradle-snatching.'

'You're jealous.'

546

'And you're wallowing.'

'Are you terribly fed up with me, Clara?'

'Let's say you remind me of Easter.'

'Egghead?'

'No. Hot and cross.'

Clara lay back on Greta's bed and looked up at the hand-painted ceiling. 'Fancy having a chandelier in a bedroom. Never in my whole life did I think I'd come to a place like this. I want to stay here for ever.'

'You should marry Mario.'

'I did wonder.' She laughed. 'But you can't set your cap at a bloke because you fancy his house.'

'Some would. Perhaps that's why my father married my mother. For money.'

'Why did you marry Dick Korda?'

Greta walked to the window, staying in the shade of a half-closed shutter. 'Dick and I didn't love, we wrestled. I think I was infatuated with my own body. On the trapeze I felt so powerful . . . there was no room to worry about danger or consequences. I was watched, admired . . .'

'Desired?'

'But my mind just . . . floated.'

'Then you came down to earth with a bang. Pregnant.'

'I hated my body then, for being female.'

'Adam's bloody rib.'

'Until I met Sam. Although I never quite managed femininity around him, either.' Greta sighed. 'He hasn't replied to my letters. I thought coming away . . .'

'. . . Absence might make his heart grow fonder?'

'I'm transparent.' She sat down heavily on the bed, making Clara bounce. 'It's worked before. And I so badly want him to believe that I could be a good mother.' Greta leaned forward, eyes intense with a thirst to know. 'You were so close to Alice, Clara. Tell me honestly, does she resemble me?'

The redundant nanny sighed. 'Her mannerisms remind me most of Katherine Sharp. But I could be wrong.'

Greta's frustration blistered. 'I have to go back. Resolve this once and for all.'

Clara sat up with weary resignation. 'Damn! I bet it's raining.'

'Oh, I do hope so. I hope it's bloody freezing.'

❖

Dear Father,
Mario tells me you are doing a bit of travelling around Europe. I hope you are enjoying yourself. I'm leaving this letter with Nonno in case you return to Venice.

After your magnificent efforts to help me, for which I am truly grateful, I'm afraid things went badly wrong, and I was hurt in a fire. I have my life, but no hair. Not the end of the world!

Alice is still missing. I've discussed your innocence at length with DI Howard. He has assured me that if you come forward to give formal evidence of the events which precipitated the death of Arthur Linden, you will not be charged. If you can prove your innocence in Alice's abduction, then you will be totally in the clear.

*Please come home to England, Father. We have both
lost so much, and life, I have learned, is fragile.
Hope this letter falls into your hands soon.
Love,
Alexandra*

❖

Fate, in true contrary fashion, blessed the least deserving.

Mary Linden never came home. Her Frenchman turned
out to be as wealthy as any greedy woman could desire, and
as dominant as a wilful woman, who despises weakness,
could crave. Mary Mary became a little lamb.

From Paris they moved to his yacht, cruising idly between
Antibes and Monte Carlo, basking in turquoise Mediterranean solitude. His body was ageing and flabby, hers even
flabbier, but soon Mary shed her orange makeup and allowed
the sun to tan her skin deep amber, leaving only lacy white
lines around the eyes to define her age. Salad, swimming, sail-
ing and sex. Life was perfect.

When her Monsieur inquired, she spoke with elaborate
fiction and a measure of sincere pain about her dear son
David, explaining that she was a widow, with the most hate-
ful mother-in-law in the world, and she didn't want to dwell
on the past, thank you very much!

Christmas in Athens. Valentine's Day in Tangiers. On
25 March, 1957, the Treaty of Rome was signed and the European Economic Community was born. Mary was there, in
Rome, when Britain was not – and she didn't give a damn.

On the June afternoon when David took his last 'A' Level
exam, she was buying opals in Majorca. She was wearing

those opals at the Casino in Funchal on the night her son and Hendo celebrated finally leaving school by getting steaming drunk in the Three Mile.

'. . . on the tree top . . .'

Greta was rocking Hazel gently.

The infant's eyes were still hyacinth-blue, although they would gradually soften to palest celadon-green. Fresh air and sunshine had chased away the jaundice, her cheeks were creamy and her coppery top knot curled in a cockscomb.

Katherine was watching the tableau thoughtfully. Had she really considered giving Greta her child? It seemed such an appalling idea now. And it was difficult not to be revolted by Greta's bald, scar-moulded head. Eventually she would be able to wear a wig, but for now her skin was still too sensitive and she spent much of the time in silk head-scarves.

'I'm so sorry, about the fire, and . . .'

'Just help me forget it, Kath. You and I have other things to discuss. Now, what are you doing for money?'

'You know what Liz and Tony are like. They turn up with things – and I don't know how to repay them.'

'Want a job?'

'Yes, but how? With Hazel to look after?'

'My grandfather wants me to settle down and has loaned me some capital to invest in a business. I've persuaded Tony to develop the land around Hisper Cottage.'

'Into what?'

'Holiday homes. Nice ones.'

'Hisper Cottage will never be the same again.'

'No. Sorry.'

'What do you want me to do?'

'Help. Muck in. What are you good at?'

'Maths, Chemistry, Physics. Not cookery.'

'Bricklaying?'

'Sorry . . .'

'Painting?'

'I could learn . . .'

'Me too. Oh, it'll be fun. Next week Clara and I are taking a house in Scarborough. We'll both help you look after Hazel. Clara is a trained nanny.'

Katherine frowned and swiftly lifted her daughter out of Greta's lap. Laying Hazel on her shoulder, she patted her back.

'She's my baby, Greta. I almost gave her up, yet now I can't let her out of my arms for a split second. Women can't really share babies. It doesn't work.'

'Of course. You're right.' Greta rose stiffly. 'It's hot. Let's get some air.'

They found Clara stomping around the field with a pad and pencil, Tony and Mustard trailing behind, two worried dogs.

'We'll put one row here, facing the sea, and the little shop next to the front gate.'

Vigorous head-shaking from Tony. 'No. Too much road. Less road, more house. Stick it here . . .' He grabbed the paper from her hand and she grabbed it back. Trouble was already brewing. Tony stormed up to Greta and swore. 'Whole thing – stupid bloody idea. I wanna peace ina my old age.'

'Come on, Tony. Let's sit down over a cup of coffee and chuck around some ideas. You can have the final say as to where the road goes, OK?'

She winked at Clara, who stuck her nose in the air.

In Hisper Cottage, they all sat around the tiny table, arguing vociferously. Their racket woke little Hazel, and Katherine lost her temper. She stood up and shouted down the rest.

'This isn't planning, it's daydreaming doll's houses. Who's going to design these chalets?'

'Bungalows! Each one will have a kitchen and . . .'

'You need an architect. Expensive, unless you ask Hendo. Have you spoken to the Council about planning permission? If you spend all this money now, when will you make a profit?'

'Well, it depends . . .'

'On what? How many weeks are there in a season? Ten? Twenty? How much will you charge?'

'Well . . .'

'How much will each unit cost to build? How many will they sleep? Greta, you need a real budget. You need a long-term building schedule and a short-term one. Folk won't pay to holiday on a building site. It may pay to get the shells up first and finish the insides over the winter. You should . . .'

Greta burst out in skull-wrinkling laughter. 'You've got the job, Kath.'

'More brains than any of us,' added Clara.

Tony, frustrated, slapped his forehead with his hand and rose from the table. As he climbed grumpily into the rusting van, Greta said, 'You must feel as if women are taking over your life.'

'No damn joke.'

'You're going to need some help in the Ristorante.'

'Bah! I likea these Yorkshire pudding people. But who can cook pasta like Tony?'

'I may just know someone.'

❖

Ten days later Lorenzo packed his bags and hugged his father. Inghilterra beckoned. The letter offered him a job assisting a chef in a Ristorante at some fashionable seaside resort. According to Alexandra Hythe, who was, after all, a Marletti, promotion could happen quickly if he worked hard enough.

With a cheerful wave he boarded the shimmering train, carrying a suitcase full of warm clothing. And waiting for him in Scarborough was a bossy girl with brown curly hair and a ginger baby.

❖

Lack of sleep is a debilitation for which there is never sufficient sympathy. Katherine felt as though someone had hold of the bridge of her nose and was pulling it mercilessly.

Hazel was still waking several times a night, feeding for a few minutes then dozing off again, but as soon as Katherine put the little terror back in her cot, the screaming started. That notorious Sharp temper! (To say nothing of Dick's. Poor Hazel was hardly destined to be placid!)

For the next few nights, before their new house became available, Greta and Clara slept in the caravan, but even they were woken by dear Hazel's screeching. During the second night, around four, Clara finally walked through the dew to Hisper Cottage. Finding the lonely teenager on the verge of losing her temper, Clara lifted the infant and suggested that Kath make some tea. A calm pair of hands, a soothing stroke of the brow, and the little one relaxed.

'Get yourself back to bed and try to sleep. I'll do the next feed, so you can have a lie-in.'

'She'll be hungry again in an hour.'

'I'll manage.'

'She's my responsibility.'

'Absolutely. And your responsibility will still be there tomorrow. How can you give her your best when you're exhausted? Let me mind her, just for tonight.'

'Just for tonight.' As Katherine's head hit the pillow she fell sound asleep, stirring slightly when Hazel snuffled, then turning over when she heard Clara clucking and cooing.

As Clara went to pick young Hazel out of her cot, she stopped suddenly. She slid her hands beneath the child, and something about the baby warmth of the sheet jolted her memory. She was back in Twin Elms, groping in Alice's bed, discovering her charge wasn't there.

The sheets. Alice's sheets had been cold. Cold!

As quietly as she could, she tiptoed downstairs with Hazel

snuffling on her shoulder. As she warmed a bottle and changed a nappy, little pictures flitted through her brain.

The peg on the back of the nursery door, where Alice's coat used to hang. Empty.

Alice had been taken some time before Dick Korda entered the house, by someone who was able to shush the baby and put her coat on.

❖

Katherine woke to the smell of frying bacon. She leapt out of bed, crying, 'Where's Hazel?' Flying past Greta at the grill, she found her tiny daughter in the garden, sleeping sweetly in her pram, tucked between pristine sheets, with Clara sitting close by, pencil and paper in her hand.

Her nightdress billowing about her, Katherine kissed Hazel's foot. 'Thank you so much, Clara. But my turn tonight.'

'Shifts?'

'You're a glutton for punishment.'

'I'm a professional.'

Katherine bent over Clara's doodlings. 'What's this? Plumbing, wiring?'

Clara looked thoughtful. 'Nothing to do with the project. It's to do with Alice. Be a dear, and ask Greta to come out. I'd like to talk to you both.'

They ate the bacon sandwiches sitting cross-legged on the lawn. After a couple of bites the food was forgotten. Clara was in full flow.

❖

Katherine wept bitterly as she left her baby. She gave Hazel a few ounces of milk and handed the little mite over to Clara, then ran out of Hisper Cottage and into Greta's new pride and joy, a Morris Minor shooting brake.

'Pull back that curtain,

so I can see the garden,' Ethel ordered, hating the sound of her own old, crabby voice. 'Why is that elm dying? How can I call the house Twin Elms, if there's only one?'

Death, her soul screamed, was totally unacceptable. She simply didn't have time for it.

'We'll plant another, Gran,' David promised.

'Who will? Don't stare at me like that. And sort out these pillows.'

'Doctor says you need looking after. I'll move back in, till you're better.'

'You will not! You're going to university. Daphne manages. Stop fussing.'

David gently repositioned Ethel's feeble frame. Even that small shuffle exhausted her. Yet, as she dozed straight back to sleep, she was refusing to believe that she might not wake up again.

❖

David was crossing the hallway when the doorbell rang. He opened the door and his heart leapt. Katherine was standing there, with her head high and her large breasts jutting. She smiled, tipped her head. And all of David's worry and sorrow surfaced in a flush of forgotten desire. Not for the first time, he wanted to hurl himself into the comfort of the younger girl's bosom.

'Gran's ill.'

'Oh, no! I came to see her. But I'm glad you're here. Can we go for a walk, before I visit Ethel?'

She took his hand. Led him out into the sunshine.

❖

Greta slid into the garden. The scarf around her bald head was as green as the grass, but her emotions were purple. Everything that Clara had said made sense.

The casement window was slightly open. She tiptoed towards it and peered in. Her aim was to sneak upstairs to the nursery, but in the sitting room she was surprised to see a sickbed, and a small shape under a rose-pink eiderdown. With no compassion for the shock she might cause, she slipped in and stood looking down at Ethel's sleeping face.

'Hello, Mrs Linden.'

It took a while for the old woman to wake. When her eyes met Greta's, she showed no surprise, only a shrewd pinch of wrinkles over brow, around mouth.

'Does a sick woman have no privacy? What do you want, woman?'

'Answers. Where is Alice?'

Ethel's face was parchment. 'Good question. You tell me.'

Jerkily, she brought a bony hand across her chest to clutch her left shoulder. She looked out of the window. There was a single tear in the corner of her eye. 'Sky's so blue today. Do you believe in Heaven?'

'No.'

'Neither do I. A bugger, isn't it?'

'Katherine's outside. She's had a baby. She's the most wonderful mother, and yet she's still only seventeen. Remember how she loved Alice? For her sake, if not for mine, tell me the truth.'

'I'm in pain, woman. Let me rest.'

'Sorry. I can't.' Greta watched the old lady's eyes close into crinkled, grey skin. 'You are the only one, you see. Dick didn't take her. I'm sure of that now. It wasn't Katherine's father, nor was it mine. And he has confirmed that it wasn't Mary.'

'Murdering bitch!' Ethel's breath was catching in her throat, the fury still fresh, trembling in her wasted muscles. 'She killed my son!'

'But what about my daughter? Did anyone kill Alice, Mrs Linden?'

One powerful word slipped between Ethel's purple lips. 'No.'

'Thank you.' Hot hope swelled in Greta's chest. It burned up her neck, scorching her scars, roaring behind her eyes, until they watered.

Frustratingly, the sick old lady seemed to be sinking towards unconsciousness.

'I'm begging.' Greta had to resist the temptation to shake her.

'Conniving bitch,' muttered Ethel. 'Planning. Alice . . . to be her ticket. A ticket to sex. With him. Pervert. Your father. Couldn't let it happen.'

Greta's heart was soaring, but the dying woman's heart began to race too hard. Papery skin around wasted face muscles screwed up. Her breath came in short pants. Suddenly, her eyes widened. She tried to sit up. Greta took her by the shoulders, but Ethel's face contorted with pain. For a few seconds she seemed suspended in unbearable agony, and then her lips became blue and her flaccid old mouth sagged like an empty sack.

Ethel Linden began to die. She took a while about it, with her head laid against Greta's breastbone, life and guilt slipping away like thieves on a still afternoon.

❖

That was how Katherine and David found them, Greta and Ethel locked in an embrace. Daphne entered the room behind them, carrying a tray.

Greta turned to David. 'I'm so sorry.'

Daphne's tray crashed to the floor.

Gently, Greta laid Ethel down and closed her eyes.

'YOU SILLY COW!' Rage shook David's body. 'She was terrified of you,' he bellowed. 'She was fine a minute ago, then you walk in – and the next minute – dear God, she's gone! What the Hell did you do?'

'I didn't hurt her. We made our peace. That's all.'

'LIAR!'

'But she was ill, David.' Katherine's face was full of horror. 'You told me she didn't have long . . .'

Suddenly David's knees buckled and the two women had

to catch him. He wept like a baby into Katherine's milk-filled breasts. In response her nipples leaked, staining her blouse.

Daphne was nervously fidgeting with a hanky. 'What shall I do?' she asked no one in particular.

Greta took charge. 'Just call the doctor, that's all. Then make David a drink.'

'Yes, yes. But I must be getting home. My man needs his dinner . . .'

'Your man will have to bloody wait.'

The doctor came and, with hasty sobriety, wrote the death certificate. Lifting the sheet over the old lady, he wrote down the undertaker's telephone number. Katherine led David away into the kitchen, catching Greta's eye as she passed, with a steely glint of accusation. But Greta closed her face, said she felt a little sick, and asked for the bathroom. As her strong long legs hopped up the stairs, Kath knew only too well that, despite this hideous tragedy, Greta was still pawing the ground like a lusty bloodhound.

A little while later Greta descended the brass-rodded staircase with appropriate solemnity. She dispatched Daft Daphne.

'We'll look after David. You go make your man's tea.'

Greta watched Ethel's naive servant close the back door. She counted twenty seconds, then softly opened the door again.

❖

Daphne crossed the lawn. As her hunched figure hastened between the elms, towards the high wall which enclosed the garden, Greta slipped out. The woman was headed for an arched wooden gate, embedded in the stonework. She lifted a bundle of keys from her overall pocket, unlocked it, slid through and closed it behind her.

Running lightly, Greta dashed to the wall and lifted the gate latch. Damn! Locked from the other side. Casting around for the next quickest route out of the garden, she realized she would have to go back around the house. It would all take too long.

So she jumped up to grasp the top of the wall and, chafing her elbows, hauled her weight up until she could peer out beyond the garden. Yes! She spotted Daphne's retreating figure, running with breast-bouncing haste across open grazing land, apparently heading for a lone cottage a distance beyond. Frustrated, Greta attempted to hitch her legs up, but her knees were already raw and her toes couldn't get a purchase.

She was rushing back to the house when she passed the great oak tree. The old swing hung empty – and tempting.

I'm not bloody Tarzan, she reminded herself. Or am I?

Jane slipped off her shoes, hitched up her skirt and leapt for the rope. A thrill of familiarity soared through her. Instinctively her arms pulled and the arches of her strong feet grabbed the rough twist. Up she pulled. Up she thrust. The rope rubbed her inner thighs raw but within seconds she was high in the branches of the tree. Straddling spiky bark, she clutched at dipping boughs and parted the leaves. The world beyond Ethel's back wall came into view.

Daphne was obviously out of breath. She slowed to a stagger, then hobbled into the cottage.

Greta, waited, swaying on the creaky branch, feeling more

uncomfortable as the minutes ticked by. Her thighs were sore. Her backside itched as she imagined how many tiny insects she had disturbed. Leaning forward, she stretched her length along the branch, gripping with forgotten muscles until her breasts hung either side of the bough, then she opened the curtain of green again.

A man, presumably Daphne's, was with her in the garden, shirtsleeves rolled above elbows, jabbing a finger in the air. He folded his arms. Daphne lifted her hands in a gesture of despair, then disappeared back into the tiny home.

Greta held her breath. She was so certain.

Instinct is a witchy thing.

A small figure was ushered out of the house. The man bent to press pale, slender arms into a little blue coat.

❖

In the kitchen Kath was stroking David's scarred face with a tenderness which only motherhood could have taught her. She kissed his salty cheeks, then his eyelids, wrapping her arms around his head as if she could somehow physically protect him from hurt. Being strong for him in his grief was a wonderful aphrodisiac, and she kissed him with passion which was laced with confounded distrust.

They clung together for a long time.

'I've got a daughter,' she whispered, lifting his chin. 'A little girl. Hazel.'

'Where?'

'Clara's looking after her.'

'Clara?'

'In Hisper Cottage.'

'Good God! Is she a nice baby?'

'Gorgeous . . .'

David was so full, so saturated with grief that he began to sob again, for his father, his gran and for Alice.

❖

Greta had no choice but to sprint around the house, down the length of the wall and across the field. As she approached the cottage, she heard a child's cry. Following the sound, she saw the little blue coat and two other figures moving through the scrub along the side of the river. Daphne was carrying a case. The man was pulling Alice. They were making a run for it!

Like a teenager, Greta sped down the bank and crashed through the undergrowth, heedless of nettles. The older couple turned desperate faces her way, then the man hauled Alice roughly under his arm and began to trot, leaving his stumbling wife to fend for herself.

Greta caught Daphne by the collar. Wrenching the woman to one side, she charged on after the man.

Daphne's husband was arthritic. Neither aggressive nor violent by nature, his ageing body failed him. He stopped to pant, dropping the child clumsily. The little girl was frightened, and crying. Brave old Tom spread his arms, standing ready to face the foe.

For a second Greta's compassion made her hesitate. She stopped to face him, ready to talk, but a sudden hefty thump between her shoulders knocked the breath out of her, and she fell to her knees. Not-so-Daft Daphne had belted her with the suitcase.

While Greta was fighting to breathe, Daphne pushed past

both her and poor Tom. Grabbing the child's hand, she hauled her away down the path.

Maddened, Greta staggered after the older woman. This time she was less polite. She wound her arms around Daphne's waist and shouted, 'Let her go!'

Daphne put up a fair fight for a while, but Greta's strength was animal. As the terrified child started running back to her Uncle TomTom, Greta heaved Daphne sideways and hurled her into the river.

Splash.

❖

'Kath?' Greta rushed into the kitchen.

The young couple separated.

'Where've you been?' asked Katherine.

'We have to go!'

'You're a mess, Greta. Skirt's all mucky . . .'

'Got stuck in a hedge. We've got to go, NOW!'

David clung to Katherine's hand, but she pulled away.

'I'll come to the funeral. But Hazel will be wondering where her mammy is.' She kissed him full on the lips. 'Promise me you won't tell anyone where I am.' He nodded – but he would break that promise tomorrow.

Greta dashed off. Kath said one last goodbye, then ran down the drive to where the car was revving.

'HURRY!' bellowed Greta. 'Get in the back!'

As Katherine opened the door, she registered a flash of blue.

'ALICE! OH, ALICE. PET LAMB!' Then, 'I'll kill David

Linden. I swear I'll kill him as dead as his own fucking grandmother.'

❖

David stood over the eerily sheeted form. He had things to
say before the undertaker arrived.

'Say hello to Dad for me. Tell him – I miss him horribly.'
Something else occurred to him. 'And if Alice is . . . if she's a
little cherub, Gran, I entrust her to your care.'

❖

Alice, however, was the picture of a traumatized child. She sat
curled up on the back seat of the car, sucking the hem of her
dress. Katherine tried to comfort her, but the child's body was
stiff and unyielding.

'Feel sick,' she mumbled.

Katherine stroked her brow, longing to hold her tight and
kiss her all over, but afraid of swamping the scared little girl.
'Oh, Alice, you don't have to be frightened any more. Auntie
Kath will look after you now. For ever. I promise.'

'Where's Nanna? Uncle TomTom said she'd gone to
Heaven.'

Katherine couldn't answer at first.

'Yes, pet lamb. Nanna's gone to Heaven.'

Through her tears, Alice stabbed her little finger towards
Greta's back. 'Dat nasty lady put my Auntie Daff in de river.
Gonna be sick.'

She began to retch.

❖

Daphne emptied the toby jug and gripped the mantelpiece. The pain in her heart was as brutal as a butcher's knife. Alice was gone. Ethel was gone. She had failed them both. What should she do? How could she betray Ethel's memory by going to the police?

Daphne had always understood that her employer was callously using her childlessness. Ethel had loaned her a child and the experience had been sweetly piercing. Now the manipulator was soundly dead. If the truth came out, the living would pay the price. What good would confessing do? She and Tom would be arrested.

Alice would never be hers again. Never.

She knew what they called her. Daft. So what if she couldn't read or write? Alice hadn't cared. Such a loving child. Such a pet.

Daphne helped her husband into his jacket. He winced. The arthritis had flared, painfully locking his elbows and shoulders. She patted him gently, then picked up the heavy suitcase, because Tom, bless him, couldn't.

Twinkle twinkle.

That's where Nanna is now, hanging her hairnet on that bendy moon, wearing a nightie made of black clouds.

'There it is, Alice! Hisper Cottage. Can you see the sea?'

Alice lifted her sleepy head from Auntie Katherine's soft bosoms and looked out of the car window. A long silver line cut the darkness in two, and there was a house shape, with four squares of orange light.

'Wanna go home.' She was tired and worried about Nanna in the sky. Auntie Kath carried her out of the car and into the funny little house. Inside, guess what, there was Nanny Blake! Alice remembered her. She made really nice cakes.

But in the house, all the ladies began to shout at one another.

AND they brought out a baby!

It was a funny baby, with a little curl on her forehead, like a doll, except that she had no teeth, just gums. Then the baby sucked a pink thing on the end of Auntie Kath's bosom. Alice went to have a closer look. When the pink thing slipped out of the baby's mouth it looked huge and wet and crinkly. Alice didn't like that bit of Auntie Kath.

Nanny Blake unbuttoned her coat, but all the time she was scolding the nasty lady who pushed Auntie Daff in the river.

❖

'Why didn't you take her straight to the police?' Clara was incensed. 'You're as much of a kidnapper as Ethel!'

'I'll ring Howard tomorrow. I promise. But you know what will happen. They'll put her in some dreadful home because Sylvia can't look after her, and Kath's dad . . .'

'. . . is in prison,' agreed Katherine. 'So they won't give Alice back to Mam. David is legally her father, but his gran has hidden her for a year. He must have known. Only a court can decide what should happen to her now, which could take ages. Meanwhile, both Greta and myself do have some moral rights.'

'But no legal ones!' Clara shouted, making Alice jump and stick out her bottom lip, so forlorn that all three women calmed down.

'How did you get Daphne to hand her over?'

Alice interrupted. 'She put Auntie Daff in de river.'

'You didn't!' Clara lost her temper all over again. 'How could you be so violent?' Automatically the nanny lifted Alice on to a kitchen chair and poured her half a cup of tea, with lots of milk.

'Daphne's hardly going to say anything. Anyway, she swam well enough. I made sure she was OK.'

'And you told her you were taking Alice to the police?'

Again, Alice spoke up for herself. 'Don't want to go to police! I'm a good girl.'

Katherine handed Hazel to Clara and took Alice on to her lap.

'Daphne begged me for time,' said Greta, 'to organize things. They've got relations in Ireland.'

'Yet another pair of fugitives! This is so sad I could scream with frustration! And Ethel – gone.'

Greta bowed her head. 'It was sudden, Clara, but mercifully quick. I hope I go like that.'

'Don't you feel any guilt?'

'I'm not sure I have anything to feel guilty about. Would it have been any different if you'd gone?'

'We'll never know. But it would have been better if it hadn't been you.'

'In hindsight, I wish we'd told Howard.'

'I never liked Daphne. But it's clear she and her man were coerced.'

Katherine spoke. 'Daphne's not that daft. She knew she was doing wrong, and that it was causing terrible pain. Old Tom always lost money at the dogs. Probably needed cash.'

'Anyway,' continued Greta, 'after I fished her out of the drink, she admitted that Ethel initially asked them to take Alice out of the way for a week or two. After that she had them shipped from pillar to post. Seems they spent some time in a cottage in Wales. In January Alice got a chest infection, so Ethel ordered them back to Corbridge.'

Katherine stroked Alice's head. 'It makes my blood boil to know that they've kept her a prisoner in that house. Hidden from everyone. No doctor. No other children to play with. Did they gag her if anyone called?'

'At least she was safe. I've imagined so many dreadful things. What if Dick . . . ?' The 'what-ifs' silenced all three women for a while.

'Just a day, Clara,' begged Greta. 'One day for Kath and me to spend with this very precious child, before they take her away from us again – probably for ever. Please.'

Clara sighed. 'Come on, Alice pet. There's a fluffy eiderdown upstairs. I'll put some cushions together and make a special little girl's nest bed. How does that sound? By, you've been having some adventures haven't you?'

❖

Alice woke when it was still dark. She climbed out of her nest and into her aunt's warm bed. She was very cuddly now, Auntie Kath, and really interested in Uncle TomTom's golden chrysanthemums and holey rhubarb buckets.

'He sounds like a lovely man. Do you remember Grandad?'

She remembered the man who used to shout. Uncle TomTom didn't shout.

'You're going to have a little holiday, by the seaside,' said Auntie Kath.

'Can I build a castle?' Then she thought a nasty thought. 'Will that pushy lady push me into the sea? Like she did Auntie Daff?'

'No! Anyway, I'll look after you.'

Alice cuddled in. She could still see the lonely little star out of the window. She didn't like to think of Auntie Daff, all soppy wet. And when she thought about Nanna in Heaven, she got a strange pain in her tummy. It made her want to cry. So she did.

❖

It was a beautiful morning. In the garden of Hisper Cottage Alice poked Hazel's rounded tummy.

'Where did that baby come from?'

'The stork brought her, in his beak.'

'What's she sucking that for?' Alice was fascinated by Katherine's elongated breast.

'To drink some milk.'

'Don't like milk any more. Am I still on a holiday?'

'Yes.'

'Will I go home soon?'

Katherine sighed. 'Oh, Alice. Wait till Grandma sees how you've grown. Remember the big bows she used to put in your hair?'

The little girl put hands on hips. 'Auntie Daff brushes my hair a hundred times every day. And Uncle TomTom grows his very own beanstalks, right up to the sky.'

Alice's hand strayed into the baby's curl. Suddenly she twirled it around her finger and pulled hard. Hazel puckered up and yelled until she was red in the face. Clara hastened over, ready to chastise, but Kath held up a restraining hand. She lifted Hazel on to her shoulder, cooing and shushing.

'You mustn't pull Hazel's hair. She's a real little girl, not a dolly. And she's your cousin.' (Or maybe your half-sister.)

Greta jumped out of the caravan. 'Morning! How are you, young lady?'

She smiled down at Alice, but was met by a cold, bold stare.

'You're an ugly witch,' the child declared imperiously.

Kath spoke quickly. 'Auntie Greta's a nice lady . . .'

There was a tiny, painful silence, then Greta smiled with her beautiful white teeth and took the stage in a dramatic pose which would have done Sophia credit. She changed her voice to be mischievous, yet mysterious.

'I confess. I am a witch. But my magic wand is broken, so I can't do naughty things today. Are you a good child or a bad child?'

'I'm vewy, vewy good.'

'And I'm very, very good – at magic spells.' Greta put her hand in her pocket, then walked across to Clara. She lifted the nanny's hairnet and pulled a small apple out of her ear. The circus clowns had taught her a trick or two. She gave Alice the apple. 'Now, I'm going to make a new wand. I have to find a very special stick and put a spell on it. Where is my spell book? Do you know any magic words, Alice? Can you help me?'

'I can make my own magic wand.'

'Good idea.'

'And I'll magic you into a wabbit.'

'And I'll magic you into a fairy. Or maybe a mermaid.'

Alice held up a warning finger. 'You not gonna push me into the water!'

'I promise,' said Greta seriously.

Thus, fate was challenged. And the gypsy who thought she could tell fortunes – could not.

❖

The phone call to Howard was never made that day. Alice followed Greta around like a shadow, waving a painted twig. Drawing on Sophia's legacy of imagination and performance, at one point Greta proclaimed herself to be Cinderella's Fairy Godmother, Kath an Ugly Sister, and poor Nanny Blake the Wicked Stepmother. There was much laughter. Stolen fun and stolen, precious moments. For Greta, this magical day felt like the last page of a wonderful book, the first day of heaven, the blinding light, the In Paradisum, a righteous Amen.

Greta's morality was instinctive, never lawful. She didn't even consider the crime she was committing.

But Katherine did. Yet she worried about the thought of Alice being institutionalized. And so she allowed two more days to slip by, while Greta and Alice searched among the rocks for a Golden Crab who could grant wishes.

A spell was cast over Hisper Cottage. A shimmering, fragile bubble painted with rainbows, floating on a sea breeze.

❖

On Friday morning, Hendo sat on his back doorstep, a bottle of Brown in one hand and a fag in the other. He took a long drag and pursed his full red lips to puff rings. It was odd not to be at school, but, after one last choked rendition of 'Lord dismiss us with thy blessing', several weeks had passed waiting for 'A' Level results. He was expecting good grades after an extra year in the Upper Sixth. His chosen career seemed tantalizingly reachable, success dangling juicily, a mere swipe away.

Some of his mates were now serving apprenticeships; others were doing National Service. Conscription was to end in 1960. Now that Alan was at university, even he wouldn't be called up.

'Nineteen,' Hendo reflected aloud. 'A broken man. Never destined to be Biggles, or Davy Crockett, or the Lone Ranger. Hi ho, Silver! More like the bleed'n Circus Boy.' His hip joint was hurting and he was sorry for himself.

Sliding into his royal blue, satin-collared jacket, Hendo swaggered up to Alan's house. By the time he arrived his bad leg was growling and the rock-and-roll, bandy gait had deteriorated to an old man's limp.

Alan was cranking his car. A brick rested on the accelerator.

'Fancy a pint up the Club later?'

'If I can get this jalopy going. Here . . .' he handed Hendo the crank, '. . . you turn her while I rev.' Alan removed the brick and started toeing the throttle.

'Give it a good hard wang.'

Hendo wound the crank but the engine refused to fire. 'Where you off?'

'Collecting Sylvia from hospital.'

'Bloody hell. They're lett'n her oot?'

'It's a hospital, not a prison. Howay, Hendo. Give it some welly.'

'Let's hope they know what they're doing.'

The engine spluttered, then died. Hendo pulled the crank out and looked at it as if it might be broken.

'She's getting better.'

'Better isn't cured, though. Is she safe?'

'What an ignorant prat you can be! Bugger off.'

'Bugger off yourself.'

Hendo reinserted the crank and gave it a vicious swing. The car fired and Alan revved hard. The big lad came to the car window.

'How's Mrs Sharp gonna cope?'

'Dunno.'

'Wharaboot the vet?'

'Off the scene. Permanently. So Sylvia's got to come home.'

'Does Syl understand? You kna. What she did?'

'Yes, she does. I'm sure she does.'

'Go careful, son. Just go careful.'

Katherine hauled herself out of the icy waves, skin puckering with goose pimples, seawater running down her legs. Instead of rushing for her towel, she wrapped her arms around her torso and watched Alice, who stood on the wide, wet sand, with her dress tucked in her knickers. Further up the beach, Greta was also watching. Alice was staring down at her own feet, at rillets of water trickling between her toes. It struck Katherine that the toddler's quiet thoughtfulness was a sign of a change, an awakening, perhaps, into that period of childhood when memories are laid down in a fresh, eager mind, memories which can last a lifetime.

A lump formed in Katherine's throat. 'I'm sorry, pet,' she whispered. Shivering, she approached little Alice, who looked up and did not smile.

Clara was sitting outside Hisper Cottage, shuggling the pram. As Katherine approached, the nanny raised a finger to her lips.

'Shh! Hazel's just dropping off. Where's Alice and Greta?'

'Hunting for crabs. Any tea?'

'In the pot. Go and get dressed. I need to go out.'

'Where?'

'Scarborough. On the bus.' Clara sniffed, long and hard. 'Police station.'

'You needn't.'

'I need.'

'But . . .'

'You're being naive and selfish, hiding Alice from the law. And here in Tony's cottage, when he doesn't even know! If you're caught, they'll assume he helped you. Katherine, he'll go to prison. I will go to prison. Somebody has to start getting sensible. And fast!'

'Monday.' Katherine went to her coat pocket and drew out three envelopes. 'I may be selfish, Clara, but I'm not stupid. I wrote these last night. I want them to arrive Monday morning. One to Howard, one to Mam, one to David. I thought if I wrote it all down, explained that I'm worried about them putting Alice into some orphanage, they'll understand why I hesitated.'

'They'll come down on you like a ton of bricks!'

'I know. They'll think it was me who took her in the first place, and even when I explain about Ethel, they'll think I was part of her plan. It could take months to prove I'm innocent.' She handed the letters to Clara. 'Go to Scarborough. Post them. By the time they're delivered on Monday we'll be on our way to Newcastle, with Alice. But while you're in town, could you please see Tony and Liz? We need their help. Somehow I have to tell Greta what I've done, and stop her from doing anything daft.'

'Like doing a bunk with Alice.'

'It wouldn't exactly be out of character.'

❖

Liz was in the Ristorante kitchen making apple pies. Clara removed her coat, washed her hands and seized the rolling pin.

'Get Tony in. We need to talk.'

The pastry was as thin as paper by the time she'd told her story.

'You don't know young Sylvia, do you?' asked Liz sadly. 'I watched that lass nearly die of 'eartbreak and loneliness.'

Tony looked sallow and sad. 'Greta always too passionate. Too desperate. I threaten to tell her Nonno. This will return her senses. I hope. Why you not bring child to Scarborough police?'

'Kath thinks it will be better to take her straight to DI Howard, in Gosforth. And it's Sunday tomorrow, so she wants to give Greta one last day with Alice. But she's frightened that Greta might . . .'

'Right!' Liz wiped her hands and took off her apron. 'Young Lorenzo and Florrie can manage here for a couple of hours.'

❖

MONDAY. Nanny Blake told Alice the holiday would be over on MONDAY.

A lady visited, with hair like a silver crown, and teeth that kept dropping up and down. She cuddled Auntie Kath. But a big, fat man with a huge moustache came in and shouted at Fairy Godmother. Her face went red and she shouted back. VERY LOUD! Then the fat man blew his nose on a spotty hanky and touched Alice's hair with his snotty hand.

Alice was frightened of MONDAY.

❖

Hendo was very drunk.

The Working Men's Club was a dark cavern of smoke. Clean-scrubbed miners were rock-and-rolling with their wives. Hendo's world was rock-and-rolling too. He had supped seven snakies and his whole stomach was one big curdle. The luminous bar was a lighthouse in a stormy sea. Everything else swam in a haze of rubbery chair backs and weaving trouser legs. The world was tipping, and when he tried to take a step, the floor smacked him in the gob.

He lay there, looking at Sylvia's legs, feeling a sudden rush of affection for them. Nice legs. For a schizophrenic.

❖

Sylvia smiled as she helped Alan prop Hendo against a wall. I'm normal, she thought. Normal!

Alice's MONDAY

never happened.

Early on Sunday, while Katherine's letters rested in slots in Gosforth Post Office, Ernest Wood was frying black pudding when someone knocked on his door.

'Better be an emergency! I'm allowed one day off.'

A man was leaning on a stick, his head held up like a duck, the best effort he could make to stand tall.

'My name is Tom Charlton.'

❖

Howard was snoring when the telephone rang. Once he had assimilated Ernest Wood's words, his whole body began to flail. His hands couldn't find his socks. His feet couldn't find his trouser legs. In his dash to the toilet, he stubbed his toe.

❖

It was Butterwell who hauled David Linden in.

Poor, naive David honestly denied all knowledge of his

grandmother's crime – the most unforgivable, incomprehensible crime – against himself. Now even Katherine had cheated him, stealing Alice from right under his nose.

Dazed, staring down a horrific chasm of betrayals, David told Howard that the missing Katherine Sharp had befriended and aided Greta, and that they were probably in Scarborough. He wanted to dash there himself, to get his little girl, but Howard struck a better deal with him and told him to be back at the station in an hour.

David spent that hour in Hendo's house, where he cried on Mrs Henderson's shoulder because there was no one else to hold him. Hendo's dad rushed into the kitchen to make him a spam and pickle sandwich.

❖

Howard, meanwhile, thought he might have a heart attack. He telephoned his colleagues in Scarborough and told them to mount surveillance around Hisper Cottage until he got there. 'Don't go in with clodhoppers. Needs very careful handling. The bairn must be protected. She might be frightened, she might be hard to lure away from Katherine, so I'll bring her dad and her grandma. Hythe's a slippery bitch. One whiff of you lot and she'll scarper.'

Twenty-five minutes later Howard had confirmation that Hisper Cottage was certainly populated by several women and a little girl. He and Butterwell went straight round to Violet's new flat, where he was shocked to find Sylvia calmly playing records with Alan Watson. Butterwell smoothly distracted the young pair with blether about the Everly Brothers, while the Inspector drew Violet into the kitchen.

'How's Sylvia doing?'

'Tablets keep her calm. Nice, even. Alan brings out the best . . . why are you here?'

'News. Best not tell her yet.'

'Which one?' Violet began trembling all over.

'Both. Alice and Katherine. It's good news.'

A noise came from Violet's throat. She began to hup, hup, hup, high in her chest.

❖

Alan was already suspicious of Butterwell's bumbling. When he saw Violet's red eyes and Howard's tight lips, he knew something was afoot.

'Just popping out,' Violet said. 'Inspector needs a favour.'

'A favour?' Sylvia faced them with chill calm. 'A body to identify?'

'No, lass. No.' Violet stopped abruptly. Then she opened her arms and tried to hug her daughter, who stood as stiff as a corpse.

'It's to do with Ethel. I told you David's gran died last week? Well, something needs sorting out.'

After they'd left, Sylvia turned on Alan. 'What's so bad they won't tell me?'

'If it's about Alice, David will know. I'll find him. You stay here. I promise I'll come back and tell you.'

David was not at home, so Alan drove round to see Hendo. Mrs Henderson was weepy and even Mr Henderson's face was mottled. When they told him that David had gone to fetch Alice, Alan's Adam's apple began to hurt.

Hendo was so deeply embarrassed at his friend's tears that

he began to giggle nervously, wondering why he was the only one who couldn't cry.

But Alan was getting fierce. 'What about Sylvia? Why haven't they told her? She's Alice's mother – and after everything she's been through . . .'

'Aye, but Sylvia's crackers.'

❖

Butterwell drove. In the back seat, David and Violet sat, silently emotional. All through the tedious sprint down to Yorkshire, Howard frowned. In front of his narrowed eyes was Alexandra Hythe, the wretched female whose face wore holes in his dreams, whose slender, scarred neck needed throttling. He prayed to God that the Yorkshire boys were keeping a low profile.

There was to be a swift and concise briefing at Scarborough police station, before any action. Howard needed control. His instincts were surging.

❖

Alan drove as fast as he dared, while Hendo held a bowl on his lap, the snakies still curdling in his stomach. He wasn't sure it had been right to tell Sylvia, and he was even less sure about bringing her, but Alan always had an extreme sense of justice. Anyway, it was his car.

Sylvia sat calmly in the back seat, reading the map.

Hendo was right to worry. Sylvia had stopped taking her tablets. Now that she had escaped the hospital, she needed to FEEL again. To feel something. Anything. And Fuggerit wanted to find poor Dothy.

Clouds were rolling inland, buffeted by a north wind which whipped around Hisper Cottage, unseasonably cold, maddening the sea till it spumed as far as the eye could see. Greta stretched her arms to embrace the damp gusts. This was a morning to make the most of, a dull day when she could inhale the tangy air without flinching at fiery pricks across her skull. Wrapping a red and white spotted bandeau around her head, she told Alice, 'This is a special day, so we're going to Scarborough, to ride on a toy train.'

Opposite the famous Peasholm Park, a Lilliputian steam engine pulled pretty carriages through Northstead Manor Park, past the open-air theatre, then between tennis courts and out along the cliff. Trundling along, waving passengers could trail their arms in the sea air, admiring the glorious view of waves crashing around Monkey Island.

On good days. Today the passengers huddled in their coats as the wind rocked the carriages. Alice cuddled against Greta. The little train terminated at Scalby Mills Hotel and Greta lifted Alice down. This was the most northerly part of North Bay, where a bridge crossed a burbling beck to a muddy headland.

They ate Clara's cheese sandwiches early. At the water's edge they bared their cold feet and jumped through chilly foam, then scrambled over Scalby Ness Rocks, which fanned out into the sea, black and green with slippery seaweed. Where waves tipped in and out of foaming pools, they searched for the 'Golden Crab' who would make all their dreams come true.

It was cold. The sky was racing in bruised billows over lumpy waves which rose and fell in great, glorious, crashes. Greta's scarf was brilliant red against all the greys.

She buttoned Alice's cardigan over her new daisy blouse.

❖

Alan sped through Thirsk, across to Whitby and down the coast road. Butterwell had driven down the A1, then up Sutton Bank. So when Howard's car was entering Scarborough, Alan, Hendo and Sylvia had already arrived at the track leading to Hisper Cottage.

Sylvia recognized the corner, and the bus stop.

'There it is! Hisper Cottage is down there.'

'Aye, and look, there's Plod.' Hendo pointed to a Humber Snipe parked down the lane. 'What'll we do?'

But Sylvia was already out, head bent against the wind, marching down the lane.

'Shouldn't we wait for the police to do something?'

Worried, Alan parked the car further up the road, before he and Hendo followed.

❖

My path. My sea. My cottage. MY MUSTARD!

And there he was, bounding towards her. Mustard, or the golden essence of him, conjured out of her need. He licked her hand and made little growls of welcome. As real as the rocks in the grass, he rolled on his back. She bent to stroke his pale belly.

Oh, Mustard! Don't run away . . .

Sylvia watched Mustard fade. Everything seemed to be

fading, blurring into the wind. She peered at the chunky shape of Hisper Cottage, and thought she saw Sam's silhouette at the gate.

Panicking, she turned and stumbled back towards Alan's arms. 'I think Sam's here!'

He frowned. 'No, pet. He won't be. Trust me. You wait in the car while we do a recce.' Small and nimble, he began scuttling crabwise through the whipping broom.

Hendo, however, said, 'Well, a'm just gonna knock on the bloody door. Divent see why not.'

Sylvia could not go back to the car. She ran a little way up her favourite path and threw herself into the rough grass, to watch. Mustard came back and lay down beside her, his coat separating in the wind. She shivered. Rain began to spit at the roof of Hisper Cottage. She could just make out Alan crouching, and Hendo peering through the windows. The big lad knocked. The door opened. He went in.

Then the wind began to whistle

and the whistle became a familiar tune.

Pack up your troubles in your old kit bag, and smile . . .

The voice came from behind her.

Hello, Sylvia.

It wasn't Sam's voice.

She turned slowly and looked up into the shuddering gloom where clouds were scudding across the shoulders of a tall, slender man. He was monochromatic. Cream and brown. His peaked cap sat jauntily, his angular uniform stiff and unyielding in the bluster. A moustache was smudged across his features. When he spoke, his fixed smile didn't move. 'Well, lass. It's been a long time.'

He had no name. No substance. But he was once Sylvia's only friend. And he used to live on the mantelpiece of Hisper Cottage.

Two policemen emerged from the cottage, holding Clara Blake firmly between them. Hendo was escorted out by another policeman. His indignant voice carried on the wind. 'A've done nowt wrong, man!'

When they had driven off, Alan crawled up towards Sylvia, to find her staring vacantly into space. 'Howay!' he hissed. 'There's another copper around the back. Why've they taken Hendo?' Alan was utterly agitated. 'Are they watching us now?'

Sylvia nodded. 'Tony. We'll find Tony. This way,' she pointed, 'up the track and down the back of the field.' Alan scuttled off. He did not see Sylvia run her hands through a prickly patch of gorse, whispering. 'I'll come back for you, Mustard. Be a good boy.'

In the safety of the car, Alan spoke carefully. 'Syl, pet. Sam can't possibly be here. I put off telling you, because I knew it would hurt . . .'

'I don't hurt any more.'

'He's gone to Australia. Got a trial job, doctoring wallabies.'

❖

'Is this the magic pool?'

'Nearer the cliffs, in a tiny cave, that's where we'll find him.'

The day was darkening, the northerly pressing the cloudbank hard into the coastline. Alice seemed content and Greta was enjoying the moody atmosphere, so she stayed out on the rocks, savouring the cold shudders over her scalp and shoulders, while most folk were hurrying back across the bridge, towards the beach huts or the Corner Café.

Some miles out in the North Sea, it had begun to rain hard. At the centre of the meteorological depression, patters and plops feathered the churning, blackening waves.

Still Greta and Alice poked and probed, moving from stone to stone, legs stretched, arms reaching to grab and balance. After a while Alice shivered, and Greta straightened up, realizing that they had gone quite a long way around the point.

'Oh dear,' she said, 'you're getting chilly. We'd better get back.'

But Alice was consumed by her quest for the Golden Crab.

'Is he really magic? Will he give me a wish?'

'Of course. But you must hold your secret close to your heart.'

'Will you wish too?'

'Oh yes. I've something very special to wish for today.'

❖

The Ristorante, steamily fragrant with garlic, cheese and tomatoes, was packed with holidaymakers.

Sylvia and Tony faced each other. His brow was sorrowful. This girl, whom he had once loved, had pushed his Greta into the fire.

Liz tried to hug her, but was not hugged back.

Alan, as usual, was direct. 'The police are on their way.

Clara Blake has already been arrested. Sylvia has come for her daughter, Alice . . .'

At that moment three policemen entered the Ristorante. One turned the sign to CLOSED. Another said to the diners, 'Nothing to worry about, folks. Just finish your food quickly.'

Local lads, they completely ignored Sylvia and Alan, assuming they were customers.

The third policeman said, 'Antonio Torricelli, I'm arresting you in connection with the disappearance of Alice Sharp. Anything you say . . .' Tony was roughly handcuffed.

'Elizabeth Baxter, I'm arresting you in connection . . .'

Liz interrupted. 'Write this down, lad. Go on, write it down.' She did not look at Sylvia. 'They were bringin' Alice back to Gosforth tomorrow. They were. My life on it. And you don't have to make a great drama of pickin' them up. They've just gone to Scalby Mills for a last paddle.'

A last paddle.

❖

Hazel was warm and dry. The hood was up. Katherine was pushing the pram against the wind, through Northstead Manor Gardens towards the beach. Her feet felt light as she tripped under dripping branches. She was enjoying the outing, despite the weather, and although she knew things would change tomorrow, she had some faith in her own future, because she was doing the right thing. She would be taking Alice back, rescued from Ethel, even from Greta. In a way, she would be a heroine.

Things were working out well. Tony had said that afterwards she could stay here. With Hazel. By the sea. For ever.

Plans for the holiday site were taking form. She felt a sense of purpose, and a thrill of hope.

A small posse of policemen jogged past. Because she was seventeen, of course, Katherine automatically searched the dark uniforms for a handsome face.

'Someone's in trouble . . .'

She began to walk faster. Her steps quickened into long strides. Greta and Alice! She had to get there. She was running with the pram, bouncing Hazel around crazily as she swerved right and left.

The plain-clothed lads had been discreet, combing the park and North Bay. A woman matching Greta's description had been seen leaving the little train at Scalby Mills.

Cold raindrops stung Howard's face as he stood on the beach, squinting right and left. Visibility was deteriorating. He closed his mind to all logic, summonsing his secret instincts. He pictured the woman he had wasted all his sympathy on, and began to walk. When the sand ran into shale and slippery rocks made him totter, he spotted her. Out under the Ness, a tall slender shadow straddling the rocks, and a blur of a child carrying a bucket.

Alice's new lemon shorts, which Liz had bought yesterday afternoon from Boyes Store, were spattered with raindrops. Her blue cardigan was getting sodden and her long dark pigtails were stringy in the rain. One of her yellow ribbons blew off.

Greta's shirt was wet against her bra. Her modern, loose trousers clung to her thighs. Crouching on her long legs, she stretched with a liberation which defied her years. But the wind was pressing at her back.

The rocks were slippery. She held Alice's hand tightly, too engrossed in keeping her footing to look beyond the next rock, too worried about the child catching a cold to notice male figures swarming covertly along the beach. Some of the policemen were plain-clothed, others were formally uniformed, in heavy boots, clotted with sand. Clodhoppers all.

The tide advanced in giant rollers, crashing down in thunderous tonnage, bashing and sucking at pebbles, flinging seaweed across the rocks. Greta looked ruefully at the goose pimples on Alice's bare legs, then at the space between water and cliff, which was shrinking. She picked Alice up.

'Better hurry, pet. The sea is getting naughty.'

'But we haven't found him yet! You want your special wish.'

'Let's quickly shout to him. He'll hear us from his special seaweed house under the Golden Stone.'

Greta curled her strong feet around a rock and, facing the awesome waves, chanted 'Oh, Ancient Golden Crab, hear me. We have come to ask . . .'

'There's a man waving at you. Hello! I waved back, Greta. Look, he's running. What's he running for? Silly man. He'll fall over.'

Before Greta turned, she knew. A watery lick surged around her feet and a chill thudded into her heart.

'Come on!' Howard pulled Violet too fast across slippery

rocks, damning and blasting the foul weather. The sea looked ready to swallow the bloody world.

David, with his bad leg dragging, came staggering behind, but Howard had ordered the rest of the team to stay well back. Several uniforms were now moving cautiously along the base of the cliff. A few had ventured over Scalby Beck and up on to the Ness, but the pathway was treacherous in the wind and rain.

It was imperative that Howard get to Greta quickly. Had he earned her trust? Would she surrender to him?

'THERE SHE IS!' cried Violet. 'It's my Alice. It's my Alice! Oh, God! Oh, Cuth!'

❖

Sylvia's arm ached as Alan pulled her along. On the beach, people had all started facing the same direction, trying to see where the action was, as constables belted across the sand with their helmets in their hands. By the time they got to the beck, the shadowy blue uniforms began moving more stealthily.

A policeman held up his arm and ordered them to stay back.

'She's my Alice,' whimpered Sylvia, staring at the tumbling spume and the bottomless clouds, the sodden, lashing air and crashing rollers. Alan was peering through the rain, across the rocks. 'Are they out there?' His voice sounded small, weak.

Sylvia tried to feel fear. At last she began to touch it, pure, pitiless, profound. To comfort her, the nameless soldier at her side began to sing.

. . . There's a silver lining, 'neath the dark clouds shining . . .

Ducking and dodging, Sylvia ran, leaving Alan to wrestle policemen.

She saw her mam first, then David, who was limping awkwardly. Howard was right out beyond them, where the sea was white and frothy, crashing around the rocks. Sylvia squinted. In the distance was the unmistakable, shapely figure of Greta – who was carrying Alice.

The ghostly picture of mother and daughter, caught out, as close and trusting as secret lovers, excluded Sylvia in a way which would stretch from this minute to her own eternity. Dreams and hopeless longings fell like rags at her feet. Emotionally naked, she stood in a thunder of condensing moisture – and the rain tasted like acid.

I feel.

Sylvia turned her face upwards, letting the downpour stream over her face. Jade eyeshadow and black mascara ran across her cheeks as she began to pray. 'Forgive us our trespasses. Suffer little children. God, please help me!'

A golden flare shot into the sky. Tock was pointing his gun heavenward. He was dressed in black again, his wings spanned like an immense, predatory eagle. Fuggerit, however, was draped in sky-blue, the colour of highest Heaven. Safe in his arms, dimpling mischeviously, and glowing as if her body harnessed a thousand joys, was little Dothy.

Sylvia waved . . . then hesitated. She looked back through the rain at Alice and Greta, confused between her human anguish and the sight of her friends hovering just above the surging sea.

'Help me!'

The brave soldier, in his big old boots, jogged down the beach. He leapt boldly across the rocks, flinging off his jacket. From his dull sepia skin sprouted the six shimmering wings of a seraph, so bright that rainbows shot through the clouds.

As he rose into his own silver lining, Sylvia stumbled after him. But Alan had caught up, and was trying to restrain her. Sylvia pushed him off, shouting, 'Behold! He shall direct my paths.' She began to run. 'He shall send out an angel before thee . . . !'

Sprinting towards the rocks, she scrabbled seawards and found a place to balance.

The dark angels began to swoop.

The Inspector didn't even notice the deranged girl on his right. His focus was riveted on Greta and the child. Other policemen were coming up behind him. He shouted over his shoulder, 'Stay back!' Leaping awkwardly from rock to rock, he kept berating himself – clumsy! CLUMSY! Cornered like a hunted animal, she's bound to try to run. Must get to her . . . offer sympathy, understanding . . .

But Greta had no intention of running. She just wanted to protect Alice. So she held her tight to her chest and began moving back towards Howard, knowing full well that this could be the last time she would ever hold the dear soul again. Suddenly, the incoming tide surged around her thighs and she slipped. As she fell, she automatically protected Alice by lifting her away from contact with the rocks. But the little girl cried out, because she had grazed her elbow and some salty water had got into her mouth.

Greta's leg was bleeding. The back tow of the wave was surprisingly strong and it took all her refined sense of balance to scramble back to her feet and pick Alice up.

❖

Over the roar of the churning spume, the angels' voices thundered and cracked. They were hurling poetic curses at Greta, their screeches spittled with TOCKs and fuggerings. Sylvia's body was bent and shivering, but her mouth was scorched with the bubbling froth of verbal venom.

When a wave broke over her back, her eyes opened wide at the shock of the icy thrust, and suddenly

– the angels sank beneath the waves.

❖

Swirling pools were forming between the rocks. Greta saw Sylvia staggering, her long stick arms extended, and water slopping her clothes around her waist. Despite the girl's astonishing tirade, Greta shouted at her to get back to the safety of the beach.

Holding Alice high, she kept moving carefully. But the next rock was a long stretch, even for a woman who could still do the splits. Alice's arms were tight around Greta's neck, her face pressed hard against her scarred ear. So close were their faces that Greta could taste strands of her daughter's hair in her mouth. For surely this dear child was her own, flesh of flesh, her little animal body so warm and clinging that they were almost one, locked together in love and fear.

She managed a step sideways, but another wave hit her from behind. It became harder to find a secure footing with the tow tugging at her ankles. A fresh weight of water hit her backside. She hitched Alice on to her shoulders and kept trying to step from rock to rock, towards Howard. The little girl clung like a limpet, shivering, terrified of the cold water rushing at them, trusting Greta completely.

❖

Katherine had abandoned the pram and was tearing along with Hazel screaming in her arms. The beach floated before her in a wash of falling cloud. Spectators were huddled under umbrellas and macs. She heard someone say, 'They'll drown! Stupid woman . . .'

Dear God! It must be them. Greta with Alice in the water!

The rain was getting heavy. Breathless, she pushed on until a young policeman stopped her.

'My niece – out there – let me go to them!' Desperate sincerity racking her face, she begged the policeman, 'I'm Katherine Sharp!'

Clearly, he recognized the name. He was looking doubtfully at the baby in her arms.

'And that's my mam!' Katherine was pointing – but her finger fell, and her hand went to her mouth. 'Oh, God, there's Sylvia . . .'

David and Alan were also standing on the rocks. They all seemed placed on a moonscape, important characters from the movie which was her past, wrongly dropped into a slipping, stony reality.

'Take me to Howard! Please!'

Persuaded, the young constable took her elbow and ran with her across the sand.

Once they were on the rocks it was difficult to hold Hazel tight. Katherine's feet slid and her body lurched. Crouching low, she eased herself forward, using one hand to hold her baby to her chest and the other like a third leg. The policeman halted her lame-crab progress. As he held her shoulders firmly, she leaned forwards and cried out, 'Alice . . . Greta, be careful . . . Oh, Alice . . .'

Clutched to her breast, tiny Hazel's shocked cries were raw in the drizzle.

The constable was a new father himself. He took the baby out of Katherine's arms and pulled her off the rocks, saying, 'Your life is as important as anyone else's. And this baby is precious.' He took off his jacket and wrapped it around her.

❖

What the hell was Sylvia Sharp doing here? Howard turned and scowled at Violet, whose arms were reaching out like a helpless beggar. David was being propped up by Alan Watson.

Alice screamed. Once she started, she kept screaming. The sound of her petrified yelps turned stomachs.

Someone pushed a loudhailer into Howard's hand. Greta had slipped into a pool and was now up to her waist in water, with waves running across her shoulders. 'Alexandra!' Howard shouted desperately. 'Get up. Get out. Bring Alice back here. Can you hear me? Game's up, love. Bring the little girl to me.' Then he tried to calm her. 'Alice. Here's your grandma come to see you. There's nothing to be frightened of. Tell the lady to bring you out of the water.'

A wave crashed over them.

Greta managed to hoist Alice out of the water and sit her on a higher rock, but the child was screaming as water flooded around her bottom.

'Get her, someone, please!' Greta yelled.

Howard crept across the rocks towards them.

Greta gave herself a moment to breathe, then pulled herself up and found a footing where the water was shallower. Alice was waving frantically. But just as Greta managed to lift the little girl high again, another wave dashed against her back.

It ebbed, for three seconds. Her voice carried on the wind, 'I was bringing her to you. Tomorrow.'

Greta was crying.

❖

Howard tried to stretch towards Alice.

Behind him, Alan shouted. 'Hand her backwards. Backwards to me.'

But Howard couldn't reach Greta's arms.

❖

Greta looked across at Sylvia for one last time. The girl was up to her chest in water, her face white with shock. The next wave went over her head. Howard dropped his megaphone helplessly as the rip tow took Sylvia out. Her head was a russet blob in the water.

Again Greta tried to step on to the next rock. Howard

moved sideways to find a way around. The granite underfoot was so slippery that he dropped to his knees and crawled through the waves. His heart pounded painfully, and the breath was knocked out of him when penetratingly cold water bit into his testicles.

❖

Oh, the devilish greed of death.

Twenty feet out, the angels conjured their special wave, heaving it up with careless solemnity. It crested and rolled, rushing through the rain towards the beach. Howard, creeping through icy swirls, felt a drag and knew it was coming. He could do nothing.

Suddenly spume loomed over him, blocking out the light, a heavy, curling, caesious body of water sucking upwards into a great translucent wall which lifted Sylvia's bobbing head to its summit, then tipped and tumbled right over Greta, sweeping Alice away from her. The water hurled itself against the rocks with all the fearsome, rushing power of the ocean behind it, then drew back in haste as though ashamed of its ferocious outburst, taking Greta with it.

There was shrieking and screaming. Violet's anguish ripped through the rain. Alice's little body was a fleck of blue and yellow flung mercilessly on to an unreachable rock.

❖

At the edge of the sand, Hazel had stopped crying. The Constable looked down. Katherine had gone. Already in the water, she had thrown off her skirt and was diving into the waves. He shouted to his colleagues and held the unfamiliar babe tight to his cheek, comforted by the warmth of soft skin against his own.

Men in uniforms were scuttling towards Alice, throwing off jackets and shoes, dropping into pools, hauling one another along.

❖

As swiftly as a dream passes over twitching eyes, Violet prayed a thousand prayers and willed someone to save the baby. She tried to put herself in Alice's head. Be brave, my little lass, be brave. . . . And her heart cried the same message to Sylvia . . . but her heart already knew another truth.

A swimmer was slicing through the water. Violet thought it was a man. She had no idea that it was Katherine, or why the icy surge was so familiar to her.

❖

Howard kicked off his boots. As he swam, his socks slid off his ankles and the glacial swell compressed his lungs. He pulled with numbed arm muscles, pushing the water under his body, twisting left, right, swallowing salt, gagging, rising and falling, pounding at the sea until his heart felt near bursting.

He was trying to get to Alice when he saw the red spotted scarf. He reached and grabbed it. The silk clung limply to his fingers. Then he flipped into a dive and opened his eyes. Greta's lifeless form floated whitely below the surface. There was a gash across her forehead, the strange ovoid of her raw scalp catching the dim light; her eyes were open, breath escaping from the side of her mouth in a stream of tiny bubbles.

He came up for air and saw that another swimmer had reached Alice, so, gasping, he held his nose as he pulled back down again. Sinuses stinging unbearably, he felt Greta's body near his feet. He dived and wrapped an arm around her torso, then kicked and thrust until he felt air on his face and in his lungs. Two heads bobbed between the waves.

Her strange mask face moved against his cheek, and she opened her eyes. Blue. So blue. 'Leave me,' she mouthed. 'Let me go. Save Alice . . . please . . .'

'Somebody's got her, I can see . . .'

'Go help!' She thrust him away and he found himself letting go. Letting her face sink again beneath the sea which could never be as blue as those eyes.

❖

The sea covered Alice's rock and sucked her away. Clad in sodden, cumbersome uniforms, officers were flailing towards the spot, but Katherine got there first, her brown hair floating behind her. Suddenly her dark crown was replaced by a small white backside as she dived through the waves.

Howard was treading water, struggling to catch his breath. 'Find her, you fucking stupid bastards,' he bellowed at the men. 'Find the child! We can't lose her now!'

He watched the girl dive again.

A blond-haired lad was also crawling manfully through the waves. Alan Watson. Come to save Sylvia. He shouted something, then moved further out towards the heaving horizon.

On Katherine's third dive a shout went up. A second small white face broke the surface. Alice.

Where are you, Dothy?

In the end, there was no tocking.

In the end there was no Fleeing Time.

Only cold.

Only choking.

Only salt.

In the end.

And, in the end, Greta thrashed.

The Yorkshire squad was not short of courage, but the sea was like melted ice and they had to take it in turns to enter the water. Each and every one of them, when the heavy surge hit his belly, shouted out. Soaked and shivering, they combed the rocks for the bodies of Sylvia Sharp and Alexandra Hythe, keeping in a chain, signalling to one another through the rain, stumbling, twisting ankles, grazing knees, as the unstoppable tide swilled towards them.

❖

Pull elbows, pump lungs. Up with the elbows, push, push. Alice lay face down between Howard's knees. Her miniature body felt too small beneath his large hands and yet he found himself being rough in his determination to make her breathe. Drips from his wet hair, from his nose and stinging eyes, fell on to baby soft, cold skin. Lift, push. Lift, push. Grief and frustration hardened his exhausted face. He'd bungled it!

He'd killed them all. It was his fault. Alexandra was gone. He'd left her to die, to drown in the suffocating, choking brine. He must save her baby.

He could hear the coughing of the magnificent young woman who had pulled Alice from the clutches of the sea. She was on hands and knees, dripping, shivering, her chest rasping with hoarse sobs. Katherine Sharp.

'I tried, I tried.' Katherine wept. 'We were bringing her back tomorrow. I promise, we were bringing her home . . .'

❖

The young constable's arms were shaking. He helped her up and pressed Hazel to Katherine's chest. 'Brave lass.'

From the shelter of his jacket, she could see Alice under Howard's hands. So white and small, her eyes wide open, as if pleading for help to breathe.

There's sand in her lovely hair, Katherine thought. It's like black seaweed. Breathe, little darling. Please breathe.

She fastened her lips to Hazel's head and stopped breathing herself.

To her left, David stood, pale as Dracula, his black fringe dripping down his nose. Alan was next to him, wrapped in a towel, teeth chattering, hot tears flowing freely.

Kneeling in the sand – her mother.

Katherine walked forward. 'Mam.'

Violet Sharp's head lifted. She stared at the bundle which was Hazel.

❖

Rain trickled around Howard's shoulders and the wind bit his neck. The crowd waited. He was their entertainment, their magician, but – no thrills today, folks – life was something he couldn't pull out of his sleeve.

Too long.

Pull and pump.

No justice.

Pull and pump.

'She's gone, Sir.'

No God.

A hand on his shoulder. 'Sir, let me . . .' Butterwell bent down and closed the little girl's eyes.

Violet tore her gaze from Katherine and her baby. Slowly, slowly, she reached out to touch Alice, and dusted sand off her angular little shoulder. So cold! The child was lying on Butterwell's coat, her ribbon curled into her tangled hair. Violet took off her own warm cardigan and laid it softly over Alice's body.

Minutes were hours. People did strange things. Not like in films. Not wailing and fainting, but silly, pointless things like whispering, as if hushed voices and offering flasks of tea would make any difference.

A man brought Hazel's pram. The constable hid his flushed face in Hazel's blankets, as he laid her down and pulled up the hood.

Katherine curled into David's chest, although neither knew why. She gripped the fabric of his shirt, in a fist of disbelief.

And, in the rain, although no one ever knew, David wet himself.

Alan turned his back and stood looking at the sea.

Only Violet kissed the little white body, the soft white face and the wet curls. The daisies on her blouse. Her blue lips, willing them to breathe again. Roughly, she pulled Alice into her arms, pulled her wet head into her shoulder.

It was Butterwell who eventually persuaded Violet to let go. He was so tender. He drew his jacket around Alice's flaccid body and picked her up.

Violet found her feet. She turned to where Katherine stood shivering. Katherine, who had run out on them and got herself pregnant. Katherine, who had probably known where Alice was all the time. In collusion with the mad gypsy, with David Linden and the witch Ethel.

Violet licked salt off her mouth. She walked towards her daughter. She reached out – the same hand which had just stroked Alice's cold shoulder.

And she lashed at Katherine's face.

The smack was wet and cold.

Violet looked down at her own fingers. She stumbled away, lurching blindly down the beach, where she vomited into the sand. Rain pelted into her hair as she spat.

People stood helplessly watching Violet walk down to the water. Sea flowing into her shoes, she bellowed at the horizon, 'Get back here! Come and face me. The sea's too kind. I'll kill you with my own hands!'

There was an arm around her waist and a head hard

against hers; Howard was pulling her backwards out of the waves.

'Sylvia's out there too, Violet. It's time to hurt for Sylvia. To pray for her and Alice. Don't waste these moments on Alexandra Hythe.' The policeman was trembling from head to toe.

No eloquent pencil

can draw the depths of anguish nor scrawl the bleak despair which hovers over an obscenely small casket. Each bereft individual is left in tormented loneliness because human nature, for all its refinements, cannot truly share such shattering grief.

If there is a God, can he hear the plea in Violet's head, for her own swift and merciful death? If He is Merciful, why has he loaded so much horror on young Katherine's shaking shoulders? In Perfect Grace, does he look down on the handcuffs at Cuthbert's wrist and forgive the death of Arthur Linden?

Can His Love really comfort the honest confoundment in Hendo's heart as he braves the poignant hymn singing? Can it help Alan, who hangs his head unable to sing at all? Can it soothe the irrational guilt of Tony and Liz, who stand apart from the rest of the party, because they will never forgive themselves for a hundred things they might have done differently?

If there is a God and He is kind, why won't he kiss away

the nauseous ache lodged permanently between David's closed eyes?

And if Man's Law is derived from God's Law, why is it so unforgiving? Why must the stupidly complicit Daphne and kindly, arthritic Tom be locked away? Why must Clara, who once risked her life to save Alice, be questioned over and over again until she almost believes she has done something unforgivably sinful?

Where is the conscience of the reporter, Roger, who is writing notes and taking photographs? He doesn't really need to be at this funeral. He has a new job in Fleet Street.

What heathen, spiritual law gives Binnie the right to stand next to him, holding a toy trolleybus? She only saw the child once.

Should those who stayed away be pardoned? DI Howard, chasing a burglar in Heaton? Mary Linden as she lies, ignorant of all these events, scorching in the sun? Samuel Phillips, devastated and drunk in Sydney? Douglas Hythe, unaware of his daughter's drowning, presently prostituting himself in Rome, for the price of a dinner?

❖

The bodies of Alexandra Hythe and Sylvia Sharp were never recovered. Following Alice's funeral, a memorial service was planned in All Saints' Church to mark Sylvia's passing, but parishioners in the chapel near Halstone House refused Greta that dignity. She was guilty of something 'unchristian', although no one could precisely label the crime.

Tony and Liz, mercifully cleared of all charges, sent Greta's personal things to Venice, where her Nonno and

Uncle Mario prayed silently in the private chapel for the soul of their princess.

❖

Violet locked herself in the flat, as much a prisoner in her own home as Cuthbert was behind bars. Her logic was addled for a while, beyond evidence or argument, all her fevered venom directed at Katherine. The moment of Alice's death had been scorched deeper on her soul by the conviction that her younger daughter was to blame. Entangled with the wicked Greta, prostituting herself to David Linden and the unspeakably traitorous Ethel, Katherine, who so loved Alice, had found the baby and kept her for herself. If only Katherine had brought her home, Alice and Sylvia would still be alive.

How could there be any room left in Violet's heart for Hazel? Howard had told her about the baby's conception, and that disgusted her. She wasn't even convinced of the story, having spent months imagining the rebellious Katherine selling her body in London. Resisting forgiveness with all her heart, Violet buried herself in her own coffin of distrust and heaped the soil of grief over her head.

❖

About a month after the tragedy, Violet had a visitor. Butterwell.

'Where's Howard?' Violet snarled. 'Couldn't face me? Coward.'

'Mrs Sharp, this isn't really my job, but I've volunteered to come and talk to you.'

'Talk, then.'

'About Katherine.'

Violet lowered her eyes and pursed her lips.

'She's still only seventeen. And she's in trouble.'

'Trouble? I showed Howard the letter. It clearly states that she intended to bring Alice back.'

'Nevertheless. Both Katherine and Clara Blake came before the Magistrates last week, and they have taken a very dim view of it all . . .'

'A dim view.'

'Because . . . of the deaths. Katherine will have to answer for her part in it. Not because of what she did, but because of the dreadful outcome.'

'Sin is as the sinner does.'

'Mrs Sharp, the Courts can only judge these events on the evidence and reports given to them. The case is very complex. The main culprit, Ethel Linden, is dead. Daphne and Tom Charlton have been arrested. When Alexandra Hythe took Alice from them, she began a whole new crime. Katherine may be deemed to be equally culpable, or she may be considered to be an accessory, especially as she's only seventeen. But in a way, it doesn't matter, because accessories are considered just as guilty as principal criminals.'

'What'll happen to her?'

'Depends how her Mitigating Circumstances are considered. There's a lot in her favour. She was accustomed to looking after Alice alone, taking responsibility for her. And she had written several letters saying that she would bring her home.'

'So why won't she get off?'

'Because Alice died. And her sister. As a result of the delay.'

'So she might join her father, in the nick?'

'Borstal.'

She hung her head. Butterwell noticed pink scalp between permed curls.

'Violet. Your daughter needs you. Not just for her defence, but . . .' he drew a careful breath, '. . . to look after Hazel.'

'No.'

❖

Violet visited Cuthbert. He was thin and waxen, and his hair had turned a queer shade of yellow. They sat looking at each other.

How could she tell him how much she needed him? Yet Violet's need was for love, not for Cuthbert himself. He had nothing left to offer. His personality was fading with his hair.

And how could Cuthbert tell his wife that, as he lay on his bunk at night, his enfeebled soul kept drifting away from his body, passing over a murky horizon towards a pair of huge, burning gates? How could he describe the golden flames which scorched his face, his chest, his toes, his penis? He wanted to scream and scream and scream. So he kept quiet.

❖

Clara stood in the dock, thinking – I am an Accessory. A handbag. Greta's bloody handbag. But she's dead, and I'm alive. For that I should be grateful.

When they said 'Guilty' she just nodded.

Of course I'm guilty.

The judge took a long time to speak. 'Mrs Blake. You came to this Court with a commendable record of bravery. If this incident had ended happily, your crime would be less serious. But, sadly, the affair ended as badly as it possibly could. Two women and a child died. I have taken into consideration all the mitigating facts, but, quite simply, failure to report a crime permits that crime. Your punishment must reflect the dreadful gravity of the situation. I therefore sentence you . . .'

Prison. The irony was that Katherine had only been given three months in Borstal. No one had been able to speak for Clara, because they were all either accused themselves, or dead.

She left the court with her head high. Nobody would visit her. Nobody would care what happened to her, even when she was released.

– I will bear injustice with a courageous heart.

– Katherine is a child herself and she needs to look after Hazel.

– I am childless, not needed.

– I will never be allowed near children again.

– I am not a nanny. I am a handbag.

David Linden was cleared of any involvement in Alice's abduction. Howard believed that he knew nothing of his grandmother's crime and there was no evidence to prove otherwise. Daphne and Tom explained that Ethel had always insisted they keep Alice away from the house when David was visiting. Tom swore that Ethel had maintained she would eventually tell David, but never did.

Alone, confounded, David moved quietly around the Gosforth house, steeped in morbidity. At the door, Hendo and Alan were thanked and dispatched. For hours on end, David lay on his bed with a cold compress on his forehead and a hot water bottle in his neck. When the undiagnosed migraine subsided, he blew into his saxophone and drank brandy. One drunken night he lay on the cold black and white tiles of the hall, imagining the final thud of his father's fall, trying vainly to make contact with at least one of the dead.

The Salvation Army came to Twin Elms to remove Ethel's clothes and Ernest Wood helped David board up the old house. In the garden, David pushed the empty swing, then left it to hang limply in the evening shadows.

In late September he had to face his first days in King's College. He tried to cope. He sat through lectures trying to soak up knowledge. He even began to hack at his first cadaver. Like a war veteran, he tried to numb his mind.

The Marlettis searched for Douglas. Notices in *The Times*, photos passed between brothers of brothers, across Italy, Spain and France. A private investigator picked up a trail which was uncomfortably warm with tight-trousered young men. When, in October, they finally found Alexandra's father, they witnessed a crumbling man completely disintegrate. He drank until he almost drowned.

When he dried out, they advised him to return to England where, in theory, he was now free from suspicion.

They tidied the musician up and packed him off on an overnighter to Paris. On 2 November, after a tempestuous sea crossing, during which he drank half a bottle of Calvados, Douglas landed in Dover, dead drunk. His legs kept buckling. No hotelier would have him and he passed out in an alley.

When he awoke, he thought about Martin and the wrecked piano in Halstone House, and he knew he couldn't go back.

❖

The papers had milked the tragedy until it bled, especially Alexandra Hythe's dramatic double-life story. Much of it was sheer fabrication and yet the truth would have made good enough reading. Old Binnie, incensed, had her say through Roger, but he was ambitious and disloyal. He wrote about her 'sight' with his tongue in his cheek, and readers gobbled up the columns, sardonically fascinated.

❖

In bin after bin, Dick foraged for soggy newspapers, gluttonous for accounts of his wife's drowning. Greta dead! He was her next of kin! Entitled to her money, wasn't he? Why was he sleeping rough, when he should be living in a bloody mansion, like Halstone House?

Bloody Greta had cheated him again. Diddled him out of that ransom money, and then gone and killed the poor little kid.

Sitting on a kerb in a back street of Manchester, he dragged on a gutter-trodden tab-end, then hockled and spat. Unfortunately he'd sliced away any hope of making a legal claim when he knifed the two policemen.

He needed money. The bike had conked out. A few

hundred quid would buy him a hiding hole in a showman's caravan to get him across the channel to France.

Suddenly he sniggered. What about the other one? Greta's legal kid? The ALIVE one!

Dick Korda licked his gold tooth. He stood up.

'Daddy's coming.'

The Great North Road.

Mile after weary mile. Thundering lorries splashing mud over a stolen coat. Bleeding blisters, legs as heavy as tree trunks. The filth of the road in skin creases and under toenails. Body itching and scabbing. Genitals and armpits stinking.

Hunger is anger. Hate is an agony of stiff joints. Human is animal.

No talking. Just nightmares behind hedges and wet leaves to wipe a backside.

A tramp must tramp.

❖

The A1 passed through a mining village called Chilton Buildings, where a queue had formed outside a steamy chip shop. Most of the customers turned their heads as the tramp limped by, but one man, who had been in the Normandy trenches, said, 'Wait.'

The tramp weaved slowly across the road and sat waiting on a lawn beside St Aidan's Church. The kind miner brought a bundle of chips, wrapped in newspaper, and a bottle of pop.

Later that night, in a sparse copse to the east of the steady stream of headlights, the diarrhoea began.

❖

In a grim, formal office, Hazel was handed back to Katherine. The baby had put on weight with her foster parents, and she cried furiously under Kath's shower of kisses.

The young mother emerged from the office feeling slightly dazed. She had nowhere to go.

After Katherine's three dreadful months in Borstal, her mother had not softened. Christmas was only days away, and yet Violet was still rejecting both her remaining living daughter and granddaughter. Katherine hugged her own little red-topped baby, weeping with relief. She would never comprehend how mother-love could be switched off, just like that.

Placing Hazel back in the pram, she began to walk, but a dark-suited man blocked her way.

'Katherine Sharp?'

'If you're a reporter, bugger off.' She tried to push around him.

'These letters are for you.'

'What?'

'I am commissioned to hand you these envelopes, that is all. Please take them. Goodbye.'

The envelopes were in Katherine's hand before she knew it. The man jumped into a waiting taxi and was gone.

❖

In Durham, hailstones like daggers of ice struck Dick Korda's bearded face. He pulled two flea-infested coats around him and crept into a park, where he had another black shit in another puddle, then wiped his backside with laurel leaves.

❖

'What's wrong now, Linden?'

'Sorry, Mr Trent. Headache – feeling – nauseous.'

'Don't faint on us, lad.'

It wasn't the drained female cadaver making the blood pound in David's head. Nor the cold scalpel. It was simply death.

The irreversibility of Death. He fled from the truth of it, staggering out of the tilting room, down the endless corridor and into the toilet. Pain crashed in the back of his left eye and he slumped to the floor, a heap of quaking misery. He knew he had a brain tumour. He pictured his own body on the cold slab and the scalpel poised above his skull. Should he leave his body to science, or should he take it with him into oblivion?

He took a taxi home and fell into bed to endure six hours of deranged sheet-clawing, without even the energy to compose his will. And then, miraculously, the pain just drifted away. He slept. Washed out, but alive, he awoke feeling as normal and healthy as a newborn lamb.

Trent asked him what the problem was.

'I think I have a brain tumour.'

'Why do you want to be a doctor? Don't give me trite answers like, "I want to help people". Why do you, David Linden, want to practise medicine?'

'It's been my ambition since I was about ten.'

'Ambition or vocation? What, or who, planted that seed of aspiration?'

David stared at Trent's pyramid fingers, and let the all-powerful shadows of the dead come to stand around him. Dad. Gran. Alice. Then he saw his greedy, self-centred mother, and oddly, instead of being angry, he yearned for her. He wanted to tell her things, to share his losses, to hold her hand. He wanted her to witness him trying so hard.

But she wasn't there.

'I don't think I want to be a doctor at all. Sir.'

'Thank God for that. You'd have been bloody useless. Too soft. Arty type. Had a few through my hands, all romance and heroism, but in this job passions must be controlled. Nothing wrong with your brain, Linden, but Medicine takes a lot more than intelligence. So, what do you really fancy doing with your life, now that you're old enough to decide for yourself?'

David felt a great weight was lifting from his chest.

'Sounds a bit sissy, but – I don't suppose I could earn a living playing my sax?'

'Probably not, Linden. Probably not.'

That evening David packed away all his textbooks. The following morning he visited his grandmother's solicitor, then went to the bank, after which he drove into Newcastle and bought himself a Christmas present. A guitar.

❖

Janice Kirkstone passed DI Howard some sheets of heavily typed paper.

'They want to take her away from me.'

He perused the legal document. 'High falut'n jargon. What does all this drivel boil down to, Mrs Kirkstone?'

'That woman's family want my Jan.'

'The Macaronis?'

'And that bastard, her father.'

Howard winced, as if an arrow had thudded into his shoulders. 'They can't take Jan out of the country, surely.'

'My solicitor says they can – if Hythe gets custody.'

'Not my territory now.' Howard handed the paper back. 'It's down to the Courts.'

'You can't do anything?'

'Sorry, pet.'

Howard watched Janice go, her rounded shoulders tense with despair. He shivered.

❖

Cream envelope. Note paper with a gold, embossed crest. Posh!

Dear Miss Katherine Sharp.
Warm regards from my Father and me. I am
Alexandra's Uncle. My poor niece talked of you many
times with much affection. Permit us to convey much
sadness to your family. It is difficult for us to
understand such confusion about the child Alice who
has been lost to all. My father grieves. You grieve also.
We share this.

Please also permit us to express distress at the
dreadful loss of your sister, Sylvia. Your parents must be
inconsolable, and I am sure you suffer greatly. Only

now do we begin to understand the complex way our families are linked. My father and I have discussed your situation. We consider that the English law has treated you, also Clara Blake, disgracefully. We feel, on Alexandra's behalf, a responsibility of honour towards you.

Pardon me for mentioning a delicate matter. We understand that you, like Alexandra, suffered from the evil of her husband. All things we blame on him. Now you have a baby who is either the cousin or the half-sister of Alice. Alexandra had great plans for the future, that they should grow together, and we were made knowledgeable of her intention to give you a secure home and income. My father, therefore, desires to honour Alexandra's memory by providing for you and for your baby. She would have wished it.

We truly hope that this proposition does not give offence. Please write your feelings back.

Mario Marletti

Katherine opened the second envelope. A postal order for ten pounds fluttered out. She grabbed it up and unfolded the second letter.

Dear Kath,

Come to us. We love you and Hazel.

Nothing was your fault. We all made mistakes and the only way to put right, is to do right. Greta's Uncle Mario has been here. He's had a detective finding out everything that's been going on, so we know that your

Mam wouldn't look after Hazel. Don't be cross at her.
She might be too sad to love anyone for a bit.

Anyway, you'd better come back to cheer Tony up.
He keeps shouting at that poor young lad in the
kitchen. Mind you, Lorenzo's got pretty good at
shouting back. I can't stand the racket.

Come home, pet.

Love from Liz

❖

'Aw, man, it's brilliant. One big boozo.' Hendo was enjoying university, truly exhilarated by the first step on his precisely measured ladder. 'Which little Geordie lass will we catch under the mistletoe the neet?'

'You must learn to speak properly.' Alan despaired of his mate's determination to cling to his roots.

'A rinse me mooth oot with Tyne watter every morn'n.'

'You gargle with it.'

'Aye. We could bottle it and sell it to them posh bastards doon London. The Waters of Tyne.' He began to sing, 'I cannot get to my love . . .'

'Belt up, for Christ's sake!'

'Aye. Fer Christ. Cos it's Christmas.'

For the thousandth time Hendo admired the arched front porch of David's home, but his more tutored eye actually began to fault the brickwork and mismatch of styles.

'What's that bleed'n caterwaul'n?'

David opened the door casually, guitar swinging across his shoulder.

'Come on in. Listen, I can play a G chord and an A chord. Love me tender, love me true . . .'

Hendo stuck his fingers in his ears. 'Howay, son. What you need's a pint.'

After many pints the lads sang everything from rugby songs to the school anthem. David loudest of all. And when the singing stopped he was noticeably quiet. He was composing.

Goodbye lullaby . . . the stars guide your way . . .

On the stairway to . . .

To where Alice? To where, my little lass?

❖

Dick had a stroke of luck in Chester-le-Street. He lifted a wallet with over a hundred quid in it. Enough to buy a boatload of booze and maybe some liver salts. His belly was bothering him. Stupid, nagging pain. He deserved a better life than this.

The newspaper said that some big lawyer was helping the Marlettis to claim that kid in Newcastle. His own daughter for Christ's sake! A father had rights!

When he looked in the mirror in the telephone box he lifted the long hair off his face and saw that the white of his one eye had taken on a yellowish tinge.

A lucky streak is often one of life's nastier little deceits. The cancer was growing quickly.

Mario Marletti

placed a hand on Katherine's shoulder. She sensed his kindness, yet the hand was controlling, strong, and it flashed through her mind that he might be capable of great ruthlessness.

A fire crackled in the grate and a new clippy rug covered the flags. It felt familiar and safe in Hisper Cottage. Outside, the sea, the very dreadful sea, was deceitfully calm.

Her weeping at Alice's funeral, and at Sylvia's memorial service, had been acute, a reaction to shock and disbelief. Today, however, in this shared home, so close to them all, Katherine finally allowed the deeper truth its horrible voice. She stared out of the window at the vast blue and thought about two cold bodies, her sister and her friend. She tried to imagine what it would be like, to lose consciousness, to die and then slowly disintegrate . . .

A backwash of horror surged from the base of her belly. It ripped up her core and gripped her chest. She began to gasp, and only when tears began to fall did she manage to inhale.

Mario turned her face away from the sea and hugged her

so tightly that she knew the enormity of his grief too. After a while he said, 'Quiet now. You did your best. Your very best.'

Later, as Hazel slept in her old cot, they talked seriously.

'To us,' said Mario, 'family is everything. I must explain you that my father has made claim with the English Courts, on Alexandra's legal child, Jan. This name, I find it difficult, so short, so – not pretty.'

'She was called after her foster mother. Your family wants to take her away? To Italy? But you don't even know if she is Greta . . . sorry, Alexandra's real daughter.'

'This is why I must speak with you. This is why you are important. Perhaps she is my father's great-granddaughter – or perhaps she is your niece. Either way, she is family to your own baby, Hazel.'

'Jan is happy with her foster mam.'

'Her husband is in prison . . .'

'Like my father.'

'. . . and my informations say this woman leaves the child with an old lady, night and day, while she makes loving with a new man. Will this man be good to Jan? How can we take this risk?'

'The old woman. Binnie. She was Greta's friend.'

'A gypsy? I do not trust her reasons.'

'Will you get custody?'

'Perhaps. We hire expensive lawyers. The child will have a good life, who can argue? But maybe the English Law will use this mix-up of the babies to keep her from us.'

'In which case they would be making an assumption that she's Sylvia's baby. And she should go to Mam.'

'Except . . .'

'That Dad's in nick, Mam's been suspected of all sorts and I've got a record.'

'Precisely. But your mother has agreed to help us.'

'What? You talked to my mam?' Katherine vision blurred with sudden pain. 'She's agreed to seek custody of Jan, yet she ignores my baby? And me? Oh!'

'This hurts very bad?'

'Hurt begets hurt.'

'She says that when she held Jan, the child . . .' Mario cheated some comforting words, '. . . reminded her of you.'

'Bollocks.' Katherine tried to calm her furious breathing. 'So how's Mam supposed to help you?'

'Ah, Katerina. We are but animals. We either chase the prey, or trap it. My father, he teaches me to get what I desire, not by bullying, not by running fastest, but by blocking the other man's escapes.'

'Explain.'

'Your mother, she applies for custody of Jan. The Courts not like it, but they must give good reasons to say no. What reasons can they have? The home of the foster mother is exactly the same as your own. Both fathers committed of murder.'

'Manslaughter. It was an accident.'

'The Court does not know what to do, this hand, that hand, and yet they must do something. Show fairness. If they cannot give her to either one, where will she go? In orphanage? Why? When her legal mother is Alexandra? We are her family. And . . .'

'You're rich.'

Mario tipped his head.

'What about Greta's father?'

'A homosexual?' The distaste on Mario's face was plain. 'And fugitive? Who can ask him, if he cannot be found? Besides, when he was in Italy, my father ensured he signed various documents.'

'And David? He might have rights.'

'I will speak with him Saturday.'

'Oh.' Katherine's eyes filled yet again.

'You love him?'

'Pointless. Alice died because I brought her here. David will never, never forgive me. I'll never forgive myself.'

Mario picked up the soldier's photograph. 'What I must ask is not for David – is for yourself.'

'Me?'

'My father is troubled. He grows old and has, er, things . . .' Mario shrugged, '. . . to arrange with God.'

'Don't we all.'

'When my sister Sophia married in England, he is angry. Worse angry at her dying. Worst anger is at himself, for not realizing that her daughter must nurse her alone. He failed them both. When Sophia passed, he should have brought Alexandra home to Italy. Because he did not, her life became terrible. How can he be at peace?'

'He can't control everything.'

Mario smiled ruefully. 'He tries.'

'My dad loved Alice more than either Sylvia or me. Is that what your dad wants? A new princess?'

'Is this so wrong? To seek a chance to do better? Yes, he desires to know Alexandra's child. But, I worry about this – what if Jan is not a Marletti? This would be another sin. She will grow up, ask questions, and it will be my job to answer. What shall I say?'

'Truth?'

'Even for a child of rape?'

Katherine hung her head.

'Do not feel shame, Katherine. You have none. Your daughter has none. Now, from you, we ask a privilege. You are the link, the bridge, for this child. You are Sylvia's sister and Alexandra's friend. We beg that you help us in our care for her.'

'Me?'

'So that we are honourable. We give her both. Her life in Italy, for Alexandra, and for Sophia, but also, because her true mother might be Sylvia, we give her . . . you.'

'But I'm only seventeen. You want me to look after another baby? Sylvia's baby?'

'You did it before.'

❖

It was close again. The badness. Binnie could feel it in her bent back, like a dagger.

She'd crocheted Jan a little cardigan. It was made up from odd balls of wool, all different colours, crocheted into flower shapes. Binnie hoped this cardigan was pretty. She could not be sure because her cataracts blurred everything. Sometimes she felt sorry for herself, but lately the bad feeling had breathed down her neck until she hardly dared sleep. The only moments of peace she knew were while she was looking after little Jan. It was a blessing that the mother was always either working or off on a date. Binnie didn't care. The only thing that mattered was watching over the child. Keeping the evil away.

It was damp and slippery underfoot. She walked slowly. Old bones don't mend, she told herself. Must take care.

❖

Janice wondered who would finally come and take little Jan away. Wrung out with helplessness, she waited, defensive as a clawless cat. Her whole body felt ill with dismay. She found herself watching the only daughter she would ever have, filling corners of her memory with Jan's serious little face.

Jan was on the carpet, playing with her doll – but not nicely. Brow pinched with concentration, she was pushing a red crayon hard against the plastic face. There was something macabre about the picture. Caught out, the child met Janice's eye with the confidence of a spoilt child who knows she will not be punished.

Wearily, Janice sat down on the rocking chair and pulled Jan into her lap. 'What are you doing to dolly?'

The little girl smiled, a rare sunbeam across a surly face. 'She wants rosy cheeks.'

'She'll blush for ever, poor thing. Come on, it's time for bed.'

'Tell me a story!'

Janice paused. The most important gift she could give Jan now was as painless a transition as possible. Whatever her own suffering, she must prepare the little love wisely and kindly.

'Once upon a time . . .' she pressed her lips to the child's dark crown, '. . . a big bird, with very long legs and huge wings, called Mr Stork, was delivering a baby girl to a new mammy. When he got to the hospital there were two mammies waiting; he couldn't decide which one to give the baby to. Now, this was a very special baby, and Mr Stork didn't really want to leave the baby with either of them. So he chased the women away with his big snappy beak.'

'What was the baby called?'

'Mr Stork didn't give her a name. That was one problem.'

'What happened next?'

'God told Mr Stork to find a nicer mammy. So the big bird picked up the baby in his beak and flew her here . . .'

'Here?'

'To me. To be my baby.'

Little Jan stared. A fleeting maturity flashed across her face, then she dipped her head and pressed her brow against her mammy's breastbone.

Tears gathered in Janice's nose, but she carried on.

'For a while everyone lived happy ever after. But unfortunately Daddy Matthew had to go away for a long time. And then God took both of the first mammies to Heaven.'

A little voice muffled in her breasts said, 'Heaven's nice. It's got a blue castle. I'm glad they went to Heaven.'

'But the family of one of those mammies, a rich family who live far away in a sunny land, in a city where roads are rivers – they wanted the little girl to live with them.'

'Why?'

'To love her. To make her happy.'

'With lots of toys?'

'And pretty dresses.'

'So her nice mammy took her there.'

'No. Her mammy couldn't do that. The little princess had to be very brave and go on her own adventure.'

For a while little Jan said nothing. Janice rocked her and hoped she was falling asleep. But suddenly, out of the painful silence, Jan began to wail.

It was that evening when the tiny knitted teddy with the beady eyes was, at last, brought out to play.

❖

The Tyne Bridge soared overhead, giant, cold, impossible. The tramp slumped against a girder. Exhaustion was a devil's grip. Limbs were lead, chest was green phlegm, anus was a writhe of itching worms.

The Great North Road had brought the tramp all the way to Newcastle. Far enough.

❖

Mario was staying in Scarborough's Grand Hotel. He took the funicular down to the bay and hurried along to the Ristorante, with his fur collar high around his neck.

Katherine was waiting. Tony was feeding toast fingers to Hazel who was sitting up proudly in her new pushchair. Lorenzo brought them coffee. It was refreshingly Italian.

'You happy here, Lorenzo?'

The lad rolled his eyes towards Tony's back. 'OK.'

Katherine stood up, back straight, defiant. 'I'm coming with you. To Newcastle. To talk to David and Mam.' She dragged a large bag out from under the table and gripped the handle of Hazel's pushchair in readiness.

Mario blanched. The thought of travelling on the train

with a squawking baby and extra luggage felt like two burdens too many. He nudged Tony into the kitchen and hissed urgently, 'I do not carry babies and bags! My back . . .'

Tony smiled at his old friend. 'Take Lorenzo. Pay him fair. He needs money for Christmas presents.'

❖

The pushchair was awkward, especially changing trains at York, but Lorenzo managed it, plus the bags, while Katherine carried Hazel.

They travelled first class from York to Newcastle. Mario sat on the other side of the carriage and watched the two beautiful young people trying to make conversation. He noticed how large Katherine's breasts were, how her brown, curly hair shone. By contrast the baby's hair was so shockingly orange. Hazel had kicked off a sock, and Lorenzo was struggling to get it back on. The lad's hands were fine, like a woman's, his fingers dark against the child's fair skin.

Sensing he was being watched, Lorenzo looked up. He met Mario's gaze with wry maturity. And in that glance, they both remembered the night he had wheeled Alexandra home in a cart.

❖

They went to see David first. At the front door Katherine began to giggle, because she could hear him upstairs, singing his heart out. Lorenzo screwed up his face. Mario hammered on the door again, but David was so lost in his clumsy chord bashing that he didn't hear. He had progressed to Lonnie

Donegan and was nasally twanging 'Cumberland Gap' as if his life depended on it. Maybe it did.

Young Lorenzo waited for a significant Gap in the Cumberland and began to sing himself, the boisterous 'Funi, Funi, Funicular . . .' until Hazel began to join in the caterwauling.

David eventually answered the door, scowling. Clearly, he didn't like Katherine being on his doorstep. He didn't like her laughing. He didn't like the lad with her. Nor did he feel inclined to take Mario's extended hand.

While the powerful Italian was talking, Katherine tested her feelings for David. His hair was really long now, and the black lick-lock flopped greasily over one eye. Yes, he was still handsome, but the new Elvis sideburns somehow quarrelled with his arched nose, and the stitching at the corner of his mouth made him look cruel. Sadly, his lovely eyes had drooped into bruised, sleepless creases.

He had no time for Hazel. That hurt. For such an important part of their young lives they had shared a mutual love for a child – but the link had died with Alice. Their griefs had polarized them, and Hazel was nothing to David. Nor, it would seem, was Jan. As Mario explained his plans, Katherine watched David float away into his own romantic place. Perhaps he had taken a leaf out of his mother's book, losing himself – in himself.

Yes, he agreed to sign papers. No, he did not care either way. No, he did not want to stay in touch with the child. No, he did not mind if she was taken out of the country.

'David!' Katherine was getting angry. 'She might be your daughter. And I'll be looking after her.'

'So?'

Katherine was not destined to confront her mother that day. She had to confront something much worse.

Mario had gone to a solicitor in Newcastle. In Gosforth High Street, Lorenzo kept moaning about the cold, slapping his body as if he were in Siberia.

For Katherine the town cloyed with cruel nostalgia. Part fascinated, part desperate to flee, she felt memories stamping behind her and anxiety tripping in front of Hazel's pushchair.

I'm only seventeen, she thought. I should still be at the grammar school. I'm too young to look after another baby. Even with all the money in the world.

'Loz,' she asked her young companion, 'should we go and see her? Jan? I know where she lives. We can just . . . hang around, and see if she's playing outside.'

'Why?' Lorenzo would always ask direct, monosyllabic questions.

'Because I want to.'

'OK. Why?'

'I'm not ready for Mam, yet.'

'OK. Why?'

'Don't know. Look, we'll keep a low profile.'

'OK. What is it? A low . . . pile?'

'We hide. Like spies.'

'OK.'

Half an hour later they stood outside the flat where Arthur Linden met his premature end. Where an electric fire glowed. Where Binnie rocked on Janice's chair, listening to the radio, and where a little girl with long black hair sat at the table with a pot of water and a magic painting book.

Katherine and Lorenzo waited outside for a while, but none of the kids flitting in and out matched Jan's description. Hazel was beginning to complain. Her nappy needed changing.

'Damn. I'll have to go to Mam now.'

'OK.'

'She can't be cruel enough to deny her grandchild a nappy change. Can she?'

As they passed a block of garages a filthy apparition suddenly stepped out in front of them. A tramp. A stinking, vagrant with damp crawling up his ankle-long overcoat. His hair was black as ink and his lone eye held a yellowish tinge.

Despite his beard, Katherine knew him at once.

❖

Gabble, gabble, gabble. Hadn't he had enough of the Sharp women to last him a flaming lifetime? Howard was irritated by Katherine's panicky jabbering. She was panting, like a puppy after a run, and he found it somehow revolting.

Howard did not want to think about Dick Korda. Or bloody Alexandra, or Sylvia, or Alice.

'All right,' he sighed. 'I'll send someone down to have a look. But Newcastle is full of tramps. It was probably just another meths-swilling waste of humanity.'

'You don't think I'd recognize the man who raped me?'

Lorenzo began shouting in Italian. He had no idea what was happening, but he knew Katherine was frightened and needed support.

Howard was firm. 'I said it would be looked into. And don't you go pestering poor Mrs Kirkstone!'

'It's your job to protect her. And Jan. Especially Jan.'

The policeman shook his head dismissively. Kath was furious. 'Are we boring you, Inspector?' Her voice began to rise. 'Now that Greta's no longer part of the chase, you seem to have lost interest.' There was worse to get off her chest. 'Don't you feel any kind of responsibility after that shambles in Scarborough?'

Howard's face turned puce. 'Don't you feel any responsibility, Katherine Sharp? Get out of my office! Now!'

'Is there a Ladies? I need somewhere to change Hazel's nappy. You've met my daughter. She's Dick Korda's daughter, too. But you know that. I suppose one day he might come looking for her. I hope she's better protected than Jan and "poor" Mrs Kirkstone.'

Outside the police station Katherine's hand shook as she bundled Hazel into the pushchair and grabbed the handles.

'We've got to get away, Lorenzo,' she panted, starting to run. 'I've got to get Hazel away – out of Newcastle.'

She shook on the bus. She shook as they stood at the hotel, leaving a message for Mario. She shook on the train as it trundled over the High Level Bridge. She stared at the black waters of Tyne and relived the nightmare in a series of blinding flashes.

Lorenzo played innocently with Hazel, but when the little soul dozed in his lap he made the mistake of kissing her red head. Katherine's whole body contracted in revulsion. Furiously, she dragged her baby away from him.

Binnie got home at around ten-thirty. She thanked Janice's boyfriend for the lift, then hobbled into her yard. Key in the lock. Light switch behind the door. Knees aching as she pulled herself into the dim hallway.

Someone coughed behind her. Binnie jumped as if her muscles were young again.

A hoarse voice from the darkness. 'Hello, Binnie.'

Death was nearer than she'd even imagined! The old woman's legs gave way and she fell against the doorframe. The tramp swayed drunkenly, murmuring, 'Binnie, it's me. It's me.'

'Greta?'

Dick Korda spotted the uniforms and slunk back into the gutter for five days.

Howard concluded that Katherine had been a victim of her own imagination. He resolved to visit Janice Kirkstone – sometime. In all other parts of his work he was as sharp as ever; in fact his tongue had become considerably sharper. His Chief recognized a new severity in Howard's methods and approved. But the core of the man had been damaged by Alexandra Hythe.

He suppressed his spiritual intuition, refusing to think about anything he preferred not to. Only in his nightmares did he see again a pair of ice-blue eyes floating under the water.

Many years in the future, Greta would watch *Dallas* and laugh wryly when Bobby reappeared in the shower. She would say to herself, I did that. I was dead, but God renewed my contract.

That laughter was so far distant that she could never have imagined it. As she soaked in Binnie's bath, the only reality was pain and the smell of Dettol. The first sleep, on Binnie's sofa, was cruel. Too brief. Too comfortable. Too good to trust.

Staring at the fire, Greta began to stammer through her own story. She tried to describe being tossed around by the icy sea. Her physical memory could not reconjure the cold, but her nerves, having come so close to death, would not let go of it. Even as she relived those few minutes, she struggled with surges of panic, because now she recognized that death was still waiting for her, as surely as it had sucked away Sylvia.

Binnie held Greta's hand. The old lady concentrated, and tried to feel it, allowing her imagination to sink into grey salt water. Strength ebbing . . .

❖

Greta offered up her own life in exchange for Alice's. Water closed over her head and she floated down, gagging on salt. But even as she tried to surrender, her legs refused to stop kicking. Thrashing involuntarily, she kept surfacing, and she saw Katherine bring Alice's dear little face up into the rain.

Sinking back down, choking, she felt a hand under her head. She was being dragged up. Eyes stinging, she sensed air on her face. She gasped and coughed, as those merciful hands heaved and pushed her in a different direction. Instinctively her arms began to work, keeping her head above the waves. The kind hands let go. The angel was swimming away. A boy with fair hair. Alan.

Disoriented, she turned on her back, lifting and dropping with the waves. But the brutal cold was biting through each layer of live tissue, killing it, penetrating her very core, until it seemed to be clutching her heart.

God does not barter. But perhaps, in that passage through her final watery gate, the child Alice pleaded for Greta.

The tide decided, sweeping her further around the point. Her shoulders felt scraping stone. Green sea slime slid under her face. She was being dragged backwards and forwards between rocks. In and out. Give and take. Death and life.

Lying in seaweed, the agonizing thaw began.

Above were cliffs, running with mud. No caves to shelter in.

'Help!'

No one heard.

Staggering over stones, she came to a place where a path had been trodden up the cliff. She fell to her knees and crawled through the rain, slipping and gripping and vomiting salt. Even when she reached the top, she stayed on her hands and knees, creeping like an injured animal towards an exposed cornfield, where the cereal was whipping in the lashing downpour.

Greta rolled into the prickling stalks, panting. She turned on to her back, opened her mouth to the rain, trying to swill the sea away. Only the shivering kept her from passing out.

As she willed herself to keep crawling through the rasping

corn, the rain eased to drizzle. Stumbling to her feet, she found a track, and some sodden pasture where grey shapes were nuzzling the ground. They were the beach donkeys, grazing, off duty. Greta fell against a mare. The placid beast stood quietly panting hot breath down her back, its coat wet but warm.

Tucked into a lee, Greta found the donkeys' shed. Inside, she stripped off, rubbed herself down with filthy straw and slept, shivering.

Just before dawn, she dressed in her wet clothes and slipped out. The rain had stopped, but the shivering hadn't. With her arms clutched around her body, she walked towards some houses.

From a porch, Greta managed to steal a pair of wellingtons and a man's mac. The bloke was a smoker. His matches would later save her life. She smoked the first fag, but would eventually eat the rest, because stealing food would prove almost impossible.

Trousers from a washing line, and towels. A flat cap lifted from a peg in an empty chapel. As her strong legs kept walking, the shivering was replaced by sweating. Her stomach was turning inside out with hunger. On lonely tracks through Cloughton Woods, she sucked at puddles to satisfy the gnaw.

That night she lit a small fire and slept for a few hours. When she woke, her whole body ached with fever, but she staggered up into the moors, where dawn warmed the heather, releasing a scent of honey. If she could have found a bees' nest, she would have eaten the bees.

In hot sun, she lay trembling against a stony crag, wrapped in layers of towel and coat. There, barely conscious, she was worried by a sheepdog. The farmer gave her a cheese sandwich. He didn't report her. He didn't even talk, other than to ask her to move on. Greta had become a tramp.

Hunched under the mac, with the flat cap pulled over her brow, she tramped into Whitby, where she drank from taps in public toilets and sat, like a bald beggar, at the bottom of the 'Hundred and Ninety-nine Steps'.

But she couldn't stand the sight of the sea. In a town that smelled of fried fish, she foraged in dustbins, then walked on. Cars flew past her on the high open road to Middlesbrough. People saw an old tramp in wellingtons, not a famished woman.

❖

'But that was months ago,' said Binnie. 'How have you survived?'

'Lurching from kindness to kindness. To my dying day, I will never forget chips in Chilton.'

'Why didn't you ring your family? Reverse the charges?'

'I saw Sylvia drown. I didn't deserve to be rescued, yet again.'

'Why to Newcastle?'

'Katherine will have brought Alice back to her family. I have to stay close.'

'Oh, Greta. Oh, Greta!'

❖

If someone had physically flogged Greta, she might have coped better. No conscience could beat the shame out of her as she wallowed in the exhaustion of grief. Nothing was worth doing. No words worth speaking.

Binnie, angry in her own loyal way, maintained that she had been spared for a reason. For Jan.

Wearily, Greta began to indulge and explore a new darkness of penance. When Binnie was babysitting for Jan, Greta hung around outside, waiting for the little girl to dash out of the flats, on her way to the park. She watched her flying backwards and forwards on a swing, thrusting her red shoes out, her dark hair streaming behind in the wind. But Greta had learned her lesson. She never allowed herself to speak to the child who was legally hers. She just sat watching her with a masochistic ache of impossibility.

And when it rained, and Binnie had to keep the child in, Greta took off her cap and sat alone on the wall.

❖

In Durham Jail, Matthew accused Janice of flesh-mongering, of 'selling' little Jan. He didn't understand that the case was already lost.

The journey home was tedious. By the time Janice trudged up the flat stairs she felt sick with guilt and despair. The door was open. She was furious. What was the silly old woman thinking about?

'Binnie!' she called. 'Jan-Jan!'

The door slammed behind her.

She smelt him first. Turning sharply, she gasped. The tiny hall was overwhelmed with malevolence.

❖

Howard stood looking at the flat. God, he was reluctant to start all this again. Of late he had been suffering with a sinking feeling between his ribs, which he refused to accept as premonition, preferring to self-diagnose an ulcer.

So, for the last two days, he had given up smoking. Now he was eating for England.

'Butterwell, nip down the shop and get some chocolate buttons for the kid. And get me a Five Boys to go with it. And some fruit gums. Look sharp.'

A knife point

curved under Janice's jaw, nudging against tender flesh.

The stench from the fingers was foul, and as she dropped her eyes she knew total horror. The knife was already slimy, red; the filthy hand which held it, smeared with globules of blood.

JAN! What had he done with her daughter? Janice began to beg, a pathetic bleat, as her heart banged against her ribcage. Dick's face loomed above hers, scarred, pitted, one empty eye socket folded in yellowing skin, crusty white saliva caked in the corners of his mouth.

Suddenly there was a jarring crash from the sitting room. Dick's nerves jumped and the blade dug deeper as his single eye moved furiously over her shoulder. Using his other arm to crush her into his chest, he dragged Janice roughly down the corridor. There on the floor, in a pool of thick blood, lay Binnie. A wound in her side dribbled steadily, soaking crimson into the folds of her purple wool dress. Her lined old face lay hard against the rug.

Even then Janice could not scream. The whites of her eyes dodged and danced, frantically searching. Jan? My baby?

Pressed tight against his body, she felt his laugh rumble. At the open window a curtain flapped. Under it, rolling gently backwards and forwards on the floor, lay a smashed flower-pot.

Dick manoeuvred Janice towards little Jan's bedroom door.

No! Her brain screamed and she started to kick. The thought of what she might see on the other side of the door was too terrifying. She closed her eyes, scared to look.

The comfortable smell of sleeping child was drowned by the tang of alcohol. Janice allowed her gaze to fall on the bed. The little girl was there, the dark-haired child she had loved from birth, carelessly covered in a satin-trimmed blanket, for all the world asleep, her precious body still whole.

'Pack her stuff.' Dick Korda ordered. He shoved Janice forwards. Her first instinct was to go to the child, but he caught her arm and spun her away.

'PACK!'

Head twisting backwards and forwards between child and monster, Janice stuffed dresses and cardigans into a bag.

'You mustn't do this. She's just a baby.'

From a top drawer she grabbed liberty bodices.

'My kid. I'll take her if I want.'

'But where? Who'll look after her?'

'Belt up!'

'Please, please, I beg you . . .'

Dick punched her face. Janice fell on to the bed. As the pain ebbed and her vision cleared, she put her arms around her little girl's warm body. The innocent child moved slightly in her shaky embrace. She smelled of gin.

'Take me too,' Janice pleaded. 'I'll help you. I'll do everything you say – anything.'

He grabbed the front of her blouse, ripping off buttons. 'Anything?'

He hauled Janice up and pushed her against the door. Slipping the point of the knife into her gaping blouse, he sliced through her cotton bra. With his yellow-coated tongue, he licked her neck.

Frozen in terror, Janice stood stock still, head averted, watching little Jan's breathing. In, out, in, out, went her narrow chest. She thought, I'm not going to scream. I'll keep his attention on me, away from the bairn. This is not the end of the world. I'll think about it when it's over.

So she allowed it to happen. She watched the blood on his hands staining her flesh, while she fought to think straight. As he bit her nipple, she gritted her teeth and started counting. One. Two. Three. Breathe. Four. Five. Six. Breathe. Seven . . . his hips and his hard penis were grinding at her.

'Please don't. Don't,' she whispered, 'Not in front of the bairn.'

❖

Binnie could see the electric fire. It seemed to be on its side. She could see the pattern of the carpet; feel matted tufts against her cheek.

Over her cataracts came another wave of blindness, sparkling with a million incandescent stars. 'On my way to Heaven,' she thought, and it was a good feeling. Better than being awake. 'Have I done it all?' she asked herself, but before she could take stock, the 'awake' feeling surfaced again, blotting out the glory.

No fear. Just the need for the pain to be done with her. Once again she could see the electric fire lying on its side. What was that noise? Grunting. Crying. She must still be alive. Why? A final test? Destiny? To save the child?

Rolling on to her front, she inched towards the window and, clutching at the sill, pulled herself to her knees. Too tired, too tired! She pursed her lips upwards towards the open pane and tried to shout for help. The curtain billowed in her face. She almost gave up, but then, as she feebly pushed the fabric away she saw the line of plant pots. Her gnarled hand reached, grabbed and hurled. There was a crash, far below, as the pot hit the pavement some thirty feet down. Would that be enough? No. She needed something more to draw attention to her plight. The pain in her side flooded back, drowning her in its mighty cascades, and she pressed her bony knuckles towards the gouge. Blood. Warm and sticky. She pulled a glass vase into her wound and smeared it red brown, then hurled it out of the window, hearing it smash. As her heart slowed, her hand touched something soft on the floor. One of Jan's toys. Binnie stained Greta's tiny teddy bear with her own blood, and, with the last of her feeble strength, hurled it towards Heaven.

❖

Dick's moment of ecstasy came and went. Over his groan, he heard something outside. Voices. Shouts. Running footsteps out on the pavement. He rushed back into the sitting room,

648

trousers still hanging around his hips. Furious, he kicked the old woman in the ribs, causing her stab wound to gush, but Binnie knew nothing about it. She was floating in the stars.

Zipping himself, Dick looked out of the window. Below him a gang of women in curlers stood looking up at the flat.

❖

Bloodied teddy in his hand, Howard puffed up the stairs, heart pounding, legs like leaden pistons. Butterwell had gone back to the car to call for assistance, so he was on his own.

But no. He wasn't. On the first floor he was overtaken by a flying, incongruous vision. Bald head on a fluid body. A ghost.

At the top of the stairs the apparition shouted obscenities – in a female voice. As he grabbed the padded shoulder, she turned and looked at him with ice-blue eyes.

❖

A woman screeching his name, 'Dick, you bastard!'

Was Greta's voice real? Or in his head? She was dead, for Christ's sake! Dick twisted and turned like a confused bear.

There was a crash and a sound of splintering wood as the combined weight of Howard and Greta wrenched bolt from wood, plummeting them into the flat. Together they witnessed the appalling mess of blood and the shape of a dear old lady on the floor – but neither flinched.

Instinctively Dick flicked the knife and crouched.

Time froze.

Then out through the bedroom door stumbled a small child, rubbing sleepy eyes, whimpering crossly. Flourishing the knife, Dick made a grab for little Jan, pulled her under his armpit and held the blade across her chest.

'Put her down, Dick.' Serene in her moment of confrontation, Greta sauntered towards her husband. 'Even you wouldn't hurt your own child.'

'Fuck off, witch!'

'Witch?' Greta smiled slowly. 'I suppose I do look pretty gruesome. You're afraid of me, aren't you? After all those years of terrorizing, here you are, hiding behind a little kid. What's happened to the big man? A drunk. A tramp. A murderer. Trapped like a ferret.'

'Holding the ace, bitch.'

Little Jan was kicking and wriggling indignantly in Dick's grasp. When his arm tightened, she wailed like a banshee and bit his hand. But he shifted his hold, bringing her across his chest, shaking the tot like a bundle of sticks. Jan's kicking became frantic and one heel flew backwards between his legs, walloping him in the crotch.

Dick bellowed and dropped her unceremoniously. Holding his genitals with his left hand, his knife slashed through the air in a frenzied effort to defend himself. As little Janice crawled away, he lunged at Greta, who dodged the blade but not quickly enough. It tore the flesh of her upper arm, leaving a bloodied flap of skin. Simultaneously Howard jumped, grabbing Dick's wrist and twisting it. The knife clattered to the floor and Howard kicked it across the carpet.

While the two men wrestled, Greta fell to her knees. Crawling, she followed the weapon. But little Jan had got there first. The innocent child stood huddled in a corner, holding the bloody handle in her miniature fist, looking at it with an unfathomable expression in her blue eyes.

'Give it to me. Good girl,' hissed Greta.

'Sore! Nasty!'

Greta heard a bone-breaking crunch as Howard hit the floor. Swiftly, with her good arm, she snatched the blade from the child and pushed her away. Reflexes sharp as the knife in her hand, she turned to see Dick advancing. On her knees, injured arm dangling loosely at her side, Greta made no decisions. It just happened. Powerful shoulder muscles flexed and the blade swung through the air, entering Dick's abdomen soundlessly.

Dick the Devil fell, and rolled in the puddle of Binnie's blood, his own mingling with hers, soaking into the carpet.

Greta stumbled, her reddened hand over her mouth. The child began to scream.

❖

DC Butterwell had only just arrived, pushing through the chaotic crowd of whimpering women in the doorway. When he saw the slaughter and mayhem, he instinctively picked up little Jan. Large and sure-handed, he soothed the child, and tried to make sense of what he was seeing.

Blood was splattered in arcs across the wallpaper, drizzling down chair legs.

Janice Kirkstone emerged from the bedroom. Her blouse and bra were ripped. One nipple hung helplessly immodest. Eyes like rolling marbles, she was searching for her little daughter, but as she reached out for Jan, she slipped to her knees, falling at Butterwell's feet.

Very gently, the policeman stroked little Jan's dark, tousled head and handed her to one of the women. Then he lifted Janice from the floor and motioned another woman to lead her away.

He looked across the butchery to where his boss was staring at the woman called Alexandra Hythe, who should, by rights, have been eaten by fish. Howard seemed mesmerized. He wasn't functioning.

So it was Butterwell who checked Binnie's pulse and shook his head; Butterwell who stepped over the body of Dick Korda to grab Greta's arm and snap handcuffs on her wrists.

Lifting his chin, the junior policeman sniffed deeply, turned to Howard and raised an insolent eyebrow.

Part Three

Mister Stork's Folly

was Jan's secret, a story which explained things. She liked to escape into the fantasy, imagining herself being flown from mother to mother in the beak of a large bird.

When, at seven, her young soul began to recognize itself, she perceived her life to be as fabulous as Dorothy's in the Land of Oz. In her blurred memory, she could recall a day when, just like Judy Garland, she had walked through a blood-smeared field of sleepy-making red flowers. But in her own story, the green-faced Witch was bald, Tinman carried handcuffs, and Scarecrow flopped on the floor with a knife stuck in him.

Oddly, everyone else in her life seemed to be reading stories from different books in different languages.

Mamma is in Heaven. That was one story. No, it's Padre who's in Heaven. Except Zio Lorenzo said there was another place, like Heaven, but hotter, especially for people like Padre.

Actually, Mamma might not be in Heaven, she might be in another country. Not England. Not Italy. So Mamma lived either in Australia, Africa, France, Spain, Heaven, or Somewhere over the Rainbow.

Anyway, *that* mamma never wanted her in the first place. And the old mamma, Janice, had let Mr Stork fly her away to another country where people couldn't understand what she was saying, or why she was crying. A nice mamma wouldn't have done that. A nice mamma would have kept her safe, and kissed and cuddled her all day, like Zia Katherine did with Hazel.

It wasn't fair. Hazel had the best mamma and padre in the world. Even when she was really naughty, she still got a kiss goodnight. Everybody fussed Hazel. She looked so different from other babies in Venice that strangers stopped to cluck at her. Young as she was, Jan recognized flirting. Hazel had learned how to charm people, to smile and tip her head and shake her red curls and get exactly what she wanted.

It was only on their annual holidays in England that Hazel was treated with the same cautious distance which Jan felt daily.

Both girls hated England. They called it Whisperland. Or Stareyland. People looked at them as if they were photographs on a wall. Grandma Sharp was the worst. She stared all the time, as if she was looking for dirt on your face. Her own face looked like two crumpled handkerchiefs. She lived in a tiny flat, where they had to sit up at a table trying not to make crumbs.

Grampy Hythe (he refused to be called Nonno) lived in a huge house, with lots of dirty bedrooms, but they never stayed there. Lorenzo always took them to a posh hotel overlooking the River Thames. Grampy played the piano, which was – LOUD! He was tall, like a silver stick, and he stared at Jan all the time too. But he hated Hazel. She wasn't even allowed to call him Grampy, she had to call him Mister Hythe.

Sometimes, just sometimes, Grampy smiled. Never at anyone else. He smiled just for himself. Jan liked to watch him do that. She understood that feeling, when smiling hurts and the only person you really trust to share a secret with is yourself.

Here in Italy she had a special, smelly Zio, called Mario. He talked English and taught her bits of Italian. The other noisy relations babbled like parrots with hiccoughs. Jan preferred being all by herself in her white bedroom, making up stories and drawing pictures.

At bedtime Hazel's nanny, Clara, read to them both in English. Jan's head always went nicely to sleep in English, but every morning, when she woke up, the day began in bewildering Italian.

Zia Katherine didn't understand the babble either, which made Jan feel like her special English friend, to share memories and jokes with. But these days her aunt seemed cross all the time, probably because it was hot and she was hugely fat.

Zio Lorenzo was always nice, though. When he came home from work in his pale, crumpled suit, Jan's job was to pour him a glass of wine.

'Zio Loz?'

'*Si?*'

'You know I haven't got a padre?'

'*Si.*'

'Will you be my padre? My babbo?'

Jan did not understand his answer. It was full of riddles and little bits of stories which did not stick together. A week later she understood why he had not said '*Sì*'. Zia Katherine gave Zio Loz a brand-new baby of his own. A baby boy! They called him Antonio John.

❖

Alexandra Korda, known to the other prisoners as Greta, lay on her bunk, staring. The glow from the window impressed on her retinae so that, when she closed her eyes, she could see the stripes of the bars.

She was alone. The other women, alert to her physicality, her violent reputation and her armour of silence, avoided Greta. Her contrived isolation was not passive; it was a constructed alienation, useful both as defence and weapon. She rejected all attempts at conversation. In fact, she seldom spoke at all.

Tragically, her defence mechanism was also deconstructing her. Over the weeks, months and years, this elected silence had slipped over her like a depressive blanket until, gradually, the habit of locking her voice in her chest had become her normality. Now, the function of speaking was almost painful, unless she was completely alone, as she was at this rare moment.

'My body is strong. Emotionally I am withering. I need sunlight. More than food. More than water. More than love. A stretch. That's what it is. A jungle of incarcerated souls, stretching towards the light. A stretch.'

Greta slid off the bunk and touched her toes. Then, very cautiously, she began to do the splits. Her legs opened wider and wider. She breathed steadily as her muscles elongated, until her crotch was only a whisper away from concrete. Reaching her arms high above her head, she stretched her neck back, imagining the trapeze swinging only a fingertip away.

❖

At ten, Jan was writing her own stories. The hero, a boy called Petompello, rode a kangaroo which could jump so high it could sit on clouds. Whenever anyone upset Petompello, he mounted his kangaroo and leapt into the skies. From up there he could drop heavy things on people's heads. Jan's tutor in Venice, a busy, bossy little man, thought the stories were really funny.

Jan liked Venice well enough, although she preferred summers on Lake Garda. The worst part of every year was the annual spring 'holiday' in England. What sort of holiday was it, staying in a tiny cottage by the sea, doing all your own cooking and cleaning? Nanny Clara was wise – she never came along, and sometimes Zio Loz didn't come either. So Zia Katherine had to do it all, and she had no patience because baby Antonio had grown into a fat, dirty monster who needed chasing all the time. Jan had to play Snap with Hazel and do horrible things like making her own bed or washing up.

She once asked Zia Katherine why it was called Hisper Cottage.

'Lord knows, pet.'

'I know . . .'

'Go on, tell me.'

Jan took a Shakespearean stance in front of her aunt.

'Once upon a time it was called WHISPER Cottage. Because the wind whispered through the windows, and the sea whispered warnings of pirates and murderous wreckers, which frightened the little boy who used to live here. But the boy grew up to be a brave soldier. He wasn't afraid of anything, not the wind, not the sea and certainly not a whispering cottage. So, just before he went to war, he took the "W" away. On his way out, he said to his mother, "Now you must never be afraid again. The wind might whisper, but it can never knock this house down. The sea can whisper all it likes, but you are safe up here, high above the rocks. And if you hear a whisper in the night, take its W away, and say, – you're only a hisper now, and you don't scare me." So the soldier's mother rubbed away the W over the cottage door and waited bravely, all alone in Hisper Cottage, until her son came home and had his photo taken.'

Zia Katherine was staring at the picture of the soldier on the mantelpiece. Next to it were two other photographs, of a little girl and a big girl.

'Jan,' said Zia Kath, seriously, 'shall I tell you Zia Sylvia's story?'

'A true story?'

'Yes. It's called a tragedy, because it's sad.'

It was certainly sad. A horrible story. Zia Sylvia had drowned in the miserable North Sea, trying to save her little girl, Alice.

❖

In 1964 Hendo proposed to a fellow architect called Heather. She was two years older, but only half his body weight. Her ring was tiny and all the diamonds in the world were not as precious, to Hendo, as her miniature feet.

The stag night was held in the Three Mile. David sent his apologies, but Alan came up from London. The lads were now twenty-seven. They laughed and told stories and sang 'House of the Rising Sun', but they didn't really talk.

Alan preferred not to confide that once a month he boxed up a selection of second-hand books on travel, tropical plants, animals, cinema, modern history, plus various biographies, and sent them to Greta in jail.

❖

When Jan was thirteen they made an extra trip to England, for a funeral. The old lady called Liz had died.

It was wretchedly cold. Jan sat with her long black fringe hanging over her face, so that no one would try talking to her. It was interesting. Because she spoke Italian, they all assumed she couldn't understand English. Several whispering people were counting years. Seven? Eight. Nine. There seemed to be some argument about nine and ten. And whose good behaviour were they talking about?

After the funeral, they all went to Newcastle to see Hazel's old grandad who had just come out of hospital. His illness must have been bad because he'd been in that hospital for years. He looked mad – another Starer in Staryland – and said 'bloody' every other word. Grandma Sharp swore too. Jan overheard her saying, 'I can't stand him, Kath. I just don't want the miserable old bugger.'

The only good thing about that trip was a visit to the Odeon Cinema in Newcastle, where Jan was utterly enchanted by *The Sound of Music* and she knew, with absolute certainty, that somewhere in the world she had a real mamma like Maria.

❖

Alan's books were Greta's one comfort. They unlocked the cruel cage, setting her free, to swoop over lands she had never heard of, mountain ranges she would never climb and oceans she would never cross. The biographies gave her a glimpse into lives just as complex as her own, but rarely so tragic.

Beauty became something outside of herself, beyond sight, unreachable. The end of her 'stretch' looked like the end of her life – so far away that it seemed almost inconceivable.

And yet the puffing train of time rumbled through the years, on strangely silent rails, past her fortieth birthday and her forty-first until, suddenly, a distant whistle was sounding in the darkness.

❖

In the villa on Lake Garda, Jan soaked up the bliss of liberation.

She had just celebrated her fourteenth birthday and now she was allowed to roam alone around the village and the woods on the lower slopes of the mountains. In luxurious solitude, she sat beneath the trees, hypnotized by the sparkling water, letting her imagination conjure tales of her new heroine, Paula, who had golden hair, right down to her ankles, and who walked around the world naked.

Nudity fascinated her, because she never saw it. She had no idea what naked genitalia looked like, either male or female, because no one shared such an intimacy with her. She had read in the paper that, in London, some women were going topless. What must that look like? Her own chest was still flat, except for a fleshy thickening of her nipples, so even the wobble of a rounded breast was intriguing.

Boys – and what they kept in their pants – were a complete mystery. She hardly ever spoke to one. Convent school isolated her from the other boys in the Marletti family. Anyway, they were jealous because they were never invited to the villa, or spoiled with treats and nice shoes. The very fact that Mario nicknamed her Princess was enough to alienate them thoroughly.

Lorenzo's family lived in the village. They positively devoured little Antonio. Hazel was hideously jealous, but Jan had learned to slip away, to be no bother to anyone, and somehow, when she only had to talk to people for tiny moments in the day, she could manage to be sweet.

❖

She brushed off her skirt and began to climb the zigzag woodland pathway which took her up into the cooler mountain pastures. A light breeze, deliciously exhilarating, swept her hair from her brow. She climbed without stopping and reached her favourite spot, puffing healthily. Under hazy mountains the shapely lake dazzled and tiny houses buzzed with tiny people. Jan smiled in her isolation. A great happiness was welling within her, a rush of energy which clamoured for expression. Like Maria in Austria, Jan opened her arms and tried to sing. She wanted to sing, in English, that the hills were alive – but what came out was, 'In the land, where I was born, lived a man . . . who sailed the sea . . .'

At first the sound was nervous and wobbly, a breathy, jerky lyric in the clear air. Zia Kath had lots of English records which she played when Zio Loz was at work. Jan knew all the words. What else could she sing?

'Hey there, Georgy girl, swinging down the street . . .

'When you're alone and life is making you lonely, you can always go – Downtown . . .'

Zia Katherine's favourite music was from the English band The Chain. She claimed she used to know the handsome guitarist known as Link, and she played his records all the time. It was very romantic. And sad somehow.

Shy, in case her voice carried, she kept the tunes as light as feathers, half in her head, half out in the open. Singing felt odd, secret and full of emotion that was neither joy nor pain.

She sang a hymn then. It sounded so pure and powerful that it hurt and she had to stop and stare at the glistening snow on the mountaintops. Jan thought about God. Not the Cathedral God, but her own God, who was as gentle and shapeless as a cloud. She asked him about her mamma and dead padre, but he did not answer. Then she asked him about her future. Again, he said nothing. So she asked him about her past and the only pictures which would come were Mr Stork and the sleepy red field.

'I'm old enough, God, to know the truth.'

The psyche evolves, they say, in seven-year cycles. This was to be Jan's second awakening. As she descended the path alone, she entered the woods, where the mystery of the trees, the tang of pine, the dead needles under her feet, seemed more real than her life. She touched a trunk, letting her fingers know its coarse, crumbling surface. Her lips were dry, so she licked them, tasting herself, the salt on her upper lip, the sweetness of lunchtime lemonade at the corner of her mouth. Nobody could see her. She looked down at her body, at her long arms and legs, her heavy shoes and green skirt. The gathered neckline of her white blouse scratched over her newly sensitive nipples. She was changing. Everything was changing.

'We skipped the light fandango, turned cartwheels 'cross the floor . . .'

Closing her eyes, Jan inhaled. She felt as if she was breathing in her future. As she opened her eyes she noticed that the shadows were broken across the pathway by dappled pink and gold light. After the bleached day, those dancing colours, full of contrasts, seemed more alive, more vibrant than anything she had ever noticed before. The beauty of the world touched her lonely soul, and loved her. In response, her body suddenly throbbed. The pleasurable sensation brought a flush to her face, and she crossed her legs to hold on to it.

❖

Back at the villa, a strange tableau had formed on the terrace. Zio Mario sat with his head up and his chins down, like a fat orangutan. Zia Katherine was sitting next to him and Zio Loz stood behind her, with his hand on her shoulder. On another chair, with a champagne flute in her hand, was a woman with a familiar face. In Jan's heightened state of awareness, she recognized the woman immediately. The short, black hair was not real. It was a wig. And the face was the face of the bald witch.

Zio Mario told her a new story.

'Princess! Come kiss your mamma. At last she is able to return to us. Tonight we have a party. You may drink a glass of champagne.'

Jan hung her head so that her black fringe hid her eyes. Thankfully, the woman made no attempt to cuddle her. How could this creature of her nightmares, this bloody witch, be her mamma? Jan's heart seemed to be contracting in her chest, getting smaller and harder, until it felt like a golf ball under her ribs. She could not move. Visions were flashing behind her eyes, old knowledge unlocking secret places in her brain.

She was polite. 'I'm glad to meet you, Mamma.'

Nodding and smiling.

Jan's questions felt like thunder in her belly. 'Have you been in Australia?'

Again, Zio answered. 'She cannot tell us, Princess. Her work has been secret. Political.'

'You're a spy? Like James Bond?' Jan was thinking, *Licence to Kill* . . . in a field of red flowers.

Zia Katherine laughed lightly, and said, 'Actually, your mamma would have made a good spy.'

At last the woman spoke. Her lips, which looked so tight, suddenly loosened across even, white teeth. 'What a beautiful young woman you've grown into.' She coughed and licked her lips. 'So grown up . . . my dear,' she sipped from her glass, 'I've missed your childhood, which is my tragedy. Probably not yours. You've been well loved and cared for by Katherine and your Zio Mario. Someday, when you are older, I might be able to explain the reasons. But now, I so very badly want to be your mamma, part of your future . . .'

Jan thought about the good clean future she had inhaled in the woods. Fury flooded through her – already that future was soiled.

❖

A taxi stopped a few streets away from the villa. A man emerged clutching a small crocodile-skin suitcase. Everything in the case was expensive and beautifully pressed. He straightened up and extracted his wallet with a flourish. Each of his fingers was banded in gold. At his neck was a gold medallion. When the taxi driver was paid, he glided gracefully into the nearest bar and ordered a gin, which he drank with his little finger extended.

❖

A long table was laid on the terrace. Greta felt sleepy, watching the sun melt into the still lake. The effort of talking was exhausting. Even the champagne couldn't seem to loosen her tongue. Battling against her habit of silence, she felt claustrophobic. There were too many secrets around the table for easy conversation. They had already covered Nonno's funeral, Jan's education, Hazel's talents, Lorenzo's business, the hippies, the weather.

Oh, why, Greta wondered, hadn't they told Jan the truth?

Plates of food were being placed before them. The teenager who was legally her daughter sat opposite, head bowed, looking dully at her steak. A moody girl! But like whom? Dick? Sylvia? Herself?

With a massive effort, Greta rehearsed some words before speaking them. 'Have you enjoyed your trips to England? Do you like Halstone House? Is my father still playing?'

The moody teenager looked up under her fringe, which was as black as Greta's wig. Their eyes locked and a flash of something adult shot between them. Then Jan stared down at her plate. Slowly the girl picked up her knife. Her fingers changed grip, so that her fist grabbed it like a dagger. She straightened her torso, then drew the knife to shoulder height and, in a sweeping arc, stabbed down into the steak.

The plate cracked.

❖

They had said:

the child needs to forget; a swift change will blot out the blood; a clean cut is kindest, love demands sacrifice.

After all these years, Janice could still see the child's open mouth as she screamed, and still feel the texture of her red corduroy dress as it slipped out of her fingers.

The kind nurse was packing. Her latest boyfriend had dumped her for a skinny, fertile teacher, and her life felt as empty as a cold grate. So she had decided to offer her heart and hands to somewhere where they might be appreciated – the Congo.

Where ten thousand babies were crying.

Jan was told

only what they felt she needed to know. She was, after all, fourteen, and naively sheltered from sex. Yet hadn't Sylvia given birth at that age? On the other hand, how could they possibly reveal that her father might be a perverted rapist? Katherine's own secret, that Dick was Hazel's father, must be protected at all costs.

Greta, struggling to speak, allowed Katherine to explain the confusion at the Maternity Hospital in Newcastle. The women were taken aback when Jan sniggered.

They were not to know that she was retreating into the secure beak of Mr Stork, wishing he would come and drop bombs on the bloody lot of them. Jan knew the Stork was a fantasy but, having been brought up on fantasies, she had every reason to suspect this new one.

Greta excused her actions as 'postnatal depression' and Katherine tried to persuade Jan that Sylvia had only run away to avoid signing adoption papers.

Neither woman could bear to linger long over sweet Alice's story.

It was only when they talked about Janice that Jan began to tremble. She looked at Katherine as if she were a monster.

'You took me away from her? When she loved me so much?'

'Zio Mario made that decision.'

Jan's face distorted. The older women watched the girl's faith in human nature crumbling, and they could do nothing.

'You remember that day? At Janice's flat?' asked Greta quietly.

'We hoped you were young enough to forget,' said Katherine.

Jan gazed at the moonlit lake. 'Killers go to prison, then Hell.'

'But she was protecting you,' Katherine blurted. 'Dick was drinking. He'd become ill, an alcoholic, going mad, doing bad things, and she was frightened for you.'

'No.' Jan turned to stare steadily at Greta. 'That's not the reason, is it?'

Greta put her hand over her mouth. Then she slid her wig off her head and rubbed her scarred scalp. The girl's gaze was unyielding, unforgiving. It was as if Jan was older than either of them, as if she possessed a God-given clear-sightedness.

'My padre would not have hurt me. You killed him for yourself . . .' For the last time, she spat the word, '. . . Mamma.'

❖

Greta left the villa that night. She carried her case down to the bench overlooking the lake and said her goodbyes where no one could hear them.

Then she strode out. Her legs were still strong, her shoulders broad enough to hump her case along the lakeside pathway towards the station. But her soul was weak. Perhaps it always had been.

Someone was walking behind her. Not the spirit of Sophia. Nor Dick's ghost. Not even one of Sylvia's angels.

This person was very warm-fleshed. And patient. He had tracked her from prison, to Halstone House, and on to Italy.

The lake held the moon, watching.

She turned sharply. 'Who's that?'

'Who indeed, Alexandra?'

The Chain

were touring. David Linden, known to his fans as Link, was tired. As the converted bus sped up the Great North Road, he pulled the elastic out of his long black ponytail and dragged on a reefer. It eased away his tension, which was terrific for the migraine, but lousy for the songwriting. He had written all his best songs when he was in pain, but these days his emotions felt plastic, his sense of romance positively historic.

At thirty-one he was older than the others in the band by seven years. How could he be close to them? He couldn't even remember himself at twenty-four.

Tonight's concert was in Newcastle City Hall; fans would already be lining up. David – Link – hadn't been back for years. He still owned the houses in Gosforth and Corbridge. It was the rent from these which had paid for his career, so that even when other broke musicians faded away into supermarkets and offices, David had been able to keep playing and improving.

Inevitably, he was thinking about his mother, last seen in Paris, back in 1956. Was she still in France, sitting in a seedy *chambre* listening to his latest LP? Would she identify the constant twang of loneliness in his music and feel any guilt?

Nervousness was unusual in the man who was becoming a Rock Legend. Yet, as they crossed the Tyne Bridge, the suspicion that some of his old friends might be in the audience set his stomach reeling, even worse than when he had appeared on *Top of the Pops*.

In his dressing room he found a pile of fan letters. His head was throbbing, so he rolled another reefer and plucked at his acoustic for a while. An hour to wait. He began to open the envelopes.

> *Dear David,*
> *I have brought Jan to see you . . . row F . . . staying at*
> *the Turk's Head . . .*
> *Sincerely, Katherine*

❖

When, for the first time in many years, Jan grabbed her hand, Katherine felt choked, and she realized just how high her emotions were running. The crush of young, near-hysterical women in City Hall was disorienting. A stiletto heel almost punctured her big toe.

Jan was watching the other girls, just a couple of years older than herself. Katherine couldn't help noticing how different she looked. Jan's skin was healthily tanned. Her clothes were modern, but of European vogue, and her mini-skirt was decent, while lots of these young girls were brazenly showing stocking tops.

I'm getting old, thought Katherine suddenly. They all look

the same. Same pancaked faces, same pale lipstick, same painted lashes. I'm old and fat and David probably sleeps with a girl like this every night. Oh, shit, what have I done?

She rummaged in her handbag for her lipstick. Where was her mouth? She tried to guess, smeared, and pressed her lips together. At her side, Jan turned to face her. The fifteen-year-old's long, slender fingers reached for the lipstick. She took it out of Katherine's hand and calmly applied some to her own mouth. Her lips, unusually, smiled.

I've not been kind enough to her, thought Katherine. I've not tried to help her grow up. I didn't prepare her for Greta's homecoming. I was a coward. Yet, she has absorbed the truth with wisdom beyond her years. When did she become so good? Why didn't I notice?

'Will we see him afterwards, Zia?'

'I don't know. I had no idea it would be like this – all these daft, screaming girls. The stage door will be thronged. I've given him the hotel telephone number. We'll just have to hope he calls us there.'

'But will he?'

'I hope so, pet. I hope so.'

There was a sudden blast of a guitar chord. A thomp, thomp of a drum. The crowd held its breath.

❖

At the airport Lorenzo drank a whole bottle of wine. He had let Katherine go to England, primed to confront David Linden, without making a single word of complaint. Yet jealousy had kept him awake every night since. What if the old flame rekindled? What if his wife was sucked into a debauched world of pop music and drugs? Had he been taking her for granted? Had he made love to her often enough since Antonio was born?

Lorenzo always hated her trips to England, but this was the worst. He missed her hair, he decided. Also her solidity, her cooking and her quick intellect.

Katherine was his wife, his partner in every way. They matched, wit to wit, frown to frown, arm fold to arm fold, kiss to kiss. He loved her with an abiding passion which felt threatened every time she played one of Link's records.

It had taken a long courtship and a disastrous honeymoon before Lorenzo had finally won his wife's sexuality, and he certainly didn't want to lose it to some rock-and-roller.

Now Katherine was in Newcastle. At a concert. In a mini-skirt. Ready to see Link.

Lorenzo turned up his lacy shirt collar and strode on to the plane.

Two flights and several drinks later, he reached the hotel in Newcastle in a state of sublime inebriation, ready to make a complete romantic idiot of himself. But he fell asleep.

❖

The hysteria was infectious. Katherine and Jan stood on seats with the rest. As the music pounded, a forest of slender arms reached over their shoulders, towards the stage. The Chain was certainly clanging.

Katherine was mesmerized. David bounced across the stage like he once did in the schoolyard. But when he sang the ballads, her heart felt crushed in her chest. Every lyric, every poetic word, she understood. The notes touched her core. She knew David Linden so very well.

Surely he would want to speak to her. He would glance to row F and seek out her face. And he would certainly ring them at the hotel – wouldn't he?

She looked at Jan, whose face was rapt. David would know by now that the girl who might be his daughter was in Newcastle, only feet away from him. Surely, once he saw the resemblance . . . or was it her imagination?

❖

Jan knew all the songs. She sang the words under her breath. I'm like him, she thought. A poetic soul. She resolved to learn to play the guitar. They could play together, like Captain von Trapp and Liesl.

The crowd was clapping and screaming. Link signalled for quiet. He spent a second looking at the audience. Was he counting rows? Searching for her? Or for his old love, Zia Katherine?

Link rasped through his microphone, 'This next one is for a very special person.'

Jan held her breath. That's my father . . .

'For Alice.

Goodbye, lullaby . . . the stars guide your way . . .

On the stairway to . . .'

Jan heard the melancholy in David's voice, saw the tears streaming down Zia Kath's face, and felt as if Alice's blue ribbons were throttling her.

The exclusion was deliberate. Alice's song was Jan's rejection.

David did ring the Turk's Head. Unfortunately Katherine was still walking down Northumberland Street, and a drunken Lorenzo told him to fuck off.

I think I will, David decided, as the bus whisked the band off into the night. A nameless girl, young enough to be his daughter, was sucking his earlobe.

❖

Jan lay in her single hotel room. She twirled her black hair through her fingers and vowed, 'I'll write my own bloody songs!'

She did.

Oh, she (bloody) did.

Prickles of truth

get stamped on; bad memories crushed, like fly-infested blooms.

Plastic petals, white lily lies, are easier to dust, to keep clean.

Hazel slips an arm around Katherine's waist.

'I'm glad you're my mamma.' The redheaded girl is now seventeen, and almost beautiful. Having grown up enveloped in physical love, she kisses too readily.

Lorenzo tugs a bouncing curl. 'What about your padre?'

'My padre's fab.'

It isn't over, is it?

Upstairs, in a locked box, is Hazel's birth certificate. It says, 'Father Unknown'. In four months' time, when a new tragedy hits the family, she will find it.

❖

You don't get seasick, do you? We need to stand beside Hazel on the cross-Channel ferry. I warn you, the white horses are charging today. While you're hanging on the ship's rail, watch how the teenager's titian hair dances madly about her head, and try not to look down into the sea, in case you see Sylvia's tresses floating.

You're shivering.

Sorry.

Hazel's eyes, bulging like Cuthbert's, are fixed on the horizon; her neck tendons are taut as harp strings.

When she gets to London, what will the politician, Alan Watson, tell her? Will he be cautious with the truth? Will he make an urgent phone call to Hendo? Will the big lad warn Violet that Hazel is on her way to Newcastle?

A new tempest is brewing. As our ferry heaves and shudders, the saga surges.

In Venice, Jan is rushing to catch a plane to Heathrow. Tormented by her own sorrow and confoundment, she is determined to catch up with the girl who could be her half-sister.

Rejection, perversely, has blessed Jan with a generous, sad heart which can sing people to tears. Not yet twenty, having renamed herself 'Jesmond', after the place where her mother abandoned her, she has already made her first successful LP.

Imagine squeezing an uncut emerald in a tightly clenched fist. That's how Hazel holds her jealousy.

Look! The White Cliffs of Dover. We could start singing about love, laughter and peace ever after, if only Hazel wasn't as clever as her mother, as vulnerable as her aunt,

and as vicious as her father.